COLD

FALLING

WHITE

Also by G. S. Prendergast

Zero Repeat Forever

COLD

FALLING

WHITE

G. S. PRENDERGAST

SIMON & SCHUSTER

First published in Great Britain in 2019 by Simon & Schuster UK Ltd
A CBS COMPANY

First published in the USA in 2019 by Simon & Schuster Books for Young
Readers, an imprint of Simon & Schuster Children's Publishing Division

Text copyright © 2019 Gabrielle Pendergrast

1 3 5 7 9 10 8 6 4 2

Simon & Schuster UK Ltd
1st Floor,
222 Gray's Inn Road
London WC1X 8HB

www.simonandschuster.co.uk
www.simonandschuster.com.au
www.simonandschuster.co.in

Simon & Schuster Australia, Sydney
Simon & Schuster India, New Delhi

A CIP catalogue record for this book is available from the British Library.

PB ISBN 978-1-4711-5807-0
eBook ISBN 978-1-4711-5808-7

This book is a work of fiction. Names, characters, places and incidents are
either the product of the author's imagination or are used fictitiously. Any resemblance
to actual people living or dead, events or locales is entirely coincidental.

Printed and bound by CPI Group (UK) Ltd, Croydon, CR0 4YY

To all the strong girls: Audrey, Penelope, Monica, Kathy, Tess, Bronwen, and Lucy

PART ONE

FIRE

*"Nothing is so painful to the human mind as a great
and sudden change."*
—MARY SHELLEY, *FRANKENSTEIN*

I t's cold.

And silent.

And dark.

I am as weightless as a thought, as a shadow underwater. The only thing that gives me substance is the sense of filling up with . . . something. Something thick and powerful and inhuman, unearthly. I want to squirm away from it but there is nothing to squirm with. All I am is a selection of verbs: to fill, to grow, to change, to perfect. It's as though I'm being rebuilt from scratch.

Days pass like this. Lifetimes. A lonely wisp of nothing floating in a sea of . . . what's left of my mind searches for the word.

Obedience? Duty? I'm being entwined in something, as though my nerves are unraveling and tangling into some idea of . . . I can't see it. I can't hear it or smell it or taste it. It's nothing, a void, like the space left behind when something is lost. I can feel its emptiness, feel it trying to consume me, to ensnare me. But there's something else resisting it, something stubborn and intractable, something *human*.

Regret. And the idea that not every broken thing is unfix-able.

In the darkness, I sense someone with me, and though this someone is no more substantial than I am, they feel heavy, like tears of grief or remorse. Tiny yet galactic.

"Hello?" I'm not sure how I say it. I don't seem to have a mouth.

The answer comes back to me as an impression of force on matter—the particles of air vibrating from sound, the light flickering on August's hands moving as he signed.

Memory.

Oh . . . August. Get me out of here. I'm afraid. August?

XANDER

I t's not until ten days after August left Raven's body in an
abandoned hotel near Jasper that I feel her death, actually feel it, the way I felt Tucker's death and Lochie's and
Felix's and Mandy's and . . . the rest. Like boulders dropped
on me from great heights that I have to carry—first the pain
of the impact, then the weight of them. Sometimes, plodding
through the mountains, I look down at my feet and wonder
why I'm not sinking into the earth like an overloaded mule in
a muddy paddock.

August turns back to me, his hand raised palm up, a sign
I've learned is a generic question.

What's wrong?

"Nothing," I lie. I've been staring at my feet, trying to
wriggle some feeling back into them.

I've made a promise, to myself, to Raven and all the dead,
and to Topher and everyone I left behind in the failing human
sanctuary under the mountains. I just need to get out of the
Nahx occupation zone, then I can lose my mind. Get word to
the human authorities, tell them there are two hundred people
starving, running out of fuel and resolve, two hundred people

marked for death in a place where no humans are supposed to be breathing, as far as I can tell. Maybe no one will care. What's another two hundred on top of millions? On top of Raven and Tucker, and Lochie, and Felix, Mandy, Sawyer . . .

And my family. Mom. Dad and Nai Nai. Chloe. She was only thirteen.

Was. Is. She'd be fourteen now. Maybe I'll never know.

This is how I keep moving, by mentally scheduling a future freak-out, fighting not to tremble from cold, and following a seven-foot armored alien through a spring-soggy landscape that is utterly indifferent to the absence of my species. Geese fly north in neat Vs, squirrels scatter up gnarled tree trunks, big-horned sheep turn their ponderous heads to us as we pass. And the earth springs back to life, oblivious, even grateful to have this respite from human interference. The colors of spring keep me focused on my goal—the soft green of new pine needles, the silvery blue lichen on rocks, and dandelions, golden glowing dandelions everywhere.

August stops to pick them periodically, twisting their stems into his armor. I keep meaning to ask him about this but I probably wouldn't understand his answer. We don't have time to teach me his sign language.

Yes and *no* are obvious signs. And there's one he repeats daily.

Promise, he says, before turning away from me. I learned

x

6

this word the day Raven died. August means he will fulfill his promise to get me out of the Nahx-occupied territory. He promised Raven, and to him that means everything. I don't know why. What's one human boy out of millions?

A few minutes later he turns back again. *Cold?* That's another obvious sign, as some of them are.

"No. Can we just keep moving?"

I'm wearing the coat, gloves, and sidearm of a dead RCMP officer we found on the empty highway two days ago. The Mountie's rifle is slung over August's back, along with a Nahx rifle he found discarded under a shrub.

Days and nights pass like this in silence, tramping through the mountains, picking up various treasures as we find them. I find a maple leaf scarf mashed in a puddle. August wrings it out and tucks it into his armor. An hour later when he gives it back to me, it is bone dry and toasty warm, as though it has just come out of the dryer. And we find food occasionally, in between days of living with my growling stomach. I now have pockets full of chocolate bars and nuts taken from a deserted gas station.

It's been two weeks, by my count, since we left the plateau where Raven died. Now a week and a half since we laid her to rest in Jasper, wearing a silky green dress August found in a hotel room. I didn't ask questions about that either. Her own clothes were stiff with dry blood and smelled of death. I

7

suppose he only wanted to give her a little dignity in her final destination.

Ahead of me, in a patch of green, August bends to pick another dandelion, and I'm struck by the sudden weight of pure silence descending over us.

"August . . ."

He spins, hissing.

The Nahx transport is careening over our heads before he even reaches me. I dive down into an embankment without thinking, rolling until I crash to a stop among a thatch of weeds.

There's another low hiss.

"I'm here," I whisper. "Did they see us?"

Before I get an answer, the transport hurtles overhead again. August lashes out and grabs me, pulling me up by the back of my coat.

Run FAST, he says. Two more obvious signs I learned early on.

I tear away from him, off in the other direction and down toward the shallows of a creek, straining my head back to try to spot the transport just as its engine suddenly roars and howls. The high-pitched screech makes the air seem to tremble and turn everything blurry.

"Where to?!" I yell back. August crashes through the trees behind me. "Which way?"

8

We have reached a split in the creek where the sparkling water tumbles and flows around a rocky island dotted with trees.

Up, he signs.

I plow through the shallow churning creek, over logs and stones, and pull myself onto the island, collapsing in the shrubs. Just as I roll over, August appears through the trees, his dark shape blotting out the sky behind him. He blurs as he swings the Nahx rifle and points it at me.

"August . . . fuck."

Dead. DEAD! His hand slices across his neck. *DEAD!*

"What . . ."

He shoves the rifle into my chest, pushing me backward onto the ground.

DEAD! You dead!

I close my eyes as his rifle starts to whine. There's a loud hiss, and a dart thunks into the ground next to my head. I open my eyes a sliver to see August bend and retrieve the dart, breaking off its tip. He hesitates a moment before twisting my head to the side and jamming the blunt dart into my ear.

His hand smacks down over my mouth before I can complain.

Dead!

I close my eyes again. Over the low rumble of the transport engine idling and the rushing of the creek, I can hear

9

approaching footsteps, heavy footsteps splashing toward us. I hear August's armor rattle and his familiar hiss.

Another hiss answers it. At the very last moment I think I can hold my breath August nudges me hard with his boot, rolling me over onto my face in the mud. It gives me a chance to take a careful breath.

There's more hissing, and someone growls. They are angry, and I'm trying not to panic. An eternity goes past.

Finally a warm hand touches my head, resting there as I listen to the footsteps sloshing away and the engines of the transport taking off.

I take another careful breath. Then another.

"That's you, August, right?"

He pats me on the back and pulls the dart out of my ear.

As I roll over slowly, August kneels there, watching me.

Sorry, he says.

"Were those the same ones as . . . whenever it was?" A few days ago we narrowly avoided a group of Nahx by hiding in an abandoned bus. Then there was the time we nearly got spotted crossing a rail bridge. And once we missed a transport flying right over us by seconds. Our luck clearly ran out today.

I sit up and wipe my face, trying to will my heart to stop punching the inside of my rib cage.

Broken you?

"I'm not broken . . . I mean hurt. No, I'm not hurt."

August stands and looks down at me expectantly, but I'm not quite ready to get up yet. After a moment, he kneels again, resting back on his heels, and makes a bunch of signs.

"I'm sorry. I don't understand . . ."

Promise, he says with a sigh.

Three days later we catch sight of the border drones just as it's getting dark. Back at the base, our commander, Kim, told us her gathered intel suggested that there was a "web of attack drones" along the border, and I guess I pictured that more metaphorically. This actually looks like a web, a hideous web some monstrous spider has spun across miles and miles of mountains, with tiny pinpoints of light floating above the western peaks, each one projecting an array of thin beams in every direction. It delineates the Nahx occupation zone. This is the border we need to cross to get me back among my own kind, among humans.

We creep through the trees until the web is looming above us only a hundred yards away. August puts one hand on his head and taps his helmet, as though he's thinking.

"Okay," I say. "Let's head north again, or south. It can't go on forever."

Forever, he says, shaking his head slowly.

"Through it somehow, then?" I suggest. "Isn't it designed for vehicles and aircraft? Maybe we could just walk through it."

I'm not sure how someone in a full suit of armor and mask

can look doubtful, but August manages it. He bends, retrieving a heavy chunk of wood from a crumbling tree. Curling his arm back, he flings it precisely in an impressively high arc so it sails gracefully through the air. The web crackles as the wood flies right through it.

"See? It—"

In a microsecond ten of the drones have converged on the spot the log breached. I stumble back as the night is shaken by a loud crack, and a bolt of electricity shoots out from the web, incinerating the log where it landed.

"Okay. Yeah. Maybe we should . . ." I'm tugging August away before the smoke even clears.

We backtrack to a crumbling one-room cabin by a stream we passed earlier in the day. August gives me one of his lights as I spread my map out on the dirt floor. Then he does this cool thing he can do, snapping his fingers to make sparks, and starts a small fire in the remnants of the fireplace. It warms me as I study the map.

At the base, after Kim died, her son, Liam, let me look at some of the topographical and military maps showing our location and the surrounding terrain. I combined that with a couple of other travel maps and stuff I could remember from geography class into what I thought might be an escape route. It became my project, pretty much the only thing that would calm my mind in the long nights when I was sure I was going to die up there, sure we all were.

The journey I mapped out was meant to be for everyone— some two hundred survivors were going to hug the low sides of the Yellowhead Pass, keeping to the trees where possible, switching over to the service roads by the railway tracks where the highway climbed too high in elevation. I suggested we plan for a month, given that such a large group, and one including children and the elderly, would be slow.

People came to believe in the map, to believe that we could just walk out of the occupied territory and be free of the Nahx. I don't know what I was thinking. It has been hard enough for me and August to walk through the wilderness undetected. Two hundred of us would likely have been picked off by the Nahx on the second day. Maybe everyone knew this deep down, and that's why we never quite worked up the momentum to actually leave.

It's the same route that August and I took, more or less, not so much an escape route, I now realize. More of a long, pointless hike. I let my finger trail along the route, coming to a stop where I think the Nahx web comes down. We're a few miles east of the web now, and the lingering paranoia incited by our last encounter with the Nahx makes me reluctant to stop moving.

I'm exhausted. When I slow, wanting nothing more than to lie down and sleep, he just nudges me again, and we tramp on like determined elks, migrating north. August never sleeps that I can tell. He doesn't eat. Sometimes, in bright sunlight, he'll slow his pace and hold his arms out to let the sun shine down on him. Is it possible he has some kind of solar generator? That would be useful.

I wish before Raven had died I'd had more time to ask her about him. We know so little about the Nahx, even after they have occupied our planet for nearly a year. But then, maybe it's just us unfortunates who were surrendered, left behind in the occupied zones, who know nothing. Maybe in the free human territory people are already writing books and pithy think pieces about Nahx physiology.

Bulletproof. Practically immortal. Silent. Driven. Tireless. Brutally efficient. Callous.

Well, August isn't very callous. He seems to care about me, anyway.

Hungry? he signs, touching my shoulder.

"I'm fine. I'm kind of sick of chocolate bars."

I stare down at the map. If I'm not mistaken, this cabin is on the southern shore of a nameless lake about five miles west of a bridge over the Fraser River. So we'll have to backtrack. My finger traces up to the thick line of river, then above it to . . .

There's another thin line on the map. I remember drawing it on, thinking it might be handy to know it's there, though not why. It's a crazy idea and I know August won't like it, but it might work.

"There's a kind of tunnel, north of here." "Tunnel" is a nice way of saying it. It's an enormous pipe—an oil pipeline that the socially conscious kids used to think would hasten the end of the world. The only reason I know it is there is because I helped my sister draw a map for a school project about it. And like most maps I've drawn, I remembered it in enough detail to draw it again.

Now my sister's voice is in my head, reciting her report. Glancing up, I wipe my eyes quickly so August won't see.

The pipeline was supposed to go from Edmonton to the coast, but First Nations' lawsuits stopped it. So now, if I'm right, it ends in a refinery in a small town about fifty miles north of Prince George and just west of the web, outside Nahx territory.

As I think it through it seems to have too many variables and ways it could go horribly wrong. How can I get into the pipe, and how far will I have to crawl to get out? And when I arrive among humans covered in oil sludge like some creature from the deep, will they welcome me like a lost hero? It's lunacy.

But it *could* work. I mean, I think there's a small chance.

"If we head north, we can look for the p—tunnel."

Dark. Yes?

"Probably be safer in the dark. You're right."

After we leave the cabin, the hours pass uneventfully, and that makes me uneasy. It's cold as hell, though, even with the Mountie's coat and gloves. Just before dawn, when we stop for a breather, August puts his hands over my ears to warm them up. He can control his temperature somehow, up to burning hot if he's in danger or agitated. We learned that when Liam took him prisoner. Just two weeks ago, was it? It feels like centuries.

How things would have been different if Liam had listened to me. I could see August was trying to surrender peacefully. He had come to find Raven to get her safely away. But how do you reason with someone who has lost their reason? Liam and Topher and most of the rest of the ragtag militia we'd formed didn't even want to talk about plans for hiking out of the mountains in the spring. They considered themselves the holdouts of the Canadian Rockies—no retreat, no surrender.

So Liam blew our only chance. It didn't end up mattering to him. He's dead on a mountainside. Along with everyone else.

I stopped thinking about what happened to my family months ago. I saw the remains of our apartment building in Calgary—unlike other ones closer to downtown, it was a burned-out pile of bent metal and ash. If anyone was inside when the Nahx bombed it, they're dead. If they were outside, the Nahx would have darted them and left them somewhere. We didn't have time to flip over every corpse to see if it was someone I knew or my parents. My little sister. Or Nai Nai.

I shrug off August's hand.

Hours later, as my legs begin to wobble beneath me, we arrive at a small work camp. Abandoned, of course, but the detritus left behind makes me think it's the right vintage to be related to the pipeline—maybe a year or two old. We follow a deeply rutted mud road into the forest, past a few discarded bulldozer blades, truck tires, and other careless signs of human disdain for nature.

At last in a clearing we come upon a kind of excavation, and sure enough, dug into the earth is a large pipe, about four feet in diameter. I'm relieved to see its size. The pipe disappears off into the trees in either direction like a tenacious snake. August approaches it cautiously, as though it might come to life and devour us both before slithering away. The sharp metallic clang of his knuckles rapping on the pipe resonates through the trees.

Under? he signs.

"Yes. It might go underground, under rivers or whatever. Right under the drone web, I think."

He taps his temple with one finger. *Smart.*

We follow the pipeline west, and soon, cresting a rise, we get a good view of the ground level where the web comes down. It's hard to see some parts of it where it disappears into the thick forest, but there's a Nahx transport vessel parked on a nearby road.

"Do you think they know about the pipe?" I whisper.

August shrugs.

Repeat. Think. No.

"Not very smart?" I tug off my hat and scratch my greasy hair. "So maybe they won't notice anything? This could work."

August nods.

I estimate the web is about a half mile away. Pulling the crumpled map from my pocket, I spread it out on the curved metal of the pipe. I've been trying to mark our progress, noting landmarks like roads, lakes, and creeks where I can. I'm pretty sure Bear Lake, where the refinery is, is about five miles west of here.

Can I do that? Can I crawl through five miles of pipe? That's insane.

August bends to inspect a round, bolt-ringed plate on the side of the pipe, tapping it lightly.

"That's an access port, I think." We passed one of them along the way. I assume they appear at regular intervals— about a mile apart. August pinches one of the bolts and tries to turn it. I'm about to tell him we need some kind of tool when there's a rusty creak and the bolt comes away in his hand.

Jesus. I knew he was strong, but that's extraordinary.

I watch for any movement down by the web while August removes the rest of the bolts. When the last one is gone he wrenches at the plate. I stand back as he pulls it away, pretty sure that since the invasion shut down the power grid there's no pressure in the pipes anymore.

Pretty sure, but not certain.

Black sludge dribbles out onto the forest floor as the plate comes away and August lets it clank down. So no. No pressure, just some residual crude oil coating the bottom of the pipe. That will make it easy to slide along it, I guess, though fumes might be a problem; they waft out of the pipe, making the air thick and acrid.

August steps aside as I poke my head into the pipe, shining my flashlight down it either way. The danger is we'll meet some kind of blockage and have to shimmy backward and uphill to get back out. And there's the danger that we won't find another access hatch and I'll be crawling through sludge for days. And the danger the Nahx will hear us and bust us out of there before I make it to the other side.

It's a very slim chance we'll survive, but what options do I have?

The pipe is pretty wide inside—wide enough to crawl as opposed to sliding along like an eel, so that's something. By the sky, it's only about midday. The pipe goes downhill most of the way from here, so we might be able to slide like in a water park. That will save time. If it continues downhill all the way to the next hatch, the whole prospect becomes a lot more plausible.

"Do you think you could open one of these plates from the inside?" I ask.

August bends again to inspect the bolt holes, the thickness of the plate, and the bolts.

Maybe, he signs.

"The next plate should be on the other side of the web. If you can open it, I can get out there. It'll be about a mile. It might take us an hour to get there." An hour in the dark, crawling through slime.

Once I hoist myself into the pipe I find I'm able to easily maneuver around on my hands and knees. Shining my flashlight, I can see where the pipe bends downward, like a waterslide. My confidence is wavering now that I'm inside it. What if August can't get those belts undone? What if I'm wrong about those lawsuits and the pipeline bypasses the refinery and goes all the way to the coast? There's no human alive who could crawl in the dark for however long that would take. Weeks? Months?

I turn back, poking my head out. August stands there with one hand on his helmet. It would be nice if I had a choice to leave him here, because he's definitely done enough to call his promise to Raven fulfilled.

But I need him. Which is both annoying and something else. Nahx and humans are supposed to be enemies. Back at the base, Liam and Topher talked as though we could somehow drive the Nahx from the earth, wage some great battle and eradicate them like smallpox. Only an idiot would think that was an option now.

August saved Raven's life. She saved his life. He's saving my life. Maybe there's meaning to it. If we do this enough, we might be able to live with one another.

This one little bridge of trust might be bigger than any dream of great battles and victories.

"I don't think I'll be able to open the pipe from inside."

August nods and clambers into the pipe behind me. I move forward to give him room as he arranges his long limbs around him. He's too tall to crawl, but the bottom of the pipe is slippery with oil, so he should be able to pull himself along easily enough. He clicks something and a light on his shoulder turns on, its beam dancing on the slick metallic walls of the pipe.

"How long does that battery last?"

Forever, he signs. *Promise. Not scared.*

We inch along slowly. When I reach the slope in the pipe I kind of tumble down it, landing with an oily splash in the lower curve. August is much more graceful behind me, controlling his descent with his hands on the pipe walls, keeping his light steady as he reaches me.

Broken?

"No, I'm fine." I untangle myself and crawl farther into the dark. The air smells like a badly managed gas station in here, and even with my scarf pulled up over my nose I'm getting light-headed. I can't imagine a worse death than this would be. Poisoned by toxic fumes in a greasy pipe? I wonder if August will just leave my body in here. Something tells me that he wouldn't, but when I turn back to look at him easing himself along the pipe, I notice he's wheezing. Great. Maybe we'll both die in here. Archaeologists will have fun with that.

I feel along the pipe walls as we make slow progress, searching for the access hatch. It feels like we should have come across it by now. Have we already gone under the web? I thought maybe we might see some sign of it, but so far it's just been fumes and sludge and darkness. Kind of like my worst days at high school.

August's fingers close on my ankle.

"What?" I say, turning back. He holds a finger over his mouth and twists his body to face behind us. Several long seconds pass while I hold my breath. A moment later we hear the unmistakable sound of someone in metallic armor clattering down a sloping pipe. It resonates toward us like a death knell.

"Fuck!"

Fast. Fast!

He shoves me, pushing himself along with his free hand.

We reach another slope and slither down that, landing in a pile at the bottom. August hisses as we extricate ourselves, before launching me forward with another shove. The slimy mix of oil and fetid water sprays up in my face, making me press my eyes and mouth firmly closed. I'm scrambling my hands along the pipe now, desperately searching for anything that feels like the access panel.

"Did we pass it? We must have passed it!"

Over the sound of my frantic hands pounding on the metal, I can hear the progress of the other Nahx behind us. They're gaining on us.

August shoves me to the side and slithers past me, shining two lights ahead of us. He waves his hand in front of my face, closing his fingers tightly.

Grab me!

I latch onto his foot and he tugs us along, with me trying to improve our momentum any way I can. An eternity of desperate scrabbling later, August slides to a stop, his light flashing around.

"There!" It's a panel, the stubby bolts casting long shadows on the metal. August curls his fist around one and twists. Only a Nahx would have the strength to remove these bolts; it's only because of August that I have a chance of surviving. I roll over and face backward, pointing my pathetic gun into the dark.

Behind me August loosens another bolt. I hear it clang onto the concrete outside the pipe.

If I'm getting out of this pipe ever, I'm doing it here, and if here is not beyond the drone web, then this has all been for nothing. Bile rises in my throat as the combination of oil fumes and mortal fear becomes unbearable. Clang! Another bolt comes free. I haven't been keeping count. Was that three or four?

Sound carries uncannily through this pipe, and I hear a distinctive Nahx hiss as if it is right in front of me. August hears it too and grabs me by the foot, dragging me past him and pushing me down into the sludge. He twists two more bolts away, slamming the heel of his hand on them to force them out.

Another hiss resonates down the tube, followed by a growl.

August presses his back against the pipe wall and simply kicks the panel, making the metal clang loud enough for my ears to ache. All attempts at stealth are done now. The whole pipe vibrates with every kick. I'm trying not to gasp with desperation because each breath fills me with the vile fumes.

August turns and shines one of his lights down the tunnel at the approaching noise as he continues to kick.

CLANG! CLANG! I put my hands over my ears. This is truly the ringing of the bells of death. I'm done for.

Suddenly the panel gives way with a loud pop. August

dives for me, grabbing me by the sweater and shoving me out the hole. I crash to the concrete pylon, my head cracking on something hard. Dazed, I stumble upward, my fingers curled over the edges of the access hole.

"Get out of there! August!"

All I see is a blur of metal as he scrambles around in the pipe and disappears in the direction of the other Nahx.

"No! Get out! August!"

I know the plan was to leave him behind, but I never thought it would be like this. They'll kill him.

Head still spinning, I hoist myself up to the hole, leaning inside. August is a few feet away, lying prone in the circle of illumination cast by his lights, the Mountie's rifle aimed back down the pipe.

"August!"

He turns and looks at me just as three other Nahx appear around a bend in the pipe. The horrifying metallic scraping of the other Nahx slithering toward him makes my teeth chatter. I reach for him, half back in the hole, my hand flailing vainly to grab him. But he's just out of reach.

"Come with me. Come with me . . ."

He tilts his head to the side, raising one of his hands, his finger and thumb touching like he's going to snap his fingers.

"NO! No, August, don't! DON'T!"

Snap.

There's a low *whomp* as the fumes and fuel around him ignite. The bluish flame tumbles back toward me and away from him, toward the other Nahx. I recoil from the heat, feeling the hairs on my fingers singe away.

"Get out of there! August! August!"

Without looking back, he launches himself toward the other Nahx. They slide away into the flames.

The pipe starts to vibrate weirdly, but before I can even think what that means, there's a deafening crack, and suddenly I'm flying through the air with the glowing hot hole in the pipe sailing away from me. I land hard and keep my eyes open only long enough to see the inferno of ignited gas fumes shooting out the hole and back toward me like a rocket launch.

It's near dark when my eyes open again, and the forest is on fire around me. I struggle to my feet, turning on the spot, disoriented. Over the glow of the flames, I can see the drone web outlined against the billows of smoke in the sky, less than a hundred feet away. The pipe is lying in still-burning pieces scattered around the charred concrete pylons. I can barely make out that the destruction extends well past the web into the Nahx zone. That escape route, such as it was, is gone now.

In the other direction, there's a thin strip of pink along the horizon—the setting sun. The west.

I stagger that way, dodging burning trees, blinking tears from my eyes. *Home*, I think as I escape the fire. *Home*.

My home is gone. Names and faces flare in my delirium. Mom. Chloe. Toph . . . everyone is gone. "Home" is simply "humans" now. And the words don't inspire me to keep moving as I thought they might. Gravity pushes me as much as anything else. The downhill slope I'm on suggests a creek or river. I need water.

"Promise," I say out loud. My lips sting, and when I reach up to touch them I find my fingers red and blistered. My throat burns, each breath like swallowing broken glass. But I keep repeating the word like a prayer for salvation. "Promise. Promise. Promise . . ."

PART TWO

EARTH

"There is something at work in my soul which I do not understand."
—MARY SHELLEY, *FRANKENSTEIN*

S uddenly I'm no longer in the void. I'm still weightless, insubstantial as a gust of wind, but there's some resistance, something tugging at me, something beneath me, anchoring me.

It's the earth. Gravity.

I'm not alone. And I can hear.

Chuff chuff chuff.

I know that sound. Digging. Digging in rich, leafy ground, damp with snowmelt, bursting to life with spring. The smell burrows into my thoughts, a birch tree, a lake, and ashes, charcoal. The sounds and smells seem to line up in my mind until they form a picture and I know what is happening.

They're digging a grave. They're going to bury me. They're going to bury me alive! I have to stop them somehow. Move. Speak. Open my eyes.

But I have no eyes. Though I can feel the suck of gravity tethering me to the earth, I feel nothing else. No limbs. No body. I think the words "look around," and something so odd happens that it almost distracts me from my terror of being buried alive. The idea "look around" stretches out, becoming a filament that twists and twines and spirals until every part of me is encased in its web. Then some of my cells simply awaken, and processing my desire to see, they do. Not my eyes—my skin, my hair, my pores. They . . . *look around.*

It's only moving shadows that I see. Someone very tall throws an object away, then kneels and bends, tugging something bulky from a hole in the ground. There are trees all around us, and above us a sun bright enough to fill my consciousness so that everything else momentarily disappears.

By the time I can see shadows again they are walking away.

My attention drifts down to the bulky thing the shadow pulled from the hole, but before I can turn what I see into a thought, as though someone has flicked a switch, the void reclaims me.

Five Months Later

Fighting is against the rules in the refugee camps around Prince George. Outside the camps too, in the streets and alleys, wherever they let us go, in the places that aren't completely off-limits to the thousands of desperate interlopers made homeless by the Nahx. We can beg, starve, cough up our lungs, or die behind dumpsters, but God forbid we fight.

Still, fighting calms my mind. There is just enough stimulation in the movement, the color, the smells and tastes and noise to distract me from the other nonsense I think about, but not enough that I get confused and overwhelmed. A little pain helps. I know the object of martial arts is to not get hit, but sometimes I let my opponent get in a good one, just to keep things entertaining.

"Get him, Lou!"

The other kids from my refugee camp call me "Lou" because no one can be bothered to properly pronounce my surname, Liu, and I guess "Xander" is not tough enough for them. Like Alexander the Great was just some schmuck.

I duck and barely avoid a half-hearted straight jab to my forehead as the North Camp kid blinks blood from his eyes. This is nearly over.

"You're going down, northy!" someone shouts.

I step back and my boot slips on a patch of ice, sending me ass first into the powdery snow. The northy takes full advantage, jumping on me and pounding my head with his white-cold fists. Fighting outdoors at night in northern Canada is pretty stupid, but there are snack rations on the line. A week's worth of nuts, salmon jerky, dried blueberries. We South Camp miscreants can party like kings if I can just get this goober off me.

Technically this is supposed to be a fists-only fight, since our boots could do permanent damage, but we don't exactly have a referee, and as we're breaking about a thousand rules already I doubt anyone will call it. I sit up quickly and head butt the northy hard in his chin. He goes flying backward as I scramble out from under him, kip up to my feet, and fall back on him fist first.

The impact of fist on face travels up my arm and into my brain, smashing things in there, memories, knocking them down like toy soldiers.

Raven. Tucker. Felix. Sawyer. Mandy. Emily. Lochie. Liam. They're all dead. Maybe the brightness of that should have faded over the last months, over a sad and soggy spring, a hot and humorless summer, and now this winter, cold and hungry. But nothing has faded. Not even August, on fire, sliding away in the pipe as I dove for him, to stop him, to stay with him. To have *someone* left.

Topher drifts through my consciousness like a sullen ghost, and I hit the northy again, just because I can.

"He's down, Lou, hold off."

I lean back, poised, aching to keep going, but even I don't think it's cool to hit a barely conscious opponent.

"Get up, David."

"He's not getting up," I say. The adrenaline of the fight wearing off now, I'm tired, relaxed almost, and starting to process how I won. Badly. I hit him too hard.

"Bro," I say, gently slapping his face. "Wakey, wakey." He moans feebly, his eyes fluttering.

"Ah shit, troopers!" someone shouts. I look up from the insensible lump underneath me, seeing flashing lights over the top of the derelict gas station in front of the alley we're in, this week's Fight Night location.

The spectators scatter, and David's so-called friends give me a pleading, apologetic look before clomping off into the dark, their boots making clouds of snow as they run. I hear car doors slam, and shouts.

"Come on, David." I shake him. "We've got to go. Get up."

More shouting. A truck engine roars and the siren bursts to life, cutting open the silent night.

"Did I win?" David mumbles.

"Nobody won, dude." All the spoils, the promised snacks, ran off with David's campmates. "Get up. Get up."

"Hey!" Three troopers waving flashlights and rifles appear at the end of the alley. "Don't move!"

I try to drag David upward, but he slumps back as the troopers close in. I have a few milliseconds of wild impulses. I want to search his pockets. Maybe he has a working lighter or a pencil or something. I could take his socks. Socks are worth nearly as much as freedom.

"Get your hands up!"

I run instead. Three troopers, well fed and laden with gear and winter clothes, are no match for me. I've been running nonstop for the past year and a half. I can outrun these spoiled mall cops. I bend to grab my coat at the other end of the alley, ducking to the left and out of sight as two of the troopers yell after me. I catch a glimpse of the third trooper leaning over David. He's busted now, but at least he won't freeze to death. They'll take him somewhere warm and patch him up.

The dark is profound once I'm out of the alley. The reason we chose the fight location is that it's one of the few places with a little light at night, from the security beacon shining down from the hillside above the road. Now I'm running in the dark, on pure instinct. I've run through here before and only hope I remember enough to lose the troopers without smacking into a wall.

Hard left. A narrow gap between two empty stores. Nothing to sell. No money to buy anything.

Right. Through the ruins of a burned-out house. Probably someone knocked over a candle during the blackout hours. No one rebuilds anything anymore. Get burnt. Stay burnt.

Left. Two school buses parked in a vacant lot. No gas, no diesel, the military gets what there is. If you want to go to school, you walk. I stop there to catch my breath, zipping up my coat between the buses, pressed against a wheel so the troopers won't see my feet. But I lost them. I bend and peek under the bus, not seeing any flashlight beams or movement. Not hearing anything. Troopers are about as stealthy as rutting moose. I think I'm good.

Sweaty, I think, looking down at my feet. My face will be bruised tomorrow. And I'm covered in soot now too. It smells of . . .

When I turn to continue around the back of the buses, there's a large shape there. Unnaturally tall, a heavy rifle, barely visible. Like a walking shadow.

"Ah no . . ." My heart practically jumps into my mouth as I spin, running before I've even processed it.

A Nahx? Here? It's impossible. We're twenty miles inside

the human-controlled territory. We're below 2,000 feet—the so-called low country the Nahx let us keep. I look back as I emerge from the vacant lot. A smudge of shadow moves between the buses. I twist my head around as I run, trying to locate the Nahx's partner, but I don't see anyone. The adrenaline has sucked the blood from my hands and feet so it's like running on blades. Ahead of me, an ice-covered car blocks a passage between two silent apartment low-rises. I leap it headfirst, sliding over the hood and rolling to my feet on the other side.

"CODE BLACK!" I scream. Maybe someone in the apartments will have a gun or something. Behind me the shadow moves like a ghost past the car. "CODE BLACK! Someone help!"

I veer hard left again, edging down through another alley, past dumpsters and piles of trash, which any other time I would stop and scavenge, before shooting out onto the open street.

A trooper truck skids to a stop right in front of me. I'm moving so fast, I smack right into it, bouncing backward onto my ass. But I scramble away, because we're dead if that Nahx catches up with us.

"Stop!" one of them yells.

"Code black!" I wail again, but the other trooper crash tackles me. We roll into a snowdrift. "C-c-code black. Code black. There's a Nahx."

His partner spins, raising his rifle, while the other one hauls me to my feet.

"Where? Do you see one or two?"

I point back to the apartments.

"He was following me . . . there. I didn't see his partner."

We wait, counting the seconds, but nothing happens. No walking shadow, no Nahx, no brown bear, no lost moose, nothing.

Ten interminable seconds go past while the three of us wait to learn whether we live or die.

"Get him in the truck," one of the troopers says at last. "Handcuff him."

I know they don't believe me, but the speed at which we skid off gives me some satisfaction.

An hour later I'm in a dim jail cell with three drunks and someone who thinks the Nahx are fallen angels come to make us pay for our sins. There are worse theories, I guess.

There's a poster on the wall outside the cell, a stylized drawing of a giant Nahx looming over a sleepy-looking village. AVOID AND REPORT it says in bold black letters. ENGAGING WITH THE NAHX IS PROHIBITED BY LAW AND WILL BE PROSECUTED. I'm interested in the design of the poster more than its pointlessly obvious message. It's an old-style screen print—bold shapes and simple colors, black, gray, red. Most of the digital technology was disabled by electromagnetic pulses in the first siege, so we're back to propagandizing like they did during World War II. I wonder who in town had an old printing press that they dusted off and cranked into this new life.

Behind the giant Nahx on the poster, you can just see his partner, rendered as a dim gray shadow in the background against a swirling sky. I close my eyes and try to picture the Nahx I saw by the school bus. I didn't engage with it. I avoided it. I reported it. So I don't know why I'm in jail.

"Liu! You're up!" a voice says through a crackly speaker. The speaker makes me feel, of all things, nostalgia. I miss my crappy sound system at home—my phone plugged into some cheap speakers Tucker gave me. He didn't tell me until it was too late that he stole them.

I move over to the cell door as an officer unlocks it and slides it open. Following him, I read some more shabby posters on the walls of the frigid hallway. HOARD AND GO NORTH one reads—an edict to not hoard food, one that everyone ignores. Another reads HELP KEEP PEACE AND ORDER: JOIN THE ICDF. I already looked into this. You need to be at least twenty years old and to have finished high school, so that counts me out.

The officer ushers me into a cramped room, where I recognize the uniformed woman behind the desk. Captain Roopa Chaudhry, former RCMP, now part of the ICDF, the International Cooperative Defense Force, a new collective of militarized patrols responsible for policing the human-controlled regions most affected by the invasion. Peace and order, just like the poster says. They keep the refugee stew in Prince George at a slow simmer rather than a rolling boil. She sighs as I sit down.

"Xander, can't you give me a small break?"

"I can explain. I—"

She has a file. *My* file, which she flips open, pointedly interrupting me. "Fighting. *Again*. These camp rivalries are ridiculous. Buying black market liquor. *Selling* black market cigarettes. And two weeks ago you got added to the watch list for kids who are trying to join the insurgents? Because you were up by the border web? What the hell?"

"I wasn't! I don't know anything about that." A lie, but only partly. I *do* know about the insurgency, though mostly as legend. "I was just hiking."

"Hiking to within a hundred feet of the web in weather like this? That zone is restricted. By us, and by the Nahx. You were there for fun, I assume?"

"No, I was . . ." Looking for a way through, because I want out of this nightmare and I can't think of a better way than to try to get back to the people I left behind. Even though most of them are dead. Half the rumors about the insurgency are that they are already on the other side of the web, doing whatever insurgents do. If they got through, so can I. If I get through, I can go back to the base and bring everyone out.

Bring Topher out. I have to fight to keep from rolling my eyes at myself. I know it's just another weird obsession. I like getting a close look at the web because it reminds me that the things I remember actually happened. "Hunting," I finish.

"Weapons are also contraband," Captain Chaudhry says in a bored tone. "Did you have a weapon?"

"No. A lot of animals are hibernating. If you can find their dens, you can just dig them up and whack them."

"With a shovel, I presume. Where did you get the shovel? Did you steal it?"

"No!" I say it a little louder than I mean to because it's the middle of the night and I'm cold and tired and *starving*. I haven't eaten a proper meal in days because poachers took out the supply truck to the camp for the second week in a row. The elusive snack fest I fought for is now a distant memory. "There was a Nahx tonight," I say, to change the subject and as a distraction and because if there was a Nahx out there, I want someone to do something.

"About that," Captain Chaudhry says. "I sent ten men on patrol with two Humvees and we didn't find a thing. Not even tracks."

"I . . ."

"False reports of Nahx activity are also a chargeable offense, Xander. You are running out of lives here."

"But I saw one!"

"You screw around. You refuse to go to school." She shakes her head, closing my file. "Do you *want* to get moved to a work camp? Is that what's happening? You know they sleep in tents up there?"

"I don't want to be moved." I look down at my boots. They're too big for me, and I only have two pairs of socks to my name. "I swear I thought I saw a Nahx."

She's quiet for a moment. "And how often do you think you see Nahx?"

I resist the urge to rock back and forth, chew my lips, or engage in any other stereotypically crazy behavior. Hunger has kept me awake for two nights, and the truth is, when I'm tired I do sometimes see things—people I know are dead, for example, or my old dog. Or Nahx.

Captain Chaudhry is not a shrink. There's only one shrink who sees to the mental health of the thousands of refugees crammed into the camps outside Prince George. I got "counseled" in the hospital when I was juiced up on painkillers, my scorched fingers wrapped in weeping gauze. That was five months ago. Five months in a refugee camp, keeping my mouth shut, silent as a Nahx. I fight and steal, but I don't talk.

"Sometimes," I say. It's not so much a lie as my unwillingness to discuss the truth. I know what's in that file. They all think the story I raved about when they found me, blistered and incoherent, floundering in a freezing stream, is some kind of delusion. A Nahx escorted me out of the occupied territory? Nahx don't do that.

"Xander." Captain Chaudhry sighs. "There's no way through the web. We can't even get data through anymore."

"So no one is even trying? What if there are people still alive in Nahx territory?"

"There aren't."

"But what if—"

"Xander!" Her sharp tone makes me twitch, and maybe she feels bad because she softens. "People have tried. Hundreds of people have died trying to breach the web. There's no way through. It's over. We're rebuilding now. We're salvaging what the Nahx let us keep."

My hands and face are starting to hurt from the fight. I want to go home, such as my home is—a cold shipping container shared with seven other guys. This is what the Nahx let us keep.

There is a kind of fragile treaty with our taciturn new overlords. Any violent resistance against the Nahx is considered a crime, even in the human world. Those caught trying it get sent to camps a lot less comfortable than the one I live in. Ordinary infractions are still crimes here—though, on the face of it, no one, not even Captain Chaudhry, seems to really care. Drugs and prostitution are rampant. Violence is an everyday hazard. And theft, well, I would know.

But the khaki-kitted bureaucrats like Captain Chaudhry are mostly interested in the detection and prosecution of two crimes. Resistance is one of them: messing around with the mythical insurgents, diverting supplies or weapons to them; or worse, attempting to violently engage with the Nahx, whose disproportionate response to any aggression is now legendary. Resistance will get you a tent and a blunt ax in the work camps up north. The other crime, collusion with Nahx, aiding, providing comfort, all that stuff, will get you dead in a dark alley. One of the guys in my trailer claims he saw it happen.

And this is why my particular truth is so dangerous. August was both a Nahx and a rebel against the Nahx. And he was my friend.

"Are you charging me?" About half the times I get in trouble I get off completely scot-free. I'm hoping this is one of those times.

"Snow clearing. Twenty hours."

I curse under my breath.

"Want to make it forty?"

"No. But someone stole my gloves."

"They'll find you a pair. City Hall parking lot. Seven a.m. Don't be late." She looks at her watch. "There's a one a.m. patrol past the South Camp, leaving in about twenty minutes. They can give you a ride."

"Can I check the register while I wait?"

She nods sadly because I ask this every time I get brought in here. And every time there's nothing.

The register is a database, a kind of social media for the survivors of the apocalypse. Because the Nahx knocked out so much of our technology, it's pretty lo-fi. Couriers travel around the human territories with great reams of paper, and updates are entered into the few working computers by hand. The names are people who have been found alive in remote places or who have finally been counted in Vancouver or Seattle, both of which are apparently overflowing with refugees. Or dead. The register also includes names of those confirmed dead. And then there are the hundreds, the thousands of names of all those missing without a trace.

For five months I've been checking the register five months; and I haven't found a person alive that I know.

Topher is alive, on the other side of the border. At least he was alive last time I saw him. And *maybe* August is alive. Maybe. Though he would never appear on a register, of course. As for the rest, my family, my friends in Calgary, and the ones who survived with me for a time at the hidden base in the mountains, who knows?

I follow Captain Chaudhry out to the reception desk, and I swear I'm not trying to look at her ass but it does occur to me that from this angle she looks pretty well fed. I suppose that's true of all cops these days. She pulls a chair up to the computer terminal and plugs in her password. The bright red and white interface of the register pops up as I sit.

Each time I've done this my heart has skipped hard against my ribs, rattling in hopeful anticipation of the answer I never get. Has someone looked up my name in the search register since the last time I checked, maybe someone who has run out of other names? Anyone who knows me and cares about me enough to give me a bed and a home so I can get out of this rat hole?

I don't think the people of Prince George set out to make conditions so crappy in their refugee camps, but for a town of seventy thousand to suddenly be dealing with tens of thousands of refugees, with transport from the coastal areas very limited, with hardly any fuel or power . . . well, what can we expect? I still dream of the hot showers back at the base in the mountains and wonder why I ever left there. As it is, I wash in cold water, once a week, and usually in the dark. And food? It's not quite a famine yet. But I don't think that's far off.

In hindsight, it's almost funny how woefully unprepared we were for this calamity, how easily our human civilization deteriorated and decayed. Schools barely operate; hospitals offer the minimum of care. Every man-hour is dedicated to the most basic tasks of living. Or dying. In summer, when the ground was soft enough, I earned extra rations by preemptively digging mass graves because we don't want to waste fuel by burning bodies. That's fucking macabre.

Once I'm on the register's search page, I try all the usual names—Mom, Dad, Nai Nai, my sister, Chloe. Names I entered as "missing" myself. I always pause before I hit enter on Chloe's name, because if she comes up confirmed dead there will be an Oscar-worthy scene with me in the starring role. Thankfully nothing seems to have changed in that regard. That means I can still play out one of my favorite fantasies, the one where they got into the minivan and headed north, plowing through Nahx barricades, Chloe hurling obscenities and Molotov cocktails out the window, Nai Nai hanging out the other side, cursing in Mandarin. I let it run through my mind as I tick off the rest of my list. Aunt Ruby in Edmonton. Nope. The principal of my school. Nope. My karate teachers. Nope and nope. Topher and Tucker's parents. Nope.

I added Tucker and Topher's names myself too. Tucker: confirmed darted along with the date, which I'm sure of to within a day or two either side. Topher: confirmed alive on the last day I saw him, walking away from Raven's death scene on the side of the mountain. That was in spring. It's now winter again. I don't know how he and the others in the base could have survived this long. But I can hope.

Naturally I check Raven's name next. I'm not expecting anything but her name and date of death—details I added myself just after I arrived in Prince George. I've checked her entry a few times since then but gave up about two months ago. There are only so many times you want to be reminded of something like that.

But I suppose Captain Chaudhry has put me in a mood to confirm certain details. I saw Raven die. I know who was with us. I didn't imagine the silvery gray tears streaking down August's face and the awful, despondent noises he made. I'm not going crazy; although if I were, no one could blame me.

I type the letters in slowly, R A V E N B A I L E Y, and hit enter. The computer hums as its prehistoric processor retrieves the right file, the screen lighting up with blue and white columns.

At first I think I've done something wrong, because instead of a nearly blank page with just the few details I entered about Raven, what comes up is a full page with multiple connections linked to Raven's entry.

"Holy . . ."

The boxes pop up one by one, each with a line connecting them to Raven. Her mom; her stepdad, Jack; an aunt on Quadra Island; a few cousins. All added to the registry since the last time I checked.

And all alive.

My hands shake as I open a text box so I can leave a note on her listing. Jesus, what do I say? Glancing up at the clock, I see it's nearly time to find the patrol truck and go back to the camp.

My name is Xander Liu, I type quickly. *I don't know if you remember me. I'm Raven's friend from the dojo and camp. We survived for ten months after the invasion, but . . .*

I press my eyes closed for a moment, just letting my brain replay the scene for the millionth time. Blood pulsing out of Raven's stomach. Liam dead in a heap nearby. Topher walking away from her, from us, because I don't think his heart could take it.

And August, a Nahx. August holding her and trembling so hard I think I felt the mountain shake. The Nahx can cry, and they can grieve. If people knew that, I wonder if things would be different.

. . . I was with Raven when she died, I type. *If you want, I can tell you about it.*

It seems I pass a thousand years like this, floating alone and silent in a sea of nothingness, with only thoughts and remorse to keep me company. The first sign that something might be changing is a faint sense of danger, as though I can no longer trust my thoughts, that perhaps they might be a threat to me. And as soon as that coalesces into its own coherent idea, I analyze it and prepare.

Some of my thoughts might be neither real nor memories, I realize. I need to account for that. So I do. I steel myself against whatever my mind can cook up, and as soon as some unknowable measure deems me strong enough, he appears.

August.

Standing before me in full armor, as tall and graceful and intimidating and mysterious as he ever was. And beautiful. If I had a beating heart, it would flutter at the sight of him.

"I've missed you so much," I say, but no sound comes out. My words are just neurons firing in the dark tangle of my brain. August doesn't appear to notice me. He turns his face up, and the sky appears. A broken sky.

"No . . ." I feel myself say it more than hear it. "NO!" Then

I'm screaming it because I know what is coming. My weightless nothingness becomes heavy, but rather than sinking down I'm being pulled—upward, out in every direction, apart—as though all my cells are tearing themselves in two.

The desire to speak coils around me like a tremulous vine until I feel my very atoms vibrate. "August, run." It comes out as a whisper, though I try to scream. "Run away. . . ."

The shattered sky falls and I open up, splitting, and a rift spreads from my body and mind to the ground, the earth beneath us, the air; everything cracks open, revealing the shadows and death under the surface, the abyss behind the veil of life. The crack spreads along the ground, a jagged fissure creeping toward August, who remains still, as though unmoved or unknowing. *Not real,* my thoughts remind me, soothingly. It doesn't make a difference.

"Move . . ." I say, but my voice is fragmented too, gaping wide open, tearing down through me. "August!"

The fissure takes him, streaking up one leg to split open his armor through his thigh, his groin, his abdomen, chest, neck, and finally his mask and helmet, which bisect as neatly as a nutshell. There is nothing inside. Only smoke.

I try to scream as the smoke pours out of him, billowing over the fractured world and filling me, choking me. Choking . . .

My body seems to inflate like a balloon animal—head, torso, legs, feet, arms—as I'm launched out of the dream. I feel pressure on my face, as though someone is forcing something into my mouth.

I try to pull my head away but the grip on my jaw intensifies. My eyes shoot open. A dark shape looms over me, with a field of gray behind it. Now my heart pops to life, pumping hard enough to make my ribs ache. I try to yell but whatever is in my mouth prevents it. As I writhe, the dark shape moves, and something in my throat slithers out, making me cough and convulse. The dark figure ignores me, moving to the side.

Nahx. It's a Nahx. It moves over someone next to me, a boy, pushing him onto his back. A dull gray light from a featureless night sky illuminates the Nahx as it pries the boy's mouth open. His head flops to the side, facing me.

"T . . . T . . ." I struggle to find the word, the boy's name. It's rumbling somewhere, hidden until it's as if I drive a bolt of rage through a wall and it crumbles and suddenly the name is there, along with every other thing I ever knew. "Topher," I say at last, but that's wrong. The other name comes to me instantly, even though I know it's impossible. "Tucker . . . Tucker!" Everything rushes back with that word.

It's *Tucker*. Is this real? How can it be Tucker?

His body moves, his chest expanding as the Nahx inflates his lungs with a small pump. But his eyes remain closed. The Nahx prods him, shaking him roughly.

"Wake up," I say. "Wake up, Tucker." I yank on the shackles

binding me to him with a long wire attached at our wrists. "Come on, wake up. Wake up."

The Nahx smacks him hard on the chest once, then again. After the third smack Tucker makes a noise—a muffled cough. Then he starts to twitch and writhe. The Nahx grabs the tube in his throat and tugs it out. He pulls Tucker up by the shirt. I slide over and support him, my arm behind his back.

"Wake up, please, wake up."

Tucker convulses and explosively coughs out a spray of gray goo. His eyes open, widening as he looks down at his bare feet. The Nahx hisses and makes a hand gesture.

Good.

Yes. Signs. They speak with signs. I know this. I watch it . . . her walk a short distance away, noticing her wheezing breath. The night is deep and heavy but my vision is starting to clear as though the darkness is siphoning out of my eyes. The Nahx bends over another lifeless body, repeating the treatment with the tube and pump. She's reviving someone else.

Tucker slumps into me, breathing heavily and moving slowly, testing his limbs. I put my free hand on his head, feeling the softness of his wavy brown hair, the stubble on his chin. He's wearing the camp T-shirt and shorts we buried him in, and mud and grime are worn into his clothes, his hair, in between his toes and fingers. Even his lips are smeared with it. But he's alive.

We buried him alive. Oh God.

I try to think back, to put events in the proper order, and find facts and images spread out in sharp formations, like a precisely disciplined army. The Nahx invaded. One of them killed Tucker with a dart. We buried him. We hid from the Nahx for a long time, and then . . .

"August," I say. And before I have a chance to think it might not be wise, I yell out into the dark. "AUGUST! AUGUST?!"

The female Nahx turns from her patient, ten feet away. She hisses lightly, as though telling me to be quiet.

He's not here. August is not here. If he were nearby, he would be at my side.

August saved my life, and then?

I look down at my body. I don't recognize any of the clothes I'm wearing. A silky green dress over black jeans? A leather jacket? High lace-up boots? None of this is even familiar. I look around. I don't think we're in the mountains anymore. Reaching down, I feel the ground we sit on, gathering a handful to inspect.

It's snow mixed with sand.

Where are we? A sandy desert covered with snow? Are we even on earth?

My thoughts are racing, which is something I should be used to, but this is nothing like my normal agitated mind. Everything has somewhere to go suddenly, as though a tangle of wires in an old trunk has finally been untangled, and everything has been plugged in, and megawatts of electricity are surging through the wires, lighting up my brain like Las Vegas.

New clothes. Sand. Snow. Night. Tucker. Nahx. August . . .

The Nahx makes a noise, like a wheeze, but when I turn I realize it's another Nahx, farther away. There are several, I now see, all of them bending over prone humans, trying to revive them. Above us, in the deep gray sky, dark ships appear, hissing as they descend.

I turn back to Tuck, who blinks and twitches his head from side to side. He looks down at our bound wrists, shaking them a bit.

I recognize the shackles. The Nahx carry them tucked away in their armor. They are light, with slightly sharp edges to deter pulling at them. The lightness doesn't reflect their strength, though. I remember tugging and biting at them, one wrist shackled to a bedpost. The thought fills me fleetingly with rage, even though I know August was only trying to help me. He saved my life, again and again. August came for me at the base in the mountains. He was taken prisoner. He killed someone—Emily.

Emily. Who . . . yeah. Tucker was my boyfriend. He cheated on me with Emily. And lied about it, over and over. Emily is dead.

August killed her.

August and I escaped the base, and some people followed us. Who? Topher, of course. Of course Topher would come after me. And Xander. Xander hardly left Topher's side if he could help it.

And Liam. Who is dead. Really dead.

A replay of that moment surfaces in my memories like it's nothing to watch someone get shot in the head. I can see each individual droplet of blood spray as though it happened in super-slow-motion.

August blew Liam's brains out.

And he did it for me. It was revenge after Liam shot me with an arrow, which went through my spine. I lay in August's arms, my blood pouring out of me, barely able to move, an inferno of pain consuming me.

I *died*. I died in his arms.

So what am I doing here? Sometime between that moment and now August changed my clothes, dug up Tucker, and shackled me to him? Why?

Tucker tugs at the shackles connecting us. "Who are you?" he asks.

The flurry of reorganization in my thoughts seems to glitch. "I'm . . . you don't know me?"

He shakes his head, looking down at his muddy clothes. It occurs to me how cold it is, and he's only in a T-shirt and shorts. Even I'm not dressed for cold like this, but somehow it doesn't seem to affect either of us. I feel my face and reach over to feel Tucker's. We feel warm. Tucker puts his hand over mine, his gaze fixing on me.

"Oh, Tucker . . ." I can't help saying it. I dreamed of this for so long, of seeing him alive and breathing again, and he looks almost exactly like I remember, beautiful and wild, his long matted hair falling into his dusky eyes, though he's different too. I don't know whether it's the light, maybe the reflection of the sky on the snow, but he looks *metallic*, almost as though . . .

Behind us I hear coughing as another human is revived. And around us, others get shakily to their feet.

"Does anyone know what is going on?" I yell, and many faces turn to me, looking more annoyed than concerned that we've all just been raised from the dead on what appears to be another planet. There are Nahx everywhere, though they are moving slowly, dolefully, their wheezing, rattling breath and the crunch of their boots in the snow and sand the only sound.

"Does anyone know where we are?" More blank looks.

Suddenly a series of lights flashes on, illuminating the large ships now hovering low over the rolling terrain. I stand, pulling Tucker up with me. He tugs away, moving toward one of the lights as the other humans around us head in the same direction. As my eyes adjust to the glare I see that the lights are outlining the cargo bay doors of the large

Nahx transports. Humans are obediently marching up the gangplanks in neat lines.

"Oh, hell no . . ." I turn and run in the other direction, barely aware that Tucker is still attached to me.

"Stop!" he says, tugging me back.

I keep running, Tucker dragging after me, until the crowds of humans start to thin. When we reach a small clearing Tucker leaps forward and tackles me. We roll down a dune, tangled in the wire that connects us, coming to a stop in a thicket of scrub.

"What are you doing?!" I say, shoving him off me.

"We need to go with the others."

"Go? Go where? Do you even know?"

He looks lost for a moment. "No."

"So you were just going to get on a spaceship and hope for the best?"

He stands with me, shaking snow and sand off his clothes and body. I can see he's confused, but I know stubborn, know-it-all Tucker is in there somewhere, because rather than just going along with me, he's going to argue.

"What was *your* idea, then? Just run off?"

"Damn right it is. You've lost the plot, obviously. You need to trust me."

"No. I need to get on one of those ships." His voice sounds hollow, like he's medicated.

"With the Nahx? Do you even remember what the Nahx are?"

He looks back at the ships in the distance, at the Nahx herding the humans on board like cattle, and shakes his head a little.

"Aliens, Tucker," I say, even though I know that's not quite right. It seems simplest for now. "They are aliens. Look at me."

He turns back to look at me, his eyebrows now furrowed with worry.

"We're humans. They attacked our planet. You don't remember that?"

He shakes his head, but I can see that his discomfort is growing, his chest rising and falling with deep, panicked breaths. I don't really think we have time for a lesson in Nahx-era earth history, but if that's what it takes to get him to come with me . . .

Suddenly a Nahx appears over the crest of a dune, their weapon raised.

"Oh no . . . " I spin to run in the other direction, but two more Nahx have us encircled. I edge us downhill. Out of the corner of my eye I can see darkness at the bottom of the hill. Trees? A forest? That would improve our chances of getting away.

The first Nahx leaps at me. A kind of shimmer flows at light speed through my cells and I react instinctively, spinning fast, the green dress swirling around me as I whack him in the head with a flying kick like I've never landed in my life. He goes sailing back, landing about ten feet away, his armor clattering as he falls. A kick like that would have knocked even a big human out cold, or killed him, but the Nahx rolls over with a hiss and jumps to his feet. When he lands he has sharp black Nahx knives in each hand. The defensive blades in his face quiver, one of them now bent by my boot into a permanent sneer.

"Oh fuck."

Behind him more Nahx emerge over the rise. Seeing us, they barrel down the hill. Two of them have nasty-looking rifles—not dart rifles, something else.

"Run!" I scream.

This time Tucker doesn't hesitate. We half run and half fall down the hill, dodging between two Nahx who come at us from either side. Seconds later we're in the trees, running unbelievably fast, leaping over debris, the branches flying past us. I don't have to time to think on this, on my newfound strength and speed and what it might mean. All I'm thinking of is getting away from the Nahx. And finding August. A small part of my brain, maybe just a few neurons, is thinking about August. Every other time I've gotten out of a fight with the Nahx alive it was partly because of him. I don't understand why he's not here.

Behind us Nahx weapons start to whine as I yank Tucker to the side, around trees, under branches, weaving back and forth to make us a moving target and hard to hit. There's a *whoomph* sound and something flies past our heads, smacking into a tree in front of us. I was expecting a Nahx dart, the kind that dispatched and apparently preserved the thousands of humans we left on the dunes. But it's not a dart; it's a cylindrical metal object about the size of a soda can that smokes and rolls toward us.

"Ah shit, get down!"

Tucker seems to blur momentarily. Then he grabs me around the waist and jumps a good thirty feet through the air as whatever the thing was explodes, blowing trees to smithereens, spraying snow and wood everywhere.

Nahx grenades. Fantastic.

We hit the ground running, not looking back until the trees clear and suddenly we're on a huge expanse of flat white snow. And ice.

"Is this a lake?" I hesitate until the sound of the Nahx crashing through the trees makes me move again. Dragging Tucker over rocks and driftwood, we step onto the lake ice, finding it solid enough to keep running. I can't see the other side, but how big can a lake be, anyway?

Another Nahx grenade thunks down next to us. We veer to the side, sliding away from the explosion of water and ice. It leaves a gaping hole. Soon grenades are falling all around us, blowing apart the surface of the lake

The sky has lightened. The ice ahead of us reflects the cold white light of the overcast dawn, and there's enough dry snow for us to run reasonably well. I look back. The Nahx are just gray smudges in the distance now, not following us. The grenades have stopped.

Tucker slows a bit, grabbing my arm. I wrench it away. Now that I've got my rhythm, I feel like I could run for hours. There's no reason we can't run all the way to the other side of the lake.

The ground collapses underneath us.

"Tucker!"

He disappears first, the surface of the lake shattering and instantly turning into a churning froth of ice and water. The thin wire connecting us stretches out as I try to keep my footing on the slippery ice. Tucker surfaces, spluttering.

"Climb out!" I scream, yanking back on the wire. My feet slip as Tucker is sucked under again. "Tucker!"

Tumbling forward to my stomach I lie on the ice, my fingers slipping on the wire as Tucker surfaces once more, scrambling, grabbing at the shattering ice. His face is blue.

"Help me!" he screams, before disappearing again. The wire slips out of my fingers and I slide forward over the ice until it opens under me and I'm sucked in, sinking into the dark, disoriented by the cold and the sudden heaviness of my limbs. Turning frantically, I search for the light, the sky, or Tucker, something to swim back to, but now I don't know which way is up anymore.

XANDER

One of my trailer mates, Steve, finds me in the communal tent we use as a makeshift camp library. Early refugees stole so many books from the public library in Prince George that by the time I arrived, we were denied library cards. We're allowed to sit in there and read but only on certain days, and only if the librarians on duty aren't in a mood.

The rest of the time, this tent full of dog-eared books donated by locals has to serve as our main form of entertainment. No one has enough electricity to waste on showing movies or playing recorded music; even outside the camps the power is on only sporadically. Sometimes a few of us get together and have a live concert, though—me on harmonica, two guys with guitars, and an ancient man with a violin who usually reduces us all to tears. We're trying to maintain a stable and safe community here, but it gets harder every day.

In deprivation so pervasive I've gotten used to it, books keep me marginally sane. I'm checking a tattered copy of *Frankenstein* for bedbugs when I hear Steve clear his phlegmy throat forcefully in the tent doorway.

"Hey," I say, glancing up.

"Hey," he replies. "There are troopers looking for you at the gate."

"Troopers? For *me*? Why?"

I've been living like a monk since I finished my snow-clearing shifts, so I can't imagine what they want, unless it's to bust me for keeping the gloves.

Steve shrugs impatiently. "I don't know. They told me to find you. Are you coming or what?"

I tuck *Frankenstein* under my arm, despite its suspicious smell, and follow Steve back out of the tent.

It's stopped snowing, but the clear skies mean the air is extra cold. I duck my nose down into my coat and shove my hands in my pockets as Steve leads me back to the administration tent at the entrance to the camp. We pass groups of men smoking cigarettes, huddled in the doorways of the social tents. Never-ending card games go on in most of these tents, where men gamble for rations, cigarettes, and bus passes into town. Once I joined a game and won a new pair of socks. But then I lost them in another game and vowed to never play again.

The heaters pumping warm air into the admin tent create a cloud of haze outside across the gates that mark the entrance to the camp. The guard posted there has a steaming coffee cup in one hand and an assault rifle slung over the other arm.

Beyond him, outside the gates, I can just make out the troopers standing with a tall, bulky man. They turn as I push the chain-link gate open.

I recognize the troopers. Captain Chaudhry is one, her motherly roundness hidden by her heavy winter coat. The other is her sergeant; Grischuk is his name, and he's just as badass as he sounds. Apparently he managed to bail out of the occupied zone with a bus full of moms and babies sometime after the first siege, so he's something of a hero around here. He's not fond of misbehaving camp kids, though, and has busted me for fighting several times.

I don't know the big guy they're with, but he gives me the creeps. The guard sipping coffee is eyeing him cautiously, as though worried he might just start killing people. He reminds me of Liam in his last days, not much older than me in human years, but in hate years, he's ancient. With his shaved head, ruddy skin, and ice-colored eyes, he's everything a professional thug would aspire to.

Just as I approach, both Captain Chaudhry and Sergeant Grischuk nod their heads in my direction before stepping away. They linger quietly by the chain-link fence, almost like they don't want me to notice them.

"Xander Liu?" the big guy says, stepping toward me. I resist the urge to edge away from him.

"Yes." I take his hand as he reaches for mine.

"I'm Garvin Joel." He smiles at me as we shake and persists in holding my hand for a little longer than is comfortable.

"Garvin Joel?" Steve says. "Like—"

"Yeah," Garvin interrupts brusquely. He shakes Steve's hand without looking at him. Focusing on me, he holds out some papers.

"I've signed you out, Xander. And here's a travel permit."

"Travel to where?" I'm often confused, especially these days, but I literally have no idea what's going on.

"It's fine," Captain Chaudhry says. "It's another camp. Better . . . suited for you." Grischuk smirks at her as he lights a cigarette, but this Garvin dude ignores them, fixing me with his watery eyes. He hasn't blinked since I arrived at the gate.

"Just a bit north of here. You'll be much more comfortable." He looks doubtfully down the main row of sagging RVs and tents. "You're just a kid. There shouldn't be any kids here. We've got heat, proper beds. Hot water. Get whatever you want to bring with you. I'll wait."

Steve follows me back to the shitty section of the camp, the one I live in because I arrived months after it started filling up.

Only one of my "roommates" is in the trailer when we get there. A guy called Colin who rarely leaves his bed. He's sick with something not contagious and waiting for space to open up at the medical shelter in town. I think he'll probably die waiting. Unless someone at the shelter dies. He's in a kind of race to death, I guess, but aren't we all?

He turns over with a low mumble as I roll up my makeshift bed.

"Lou's leaving," Steve announces. Colin doesn't look very interested.

A sleeping mat knitted by kindly old ladies out of plastic shopping bags, two woolen blankets, and a pillowcase stuffed with every item of clothing I own that I'm not currently wearing. One sweater. One T-shirt. One flannel shirt. Two pairs of boxers. Harmonica. And my maple-leaf scarf. I drape it around my neck, slinging the bag over my shoulder like Santa Claus.

I toss *Frankenstein* down on Colin's bed. He doesn't even open his eyes as he wriggles one hand out, grabs the book, and pulls it under the covers.

Steve is still standing there, red-faced. "You could convince that dude to take me too."

"Why would I do that?"

We look at each other. The truth is, I don't really like Steve. He has that kind of coldness that is repellent, almost scary, like someone who might kill you in your bed for an extra serving of toast. I don't know his full story. He's got no family. I know that. And he doesn't care about me either. Like the rest of us here, he's just looking for a better place to stay.

"Forget it." He turns and strides into the glare.

"Bye, Colin," I say, hurrying after him. Colin doesn't answer.

"Lou wants me to come too," Steve says as we arrive back at the admin tent.

"No, I . . ."

As Garvin frowns at me, I notice how red his eyes are. He looks like he hasn't slept in a week. Or he hasn't *wanted* to sleep in a week, which is different.

"Are you two together?" Garvin asks.

Steve says "Yes" and I say "No" at the same time, like in one of those ridiculous comedy scenes. It's profoundly unfunny.

"I only have room for one, kid," Garvin finally says. "Sorry." He takes my sleeping bag and bedroll. "You won't need the bedding." He shoves the bundle a bit roughly into Steve's chest, like extra bedding might be an adequate consolation prize. Steve clutches it, staring at me.

I tug the maple-leaf scarf from my neck, holding it out. "Here, have this."

Steve grabs it quickly, as though he's afraid I'll change my mind. I am actually reluctant to part with it, tatty as it is. It reminds me of August. But I suppose it's time I moved on from that. If I have to obsess about dead friends, maybe I should just stick to the human ones.

Garvin starts to walk away without another word. I follow, burning with shame. Steve is younger than me and smaller and not much of a fighter. If anyone needs a better situation, it's him. But I'm not about to say anything. When I glance back, he's still standing there, made blurry by the haze of steam from the admin center. I turn away, focusing on keeping up with Garvin's hurried footsteps along the gravel road that leads out of the designated camp area. No unauthorized vehicles are allowed inside the camp, so the infrequent visitors need to park by the side of the highway, past the first set of guards.

It's not a prison. I know that. But life in a refugee camp sure feels like one. Check in. Check out. Contraband frequently gets confiscated, which usually means any scavenged food and warm clothes are redistributed to those currently in favor with the higher-ups. Permits are needed to get on the bus into town and doled out at the rate of two a week if we're lucky. No visitors past dark. No female visitors at all. No running, no fighting, no sleeping outside your designated bed. What is it about crumbling civilization that always makes freedom the first casualty?

The perimeter guards turn to us as we approach.

"Leaving?" one says, eyeing the sack over my shoulder. "You check out?"

"I checked him out," Garvin says, waving some papers around. "I'm taking him . . . farther north."

One guard glances at the papers while the other one catches my eye. "Is that okay with you, buddy?"

"Yeah. It's . . . the troopers know him," I say. Garvin smiles coolly.

"All right then."

They wave us through, down onto the highway, where the wind blows through my open collar. I wish I'd kept my scarf now. As Garvin leads me along the highway toward a few parked cars, I turn back to the guards, musing at their pathetic attempts to ensure my safety. As though if I were being abducted I would just tell them, right in front of Garvin. Is that how they think it works?

Garvin turns off the highway, down through a shallow ditch, and up onto a service road. There's a large black motorbike parked there. If this is how we're traveling now, I really regret giving up my scarf.

Garvin pulls a few things from a pack tied to the back of the bike. He hands me something wrapped in brown paper.

"Soda bread. Eat."

I'm shoving it into my mouth before I take another breath. Garvin gives me a sad smile as he watches.

"Have you ridden before? As a pillion?"

"Yeah."

"Hop on; hold on to me or the rack behind you." He hands me a helmet. "It's a long ride, and it's going to be cold. You got gloves?"

I pull them out of my pockets and zip the coat up to my

neck before donning the helmet. Then I slip my gloves on and clamber onto the bike behind Garvin.

The engine rumbles to life as Garvin eases the bike off the kickstand. We cruise along the service road for a few hundred feet, until he turns back onto the highway and heads north, barely slowing down as we ride through Prince George. A motorcycle, especially at this time of year, is enough of a novelty that people turn to look at us as we pass. I see some normal life mixed in with the end of the world. Mothers and babies cross paths with heavily armed soldiers. A man shovels the thin snow from a sidewalk across from a long line of people waiting for food handouts. Tattered-looking people burn something in what's left of a playground.

The snow and the bright gray sky make everything washed-out, as though we've all been living in a slowly fading watercolor painting. Maybe one day I'll come back here to find nothing but a blank sheet of white. When it gets too much for me I close my eyes, but then all I can see is Steve, standing in the mist, watching me walk away. And my mind turns him into Topher because that's how I work.

By the time we arrive at our destination, four hours later, some of it over snow-rutted roads that would normally be an insane choice for a motorcycle, I'm a walking Popsicle. I guess fuel efficiency outweighs potential frostbite.

A couple of guys emerge from a building.

"Get him inside and warmed up," he says as the other two help me off the bike. I can barely move. "Is the fire going?"

"Just coals," someone says.

"Build it up," Garvin says. "And feed him. He looks like a Ringwraith."

I follow the other guys into a low gray building as Garvin strides purposefully through the deep snow in the opposite direction.

"What . . ." I try to say. What is this place? Where am I? What have I signed up for? But my face is so numb, my lips won't work.

They lead me across a kind of dining hall to a pile of cushions and blankets next to a potbellied woodstove that radiates with heat from the glowing coals inside it. I lower myself stiffly onto the cushions, trying to rub feeling back into my legs. A moment later one of the guys appears with a steaming cup.

"Tea," he says. "We don't have any milk, sorry. Or sugar."

I prefer straight tea anyway, but it's too hot to drink. I ease off my mittens and take the cup, curling my fingers around the warmth and breathing in the steam to thaw my frozen nose and brain.

Another guy lays a plate of what looks like scrambled eggs on the floor beside me before wandering off without a word. The first guy kneels in front of the stove, opening its creaky door and tucking another log inside. He pokes at it for a few minutes, and soon a nice blaze rises up. The guy clangs the stove door shut and slumps back onto the cushions with a sigh.

"So, Xander, huh? I'm Dylan."

I have tea in one hand and a forkful of scrambled eggs in the other, so we don't shake hands. I nod as politely as I can, mouth full of egg and all.

"You don't talk much," Dylan says.

"Sorry," I manage. "My face is frozen."

The tea has cooled enough to drink. I take a cautious sip and set my empty plate on the floor, taking a proper look at him. He's one of those white kids with hair and eyes so dark that he might be mixed, or pass for it if he wanted, and his thick beard makes him look older too. I barely need to shave, and haven't in so long that I have long wispy hairs on my chin. Dylan would probably have to shave twice a day if he wasn't okay with looking like a lumberjack.

We both turn as the door behind us swishes open. Garvin takes care to close it behind himself before joining us by the fire. He pulls up a chair rather than sitting on the floor.

"Go see to the generator, Dyl," Garvin says. "We'll need the lights on the barge tonight."

Dylan stands and heads back out the door.

"So you really don't know who I am," Garvin says to me.

I look at him. The light from the windows is dimming and the fire's glow makes his face and bald head orange, as though he might burst into flames himself. But he doesn't look familiar. I shrug.

"I think I've forgotten a lot of stuff from, you know, before. Before the invasion."

Garvin looks mildly interested at this confession. "What about since? I hear you were on the other side for a while."

"About ten months, yeah."

He stares at me for a moment as the scrambled eggs gurgle in my stomach.

"You went under the web in a pipeline?"

My teacup rattles as I set it down on the plate.

"How did you know that?"

"Two days after you were found, the Nahx blew up three more pipes under the web, including one so small a weasel couldn't get through it. It was the first time they had bombed anything in ages, so there was a lot of chatter about it." He shrugs, making his coat stretch over his meaty shoulders. "I put two and two together."

I stare down at my empty cup.

"One day you'll have to tell me how you got into the pipe. And out," Garvin says. "I bet it's quite the story."

I just nod. He leans back in his chair, stretching.

"Listen. Here's the thing. We find the less we know about each other, the better. Some of the guys here have done . . . questionable things. Not entirely legal things, even before the invasion." He chuckles, his breath low and raspy. "About a quarter of the boys busted out of a juvie jail west of here."

"Jeez."

"What I'm saying is, you might want to keep your story to yourself. I already know some stuff about you that the others might not be so accommodating about."

I'm starting to feel a bit defensive, and the small amount of doubt I arrived with has grown to me thinking I might have inadvertently taken a bit part in *Lord of the Flies*.

"What stuff about me?"

"We can talk about it later. Don't worry. I'll keep an eye on you."

"I can take care of myself."

Garvin grins in a way that makes me feel a bit queasy. "I heard that about you," he says. "You fought for money down at the camp?"

"Not money. Food. A couple of times in self-defense."

"You broke someone's nose."

I almost smile at the memory. Homophobic douchebag got kicks out of roughing up boys half his size. I coldcocked him in line for breakfast one morning. He landed facedown. "Deserved it," I say.

Garvin is still grinning. "We don't have anyone here who can fix broken bones, so I don't want to see any fighting. If someone gives you grief, come to me. The only punishment for breaking rules is expulsion. One strike, you're out."

"What are the other rules?"

"No stealing. Keep a tight lip with outsiders. Do what I tell you in everything else."

He studies me, while I try to keep my face as neutral as possible. In normal times his deal would sound like a tyrannical regime best avoided, but these days it seems all regimes are tyrannical.

"What do I get out of it?"

"A proper warm bed in heated quarters. Better food. And a purpose."

"What purpose?"

He sniffs. I get the feeling he's done sizing me up. "We'll get to that."

He stands and beckons for me to follow. Outside, the sun has dipped below the horizon and the air grown even colder. I tuck my hands into my pockets as I follow Garvin across a kind of forecourt. Tall industrial buildings rise up on either side of us as we turn and head down a dim lane between two lower buildings. There's an air of finality to the desertion here. Snow piles up on shapes that might once have been useful equipment or supplies. It smells woody, though, like shop class in school, sawdust and pine.

Following Garvin's brisk pace through well-trodden snow helps me to warm up a bit.

"How many people are here?" I ask.

"Only twenty," he says. "Twenty-one now."

"And it's just guys?"

"We had a couple of girls, but they went down to Kelowna over the summer. I think one of them was knocked up." Garvin pushes a door open, leading me into another warm hall. We cross it and go through another set of doors that leads to an enclosed gangplank.

"Logger accommodation," Garvin says when he sees me checking out the scene. "It's a pretty sweet setup that used to chug up and down the reservoir during the season."

"What happened to the loggers?"

"They legged it when the Nahx landed up in the hills. Survivors in town were evacked. Their loss is our gain."

We step out onto the deck of what looks like a miniature cruise ship, only lower, flatter, almost like a river barge. As we walk along the deck, dim lights flicker to life above us, and a low rumble vibrates the floor under our feet.

"We normally don't keep the lights on every day. Do you have a flashlight?"

I shake my head.

"We'll get you one. The cabins are heated, but coolish, you

know. We don't want to waste fuel. But there are two hundred beds and only twenty of us, so you can basically have ten blankets if that's your thing."

We turn into a long, narrow hallway. Five doors along, Garvin pushes a door open.

"Home sweet home," he says as he flicks on an overhead light and points around the room. "Bed, desk, a little toilet and sink. You're going to share with Dylan. You met him earlier."

I've never been on a cruise ship but I've seen enough commercials for them, and the room is just like cabins in the ads. Two white beds piled with fluffy blankets, a side table, a desk. There's even a TV.

"Not much to watch," Garvin says, pointing at it as though he read my mind. He takes my meager belongings from me and tosses them into a tiny closet. Then he pulls out the desk chair and sits down. I sit on one of the beds.

"When you were on the other side, did you get our videos over there?" he asks "We had reports you could pick them up in Manitoba sometimes, on the other side of the red zone."

"The videos? You mean the Nahx kill videos? That was all we got, pretty much. The only way we knew anything."

Garvin nods, satisfied.

Wait. *Our* videos?

"That was you? You broadcast those?"

"We *made* them. Did you see the one where the Nahx gets beheaded?"

Even though this cabin is warmer than anywhere I've been in weeks, I get a chill. There was a time when I would have been thrilled to meet the maker of that video or any of the nastier NKVs. We watched them back under the mountains, dreaming of the day when we might have a chance to video our own revenge on the species that took our planet. I went sour on them before most of the other guys, but I watched them, especially the one he's referring to, the one where a group of men taunt and finally behead a female Nahx.

"I saw that one, yeah. A few times."

"That was me," Garvin says. "With the machete. That was me."

"Okay." I can see he's disappointed by my lack of enthusiasm. "Sorry. I haven't seen those videos, or anything like that, in a while."

Garvin recovers from his disappointment. "No. They're outlawed in Prince George; in a lot of places, actually. I mean, people still find them, but not in the camps. Were you friends with any locals?"

"No. I kept to myself mostly."

He nods as though he approves.

"How much do you know about . . ." He waves his hand around. "Everything that's going on?"

I shrug. The information we got on the other side of the web was very limited, but since I've been on this side, I think I've been brought up to speed. "As much as anyone else, I guess."

"Anyone else doesn't know very much," Garvin says. "The official picture is of a human population well and truly conquered and obediently abiding by the treaty. Is that pretty much your impression?"

"Yeah."

"And are you okay with that?"

"No. The treaty totally fucked us on the other side of the web. I barely got out. None of my friends did." It feels so good to say this out loud that I get a slight buzz.

Garvin's eyes seem to drill into me as he nods approvingly.

"What you're going to learn here is that there is a lot of *unofficial* information out there too, if you know where to look."

"Like what?"

"Well, everyone acts like the darting only happened to other people. But people got darted on this side of the web too. Not many, but some. And about a month ago the Nahx marched right through the web like it was nothing and collected as many bodies as they could."

He looks at me as though he expects a very specific reaction.

"That's . . . messed up," I manage.

"Yep, busted into morgues and labs and all. Darted anyone who tried to resist and hauled them off too."

"I never heard anything about that."

"Like I said. Unofficial information. And there's more. Like this isn't the only web. And not all the webs are in high altitudes." He smirks at me. "Does that surprise you?"

"The Nahx . . ." I pause, taking my time, because I'm in danger of revealing that I know more than I should about the Nahx. "I thought they preferred high altitudes. Didn't they pretty much leave lower altitudes alone?"

"They did most of their killing, their darting, in high altitudes, but for whatever reason it appears they fancied a few other places. No one knows why so far. They're mostly pretty remote and unpopulated. Some are connected to populated high zones, like inside the same web, and some aren't. They've even put webs around places in the middle of the ocean. The web you went through covers pretty much all of Alberta and Saskatchewan, up north all the way to Yellowknife, and down south past Denver to New Mexico. It's massive, but there are some smaller webs too. Some in Siberia, for example."

"That's weird."

"Isn't it? They're tricky bastards, the Nahx. Not very forthcoming with their intentions."

I nod, looking at my slowly thawing feet, and don't say anything else for fear of revealing too much. But enough time passes that I start to feel like Garvin is waiting for me to speak again.

"Why am I here?" I ask.

Garvin chuckles. "I was wondering when you'd ask that. Do you know where we are?"

"Williston Lake?"

"Good guess," Garvin says. "We're just west of Mackenzie. This was a pulp mill. The border web comes down just east of town. Not much Nahx activity this side of the grid. But enough to be interesting."

It takes a moment for that to sink in. "You're still making the videos?" I ask.

"When we can." He stands. "You should get some rest. There's only cold water on board but tomorrow you can have a hot shower in the mill."

"Okay." The soft bed does feel inviting. And I haven't slept properly in months. Though why that would change now I don't know.

"Is this the resistance? Like you guys are insurgents, right?"

"Partly."

Now I'm mildly annoyed at Captain Chaudhry for yanking my chain. Obviously she never cared that I was trying to join the insurgents if she handed me right over to them. "Dozens of guys in the camps want to join up. That's all they talk about. Why did you want me?"

Garvin turns in the doorway, leaning on the frame.

"Do you hate the Nahx?"

"Yes," I lie, because I know that's what he wants to hear. And self-preservation wins over honesty every time.

He nods, with another unsettling grin. "That will have to do for now. Sleep well."

RAVEN

I'm floating in an empty space that's starting to feel familiar, even welcoming, but the feeling doesn't last. Too quickly I get that sense of the world breaking open again, of reality fracturing and parts of me getting sucked into the void behind the fissures and cracks.

And something waiting there for me. Something awful.

My eyes snap open. The gray mask of a Nahx fills my vision. His hand is on my face.

"August?" My fleeting joy quickly dissipates. The armor plates on the Nahx's face pulse, revealing the sharp defensive spines. This is not August. This is the one I kicked back on the dunes, with the blade permanently bent into a sneer. His hand slips down around my throat as I tense up, shoving upward and encountering the hard armor of his chest.

"Get off me!" Choking, coughing up water, I try to wriggle backward. The sneering Nahx kneels over me, one knee on either side of my hips. I lash one hand up to his face and clamp the other around his wrist. With a hard push I'm able to destabilize him enough for his grip on my throat to loosen. I slide back, threading one leg from between his knees and wrapping it around his neck. I twist my torso and he goes down with a crack of his helmet on the hard floor. As I scramble away, he leaps after me, his weight shoving my arms out from under me. I slip down, smacking my chin.

In front of me, in my blurred vision, I see a metal bar and grab onto it, pulling myself forward. The Nahx slides with me, his head slamming against something hard as I skid underneath. While the Nahx is momentarily stunned, I untangle myself from his limbs, roll away, and leap to my feet. The Nahx swings his leg around, trying to trip me, but I dodge him. With a growl he lunges for me again, pressing my back against something not quite solid—a wall? It seems to bend and crackle with the pressure. There's a pulse of electricity and we both reel back, tumbling to the floor. I use the momentum of our fall to swing the Nahx under me. Sitting back, I punch him hard. Then I grab his face, smacking his head on the floor over and over. The blades hiss out of his armored mask again, cutting into my hand, but I don't let go. He grips my elbows, squeezing until I hear my bones creak. I wince, and that's all he needs to slither out from under me. His fist catches my chin, sending me flying backward. Shaking the stars from my eyes, I see him lunge over me again, fists raised.

"Fifth! Stop that! Stop it at once!"

He reacts, hesitating, and I use the opportunity leap to my feet, poised to fight. As the Nahx steps back I realize he's at least twice my size, in height and breadth. I don't know how he didn't kill me.

"Who gave you permission to touch her?"

I turn toward the voice but can't find its source, though I'm finally able to take in my surroundings—a featureless gray room, empty but for a narrow steel bench fixed along one wall.

As I turn, one of the walls crackles with electricity, before it fades and vanishes, revealing another identical room. Tucker leaps off a bench, staring at me. In proper light, his skin and hair are slightly metallic. Looking down at his bare feet, I see his toenails are silver.

"What's going on? Where are we?"

"Fifth, return to your post."

The sneering Nahx strides across the cell to stand against the far wall. Just as he takes his position, part of the wall shimmers and fades like a wisp of smoke. There's another Nahx there, this one a female, I think; she's a bit smaller than the sneering one. And next to her, a human male.

The human is very tall, nearly as tall as the Nahx standing on either side of the door, but lacks the grayish coloring that August had, or even the weird metallic highlights that Tucker has. He still manages to look not quite alive, though. His eyes are unfocused, his longish brown hair limp. When he moves there's something odd . . .

With a rush of recognition everything I'm seeing seems to

slot into place in my head, and a word emerges. *Puppet.* This creature is some kind of puppet. As my eyes adjust to the glare from the open door I notice a small swarm of what look like fireflies hovering around his head. They vibrate as he speaks.

"Why is it that whenever we bring a *snezjinka* into a cell, chaos ensues?"

I file away the unknown word. Whatever this thing is, it creeps me out.

"Sit," he says.

We both edge back and sit on the bench, the cool metal making me notice the silvery blood on my hand for the first time.

"You're hurt," Tucker says, reaching for me.

"It's fine." As I wipe my hand on the green satin of my dress, I see that the bleeding has stopped. I feel that weird shimmery swoosh through my body again, and almost before my eyes, the wounds close as my skin knits back together.

"Small wounds will do that," the puppet says. "Larger ones take longer. Grievous wounds will put you out for several days, sometimes weeks, but you'll recover from most things eventually." His mouth curves into what might be a smile on something more human. On him it looks like badly executed Claymation.

"Am I supposed to be happy about that?" I snap. I don't like the way Tucker is just sitting there like a zombie. And I don't like this puppet and his abusive guard. And the fireflies swirling around his head are making me dizzy. A few of them drift away from the cloud and buzz lazily up to the ceiling.

"Happy to be nearly immortal?" The cloud of light trembles as the thing speaks again. "Free of disease, free of the slow decline of time, practically indestructible? That doesn't make you happy?"

"No." It's a lie, but I don't want to give him the satisfaction.

The fireflies vibrate, the cloud shifting to the left and to the right as the puppet looks at Tucker.

"You humans remain inscrutable, even perfected like this."

"What did you do to us?"

The puppet-human looks at us again, the cloud of lights waving from side to side. He fixes his gaze on me.

"What is your name?"

"Raven."

"And . . . ?" He turns to Tucker, who is still sitting quietly. "What is your name?"

Tucker glances at me blankly but says nothing.

"His name is Tucker," I answer for him.

The puppet sneers at me, his unnatural face made all the more monstrous with disdain, and the cloud of lights seems to throb and its color intensifies to lurid yellow. "This one is incompletely processed."

It happens so fast, I barely see it. The female Nahx leaps at me, one hand closed in a fist, the other wielding a black knife. But before she makes contact Tucker springs up to wrap his legs around her throat. By the time they both hit the steel floor, Tucker has the black knife jammed neatly in between the armor plates on her neck.

Her partner, the Nahx with the sneer, lunges forward, but the puppet holds him back with a hand on his chest.

"That's enough, Fifth. Don't damage this one."

"You don't touch her!" Tucker growls, and pulls the knife out of the female Nahx's twitching body.

"Give me the knife . . . Tucker."

Tucker tosses the silvery-bloodied knife away. It clangs on the floor.

"Your protective instincts are well honed," the puppet says. "But you're very obedient. Sit down."

Tucker returns to the bench beside me and sits there staring forward, as though he hasn't just killed someone on my behalf.

As I turn away from him and watch the other Nahx, the male, my heart crumples at his rocking posture—his left hand raised to waist height and reaching out, his other hand clenched in a fist. He growls but it comes out staccato, almost as though he's choking. More than maybe any human on earth, I understand the Nahx capacity for sorrow, and this one has just had his heart broken.

The puppet turns and looks at him with a disdainful flick of his head. "Grief is beneath your rank, Fifth. Take Third down to cold storage. She may recover."

Fifth. Third. Rank. Something becomes clear to me after all this time. August's name wasn't actually August. And it wasn't a name. It's a rank. Eighth.

I gave him a name. That seems like more responsibility than I deserved.

Fifth leaves, dragging the girl Nahx ungracefully behind him by her foot. She leaves a streak of dark, silvery blood on the floor. With his free hand he makes two signs I recognize.

Sorry. One.

The puppet only sniffs, the cloud of light contracting around him.

"First?" I ask. "Is that your name? Your rank?"

He turns slowly, his eyes narrowed. "We told our soldiers not to dart humans in the head."

"What does that mean? What difference does that make?"

First picks up the knife and steps back until he's outlined by the bright opening in the wall. The cloud follows him out as the opening contracts, disappearing around his last words.

"Perhaps you'll find out."

I stare at the blank wall for a few seconds as everything that just happened seems to sear into my thoughts.

"Are you all right?" Tucker asks behind me.

"Yes, I'm fine. But you . . ." I don't finish my thought. I've never needed Tucker to defend me, and I certainly don't now if I'm as strong as I feel. But if he's feeling protective toward me, maybe that's because he remembers us in some way, remembers what we had. And maybe we could go back to that, if only for a day, or an hour. It would be as if none of this had happened. The idea makes me grind my teeth. Why does he still have this effect on me, after everything? I want him to put his arms around me. And I also want to strangle him.

"I'm super strong," he says. "Did you see how far I jumped with you in the forest? When that grenade went off? That felt weird."

"Weird how?" I think I know what he means.

"Like I knew I needed to jump that far and suddenly I could. Almost like . . . my *thoughts* made me able to." He shakes his head, frowning. "And we could run so fast. Did you see that?"

I turn and look at him, taking in the weird silvery pallor of his skin, the metallic gloss over his brown eyes. He's still the same pretty white boy, but harder somehow, more detached. Worst of all, he's talking like a six-year-old who doesn't remember who I am and clearly doesn't care at all that we're in mortal danger.

"How do you know you haven't always been able to run like that?" I ask. I hope that doesn't come across as unkind. He doesn't seem to care.

"I don't know. I feel like I was different before. More like a normal human."

"So you remember normal humans. Do you remember your family or your friends? Anything?"

He gazes at me for a long time, innocently at first, but then after a few seconds there's a flash of something and he looks me up and down, like he's checking me out at a party. He smirks a little.

"You do look kind of familiar. Did we know each other?"

I nod, but I have to turn away. I suppose in a way it's better, simpler. At least I won't have to explain how we loved each other and how he betrayed me and how I buried him alive. Where would I even start?

Before we can discuss this further the door dematerializes again. Tucker and I leap to our feet as the sneering Nahx, the Fifth, steps into the cell. He points something at us, there's a blinding flash of light, and everything burns.

When I shake back to my senses I'm being dragged in shackles across a wide-open landing bay. Through blurred vision Nahx transports appear, one after another, landing, taking off, being boarded or loaded with God knows what.

"Wh-wh—" My face feels numb. It's hard to get the words out. "Where's Tucker? Where are you taking me?" I try to struggle, swinging my legs up, but I see they are bound too, so I'm immobilized. "Tucker!" I twist my head around, but it seems it's just the sneering Nahx and me.

The landing bay is huge. Thousands of Nahx march around, boarding or disembarking from transports. There are huge racks of Nahx rifles and other weapons. And tiny pinpoints of light float everywhere, some in clouds and some by themselves.

"August . . ." It comes out slurred. I think I might have gotten punched in the mouth at some point. "AUGUST!" None of the Nahx reacts.

The sneering Nahx drags me too close to a weapons rack, slamming me into it painfully as he pulls me onto a transport. He locks my wrist shackles onto a row of metal rings in the cargo bay.

The transport launches so abruptly, I slip to the floor, the gravity of our ascent yanking my arms painfully. As our climb accelerates, my shoulders feel like they they're being torn open. I struggle to gain my footing, and get into a position where my arms aren't being wrenched.

The transport banks, jostling me against the wall. I pull myself up with one of the other rings and lean over as far as I can to see into the cockpit. Sneerface clings to a handhold above the archway while two other Nahx pilot. He turns to me, the blades in his face flicking out menacingly.

I tense as the transport straightens out and he steps back into the hold toward me. Despite his obvious dislike, he reminds me of August, who I'll probably never see again.

I want to close my eyes, but I don't trust this sneering Nahx.

He hisses at me and turns back to the cockpit, signing. I catch the word *open* and what I think are some numbers, but the rest is too fast for me to interpret. A few minutes later I can feel the transport decelerate. The engine whines as we begin to descend. Sneerface returns to the hold, activating a control panel by the door. It swooshes open, filling the hold with gusts of freezing air.

One of the tiny lights from the hangar hovers near the ceiling of the transport, being buffeted in the wind, before dipping down to buzz around my face. I wonder if they meant to join this journey or got trapped in here by accident; they seem to be on their own. The way they float in front of me makes me feel like they are studying me, sizing me up somehow, but they zip away when Sneerface approaches me again.

He releases my wrists and feet and drags me to the door. The air blowing in is frigid, and all I can see outside is white. The Nahx latches a winching cable to his armor as the transport slowly descends through the clouds. Soon I can start to make out detail on the ground—trees, rolling hills, a frozen lake. I'm pretty sure I'm being returned to where I was revived.

As the transport hovers over the sand dunes, I can make out some human shapes lying far below in the snow. Dead?

Rejected? Defective? *Incompletely processed?* I think I might be about to join them one way or another.

The little light lingers around the edge of the door, holding position despite the wind whipping my curls across my face. The Nahx yanks me forward, grabbing me by the front of my jacket. He signs with one hand, the sneering blade on his face reflecting the snow glare from hundreds of feet below us.

Good-bye.

"No! No!" My hand lashes out, trying to find something to grab on to. The light creature pops back into my field of vision, and my fingers close around them just as I fall.

My brain tries to estimate how long I have left before I slam into the ground, and I find it counting down, in bizarrely precise milliseconds and meters, even though I know it's not enough to come up with any other option than to die on impact. Have all my efforts been for nothing? I didn't save Tucker, I didn't save Topher or Xander or even August. I never got to say the things I wanted to say to my parents. I'm not going to save the world or ever have a chance to be a hero. I'm going to die.

The last thing I think of is August and how hard he tried too.

XANDER

Three days pass without me being any closer to knowing what the hell I am doing in Garvin Joel's testosterone-fueled enclave by the lake. My roommate, Dylan, shows me around; I get a shower, some new clothes, plenty of food.

What I do learn is mostly banalities. Why do we eat so many eggs? Garvin and his gang looted a chicken farm. The chickens live off our scraps in the boiler room. The rest of the food and supplies are mainly scavenged from the nearby town of Mackenzie, which was evacuated during the first attacks. Just like we did from the base in the mountains, teams of raiders go on sorties, looking for anything of value. I feel like I've landed on a snake and slithered back to where I started.

I've been introduced to everyone and tried to remember names, but so far no one seems to have any expectations of me other than to eat and sleep. No one asks any questions. It's almost too good to be true, and probably stupid for me to let my guard down, but I'm so hungry and tired that I just meet those low expectations. I learn people's names. I eat eggs and potatoes. I sleep in a comfortable bed. I don't ask questions.

On the third night I wake up in the dark and have that

disorienting feeling of not knowing what day it is or where exactly I am. In the faint glow of the moon through the high window I can see Dylan in the other bed, sitting up. He has one hand over his mouth.

"Dylan? Are you okay?"

He takes a few seconds, finally peeling his hand from his mouth. "Fine." His voice is shaky. "Nightmare."

"Nahx?"

He nods, wiping his face on the sheets.

"I get those too." I'm pretty sure his aren't like mine, though, fraught with the conflict of friend and foe. Mostly in the nightmares I'm watching August burn alive. "Do you want to talk about it?"

"No."

"Do you want to go back to sleep?"

He laughs. "No."

I lean back on my pillow, tucking the pile of blankets into place. We have some heat on the barge, but not a whole lot. It's still cold enough for us to sleep in our clothes. I'm even wearing a tuque.

"I heard you came from the other side," Dylan says after a moment. "That's wild."

"Yeah." I'm surprised no one has asked me about this before.

"You were at some hidden military base. What was that like?"

"It was all right. Warm. Where did you hear this?"

"Garvin told me. We're not supposed to bug you about it, though."

"I don't mind."

"Were there a lot of weapons there?"

"Some. Enough." Now I'm wondering how Garvin knows this about me. It wasn't a secret, exactly, but it wasn't something I talked about a lot either. Someone who escaped the occupation zone was enough of a novelty to draw attention. And that was the last thing I wanted.

"What kind of weapons?"

"Guns, rifles, you know."

"Garvin has a grenade launcher. Like a bazooka."

I turn to him. He has a huge grin on his face.

"For real? Where did he get that?"

There's another moment of silence, one too long to not mean anything.

"I was with this military convoy," Dylan says. "We were coming up east of Spokane during the first siege, a bunch of cars following these army trucks along a remote road. They thought it would be safer. But we got hit. By the Nahx."

I can tell it's hard for him to talk about this so I just let him take his time. Seconds tick past. He wipes his face again.

"I was the only one who . . . you know . . . didn't get darted."

I count in my head to fill up the silence. It's like I'm measuring his trauma. It takes ten seconds to get to the next detail.

"I was in the trunk. We had one of those cars where you can pull down the back seat and get at the trunk. My brothers pushed me back there and piled a bunch of crap on the seat."

Twenty seconds, each one like a hypodermic needle in the heart.

"I waited in there for two days. When I got out everyone was dead. My . . . my brothers were dead in the front seat. So I pulled their bodies out and took the car. Kept going until I found another convoy. I figured I'd join them, and if we got attacked, I'd just let the Nahx dart me."

I don't even know how much time passes before he talks again. It feels like an hour.

"Anyway. We made it to Kelowna and I was in a camp there, you know, when Garvin got word around that he'd take any guys who had something to offer. Information or whatever. So I told him I knew where a bunch of weapons were. He went down there, salvaged everything he could, and picked me up on the way back through." He exhales, not quite a sigh but more than a breath. "He's a man of his word."

That last sentence gives me a chill. Garvin hasn't made any real promises to me yet. I have a feeling that when they come, he'll be looking for something in return.

"So you're amassing weapons here? That's what Garvin wants?"

"Among other things. Hasn't he given you the list?"

"What list?"

Dylan lowers his voice to an ominous rumble. "*THE* list. All the stuff we're supposed to look out for when we're out on raids. Weapons and ammo are high priorities, but there are some funny things on there too. Coffee. Jell-O mix. Allergy pills. He has a running offer of two days off chores for anyone who brings back a pound of butter. We have barrels of flour from the bakery and pizza place in town, and as many eggs as we can eat. But no butter. It's kind of heartbreaking."

"So this is what you guys do? Just patrol around looking for stuff to scavenge?"

He frowns at me. I didn't mean to make it sound so pitiful, but before I can apologize, he puffs himself up, even under his fluffy blankets.

"Nahx. We patrol around looking for Nahx."

"To kill? And make videos?"

He nods, now thoughtful.

Something happens to the clouds and moon outside, and the light in my cabin changes, turning everything blue-gray, including Dylan. The terror of the dream seems have dissipated, and with it something that made him seem like a fully functional human. He looks dead now as he lies back on his pillow, resting his head in his hands.

"Xander," he says after a moment. "Can I give you some advice?"

"Okay," I answer warily.

He takes his time, parsing each word, as though he's typing them out on an ancient typewriter.

"I get . . . let's call it a *vibe* from you."

"Okay."

"I mean, I don't care. There's nothing wrong with it. It's just that some of the other guys can be real dicks. And I don't want you to get into problems with them."

I have a pretty good idea of what he's talking about, but I don't feel like helping him out.

"What is the nature of this 'vibe'?" I ask.

He rolls over, and I do the same until we are looking at each other over the two feet that separates our beds. I could reach out and touch his face. In the dark, I can see him smile.

"I'm just saying you might want to chill with it, a bit."

"The *vibe*?"

"Yeah."

I can't help sighing as I roll over onto my back. I could drag it out, this euphemism game, but now I'm just annoyed with Dylan and his nightmares and his vibe. I wish I'd been given a private cabin.

"This vibe is gay, right?"

He snort-laughs, plumping his pillow, probably as an excuse to turn away from me. "Am I wrong?"

"I mean, bisexual, I guess, if you need terminology." I've never said this out loud before, not even to . . .

Well. I'm beyond pissed off that this hairy American is the one who hears it first. I can think of twenty people who would have been better choices.

Pretty sure most of them are dead, though.

"Whatever, man, it's cool with me," Dylan says. "I'm from Seattle. It's the other guys you need to worry about."

I don't quite understand how twenty young guys isolated in a postapocalyptic rebel enclave can be so uptight, but I guess I don't have much choice but to play along. I can defend myself. I know I could take any of these slobs. But who wants to fight in a place like this? And anyway, Garvin said fighting would get me sent back to the refugee camp.

"Thanks for the warning."

"Not a warning, bro. Just advice."

I don't really see the difference, but I keep that to myself too.

Dylan closes his eyes, as though having gotten a few things off his chest, he can now sleep. Meanwhile I'm wide-awake and staring at the ceiling, trying to let my mind run loose. Lately my thoughts don't seem to go anywhere. I live another day. Repeat. Repeat. Then I die. Probably sooner rather than later.

Maybe the horror that's been building up in my head doesn't

leave room for anything else. Raven bleeding to death. August getting blown to bits. Felix's dead eyes. Lochie's twisted neck. Liam's head . . . just . . . like a really morbid merry-go-round.

I think I drift off at last, but what seems like seconds later, Dylan is shaking me awake, leaning over me with a big grin on his face.

"Wanna have some fun?"

"What? No! What?"

He yanks my blankets off, but before I can protest, two other guys are crammed into the cabin and dragging me out of bed. I'm preparing to defend myself when one of them hands me my coat.

"Where are your boots?" he says. The other one tosses them at me. I pull them on. So we're taking the fight outside? That's annoying. It's freezing out there. I stand up, jamming my arms into the sleeves of my coat. When I turn, one of the guys shoves a rifle into my chest.

"What's this for?"

"You know how to use it, right?"

"Yeah, but . . ."

"Come on."

I follow them out of our cabin and into the dark hallway. Someone clicks on a flashlight, waving the beam around as a few other guys emerge from their cabins, dressed for a winter night like I am.

I can barely see, but I feel around, trying to check out my rifle.

"Is this a laser sight?"

Dylan huffs next to me. "Nice, right? US military. These are the ones I hooked us up with."

I check the safety, making sure it's firmly in place, then flick on the laser sight. A red beam joins the flashlight dancing on the walls as we walk. I click it off before testing the tactical flashlight mounted on the barrel. Pretty sweet weapon, actually. A year ago I would have been delighted with it. Now it just makes me feel dead. Preemptively dead, like how people who carry rifles around usually end up.

"What are we hunting?"

There are five boys with us now. They all dissolve into chuckles.

"Dude, panda bears!"

That just makes them snicker even more.

"Mobbs spotted a Nahx out by the airstrip."

I skid to a stop. The others carry on a few paces before turning.

"Are you kid—a single Nahx? Where's its partner?"

Two guys shrug.

"We have to know where its partner is or we'll get ambushed."

One of the guys leans toward me. He's broad and tall and

has one of those mashed-looking noses, like he's a boxer or rugby player. I try, as casually as I can, to sling my rifle's strap over my back so I can have my hands free.

"Are you chicken?" the broad one says. I'm assuming this is Mobbs. He *looks* like a Mobbs.

"No. But I'm not crazy either."

"This is what we do, Xander," Dylan says. "This is the deal."

I notice one of the guys has a small video camera instead of a rifle.

"Where's Garvin?" I ask.

"He's with the other guys out by the fence."

I've lost track of who is talking.

"Go back to bed if you're going to pussy out."

Mobbs. That was Mobbs.

"I'm not going to pussy out. I'm just . . . I just woke up. Give me a break." I pull my rifle from behind my back, pointing it down and checking the clip, the chamber, and the safety again. Snap. Crunch. Click. All very professional and badass. I haven't held a rifle for nearly six months, but I guess it's a bit like riding a bike.

A couple of the other guys whoop as we break into a run down to the end of the hallway. We turn onto the enclosed gangplank and emerge into the cold forecourt. It's snowing lightly, which makes the night deceptively quiet and peaceful. Circling around a building, we turn back toward the lake, silently following the shore. When we reach the high fence that marks the boundary of the mill's administration area, Mobbs calls us to a stop.

"It was outside the fence moving east," he whispers. "Dylan, you take Xander and Michael across through the grinding shed to the south side, then follow the fence north. The rest of us will go the other way."

We split up. Dylan, Michael, and I turn away from the admin buildings and into the mill proper, the smokestacks looming over us like haunted castles as we pass. Dylan turns us down between them to a set of doors at the end. Retrieving a key, he unlocks one and pushes it open, leading us into a long, narrow shed. Two huge machines line either side, flanking a walkway between them that disappears into darkness. Dylan snaps his flashlight to his rifle, flicking it on.

Our footsteps kick up clouds of dust, which meld with our foggy breath to create wisps and ghosts that drift across our flashlight beams. My eyes dart around. I don't know if I should remind Dylan that a Nahx could easily jump the perimeter fence if they wanted to, or just tear it open. Surely if these guys have been hunting them, they would know that.

I'm not sure what a grinding shed is, but the machinery is gigantic and menacing, made of bolts and cogs and chimneys. It looks like something out of a steampunk fantasy, complicated-looking, strangely shaped, and bulky. And dark.

If a Nahx wanted to hide in here, they could just press them-selves against a machine and they might blend right in.

Neck, I think, *shoulder joints, knees.* A good knee shot makes them fall. A neck hit and they don't get up. Not right away, at least. Dylan turns us down another aisle, this one weakly illuminated by a set of open doors to the outside down at the end. He stops us, holding one fist up. When he turns back to us his eyes are wide.

"What?" I whisper.

"Supposed to be locked," he hisses.

This is what happens when you *try* to find a Nahx in the night.

Dylan looks like he's going to pee himself; the other guy with the camera still hasn't opened his mouth. Meanwhile my mind has clicked into high gear, which can be helpful in moments like this because I can think of all possible outcomes at once. About 70 percent of them are imminent death, but that's just normal operating procedure. Thirty percent are ways to get out of it.

"Back-to-back," I say, tugging Dylan behind me and turn-ing him so he's facing away. "Cameraman, what's your name again?"

"Michael."

"Stay between us, Michael. We're going to go back the way we came."

I click on the tactical light on my rifle, shining it down on the floor. Our three sets of footsteps in the dust wind back along the walkway before turning down the center of the shed. There are no other footprints here, which makes sense. If there's a Nahx in here, they turned left or right inside the back entrance, which means they could be anywhere.

"Did you lock that door we came in?" I whisper, looking back. Dylan nods without turning. He has his rifle raised; the beam of his flashlight shakes on the walls and machinery.

"If there's a Nahx in here, he already knows we're here too," I say.

"So we ambush him," Dylan says. "Find his tracks."

That's a crazy idea, but it's also part of every scenario I can think of that has us making it out alive.

We edge back down the passage to the central aisle. I shine my flashlight back along the way we came in, seeing only our footprints there too. Along the other way is undisturbed dust.

"Are you sure that door was supposed to be locked?"

"Yes," Dylan says tightly. "Garvin put locks on everything for this exact reason."

There's a loud bang and the sound of glass breaking from the other end of the shed. Michael swings his camera around, nearly clocking me in the head. Dylan reaches past him to give me a shove, but I'm already running, on pure instinct. The feel of having a rifle in my hands again has turned me back into a soldier, a survivor. A killer even, maybe. Will I take out this Nahx if I get a shot?

The door we came in through is mangled and torn from its hinges—a heavy, oversize metal door, crumbled on the floor like a discarded tissue. Of course I know how strong the Nahx are, so this is just a reminder. I edge forward, every muscle in my body clenched, and poke my head out the demolished doorway. Tracks in the snow lead away from the door in both directions—our tracks and the long strides of the Nahx's distinctive armored boots, his tracks disappearing along the front of the grinder shed and in between the stacks of logs left behind when the mill was abandoned.

"It's heading toward the barge," I say. "Is anyone left there?"

"Just a sentry. AJ."

"Is he armed?"

Dylan nods.

I need to think, but I don't have time. This Nahx is behaving strangely. It knew we were in the grinder shed. With only two exits, it would have been easy to corner us and take us out. It's almost as though it didn't want to.

Gunfire draws us into the log stacks, running practically blind through slushy piles of snow and sawdust, following the Nahx's footprints. They stop abruptly when we reach the end of the log yard and the high fence.

I spin, pointing my rifle and light left, right, back the way we came.

"Where'd it go?" Dylan says. "Michael, did you see anything?"

Michael's eyes are fixed on the viewfinder of his camera as he shakes his head. I've got to admire his commitment.

"Who is shooting?!" I shout. Some indistinct yelling from the direction of the lake is the only reply. I tug Dylan back between the log piles. "Let's circle back."

We turn and run back down through the slush. Just before we reach the end of the logs a shadow flashes across above us, from one stack to the other.

Dylan spins, raising his rifle. "Was that . . . ?"

I strain to see. High above us, on top of one of the stacks of logs, a shadow moves lengthwise, away from us, before leaping to the next stack, its shape outlined against the gray sky.

"Did you get that?" Dylan asks.

Michael is actually smiling. "Uh-huh."

These guys are crazy.

Dylan leads us out of the log piles, edging along the ends of the trunks until we're two rows over. We slide to the ground, rifles and camera raised, trying to be as quiet as we can while we gasp for breath. I start to speak but Dylan pulls me back, hand over my mouth. Michael turns the camera on us and holds it there a bit too long for my comfort. Dylan nudges the barrel of his rifle up toward the top of the log pile, about halfway down the row. If he hadn't drawn my attention to it, I would have thought it was just a misshapen log.

But it's the Nahx, pressed down on the logs. I strain to see, but I don't even think his rifle is aimed at us. He's not moving, though from the position of his head, I think he's watching us.

"Take the shot," Dylan whispers. "He can barely see where you are from that angle."

He's right. One of the logs is jutting out, giving me some cover. Slipping down until I'm lying in the muck, I painstakingly nudge my rifle over so the barrel is poking between two logs. I have to hold my head in an intensely uncomfortable position to get my eye to the scope, but once I've contorted myself sufficiently I have the Nahx right in the crosshairs. The top of his skull, I think, which won't work. Even the high-caliber bullets bounce off their helmets. But if he moves his head . . .

"Take it, Xander," Dylan says. "You got him."

My finger curls around the trigger as I click on the laser sight with my other hand. A bright red dot appears on the Nahx's head. He reacts as though the laser burns him, jerking his head up and scrambling backward over the logs. The red dot glows just under his chin. Perfect.

"Take him, bro! Take the shot!"

I hesitate. I don't know why except that this seems all wrong. This Nahx shouldn't be alone. He hasn't taken a shot at us. In fact it's almost as though he's been avoiding us, which makes no sense. The Nahx are brazen. They openly stalk and kill. Stealth is not really their thing, especially when they're not even shooting.

"Xander . . ."

The Nahx drops out of sight.

Dylan curses and pushes me off him, leaping up with his rifle raised, running back down the row. Michael chases after him without a word.

"Wait!" I yell.

Dylan shouts back. "Go around! Cut him off!"

Before I can move the Nahx reappears, jumping down from the top of the log stack, landing between Michael and Dylan with the force of a cluster bomb. They go flying in opposite directions, Dylan rolling toward me. I'm on my feet and firing at the Nahx before I have a chance to think. Bullets ping off his armor as he suddenly turns, leaps right over Michael, who is miraculously somehow still filming, and runs back toward the fence.

"Yeah, you better run, motherfucker!" Dylan yells after him. Both he and the Nahx raise their weapons at the same time and I hear a million different things suddenly—Dylan's rifle firing, the whine of the Nahx rifle, shouting coming from somewhere, my heart beating in my skull, Michael finally making noise, going, "Oh my God, oh my God," and a kind of sharp hiss as the Nahx fires a dart. I grab Dylan by the coat and pull him down just as the Nahx gracefully leaps the perimeter fence and runs; with three or four long strides he's gone, disappearing into the dark.

"Xander!" It's Michael's raspy voice. I spin around to see Dylan cradling his bare hand. A Nahx dart lies on the ground next to him. A dark spiderweb of black veins is spreading out from his palm.

"He blocked it," Michael says. "It would have hit me." Unbelievably he's still filming, talking at me through his camera like a rogue reporter in a war zone.

People are shouting somewhere. Dylan is hyperventilating. I fall down on my knees next to him, tearing open his coat and pulling it off. Stripping my scarf off, I tie a tight tourniquet around his upper arm before peeling back his sweater sleeve. A thin sliver of Nahx toxin is inching up his wrist.

"Move out of the way!" Garvin's voice bellows as he charges on us. As I tumble backward Dylan reaches for me with his good hand. I take it and squeeze as hard as I can, as though maybe I can pull him away from the inevitable. He turns to look at me, stricken, and I watch his face because I don't want to see what I know is going to happen next.

Garvin raises his machete, bringing it flying down, and cuts Dylan's arm off just below the elbow, while I'm frozen, holding on to Dylan, letting him scream for both of us.

RAVEN

Wherever I am, the sky is beautiful. It cycles through sparkling, fluorescent blue, soft misty mauve and pink, and deep velvety indigo streamed with ribbons of aurora borealis and sprinkled with stars.

If I'm on earth. The northern lights might be called something else on other planets. The sun, or something like it, rises and falls, bringing short days and long nights. I can't actually see the sun because it's low on the horizon over my right shoulder and I can't turn my head. I can't move at all.

Only one sun, though, as far as I can tell; that's a good sign.

I try to keep my eyes open, though it hurts. If I close my eyes, I drift into unconsciousness, and the gaping, jagged hole in the universe is waiting for me, crackling with lightning, pulling my molecules apart. I wake with an agonizing jolt, salt tears stinging me.

At night the darkness is profound, despite the colorful sky. The little firefly creature I stole from the Nahx transport hovers over me some of the time, my only company. They bathe me in a tiny circle of bluish light, like a miniature UV bulb.

"Blue," I say one night, though the effort makes my lips burn.

The light flickers happily, dancing off. Though my thoughts are tangled and swirling, I note that as the creature's name and file it away. *Blue.* I want to ask them to come back, because I'm lonely, but now I can't make my mouth or tongue move.

The next day it snows. The flakes melt on my face, but I think my body gets coated in a thick white blanket, as though I'm becoming part of the landscape. I manage to open my mouth, which is difficult with what I think is a broken jaw, to let snowflakes wet my parched tongue, more to relieve the discomfort than from any desire to survive. My inability to move, and the scorching fire that lances through every inch of my flesh, suggests that I'm grievously injured. So I wait in agony, expecting the trauma of my fall to finish me off, hoping it does.

I've lost everything. It's time to give up. The Nahx won. We lost.

I lost.

Everything.

My eyes drift shut and capture another terrifying glimpse of the crackling, stygian rift before snapping open again. The tiny light floats above me, pulsing, seeming to say *Stay awake.*

I try to say "Okay, Blue," but all that comes out is a hoarse moan.

Things are *moving* inside me. Bones, muscles, sinew, and cartilage are tugging, pulling themselves back into order.

117

Blood is churning through my veins and arteries like lava, pouring into holes left by shattered ribs and crushed vertebrae. My spine is like a glowing-hot spike from my brain to my pelvis. My head is still fragmented—part of it working on reconstructing my skull, part of it occupied with a kind of reorganization of my brain, as though everything I've ever seen or thought or learned is being catalogued and shelved in a more practical order. Maybe this is just a side effect of whatever is happening to my bones, less physically painful but with its own kind of anguish. Thoughts and memories are as clear as a movie screen as they get sorted. So I watch it again. All of it—every mistake, everything, everyone I've lost. I see Mom and Jack. And Topher and Tucker. And August.

August carrying me. August feeding me. August holding me while I bled to . . .

Blue bops me on the nose as my eyes droop.

"Yeah . . ." I manage, though it gurgles a bit. "M'wake."

I understand what is happening. I am being reconstructed, body and soul. Whatever is in the darts, whatever turned my blood silver and made me a superhuman, knows how my body parts are supposed to fit together and is slowly dragging them back into place. When this started, in the first few hours, I was sure the pain would drive me mad, but now that a few days have passed, I've grown used to it, which in itself is a fascinating discovery.

On the fifth day, just as the bright sky begins to fade into twilight, I suddenly vomit, which would be less catastrophic if I wasn't stuck lying on my back. Blue zips into my field of vision and vibrates as I choke and cough, before they zip away. I painstakingly turn my head, but the movement causes me to vomit again, my nose and mouth filling with rancid fluid. When some of it dribbles onto the snow beside my head I see that it's dark silver. Like my blood is now? I'm vomiting blood. That can't be good.

With supreme effort, I roll onto my side as I hear footsteps crunch through the snow. Seconds later a Nahx arrives on the dune above me. With the bright sky behind him, all I can see at first is his outline—slender, broad shouldered, very tall.

"August?" My voice is barely above a murmur.

He doesn't answer, but as he steps down the dune toward me I see I've made a mistake. This isn't August. This one is skinnier, gangly, with the loping gait of an awkward teenager. He limps a little as he approaches, glancing down at me for a few seconds, his head tilted to the side. Blue drifts next to him as he approaches.

He drops to one knee, reaching out to touch my head, letting his hands slide down onto my shoulders and arm. After a few seconds he leans back, wriggling his fingers in front of me.

Explain.

My teeth feel a bit loose, but I manage to speak. "Explain?"

No. Move hand. Like this.

I wriggle my fingers to match his demonstration.

Move feet.

I obey, but the effort sends searing pain up my legs and spine. The Nahx ignores my moans, reaching under my back to lift me into a sitting position. The agony of that small amount of movement sets off a bout of uncontrolled trembling. The Nahx seems unperturbed by this. He sits back on his heels and watches me as my aching teeth chatter and my eyes run with stinging tears. Blue lands on my bent knee and flickers there just as I vomit again and eject a stream of gray sludge onto the ground between my legs.

"I think I'm dying," I croak. The Nahx shakes his head.

No. Sick. You're letting the sickness out.

I gingerly lean my weight onto my hands in the cold snow and edge myself backward away from the puddle of puke. The pain of that is unexpectedly manageable.

"I'm not dying?"

The Nahx shakes his head again as Blue floats up and zips from side to side.

"Well, shit." I'm slightly disappointed to receive that unexpectedly optimistic prognosis. "What does 'letting the sickness out' mean?"

The Nahx tilts his head to the side, which is so reminiscent of August that I have to flick my eyes away for a second.

Parts of you died, he says, pointing at the puddle of vomit. *You threw them out and made new parts.*

I look at Blue, who bounces in agreement.

"Is that normal?"

They bounce again.

The Nahx, making a little hissing sound, signs at me.

You understand my language?

"Yes. It's kind of a long story. Help me up." After he drags me upright, it takes every reserve of willpower to take a single delicate step. My body is still burning, inside and out, but I'm moving at least, even though the pressure of my feet on the soft sand is like standing on coals.

You're not broken. I go now, the Nahx says.

As he walks away, I see the reason for his limp. Parts of the armor over his thigh and knee are dented and cracked, the segmented plates no longer fitting neatly together. Beyond him, I can see other Nahx, scattered over the rolling dunes, some wandering, some kneeling with their heads down. When I crane my neck, painfully stretching to see over the rising and dipping hills, I spot some Nahx shapes lying in the snow, seemingly dead. Some of the dead appear to be human too, or formerly human, like me.

"Wait," I call after him. "Wait! I want to ask you something!"

Blue floats with me. We catch up to the Nahx just as he bends over one of the dead. Clicking something in his armor, he removes some kind of small tool and proceeds to poke at the dead Nahx's knee. Seconds later one of the armor plates comes away, then another. The limping Nahx uses the plates to replace the damaged parts of his own armor. I watch, fascinated by the thin, tentacle-like tendrils that wriggle out from the Nahx's knee, knitting together the undamaged plates and sucking them into place. It looks alive somehow, almost sentient, though that idea is too terrifying to dwell on.

"Are they dead?" I ask, pointing to the body in the snow. "How can you tell if they're dead?"

Feel cold, the limping Nahx says. He lays his hand over the other one's head, chest, and thigh.

I kneel and do the same. The dead one's armor is frigid, even colder than the surrounding winter air, if that's possible.

The limping one reaches over the body and touches me gently, with another question hand.

Who are you?

"Raven," I say. "What's your name?"

No, he says. Then, *Tenth.*

"That's your rank, right?" He nods. "Don't you have a name?"

No, he says again. Then he makes my sign name.

Night color bird.

"That's right. Raven."

Blue swirls between us, as though to say *Pay attention to me!* Tenth recoils when they get too close, stumbling backward.

"They won't hurt you," I say. "I think they just want to be introduced. Blue, this is Tenth, I'm Raven, and apparently the three of us are reenacting Milton's *Paradise Lost*."

Tenth tilts his head again, raising a question hand.

"Sorry. My mother is an English teacher. *Paradise Lost* is an epic poem about . . . oh, never mind."

Tenth shrugs and reaches back down to the dead one, clicking something on its helmet. There's a slurping noise, and a gush of oily fluid pours out around its head. Tenth pulls the mask away, revealing the Nahx's dead face.

A girl, I think, though I suppose when you're a mind-controlled soldier with only one goal, what does it really matter? Her features are quite delicate, with an upturned nose and small, pursed lips. Blood or tears dribble from her nostrils and half-opened eyes; their irises are milky gray. Her eyebrows are heavy, glossy, metallic, and fixed in a stony frown, and she's a bit gaunt, as though malnourished. She looks nothing like August, which is both a relief and a mystery. Whoever these creatures are, whatever they are derived from, it's human; that is obvious. What kind of human, though? Where did they come from?

She looks young, which makes me sad.

Tenth wrenches on her mask, pulling the plates apart and removing a small pin-like object. He wedges it into his own mask with some force around the jawline. Seconds later, the defensive blades flick out on his face before retracting. He flicks them out again, feeling his face with his hand. I turn back down to the dead girl.

"Why did she die?"

He shrugs, standing. After a second he holds a hand down to me and hoists me up. Then he turns and walks away. His limp seems to have improved. I follow him, feeling bad about leaving the dead girl, but I suppose there's nothing I can do for her now. Blue zips along beside me.

The wind whips through the long green dress as I stumble over the dunes. Catching up, I notice Tenth's breathing. He is wheezing heavily.

"This is too low for you, right? The elevation? The air is too thick or something? Where are we?"

He shrugs without stopping, tromping along, leaving deep footprints.

You wanted to ask a question? he signs.

"Yes! Have you seen a . . . another one. One like you. His rank is Eighth. He has a star-shaped scar here." I tap my shoulder, then my chest over my heart. "And another one here."

Tenth shakes his head.

There are no Eighths here.

"Where would the Eighths be? Somewhere special?" I turn to Blue. "A ship or another place?"

Blue draws a large slow circle in the air.

Repeat me, Tenth says. *I don't know.* He shakes his head with a little sigh and starts moving again. We trudge on in silence, passing many more fallen Nahx—I check each one for August's distinctive scars but don't find them. We see quite a few dead humans too, or what passes for humans. Tugging Tenth to a stop, I bend to examine one, an older woman. She's cold and, like the dead Nahx, has silvery fluid dripping from her eyes and nose, even her ears. Blue buzzes around her head, as though examining her. When I touch the dead woman's face, her skin crumbles into fine metallic powder under my fingers, like a sand sculpture.

"Oh God!" I recoil so quickly, I tumble back. Tenth helps me to my feet.

"What happened to her? Are they all like that? All these dead ones?"

Cold falling white broken, he signs. *Dead.*

"Snow? Snowflakes? Why do you call her a snowflake?"

You are a Snowflake too. Different. Not a clone, like me.

"Oh! We're Snowflakes because we're each unique?"

Yes.

"'Snowflake' is kind of an insult. Or it used to be. It meant someone who thinks they are special. Or delicate."

Blue seems excited by this. They flicker and bounce. Are they laughing?

Broken fast easy? Tenth says.

"Delicate, yes."

He flicks his head back a few times. *Humans are delicate but Snowflakes are not delicate. You are not delicate. You fell and now you're walking.*

"Yes. I suppose that's true." I'm not sure I like being put in a different category than humans. "I felt kind of delicate for a while after I landed."

He flicks his head back again, laughing with me as he resumes his inexorable trudging. I follow him, thinking of August and one of the last things he said to me: *Maybe snowflakes will rise and time will stop moving.* Is it possible I misunderstood him? Was he talking about this? Trying to warn me? And something else slots into place. I think of what the First called us on the ship: *snezjinka.* I think that must mean "snowflake." But in what language?

Why are you looking for the Eighth? Tenth asks.

"He's my friend."

Tenth tilts his head to the side again. *You and Eighth are friends?*

"Yes. It's complicated. He saved my life. More than once."

Eighth helped a human?

"Yes."

Tenth lets out a hard, disapproving puff of breath. And Blue's light dims, as though they agree.

That is forbidden, Tenth says.

"Neither of us was much for rules."

He puts one hand on top of his head, appearing to think about this for a moment. Blue hovers in front of his face.

It is not forbidden to help Snowflakes, he signs at last.

Blue bobs in agreement.

"Well, that's good, I guess. I wouldn't want you to get into trouble."

I will help find Eighth.

I'm starting to see the sign for *Eighth* as *August*. Now I wonder who I should be looking for. Something happened to me between dying in August's arms and waking up on the dunes. My clothes were changed. Tucker was dug out of his grave under the tree and shackled to me. And we were moved to wherever we are. Who arranged all this if it wasn't August? And if he left me with Tuck, doesn't that mean . . . ?

Isn't Tucker the person I should be looking for? And when I find him, then what? He doesn't remember who I am.

Abruptly, Tenth turns and heads into the trees, flicking on a light when the dense branches draw darkness around us. Blue lingers close to me, floating over my right shoulder. We emerge after a few minutes, back on the shore of the lake.

"I need to get back to . . . I was in this place," I say. "It was very large, with thousands of Nahx and transports taking off. Where is that?"

I don't know.

"Blue? Do you know?"

They zip from side to side.

"No? Where are we going, then? I was following you!"

Humans, Tenth says. It's a distinctive sign. I saw August say it enough times.

"Where are humans? Around here?"

He points across the lake.

"Last time I tried to cross the lake I went for an unscheduled swim."

It's colder now. The water is hard.

I'm extremely reluctant to go through the ice again, but curiosity gets the better of me. If there are humans here somehow, then they'll know where we are. They might know where the Nahx bases are.

We set out. Tenth was right; the surface ice is solid, and so clear in some places that I can look into the murky water below. Tenth walks surefootedly, his segmented boots easily finding purchase on the ice, while I keep to the patches of snow as much as possible. These boots that August picked out for me are comfortable, even fashionable, but not designed for ice. As for Blue, they seem unsure too, and settle on my shoulder, flickering there like a rhinestone.

It's slow going. My bones and muscles are still burning from my healing injuries. I've had broken bones and torn muscles before, but the healing process for those was just intense pain, followed by slowly abating ache. This is more like heat than pain now, almost like the feeling of mixed pleasure and sting you get from slowly sliding down into a too-hot bath. It's something to do with my new blood, with the darts and the way we've been changed. "Practically immortal" is how the creepy First described it. I should be thrilled, but all I can think about is that if we need to be practically immortal, whatever they've got in store for us must be practically unstoppable. The cataclysmic rifts from my vision threaten at the edges of my churning thoughts.

Darkness falls, and a few hours later a full moon rises. *Our* moon. The relief I feel that I've confirmed we're still on earth is so palpable that it's practically intoxicating. I can't help giggling. Then I'm shaking, my peals of laughter ringing across the ice. Tenth turns to look at me, one of his hands upturned.

"The moon," I say. I'm wiping tears from my cheeks by this time. "It's a relief to know we're still on earth."

Where else would we be?

Blue floats up and flickers, casting their light in a pale blue circle around us.

"On another planet, of course. On your planet."

This is my planet. Tenth points down at the ice as he signs. God. I'm suddenly reminded of the countless conversations with strangers I've had: "Where are you from?" "Calgary." "No, I mean where are you really from?" "Calgary." "No, but where is your *family* from?" And so on. I was about to clarify that I was referring to whoever created him. His *family*, so to speak.

"Never mind," I say instead.

The sky begins to lighten just as the opposite shore comes into focus through the ice haze. As we get closer and it gets lighter, I start to realize my vision must have been enhanced along with the rest of me. I can't zoom in or do anything cool like that, but I can pick out a lot of detail on the distant shore, even in the low dawn light. As I muse on this, I become aware of my sense of smell too, and how I'm able to process a multitude of smells in detail. The slightly fishy smell of the ice at my feet, the distinctive way the Nahx smell, like charcoal or ashes. Beyond that I smell a wood fire and something cooking. A thin wisp of smoke just past the shore confirms it. There are humans there.

Tenth leads us directly toward the smoke, while I wonder if it's such a good idea. Humans and Nahx are still at war, aren't they? And in my changed state, whose side am I on? Each hour that passes, I feel less human. I've been walking for hours on bones that were smashed to pieces a few days ago and I'm not tired. Even the burning sensation has gone away, replaced with a kind of electricity. I want to run, actually. I want to leap and break things.

And I have a tiny alien perched on my shoulder. That's not normal either.

The lake ice merges with a jumble of driftwood and rocks on the shore. Tenth scrambles over them, pulling himself into the trees, and Blue floats after him while I catch up. I don't bother to scramble, though. I simply bend my knees, feeling a shimmer of energy spread out from my mind and coil up in my muscles and bones. Then I leap, a good twenty feet up to the thicket. Tenth steps out of the way as I land. I feel like I deserve praise for nailing such an extraordinary jump, but neither Tenth nor Blue seems impressed. Tenth turns and I follow him farther into the trees, with Blue drifting behind us. A few minutes later I smell something new, a recognizable smell. It's a human.

I haven't met a new human since Liam brought us to the base in the mountains months and months ago. There were over two hundred of us there, and though I resisted becoming close to more than a few of them, I knew them. But this is someone unfamiliar.

Tenth curls his fingers around my arm, stopping me.

"Blue, maybe you should hide," I say. I feel them settle behind my ear with a low buzz.

One human, Tenth signs.

Whoever it is, they're stupid for being out in the woods by themselves.

"You're not going to dart them, right?"

Tenth slows. The smell of campfire and human and cooking

food is strong now, almost cloying. I can smell death on this human, decay, mortality. They smell imperfect.

"Don't take another step. Don't you even move." A young woman's voice. I'm relieved to hear English and a familiar accent. She sounds a bit like one of my Métis stepcousins. The crunch of a rifle bolt being pulled back is less reassuring. I can hear it so clearly over the light wind rustling the bare branches that it's almost musical. When I turn, Tenth has disappeared. I mean he *vanished* without so much as a whisper. I glance down at the snow, just to confirm to myself that he was even there. His footprints just stop. Did he jump? Where is he?

A young woman emerges from the trees, pointing a rifle straight at my head.

"I know what you are. I saw you with that Nahx on the lake." She spits down on the ground between us, cursing in French. "And that ghost fly or whatever it is."

I put my hands up. "I just need some help."

"Help? You're one of *them*."

"You've seen others? Like me? Where did they go?"

She takes another step toward me, coming out of the shadows. She's about my age, with short, choppy brown hair and a ruddy face smudged with dirt.

"Have you been up here since the invasion?"

"We've always been here, freak."

She's shaking so hard, she can barely hold the rifle.

"You don't need to be scared. I'm not going to hurt you or anyone. I just need some information."

"I'm not telling you anything. *Shipwaytay*. Get off our land."

I'm starting to feel impatient with her, and I actually have this thought: *Humans are so irrational.* And that scares me a little. I'm not ready to be done with being a human. And yet I am. Humans are unreasonable, weak, petty. And I'm something else. I don't feel superior—far from it. But I feel removed.

"Where did the others go? The others like me. Did you see them?"

There's a noise from behind me, causing the girl to twitch her aim over to a blur of gray. Tenth dives for her rifle, grabbing it by the barrel. She fires it as he pulls it away. I don't even think; I veer backward, my hand flies up reflexively, and when I look back, Tenth has the rifle aimed at the girl, she's kneeling down with her hands up, gasping, Blue is angrily buzzing between us, and I have a bullet in my hand.

Like, I'm *holding* a bullet.

I caught it.

The heat of it, the smell of gunpowder, the feel of the metal, and the tingling of my cells give me focus. We need to move on, get off the girl's land as she insisted. I turn back to her, unmoved by the terror in her eyes.

"East," the girl spits. "In Black Lake. There's some kind of ship in the lake."

"In the lake? The ship landed there?"

"No . . ." She looks uneasy, her eyes darting between us. "It's just kind of parked in the middle of the lake. It's huge, like five miles across."

I turn back to Tenth. "Does that sound right?"

He nods. Blue bobs up and down.

"How far is it?"

"About a hundred miles. Follow the lake to Stony Rapids, then take the road south to the Black Lake Nation. The ship is east of the community."

"There are people still there? In the community?"

The girl nods.

"Why didn't they get darted if the Nahx are right there?"

She stands slowly, her hands still raised. "I don't know. And you don't want to fuck with them either. They don't play. Not with Nahx, and not with whatever you are."

I feel my impatience turning into anger, and I know I need to get away from her. Next to me Tenth has started to growl deeply, a low rumbling that resonates out of his armor. This is part of who we are now—perpetually fed up with humans.

I yank the girl's rifle out of Tenth's hands, unload the rounds onto the frozen ground, and toss it back down at her feet.

"Do you have communications?" I ask.

She shakes her head.

"Are you going to survive here? Do you need anything?" I look around. Now that the day has brightened I can see buildings through the trees. Not quite a town, but shelter for a few people. "Are you here by yourself?"

She doesn't answer, instead snatching up the rifle and starting to load it with rounds she has in her pockets.

"We're going," I say, backing off. I pull Tenth along with me. When we're fifty feet away I turn back. The girl is still there, barely visible through the thick trees, rifle raised, watching.

"Fuel!" she shouts. "We need fuel!"

"I'll see what I can do!" I shout back, grateful for the chance at a friendly exchange with a human being, maybe my last one.

The next time I look back, a few minutes later, the girl is gone.

XANDER

After breakfast, unexpectedly, Garvin recruits me to the team that's going with him up to the transmitter. I only watched the video of Dylan getting his hand amputated once, but from the exuberant way the other boys talk about it, I'm not surprised that Garvin expects it to be one of his biggest hits. Now that he's edited it into a nice downloadable size, it's time to send it out into the world.

Rugged up like arctic explorers, we hike east for two hours, skirting the town and heading uphill, first on a snow-covered gravel road, then via a narrow track through the trees. It's quiet in a way only snowy mountain paths can be quiet. There are no birds—they have flown south, unhindered by the new rules about travel passes and permits. Though it's bitingly cold, there's very little wind, and our footfalls are muted in the soft snow.

Logan and Michael aren't very talkative, but Garvin lets them trail ahead, hanging back with me until there's a good distance between us. It's been a week since he got back from taking Dylan to the hospital and we've hardly spoken. I'm not sure if I've been avoiding him or he's been avoiding me. But he seems to want to talk now.

"How are you feeling, Xander?"

"Fine. Okay."

"I can move you into a different cabin if you don't want to be alone."

"No, it's fine. How is Dylan doing?"

"He's getting better." We walk on silently. The rhythm of our footsteps in the snow, the soft crunching, is hypnotic. I listen to it for a moment, thinking of following Nahx footprints and what happens when you catch up to them.

"He'd be dead if it wasn't for you," Garvin says.

The word "dead" hangs there, and for the life of me I can't figure out what it even means. Does Garvin mean dead as in dead or dead as in darted? Because I'm almost sure those are two different things, but I don't know how to broach that with him or anyone else.

"Has anyone seen that Nahx again?" I ask.

"We tracked it back up to Mugaha Creek but lost the trail. It was heading away from the enclave, though, to the east. We don't think we'll see it again."

"You're not worried he'll bring back a squadron?"

Garvin shakes his head. "All we've seen on this side is lone pairs or singles for nearly a year. I think they accidentally got left behind when the Nahx activated the web. They remind me of those Japanese soldiers after World War Two. You know, the ones on the remote islands or whatever, who don't know the war is over?"

"The war *isn't* over," I say. Either Logan or Michael coughs.

"Isn't it?" Garvin says. "We surrendered." He grins at me. I almost expect him to wink. I look up at the sound of more coughing. Logan is bent over, hacking. He spits a blob of phlegm into the trees.

"Dude, that's gross," Michael says.

"Where do you even get cigarettes now?" I ask as we catch up to them.

"People send stuff to us," Logan says. Unbelievably, he tugs his gloves off and lights another one. Apparently some people don't care how they die. I'm reminded of Colin, back in the refugee camp, who has something eating away at his insides.

"Why do people send you stuff?" I ask Garvin as we trudge on, letting Michael and Logan take rear guard.

"Fans of our work," Garvin says. "There are weekly deliveries—most weeks—down in Prince George. I have a guy down there who makes sure things marked for us get set aside. I guess people appreciate what we're doing up here."

"Killing Nahx?" I'm trying to hide my incredulity, and probably failing.

"Making videos of killing Nahx. You think Hollywood is still churning out blockbusters? Los Angeles has no power and no water. And anyway, who wants to watch fake fantasies when they can watch the real thing?"

I guess I'm not very good at hiding anything anymore. Garvin puts his hand on my shoulder, which reminds me of the way August used to do that, the way all Nahx walk with their partners. But Garvin only squeezes for second, in a fatherly way, before letting go.

"It's a lot to take in, kid, I know."

"It's fine."

"I can get word down to Vancouver, get something special for you in our next delivery."

"Like what?"

"Girlie magazines?" Michael says behinds us.

"Boy-ie magazines?" Logan adds. They dissolve into giggles.

"Logan!" Garvin snaps, making them both shut their stupid mouths. "Take point. And put that cigarette out. Michael, you stay where you are and shut up."

They obey, chastened. Logan jogs up ahead of us while Michael lingers behind, muttering, until Garvin gives him a dirty look.

Garvin talks to me in low tones. "Candy? There's not much chocolate but there's roaring trade in maple brittle and peanut fudge in Vancouver. Or liquor? I discourage drinking, for obvious reasons." He flicks his head back and glares at Michael again. "But I can make an exception. We had a case of homemade wine sent up over the summer. Maybe we could get more."

"I don't really like wine. I don't need anything." Though the candy sounds good, I don't like the idea of being Garvin's favorite son, for whatever reasons he has. It won't last, for one thing. Stuff like that never does.

"LOGAN!" Garvin suddenly bellows, making us skid to a stop. "You walked right past it." He points to an unexceptional tree. Only when I step closer do I see three lines carved into it, as though it's been marked by some kind of beast. Garvin makes a disdainful noise in Logan's direction and barrels off the path into the trees.

We emerge through the tree line about twenty minutes later, puffing with the effort of the uphill climb. The terrain is rocky, made treacherous by its coating of ice and snow, even in my sturdy new boots. I nearly wipe out three times before it occurs to me to follow in Garvin's footprints. He knows the way, knows secure footholds where the rock is rough enough to provide adequate purchase. Turning back, I see that Logan and Michael aren't struggling either. They've been this way before.

We come around a bend, and the rocky surface changes to a landscape of brutal cracks and wide crevasses, as though some giant hammer has smashed the mountain from above. Ahead of me, Garvin deftly leaps over one crevasse, then another. On the third leap he drops out of sight.

"Whoa. Garvin?"

I jump the two crevasses, stopping short at the lip of the third. Garvin is about eight feet below, crouching in the deep snow.

"Down you go," Logan says, coming up behind me.

I jump, poised to roll when I land if needed, but the snow is deep enough to cushion my fall. Logan and Michael jump down after me, their arrivals marked only by the soft *whoomph* they make when they land.

The crevasse narrows as Garvin leads us along, and we have to duck to avoid rocky outcrops and overhangs. Soon we're edging through a passage so narrow, Logan and Michael have to take off their packs and drag them along behind them. The crevasse is deeper by this point too, and the light of the gray day has diminished to a thin lightning-shaped strip above us. Finally even that disappears, and we creep through a low rocky tunnel before emerging into a large, light-filled basin, which is surrounded by high craggy walls. Beyond the walls, to the east, the filaments of the Nahx web glow across the cloud-heavy sky.

Mobbs and another guy whose name I think is AJ look up from a small campfire as we approach. Behind them, about two hundred feet up a steep escarpment, is a radio transmission tower and a small shack. Both are equipped with solar panels. Garvin pulls a USB drive from his pocket and hands it to Michael, looking at his watch.

"Upload it, test the transmitter. Wait for the break, then blast it."

"I know. I know," Michael says. Logan follows him up the slope.

"What's the break?"

Garvin leads me to the campfire, where we dump our packs as Mobbs and AJ gather theirs and wander wordlessly away toward the crevasse.

"You got our broadcasts on the other side? And the emergency stuff? Only for about an hour a day, right? Around noon?"

"Yeah."

"The Nahx use a jammer. A massive signal emitter that jams most wireless communication. No one knows how it works, but it seems to be connected to the web somehow." He grins at me. "But something, or someone, uses a canceling frequency to break through the jammer signal. No one knows how that works either, but it gives us about thirty minutes to an hour, most days, to stream video."

"Do you get anything back? From the other side, I mean?"

"Early on we did. But not recently. Everyone is dead." He shoves another log into the fire before realizing what he's said. "Sorry." I can tell it costs him to say that, but that knowledge doesn't really help.

The fire blazes up, making it warm enough for me to take

off my gloves. I hold my hands forward, letting the warmth sink into my fingers.

"So, one of our guys was on the crew that found you, did you know that?" Garvin asks.

"Found me? You mean back in May? Just after I crossed?"

Garvin nods encouragingly. If this is what he wants to talk about, my rescue, he'll be disappointed.

"I don't remember much of that," I say. "I was delirious, they told me. Raving nonsense for three days."

"Was it nonsense?" Garvin asks intently. He lets a silence grow around us, one I'm sure he wants me to fill up. "I'm pretty curious about this base you were at. North of Jasper?"

I shrug. Precisely what I told the people who found me is lost in the mists of my delirium. I know no one believed me about the base, though, not even military types. Apparently it was such a top-secret operation that hardly anyone knew it existed.

"I can show you on a map. And if we could get through the web, we could go there and get those people out." Get Topher out, I'm thinking, if he stuck around. Maybe he left the human race behind, like Raven did.

"I don't think anyone is thinking about getting through the web."

"Why not?"

He shakes his head. "Things have changed on this side, after the surrender especially. The focus became . . . narrowed."

"On *this* side?" I don't mean for it to come out so accusingly, but it does. "Was it that easy to just sell us out?"

Garvin remains calm, rubbing his tattooed hands on the knees of his snow pants. "On survival." His tone is patient now. "On rebuilding, and hanging on to what we had left. You know the Nahx took control of most of the hydropower stations, right? And several of the coal and nuclear stations too down in the States."

"So?"

"So. Hardly any power. Rolling blackouts. Whole areas cut off. And communications are messed up because of the jammer. Not nearly enough food. Transport is fucked because there's almost no fuel. You know that expression 'bombed back to the Middle Ages'? That's what happened to us."

"That's not a very good excuse. I had eight friends with me when the Nahx attacked. Seven of them are dead."

"Everybody is singing the same song, kid. Dylan is not the first of us to get darted. The others are dead. I know well enough what it's like to be in close company with Nahx," Garvin says. "The buzzing way they breathe. The smell—like ashes or charcoal. The signs they use."

He studies me as I try not to react. I'd like to change the subject to just about anything. I can't get August out of my head. Every time I hear a twig snap or a door click closed I think of the sparks he made by snapping his fingers, and the way he did it to set himself and those other Nahx on fire, to blow them all up.

He did it to help me get away.

Garvin watches me, as though he can see into my mind like I'm a zoetrope.

"You've been in close company with a Nahx, haven't you?"

"It's against the law, isn't it?"

"What is?" He knows what I'm talking about but wants me to spell it out.

"What you do. Hunting and killing them. You're supposed to 'avoid and report.' Aren't you worried you'll get arrested or something?"

"No. I'm not. It doesn't take much to buy off cops, and no one else cares. Not even the Nahx." He clears his throat forcefully and leans forward again. "But helping the Nahx—people care about that. That will get you killed."

I focus on keeping my expression calm. I haven't done anything wrong. Not really. At least nothing Garvin could ever find out.

"I . . . I don't know what you're talking about."

"How did you get through the web, Xander?"

I wipe my face and surreptitiously glance up toward the signal tower.

"I went through a pipeline, like you said. It went right

under the web. But the Nahx came after me and blew it up."

"Right. Just a bit south of here. Pretty far from Jasper. You walked halfway across the mountains by yourself?"

"Yes."

Garvin leans forward and takes me by the knees, his chunky fingers digging in just enough that I can feel pressure on my bones. "Listen to me. You're safe here. We don't follow the law either way. Our goals are . . . different."

Despite my best efforts, I've started to shake. "Okay. But—"

He holds a finger up, silencing me. "When James picked you up, you were raving about a Nahx. A single Nahx you traveled with. Who helped you. Is that true?"

I take a breath. "Yes."

Garvin sighs with satisfaction. "You befriended it? Him? Her?"

"Him."

"Where is he?"

"Dead." Supreme concentration is the only thing that keeps me from sobbing it out. August is dead. My last friend on earth, unless I can find Topher again one day. Everyone is dead.

Garvin nods and loosens his grip on my knees, patting me almost sympathetically before leaning back.

"All right, Xander. You don't need to be worried. No one here is going to judge you for doing what was necessary to save your own skin."

I just nod. I'm not sure who was trying to save whom anymore.

"I have one last question, and then I want you to meet someone."

I nod again. Maybe I'll just stop speaking altogether.

"This Nahx friend of yours, who helped you," he says, fixing his eyes on mine. "Did you learn his sign language?"

"Yes. Some of it."

This time his satisfaction is palpable. He practically fist pumps, leaping to his feet and beckoning me to follow him across the wide basin to the sheer wall of rock. We squeeze through another crevasse into a dim cave of rock and ice. Digging a lighter from his pocket, he bends to light a small kerosene lamp. It casts a yellow light over the rock and ice walls.

"Sometimes she tries to jump out at you," Garvin says, not taking his eyes off the shadowy edges where the cave ceiling curves down to crawling height.

"Who?"

There's a low hiss, a rattle of heavy chain, and the scrape of metal on rock, and something moves in the dark. I step backward without thinking, but Garvin stops me.

"She can't hurt you. Not in her condition."

Garvin squats, lifting the lamp to shine into the low rift at the back of the cave. And there, kneeling in the dark, her arms pulled to either side by thick chains bolted into the stone, is a Nahx.

Her head is hanging wearily, but even though I can't see her eyes through her mask, I can tell she's watching us as Garvin sets down the lamp and beckons me forward. As my eyes adjust to the light, I note with horror the pools of dark blood on the floor of the cave—one beneath her knees, and one beneath each of her forearms. I step closer, tugging my own flashlight from my pocket and clicking it on.

"God . . ." I whisper it without thinking. I've seen enough of Garvin and his crew to know how I'm supposed to feel about this. Rationally thinking, maybe I could just ask to be taken back to Prince George and forget any of this ever happened. But irrational thinking is my specialty. And that tells me that I'm just as likely to get banished out into the snow if I make a scene.

The cave smells, the characteristic smoky, chemical smell of the Nahx, but mixed with rot and death. As Garvin moves the lantern I can see the Nahx has heavy metal bolts piercing both wrists and one knee, shackling her in place, imprisoning her through her very flesh. Is she dying, this Nahx? Surely the wounds must be infected.

"How long have you had it . . . her?" I ask, swallowing a sour taste in the back of my mouth.

"Three weeks."

The Nahx's head shoots up at this. She growls as I kneel next to Garvin, both of us still keeping our distance. The way she's chained, it doesn't look like she'd be able to lie down or sit, and she couldn't stand because the cave ceiling is too low.

"Have you fed her? Or given her water?"

"They don't need to eat."

Three weeks. They've had her here for three weeks, chained up, unable to move, to sleep, sit, or stand, with no food or water. I can feel her eyes on me as I take it in, but after a few seconds, she lowers her head again as though she's done with me.

Garvin shimmies backward out of the cave, and I follow him.

"What do you think?" he asks me as we straighten up.

"Did you kill her partner?" I ask.

"We thought we did. But when we went back for his body two days later, it was gone. I think it might have been the one that got Dylan."

"He's looking for her?"

Garvin shrugs pretty calmly for someone so in danger of being killed in his sleep. I think about the tracks we've left in the snow leading up here, tracks all the way back to the pulp mill.

"Jesus, Garvin, he'll destroy us if he finds her like this. You have no idea how loyal they are."

Garvin considers me with a thoughtful expression. "And

149

you do? How close were you with the Nahx who crossed with you?"

"He didn't cross with me. He . . . accompanied me to the web. That's it. I wasn't trying to get him across to our side. He didn't want to cross."

He looks like he doesn't believe me, which just reinforces how tenuous my situation here is. And also how much Garvin must think he needs me. He wouldn't bring someone he didn't trust here without a good reason.

"You want me to talk to her? Interrogate her?"

"Among other things."

"What things?"

Garvin's face is permanently fixed in a *not sure how much I should tell you* expression. He's been looking at me that way since the moment I clapped eyes on him back in Prince George, and it's really starting to piss me off.

"Look, Garvin, I can't get on board with whatever it is that you want me to do if you don't trust me. Where am I going to go?" I look around the snow and rocks for emphasis. "If you're not sure about me, take me back to Prince George, and we can call it a day."

Garvin turns and glances at Michael and Logan, who are now watching us with interest, sitting bundled up by the fire, their rifles in their laps.

"Okay," he finally says. "If you could talk to her, get some information, that's going to help us. We need to know where their bases are. We need to know if there is another way through the web. We need to know especially about their operations on this side. Are there any bases, headquarters? Was she trying to get to one? Where are they?"

"So you can attack them?"

"Damn right so we can attack them. That okay with you?"

"Of course. Why wouldn't it be?"

"It occurs to me that you must have been pretty friendly with the Nahx who got you across the mountains."

"He was different. And we weren't friendly. We just . . . had a deal."

Garvin slings his rifle over his back and crosses his arms. "So make a deal with this one," he says, pointing his thumb back into the cave. "She gives us information, everything she knows."

"What does she get out of the deal?"

Logan and Michael scoff until Garvin shoots them a dirty look.

"What did your Nahx friend get out of your deal?" Garvin asks.

"Nothing," I answer. "He died."

Garvin nods. The satisfaction in his expression gives me a chill beyond the numb coldness that has already settled into my bones.

"Make sure she knows that," Garvin says, turning away from the cave. "Make it sound like *you* killed him. Maybe that will motivate her to talk."

"She can't talk with her arms stretched out like that. Some of their signs need two hands."

"That's your problem," Garvin says. He packs a pot with snow and sets it on the fire. Digging in his pockets, he pulls out a few tea bags.

"Will you let her go?" I ask. "If she gives you the information you want, will you let her go?"

"You think we can trust her? After the way we've treated her?" He seems almost amused by this.

"So you're going to kill her anyway?"

Garvin stirs the tea into the steaming pot. "We're all going to die sometime," he says.

He's right about that, at least. From his expectant expression I guess he wants me to start right away. I'm not enthusiastic, but on the other hand, I'd like to get a better look at the prisoner. I stand up, ignoring Michael and Logan's jeering, and squeeze back through the crack in the rock. Poking my head into the cave, I strain to see the Nahx where she kneels in the dark. She turns her head up at me, letting out a low growl. Thinking of the pain she must be in with those spikes through her wrists and knees makes my breakfast threaten to come back.

"My name is Xander," I say, kneeling just inside the entrance. I draw a Z in the air the way August did. "Xander, see? You could make it with your fingers. What's your name?"

She ignores me.

"We just want to talk to you," I say. "I think you can understand me, can't you? And I know some of your signs."

I edge forward a few inches, moving the lamp with me.

"Look, this one—*please*. And this, *sorry*." I do the signs. They're similar, and I'm slightly concerned I may have transposed them, but if I did, the Nahx makes no move to correct me. She still hasn't stirred, though I get the sense that she has turned her eyes up and is watching me.

"I know you can't make the signs properly, chained up like that, but if you just do the hand part, maybe I might be able to understand. *Please?*" I repeat the sign, a closed fist pressed into the chest. "*Please?*"

It happens so fast, I don't even see how she does it, but suddenly the little lamp is flying through the air. It explodes on the cave wall, showering me with flaming oil.

"Fuck!" I lurch backward, just barely avoiding a face full of fire as I crash against the rock. My snow pants are burning and I'm screaming, trying to tear them off, while outside the cave I hear Garvin yelling, "Xander!? What happened?"

I'm swearing and rolling and trying to twist out of my pants when Garvin and Logan burst in, rifles trained on the

Nahx, who has retreated back under her overhang.

"Get down!" Logan screams. "Get the fuck down! Let me see your hands!"

The Nahx curls her legs under herself and kneels, palms facing down, her head hanging.

Garvin tears off his coat and beats the fire out as I manage to shove my burning pants away.

"What did she do?" he asks.

"Nothing," I lie. "I knocked the lamp over."

The Nahx glances up at me and flicks her head back a couple of times. I know what that means. She's *laughing*. Laughing at setting me on fire.

I cough and blink away the burning of the smoke in my eyes. The cave now smells of kerosene, burnt polyester, and humiliation. One leg of my snow pants is scorched and shredded.

Garvin lowers his rifle and looks at me with a wry smile.

"Call it a day?" he says, holding a hand down.

I take his hand and struggle upward, careful not to hit my head again on the cave ceiling. Logan, apparently satisfied that the Nahx is done misbehaving for the time being, lowers his rifle and backs away. As we exit, he flicks on his flashlight, scanning the cave. Garvin steps back inside to gather the remains of the lamp and my shredded snow pants.

I turn as Logan ushers me out, taking a last look at the

Nahx cowering in the dark. I can just make out one of her hands moving in a familiar flat, chopping shape, pointed at her chest as she flicks her head back again.

Sorry.

She doesn't seem very sorry, to be honest, but I'll take it.

RAVEN

The ship is exactly where the girl said it would be, and exactly as large, rising out of the frozen lake like a colossal leviathan. Unlike the Nahx transports, which are triangular and black, this massive ship has rounded silvery walls curving up at least twenty stories above the surface, almost disappearing into the sky. No entrances are apparent—the curved walls are featureless but for some rows of lights lining the very top.

The size of it is horrifying. In the first hours after the invasion, there were news reports of giant ships suddenly appearing over Canada and America, Peru, India, various North African and European countries. Ships like this one? This is *huge*, and if this is only one of many, then . . .

Doubt has been entirely absent from my mind-set the past few days, as we trudged along the shore of the endless lake with a single-mindedness that felt both unfamiliar and unsettling. Whenever my resolve seemed to flag, due to boredom more than fatigue, new reserves of focus would spring up as if from nowhere. It was as though my mind had set a goal and my whole body would see that goal achieved. But now, seeing the size of the ship, watching the Nahx transports flying in or out, even noting the way the snow around the ship is tamped down as though by thousands upon thousands of feet, my doubt flares back to life. I hesitate at the edge of the ice.

Tenth wriggles his fingers in front of his mouth.

What's wrong?

Now my doubts unleash like a cascade. Why did I come back here? To look for August? To find Tucker and get him out? I should be running in the other direction, away from whatever the Nahx and their firefly overlords have planned for us, not toward it. I feel like I've been in a trance, and I don't know whether its source is my loyalty to my friends or whatever has been done to my body and brain. Who is controlling me right now? Am I here to help August and Tucker escape or simply to report for duty?

Blue buzzes near my right ear and draws a big slow circle when I turn to them. I take a step back, trying to rein in my unease.

Tenth, who has turned away, hisses. I spin and see him pointing in the other direction, where the sky is soft purple and the unmistakable dark shape of a Nahx transport approaches us. As we watch, the transport banks and veers back toward us, coming to land on the ice. Blue, who has been hovering around my head, disappears into the front pocket of my jacket as two Nahx appear in the hatch. Tenth takes my shoulder, gently nudging me on board.

It's a larger transport than the one I was previously on. The hold of this one is wide and open and crowded with humans. Altered, upgraded humans like me, their hair and skin various metallic shades. What might once have been white or brown, blond, brunet, or rich, deep black is now coated with a glittery sheen. Even the eyes that turn up to me look glossy and pearlized, like frosted nail polish. I haven't seen a mirror since I rose from the dead, so all I can see of myself is the coppery skin on my hands and the tendrils of my hair streaked with silver and bronze. Looking around at the others, I wouldn't say we're frightening to look at so much as intimidating. There's something cold and hard, almost machinelike, about us. Not so much Snowflakes as *shuriken*, ninja throwing stars like the homemade one that got Tucker banned from the dojo for a month. He's lucky he wasn't arrested then and there.

Tenth disappears into the cockpit, so I sit near the wall among a group of silent Snowflakes. One of them looks me up and down as I get comfortable.

"Straggler? Me too," she says vacantly.

Some of the other humans are filthy, covered in mud, their hair matted. One appears to be speckled with bird shit. I see torn, ragged clothes and an array of seasonal attire. One older woman is in a swimsuit and bathrobe. Others are in pajamas. Many are barefoot. These people have been as good as dead for months, more than a year, some of them. They wear the same impassive expression as the woman who spoke to me. I turn back to her.

"Straggler?" she repeats. "Me too." Then she turns away, her silver eyes glassy.

As the transport shakes and lifts off I watch the sky through the open hatch and see the first tendrils of the aurora just drifting in from the north. Abruptly, my view is blacked out by something as the transport descends again. Seconds later we land with a crunch. The woman who spoke is jostled against me.

"Straggler?" she says for a third time. "Me too."

Of everything I've seen so far since my rebirth, this makes me the saddest. She doesn't even know how lost she is. Are these the only words she remembers?

"What's your name?" I try.

She just frowns at me, not concerned so much as angry at me for bothering her with trivialities. Who needs a name when you've been made immortal? My ears start to ring.

Four Nahx emerge from the cockpit, ushering us back through the hatch. In the tussle of the crowd I lose sight of Tenth, or maybe he's just lost interest in me, now that he's back with his own people. I suddenly feel vulnerable without him, not physically so much as emotionally. I'd like to have someone beside me that's not this woman who can only repeat the same inane greeting over and over. Glancing down at my pocket, I can just see Blue's faint glow, and take comfort from it. They don't seem to want to leave me, and right now I need all the friends I can get.

We step down off the ramp and into a wide-open arena-like space, so wide that I can barely see to the edges, and know they exist only because of the high curved walls of the ship rising over us. Crowded around us are thousands and thousands of other humans, their shimmering faces reflecting harsh artificial lights shining down from every side. We are outside, standing on snow and ice again, with the ship surrounding us, and the dark sky above. So the ship is some kind of torus shape? I'm disoriented for a moment—the crowd is so large and the space so wide that the scale of the ship is suddenly hard to process. Five miles across? That's what the girl back in the forest said, and that seems about right. There's a giant park in Calgary that we used to snowshoe in. Bigger than that.

And full of people, prisoners, though you wouldn't know by the tranquil mood. As the new arrivals disperse into the crowd, I notice most faces share that dull expression. Tucker had it too, when we awoke on the dunes, as though he hadn't a care in the world. I'm envious, in a way. I can see I have little choice in whatever is happening here. It might be nice to not care.

At the center of the arena, a bright sphere glows above the crowd, its surface marked by patches of blue, green, and red and pinpoints of piercing white. None of the other humans seem particularly interested in it, but even from a distance, something about it looks familiar to me. As I get closer I see why. It's the earth, the traditional political borders marking countries neglected in favor of red patches representing the Nahx occupations. The rest of the land is green, the oceans blue. There are bright white lights seemingly at random points, some inside the Nahx zones, some outside. A few are even over the oceans. Their locations mean nothing to me, though I note there is one in Northern Saskatchewan, which could be where we are. Maybe the bright lights indicate where these giant ships are located.

It doesn't make sense that some would be outside Nahx zones, unless the Nahx plan on claiming more territory. Is that going to be my mission, to help the Nahx take over the rest of the world? The idea should be abhorrent to me, but it has a strange appeal, fitting into my brain like a puzzle piece, as though I've put together the whole horror of human history and this is the logical conclusion.

I stare up at the globe, trying to let myself be pulled into resignation—that would be so much easier—but apparently there's still a kernel of resistance in me, because the only clear emotion I can drum up is anger. Whatever is happening, none of us had any say in the matter, and that is unfair.

Yes. Unfair. I need to tattoo that word on my cerebral

cortex. I'm still a human being, despite everything.

Turning away from the globe, I see that the huge crowd is being herded into militaristic groups and lines. I join one group, shuffling into place behind an older white woman with short gray hair that shines like it's coated with glitter paint. Turning, I meet the eye of the person behind me, a dark-skinned black man who acknowledges me only with a blink of his glossy, obsidian eyes.

"What's your name?" I ask, and when he doesn't answer I try again in French. "*Quel est?*"

He blinks again, though a flash of something crosses his face, maybe just because he's annoyed with irrelevant questions too.

Nahx patrol up and down the neat lines, watchful, as though they expect trouble. Above them, swarms of firefly creatures float around, occasionally coalescing into clouds as though to confer before drifting apart again. I watch, trying not to be obvious, as one of the clouds buzzes angrily around the head of a Nahx who is dragging a girl roughly by the arm. The Nahx releases the girl and she scampers away, disappearing into one of the formations.

Sorry, the Nahx directs to the cloud of lights, before turning and marching in the other direction, as though eager to escape further reprobation. So the Nahx defer to these creatures? Do they defer to single ones like Blue too? That could be useful. I file that away to ponder later.

When the lines are formed, an eerie stillness falls over the crowd. I study their number, and although there seem to be all ages and races and every variety of size and shape, suddenly the word Tenth used for us makes deeper sense. Snowflakes. Each one of us an individual among countless others. Unique but insignificant.

No one twitches or fidgets; they barely seem to breathe. I twist to look behind me, to scan the crowd for any sign of life, and the black man hisses at me, barely audibly. No words, just a hiss, like an irritated cat. Turning back, I face the front, waiting, because I can sense something is about to happen.

Some kind of alarm suddenly pierces the silence, though it's nothing like a siren or any other kind of human alarm. It's deep, so low pitched that I'm pretty sure a normal human might not be able to hear it. The throbbing noise gets inside me, and that feels so invasive that I struggle not to dive away and run, measuring my breaths, curling my hands into fists.

Invincible yet terrified. I wonder whether I wasn't better off as a delicate little human, as breakable as the stem of a flower. At least then I had some choice about my destiny, even if it was only fight or die. But I shake that thought away. I'm not supposed to be here. I'm not supposed to be as aware as I am, that's clear now. And I've managed to befriend both Blue and Tenth. I can use that against the Nahx, against whoever this enemy is.

I could be the only chance the human race has right now. I don't know why, but that thought makes me feel even more alone. And annoyed.

I curse under my breath. The woman in front of me turns and glares me into silence, forcing me to press my lips together and listen to my thoughts, which naturally stray to August. August left me on those dunes. August must have shackled me to Tucker. Everything suggests he not only gave me up willingly but was happy for me to be drawn into whatever this is. That seems . . . so out of character for him. Something is not right.

The low groaning signal changes, taking shape as repeated words, at first just a muddle of sounds layered over one another. It takes a few seconds to realize that it is several languages spoken at once. Though it should be impossible, my brain homes in on the English and the French, parsing them out from the chaotic din.

"Be seated."

Every human sits as one, like a wave resonating out to the edges of the crowd. The sight of it, of how easily these Snowflakes are instructed, enlivens the rebel in me. I remain standing, defiant, and note with some satisfaction that a few others scattered far across the crowd do the same. Spinning, I see four or five, and maybe a few more distant specks, standing up like beacons of resistance. One slender, shaggy-haired boy stands not far from me, looking nervous but proud.

The black man, cross-legged behind me, scowls up, horrified.

"Sit *down!*" he says through gritted teeth.

The humans sitting around me recoil as five Nahx come barreling out from the dark space beneath the globe. They veer off before I have time to react, and one of them connects his fist with the defiant boy's face so suddenly and hard that the crack of skull bones echoes across the arena. He collapses like a rag doll as the humans around him scatter.

A deeper silence falls over the crowd. Where before there was a kind of hum of anticipation, now there is a deathly pall, a collective holding of breath as one of the Nahx drags the motionless boy away by his foot, facedown. His head flops over as they pass us, his face a concave, misshapen mass of blood and bone, all the features, eyes, nose, mouth, teeth reduced to red mush. But he's alive. I can see his fingers clenching and unclenching, trying to claw at the bloody ice beneath him.

No one moves until they disappear back into the darkness.

"*Be seated,*" the voice intones again.

I slip down, chastened by the image of the boy's ruined face flaring behind my eyes. Will he heal like that, mangled and deformed? I think back to my days on the sand dunes, my bones on fire inside me, dreaming of death. I wouldn't wish that on anyone.

The multilingual voice continues, oblivious to my distress.

"You are superior to the organic humans. Do not concern your-selves with their petty disputes. Keep to your task, your mission."

The voice falls silent. A few of the humans near me look around, astonished.

"Your directives are simple. Follow them. Directive one: Take care of your body."

The humans around me start to shuffle nervously, some of them holding on to one another.

"Decapitation is terminal. Explosive disintegration is terminal. Defend yourselves against violence. Do not kill humans unless abso-lutely necessary. Conflict with them does not serve your directives. They are irrelevant to your directives."

Even over the noise of the loudspeaker, I can hear the man behind me breathing, fast and scared.

"Directive two: Remain at your station. You are the sentinels of your assigned fissure. You are not needed at other locations unless instructed."

The word "fissure" jars me. Is this what I saw in my visions and still see when I close my eyes, the dark rift that seems to pull apart my molecules? I become unnaturally aware of my heart pounding, making the blood rush in my ears. These are the answers I've been seeking, at least some of them. But I don't want it to be true. We've been turned into some kind of army? An army against who? Something coming from this rift? This fissure? Each answer contains more questions.

"Directive three: Obey commands. Those who disobey will be discarded and replaced."

Conveniently, we've just been shown a demonstration of this. I doubt any of us will forget it. As the voice speaks again I note its accent. It's artificial, of that I'm almost sure, but it also almost sounds like someone who has learned very precise speech at a very posh school. "Formal" is the only way I can put my assessment into words.

"Directive four: Destroy threats. Use any means. Use bodily force. Weapons will be adapted as needed. You will be deployed as needed."

The announcement continues in French and some other languages for a few seconds after the English is done. There's a pause during which I'm convinced the disembodied voice will ask *"Any questions?"* and then all hell will break loose. But the silence just goes on and on.

The man behind me whispers to no one in particular. "Are *we* the weapons?"

He might be on to something. I *feel* like a weapon. I don't tire. I don't seem to need food. I heal quickly from wounds and injuries that would kill a normal human. And I feel intensely focused, right now on gathering intel and making a plan to find Tucker and August, but I wonder if that might change. If the Nahx have some purpose for us, if they give us instructions or directives, will those become my focus?

"Are *we* the weapons?" the man behind me asks again, and I'm struck by how insightful this question is for someone who doesn't even know his own name. He looks at me as I turn back to him.

"We're the sentinels," I say. I've always liked that word, and I certainly prefer it to "Snowflakes" with what that implies. Snowflakes, for all their uniqueness, melt in the slightest heat.

Sentinel. The word slices a path through my consciousness, like a signature carved with a blade. And the churning chaos of my thoughts seems to organize itself around it, trillions of neurons and impulses lining up like soldiers who now know their purpose. We are sentinels. But of what? For what? And, most important, *against* what? What is coming through that hellish rift, the one I see in my dreams?

I have a sudden urge to scream and scream, rage and helplessness threatening to bubble out as formless noise, a wordless plea to the multicolored sky to do something, maybe just fall down on us, envelop us in a blanket of darkness and swaths of light. The full horror of what we are is dawning on me: an immortal slave army. It's like something out of an ancient myth.

Miraculously I manage to contain my urge to scream and repurpose it as the determination to move. Curling my feet under me, I stand. The other sentinels around me glance up, alarmed, but no one voices any objection. The only sounds remain the eerie night, the crunching of the ice under my feet as I shift my weight from one foot to the other, and the whispering sky.

When the noise takes the shape of my name, as though something in that distant sky is calling out to me, I'm sure I'm losing my mind at last.

"Rave! Rave!"

Wait.

That's not coming from the sky. A girl's voice. I spin around, searching the crowd, and see that several other people have stood up. One of them hurtles toward me, a blur of khaki, leaping over people where they sit.

"Raven!"

A group of sentinels stands as though to stop her and she disappears in a tangle of bodies. I step out of my formation, moving down the open aisle, dodging the hands of people who can think only of stopping me. At last the girl-shaped blur emerges into the aisle, a hundred feet ahead of me, with the bright light of the globe glowing behind her, turning her short hair into a halo.

"Raven! Holy shit!" she shouts as she runs for me, stopping a few feet away as we stare at each other. She's taller than me, dressed in survival gear, khakis and boots and even a utility belt still strapped around her, though no weapon that I can see. Her face is ruddy with cold, and one of her eyes has a pearlized gray iris, like the eyes of so many others around us. Her other eye is solid silver—not just the iris, the whole eyeball, like a ball bearing lodged in her face. The skin around it is streaked with fine gray lines like a spiderweb.

"Mandy?" The last time I saw her she was dead on the floor of a drugstore, a Nahx dart in her eye. That was minutes before August saved my life and everything went in a direction no one could have anticipated. "Mandy." I repeat her name, because maybe she's a hallucination.

She throws her arms around me.

I let her hold me for a few seconds because I need a hug, even though from my perspective it's been only about a week since August hugged me back at the base. The day I rescued him. Or he rescued me. And I died. Or not.

I let Mandy hug me because it makes me feel less like I'm literally going to fall apart.

"God, you're the first person I've seen that I even recognize," she says when she pulls back.

"Same," I say, though that's not quite right. "But you *do* recognize me?"

"Yeah, yeah," she says, putting her arm around me and leading me along the open aisle. "Most of these people don't even know who they are. I don't know why. I don't know why I do either. And you do? You remember everything?"

"I remember more than everything." The moment I say it,

I realize how true it is. Details have been pouring through my brain for the past few days that I can't possibly remember as clearly as they appear. "I feel like if someone asked me to recite the entire Harry Potter series word for word, I could do it and not make a mistake."

"Me too," Mandy says, nodding. "And that would be very entertaining, but we should talk."

As she leads me away from the crowd to the clear areas near the walls of the ship, I glance down into my pocket again, where Blue's light is barely visible. Probably best if I keep them to myself for now, so I surreptitiously zip the pocket almost the whole way closed.

Mandy and I go over the last few days in low tones as we walk. She's not surprised to hear that Tucker is alive.

"That's the first thing I thought of when I woke up," she says. "We buried him alive. God."

"Thankfully, he doesn't remember it. Or anything."

Mandy stops. Turning me and taking me by the shoulders, she studies me with an intent look.

"I'm fine," I say. I know what she's thinking. "I mean, I'm freaked out, but I'm fine. I'm worried about Tucker."

"I've been looking for him too," Mandy says. "And Felix and Lochie. Who else got darted after me?"

"Sawyer. Britney, remember her?"

"Not Liam?"

171

"No. He died, the ordinary way. So did Emily." I don't offer any more details, and thankfully she doesn't ask for them. How on earth can I explain August to her? "Kim's dead too."

She blinks once and appears to process these calamities in an instant. "What about Topher and Xander?"

"They were alive the last time I saw them. That was in spring. But I don't know . . ."

"It's winter now," Mandy says. "Around November, I think, and we're in Northern Saskatchewan. Did you wake up on the dunes too?"

"Yeah."

"Athabasca Sand Dunes. Just south of Uranium City."

"How far is that from the base?" I ask. I'm still trying desperately to piece together how I got here.

"About six hundred miles as the crow flies," she says. "And you'd have to fly, as there's no roads up here. Not in winter, anyway."

"They must have brought us in transports."

"I don't remember that." She shrugs. "Oddly, I *do* remember some other stuff. I remember lying in that store, with snow blowing through the open window. But . . ."

"What?"

"It's so strange, like a weird dream. But it was almost like I was seeing without eyes. Like my *skin* could see."

"The same thing happened to me. I think our skin *can* see."

"And my eye," she says, pointing to the silver orb where an ordinary gray eye used to be. "I haven't managed to find a mirror yet. But there's something weird about it, right?"

I bite my lip. How do you tell someone they have a ball bearing for an eyeball? "It's silver. Metallic."

"I thought so. I can see all kinds of things with it. Radio waves. Infrared. Ultraviolet. I feel like a bee."

We arrive at the edge of the wide arena, where the metal walls of the ship curve down, terminating in terraced levels, almost like bleachers, that connect the walls to the snowy surface of the lake. Mandy leads me up to the top level, where the wind has left a clear patch on the metal terrace.

I lean back on the wall as I slide down next to her, and feel not only warmth but also vibration. Bizarrely, I recognize something about the vibration. The frequency? It's like the vibrations I felt the time I examined August's rifle. While this is the sort of thing that should be just a hunch, my brain insists that the vibrations are *exactly* the same, as though the weapons and even the darts are made of the same stuff as the wall. Maybe the Nahx armor is made of it too. I turn my head, pressing my nose into the wall, and sniff.

"You smell it, huh?" Mandy says. "Smell your skin."

I pull back the sleeve of my jacket and sniff again. The scent is not strong but it's there, the familiar smoky smell, almost like charcoal. Whatever this is, it's part of the entire project—the ships, the Nahx, their armor, their weapons. Maybe even the toxin in the darts. And me now.

"You know what else is weird?" Mandy asks.

"What?"

"I can pick out individual elements in the wall. When I first smelled it I thought it was just garbage words rolling around in my head. But I realize now it was like a chemical analysis, like my nasal cells *know* the words somehow."

"Yeah. Same. I could do it with the smell of the lake. I thought it was nonsense too. But it wasn't."

"Carbon," Mandy says.

"And sulfur. Nitrogen." A grade-ten chem lab comes back to haunt me, as clear as if the beakers and the periodic table were in front of me.

I don't say what I'm really thinking, which is that it smells familiar, from even before the invasion. My brain grabs that thought but can't find anywhere to file it.

I smell my skin again. "So we're part of it now?" I ask. "Whatever this is?"

Mandy shrugs. "Why do you think we can remember who we are and everyone else can't?"

"I have a theory."

She turns to face me, sitting cross-legged.

"Okay, so when I was in the detention cell, after Tucker and I made a run for it, one of the Nahx said something about how their soldiers weren't supposed to dart people in the head. Have you seen any talking Nahx, ones without armor? This one seemed to be a leader. The other ones called him 'First.'"

She nods. "The ones with the clouds of light operating them? I've seen a few around. Why do you think they didn't want us nailed in the head?"

"I think if the dart injures you enough to"—I make air quotes—"'die,' the toxin preserves your brain as is or something, rather than erasing it. Because I was almost dead when I got darted, so maybe that's why it didn't work on me either."

"That's a good theory. I'm assuming it's some kind of nanotech. Maybe it was programmed to . . . attach to neurotransmitters or something. If your brain is dead, it has nothing to attach to, so it can't do its job?"

I nod. "Or it assumes your brain is already erased so it doesn't bother?"

"How did you get darted when you were nearly dead?"

"Oh, it was just"—*a desperate attempt to save my life by a Nahx who was in love with me* is what I *don't* say—"a fight, you know. An ambush. Very messy. I took an arrow in the gut." Sounds plausible enough for now, and thankfully Mandy doesn't ask for more details, though I show her the silver scar.

"So there have to be more of us," she says instead. "More who can think and remember and know that we're human."

"There are, I'm sure. Remember that guy who got smashed

in the face for refusing to sit down? Did you see that?"

"Ah yeah. Damn. He was one."

We sit in silence for a few minutes as I try to take in the enormity of the crowd spreading out in front of us. I can't count them exactly, but things click into place to process the size and density of figures across the vast arena and come up with a number. Over two million. How will I ever find Tucker among millions?

"What do you think we should do?" Mandy asks. Her voice has changed. Mandy is practical, a survivor. She's been like that since I've known her. But every once in a while her demeanor changes and her voice gets small, as though she's showing a little bit of the lost child inside. It's almost comforting to know that hasn't changed.

"Escape, obviously."

She scoffs, gazing out at the endless crowd. I let a few seconds tick past, because it feels like it might take time to convince her.

"Do you sleep?" I finally ask. "Have you slept?"

The change in her body language is subtle, but my hyper-observant brain has no trouble processing it.

"You've seen it, haven't you?" I ask. "The thing in the sky? The . . ."

Mandy squeezes her eyes shut while I search for the word.

"Rift. The *fissure*. The thing we're supposed to guard or defend or whatever. You've seen it, right?"

She nods. "I saw it before I woke up. And again after a couple of days. I tried to sleep, but . . ."

"So what is coming through it? Must be something seriously bad to do all this." I wave around the ship, the crowd. "Listen to me." I take her hand, feeling how weirdly warm it is compared to the frigid night air. "I don't care how strong we've been made, or how invincible. Whatever is coming through has a beef with the Nahx or the firefly things. Not us."

She goes quiet as I wonder if all the Snowflakes see the dark rift when they sleep. Maybe it's just ones like us who still have brains that work.

"How are we going to get out of here?" Mandy asks. "I've walked around the whole perimeter. The only exits are well guarded by Nahx. And they go inside the ship. We'd have to get over these walls somehow."

As I look up at the wall disappearing into the dark sky hundreds of feet above us, I analyze our situation and come up with our only possible chance.

"I have an idea." I whisper it, though I doubt any of the nearby Nahx are listening. They mostly look like they are asleep on their feet. "Don't freak out, okay?"

"What do you think could possibly make me freak out at this point?"

I unzip my breast pocket, and Blue drifts up.

XANDER

Two days after my first failure with the Nahx girl, Mobbs announces after breakfast that everyone is to proceed to the south road entrance to the mill. It's hellishly cold, and nearly an hour's quick march to our destination, so we pile on layers and cram whatever snacks we can find into our pockets. As Mobbs leads us up there, I note that he's the only one armed, an assault rifle slung over his back.

"What's this about?" I ask Logan.

"If I knew, would I tell you?"

Logan's mad at me for some reason. Sometimes I feel like I'm back in seventh grade with this crowd. So much rivalry, it's a wonder any of us are still alive.

When we arrive at the gate, Garvin is waiting in the cab of one of the trucks. He calmly climbs out as we fall into a loose formation around him. Mobbs and another boy flank him, armed and scowling.

"We had a visitor late last night," Garvin announces.

The boys shuffle nervously.

"Another Nahx?" someone says.

Garvin smirks. "Not another Nahx, no," he says, pausing

for effect. "It was two fine members of the local ICDF." He pauses again. In my next blink I picture Captain Chaudhry and her sergeant standing outside the gates of the refugee camp, literally selling me to Garvin and his band of demented lost boys. I wonder what they got in return.

"Anyone care to speculate what the lovely troopers' visit was in regard to?" Garvin asks.

When no one makes any reply, he continues. "They were very curious about our friend up in the cave by the transmission tower."

There are audible gasps. We are under strict orders that the existence of the Nahx girl is not to be discussed outside the camp on the mountain, not even among ourselves. Because the law says that any Nahx sightings are to be reported to ICDF and dealt with by them and them alone, interacting with the Nahx in any way apart from immediate self-defense is discouraged in the strongest legal terms. Yeah, most of what Garvin and crew get up to walks that line, but keeping a Nahx prisoner plows right over it. As much as I'm uncomfortable about what they are doing with the girl, I would never tell anyone. I may be conflicted, but I'm not stupid. I don't know who here would be.

But Garvin apparently does. "Michael? Do you have any idea?"

"No!" Michael says, a little too quickly.

Garvin lets out a breath, creating a cloud of mist around him. "Come here, Michael."

Michael goes from zero to panic in a matter of seconds.

"I didn't do anything! I didn't . . ."

Instinctively we step away from him, as though he might be contagious. When he doesn't move, Logan and another guy drag him to Garvin, pushing him down until he falls at our leader's feet.

"Please, Garvin. I swear I didn't tell anyone! I swear!"

"Quiet!"

Michael kneels in the snow with one mittened hand pressed over his mouth as Garvin glares down at him.

"I'm not stupid. Do you think I'm stupid?"

Michael shakes his head. I can see his eyes are filling with tears.

"Does anyone here think I'm stupid?" Garvin shouts.

"No!" we shout back in unison. Michael is crying now. I've never really thought of it before, but I think he might be only about fourteen or fifteen. He doesn't look like he's ever shaved.

"Garvin . . . I . . . I'm sorry . . . I didn't . . ."

Garvin turns his face back down, looking at Michael as though he's something disgusting he found in his food.

"What did they give you?"

Michael just shakes his head, his hand back over his mouth.

"I said: What. Did. They. Give. You?"

The wind whistles over the frozen road while we wait for an answer.

Michael finally removes his hand from his mouth and mumbles something.

"What?" Garvin snaps.

"Milk." Michael practically whispers it. "Two cans of milk."

Garvin crosses his arms, making his heavy coat crinkle. "And what did you do with the milk?"

Michael hangs his head. "I drank it."

"Xander!" Garvin yells, making me jump. "What do we do with any food or drink we come across?"

"Share it," I say. That rule was drilled into me soon after I arrived.

"What is the penalty for not sharing food?"

"Two days without rations," Logan supplies.

If that's all this is, I don't know why Michael is crying. I could do two days and barely even notice. But I'm used to it.

Michael looks up at Garvin hopefully, but Garvin's mouth twists into a cold smile.

"What's the penalty for spilling secrets?"

"No!" Michael cries. He shuffles forward on his knees, pathetically, grabbing at Garvin's legs. "No, please. Please, Garvin. I'll do anything. I can get things. I can get weapons or food. I know how. Please!"

My heart is pounding. What *is* the penalty for spilling secrets?

I know we're supposed to keep tight lips around here, but I don't know what happens if we don't. Is Garvin going to kill him?

Will I just stand here and let that happen?

"Start walking," Garvin says through his teeth.

"No . . . Garvin, please . . ."

Some of the boys look down at the ground, but I force myself to watch. Garvin pulls off his gloves, setting them on the hood of the truck. At first I think he might lay hands on Michael, forgiving him like Jesus or something, which is creepy enough, but instead he just draws back and punches Michael hard in the face. He goes flying backward, blood spraying onto the snow.

Garvin steps back, reaching into his coat. His hand comes out holding a pistol. He aims it at Michael, who is struggling to stand.

"Walk."

Michael's mouth bubbles with blood as he cries formlessly, turning to look at us, pleading silently. But nobody moves.

"It's cold, Garvin," he says. "It's too cold. I'll freeze."

"Is there anyone here who was unclear on the rules?" Garvin bellows, making me twitch again. "Anyone else who didn't quite understand the need for discretion? How important it is that we maintain the separation of this"—he waves his free hand around the road, the fence and truck, the distant mill—"and *state*? Anyone having *doubts*?"

We all shake our heads.

"Good," Garvin says.

Michael sobs quietly, wiping blood from his face.

"Am I a fair man?" Garvin asks, turning back to him. "Huh? I didn't hear you. Am I fair?"

"Yes, Garvin," Michael says, his voice thick.

"Right. I'm fair. I'm not a tyrant, am I, boys?"

A few guys shake their heads. I don't move, wishing for a sudden sinkhole to open up beneath me to get me out of this.

"I'm not a tyrant. I'm a fair man. What would a fair man do in a situation like this? Huh, Michael?" He waves the gun at him, making him cringe. "Huh?"

"Give me a second chance?"

Some of the boys actually chuckle, but this is the least funny thing I've ever seen.

Garvin laughs out loud. "That's what a tyrant *might* do. But since I'm not a tyrant, I would rather have a vote. Wouldn't that be more fair? Michael?"

Michael nods. I can see him shaking from here.

"So let's vote!" Sickeningly, Garvin seems to be having fun now. "Let's start with chances. Hands up who among you thinks I should give this treasonous rat, this pathetic excuse for a man, this snot-nosed worm who sold us out for two cans of milk, a second chance!"

I raise my hand without thinking, even when I can see

that no one else does. Garvin glares at me, but turns back to Michael, who has started to cry again.

"And with another show of hands, who thinks Michael should walk?"

I lower my hand as every other hand goes up.

"Start walking," Garvin says, his face hard. He draws the safety back on the pistol.

Michael turns, sobbing, and starts to trudge away south along the road. Garvin holds the pistol aimed at him, while I try to keep from trembling. Michael staggers on the icy road but carries on, pulling up his hood, jamming his hands into his pockets.

"You're dismissed," Garvin says to the rest of us. "Xander, wait with me."

Logan and Mobbs lead everyone back toward the mill as I join Garvin on the road. Michael is now just a dark smudge in the distance, but Garvin keeps the pistol aimed at him.

"Are you going to shoot him?" I ask, emboldened by not having the other boys around.

"Would you try to stop me if I did?"

"I'm not Superman. I can't stop bullets."

Garvin laughs and clicks the safety back on. He flips the pistol and hands it to me. I slip my mitten off and take it.

"*I'm* not going to shoot him," I say, checking the safety and the clip. Old habits.

Garvin laughs again. "No one is going to shoot him. He'll probably die on the road."

"Is that the idea?"

"No. The idea is that he walks to Prince George and moves back into the cesspool I rescued him from."

"That would take days. He'll freeze."

"Like I said, he'll probably die on the way."

I look down at the pistol in my hand. It's just me and him on the road—the other guys have disappeared around the bend past the gate. When I look back up at Garvin, he's still smiling.

"Go ahead and shoot me. Shoot me, take the truck. I just filled it. Plenty of fuel to go after Michael, pick him up. Both of you can head down to Prince George. If you don't, like I said . . ." He mimes slitting his own throat.

I'm frozen to the spot as the weight of the pistol in my hand seems to pull me down deeper into the snow.

"It's not easy, is it, Xander?" Garvin says. He doesn't seem the least bit concerned that I could turn the gun on him at any moment, that I could kill him. "Choices. There are always so many choices. Do you remember being able to choose chocolate or vanilla? Apple or PC? Girls or boys? Remember that world?"

"No. Not really."

"No. I didn't think so. When you're in a war your choices

are much more . . . basic. Life and death. Michael's life? Or your soul? What's it going to be?" He takes a step back, holding his arms out at his sides as though he's daring me.

I don't even lift the gun up; I don't even twitch.

Garvin lets a few seconds pass before nodding slowly. He puts his hands in his pockets, coming out with the keys to the truck.

"Keep the gun, kid. I think I can trust you with it. I'm going to go and get Michael."

"What?!"

"*What?!*" he repeats, mocking me. "I'll take him back down to his refugee camp. You won't tell the other boys, will you?"

"I guess not."

Garvin climbs into the truck and starts the engine, pausing there with the door open. "You understand what it takes to be a leader, right, Xander?"

"Choices?"

He nods, grinning at me. "Get in."

"What?"

He rolls his eyes this time. "You going deaf, kid? Get in the truck. You can come with. I've got some business in town, and you can visit Dylan. Tuck that gun away, though. Don't want anyone to see that."

I have a feeling I don't have much choice in the matter. I tuck the pistol into the back of my jeans and, zipping up my

186

coat, climb into the passenger seat. We find Michael half a mile down the road, a crust of frost and frozen tears already forming on his flushed face. He's completely silent as he climbs into the back of the truck, chastened by his brush with icy death, I suppose. His silence persists all the way down to Prince George and the North Camp, where Garvin unceremoniously dumps him. I try to call out a proper farewell or "See you later" but Michael just runs up the road to the camp gates, not looking back.

"He's was too fucking fragile for our scene," Garvin says as we peel off, blowing up snow behind us. I don't respond to that. I'm feeling kind of fragile myself, and the last thing I want is for Garvin to know. He drops me in front of the hospital with instructions on where to meet him in an hour. As I trudge up to the hospital doors I consider that *not* meeting him would probably be the wisest choice. But like he said, choices are for leaders. And I'm one of his followers.

Dylan is in a ward so rank, it takes every reserve of my willpower to not reel back from the smell. Where outside the doors of the ward smells of fresh death, inside smells of old death, as though something has been festering here for weeks. There are about twenty beds lined up along both walls and several thin mattresses on the floor down at the end of the long room. I try not to make eye contact with anyone as I search for Dylan, finding him at last between an empty bed and another with an occupant who is just a lump under a thin blanket.

Dylan's eyes are closed, but when I pull over a rusty stool and sit, they open. He frowns and blinks as though he's trying to focus.

"Xander," he croaks at last. "What are you doing here?"

"Visiting you, of course. How are you doing?" I ask it because it seems right, not because I need him to tell me. I can see he's not doing well. He's pale and gray, his forehead slicked with sweat even though it's cold in here. His right arm ends with a wad of stained bandages, resting on his chest. It feels natural to take his good hand in mine and give it a squeeze. He squeezes back, weakly, but doesn't seem to want to let go.

"Not that great," he says unnecessarily. "I keep getting infections, and there's hardly any antibiotics. But the morphine is s-s-sort of nice." As though to demonstrate, he drifts off for a few seconds before coming back. "Garvin told me you met the girl," he says, his voice low.

I glance around, but everyone in earshot seems to be either unconscious or dead. "You knew about her?"

"S-s-sure. Everyone did."

"I wish someone had told me."

"You know how it is," Dylan says. "Garvin decides when people get to know stuff. " His words are starting to slur. "Don't get too attached to her."

"I won't. I know what Garvin is planning."

"Yeah. What a vid that will make." When he blinks his eyes stay shut for a few seconds before opening again. "Has Garvin finished writing her declaration yet?"

I try to measure how to respond. Garvin hasn't mentioned a video or a declaration to me, but now I can see how stupid I've been. He wants the Nahx girl to renounce her people, to confess her crimes or something. I'll translate her signs, and then Garvin, presumably, will behead her. It will be the most popular video he's ever made. I wish I could say I've never seen or heard of something like that, but of course I have, even before the invasion.

It occurs to me how tidy Nahx darts are. They're not even very painful, from what I've seen. I suppose it's not like them to make a performance out of death, unlike us humans, who make whole industries out of it.

Then again . . . maybe the Nahx darts aren't really death. The movement of this tiny thought through my brain shifts things as it passes, as though trying to clear a path through the garbage and get to the actual answer, to understand. Garvin must think the darts kill. Why else would he have amputated Dylan's arm? But maybe it's *Garvin* I don't understand.

"No," I say. "No declaration yet. I think he's still working on it."

"Mmm . . ." Dylan says. I'd like to ask him more about Garvin's plans, but his head falls to the side and moments later he's asleep. I sit there as my mind cracks open and plays a dozen possible scenarios at lightning speed. I could coldcock Garvin and take his truck. But where? Checkpoints would stop me before I got past South Camp. I could go back to South Camp, crawl back into my trailer with sickly Colin, and pretend none of this ever happened. Or I could go back to the enclave at the mill with Garvin and refuse to take part in his sadistic spectacle. Not sure how that will go down.

"Your boyfriend doing okay?"

A nurse stands at the end of the bed.

"I'm not . . . yeah. He's sleeping."

She nods, turning to leave.

"Hey," I call after her. "Do you guys have access to the register here?"

"Uh-huh."

"I thought I should check it. You know, see if any of his family has popped up. They should know"—I look back to Dylan's face, peaceful as a corpse in a coffin—"what's going on."

The nurse nods, her face grim.

A few minutes later she sits me down at a computer terminal in the reception area, clicking a few keys until the register home page pops up.

"He's a fighter," she says, resting her hand on my shoulder.

I'm already distracted by punching my password into the log-in box. "Who?"

"Your . . . Dylan," she says. "Strong young kid. He'll pull through."

"Oh yeah. I know."

"I'll leave you to it," she says before wandering off.

To my shame, I don't know Dylan's last name, so I couldn't search the register for his family if that was even my plan. Which it wasn't. I do my usual thing instead, looking for my own family and any friends I can remember. Tucker, still dead. Topher, still alive. I swallow back the meager flare of relief. If he was dead on the other side of the web, how would anyone know? When I enter Raven's name, of course I find her still dead, and the message I left for her family a few weeks ago.

And a reply.

I blink a couple of times because it's gotten so I don't quite trust my mind to not fuck with me.

But no, it's real. A message from Raven's stepfather.

Dear Xander,

Thank you for your note. Of course I remember you. At times like this, it's important to remember as much as we can. It gives Raven's mother and myself some closure to know for certain that Raven is gone, and great relief to know that you were there with her when she passed. While I would dearly love to know the details, Raven's mom will need more time. You understand. Regardless, we have discussed it and hope that you will agree to come out to Quadra Island to live with us. I see that your own family is unaccounted for and that you are living in a refugee camp. Our community here is not luxurious, but I think we can probably improve on the conditions up where you are. It's the least we can do. You were a good friend to Raven and I think it would comfort her mother to have you around. In anticipation of your agreement, I've already put in an application for two travel passes and spots for you and a friend on the bus to Vancouver and the overnight ferry north. From what we've been told, these usually take about a month to process, so, everything going to plan, we should be able to get you here by Christmas. I hope you agree to come. You can leave your answer here, but knowing how patchy the updates are, it's likely your passes will be delivered and the first I hear of your decision will be you knocking on my door. We're in a cottage at the Cape Mudge Resort. Once you get off the ferry, any of the locals will know the way. I hope to see you soon.

Jack.

Jack. He always had this disconcerting habit of code switching from casual Canadian dude to really thoughtful, patient Métis elder to intimidating legal mastermind. His note is a mix of those things. All I can do is stare at it for a few minutes, until it blurs in my vision.

It would be so easy to give up at this point. It's almost as though the universe is offering me an out—go back to the South Camp, wait for my travel permit to arrive, go to the coast. Forget about Dylan and Garvin and the Nahx girl and Colin and his dying organs. And August and Raven.

And Topher. Just forget about Topher. Pretend I have closure too, that I saw him die, that I buried him with Tucker or left him behind on the plateau with Raven. I could move in with Raven's parents and be far away from the Nahx territory and the border web. Maybe they'll let us keep the low ground and coastal areas. Maybe the treaty is solid; maybe they'll stick to it. I could go back to school and try to be a normal kid again.

I have to admit, it's tempting. But as soon as I start to picture it, doubt enters my thoughts. I can never be a normal kid again. I've gotten too used to holding a rifle. Since Garvin recruited me, I've easily slipped back into that role; maybe not quite as a soldier, much less an insurgent, but as someone involved, at least. Those lucky ones who ended up in coastal areas must find it so easy to surrender everything, not just the territory the world gave up but also the people who got left behind and our ownership of our planet. A comfortable bed, adequate food? Is that what it takes to sell out to the new world order?

I'm actually a little disappointed with Jack. But maybe that's unfair, because I'm not fully committed to turning him down either.

Jack, I write.

>*I don't know what to say. Your offer is incredibly gen-*
>*erous, and if you could see the way people live up here, you*
>*would know what it will mean for me. I'll wait for the*
>*travel papers to arrive, I guess. And see you in December.*
>*In the meantime, give Raven's mom a big hug from me. She*
>*was always so nice to Raven's karate friends, even though*
>*we must have been annoying. You should know that Raven*
>*spoke about you guys literally every day. She loved you both*
>*so much.*

>*See you soon,*
>*Xander*

It's snowing when I leave the hospital, and along the walk back to the park where I agreed to meet Garvin, a lot of the dystopian decay is covered in a blanket of soft white, making the world pretty again, if only until reality encroaches. I can't miss the lineups for fuel and firewood. It's hard not to think that some of these people won't survive the winter. But then, maybe I won't either.

Garvin waves at me from the sidewalk where he's standing next to a stack of boxes. He loads me up with as much as I can carry before leading me into the park.

"Where's the truck?" I ask.

"I traded it."

"You traded the truck?"

He just looks at me with one of those inscrutable Garvin smiles as we turn off the path. We follow a trail of footprints in the snow for a few minutes, before ducking through a dense grove of young trees to an open field on the other side.

There's a helicopter parked there. A heavyset guy in winter camouflage is bent over the engine as we approach.

"How does she look?"

"Top-notch," the heavyset guy says. Garvin introduces him as Brad.

"Formerly of Cascade Heli-ski," he adds.

"Not much call for heli-skiing tours anymore," Brad says.

"Welcome Brad to the resistance, Xander," Garvin says as we board and buckle up.

I mumble something that I'm sure he doesn't hear, because he's powering up the rotors. No one offers me a headset, so I watch from the back seat as Garvin and Brad talk about something I'm apparently not supposed to hear. The journey takes only a bit over an hour, flying low over land made featureless by new snow.

Garvin's whole crew greets us on the airstrip as Brad brings the helicopter down. The mood is jubilant, with everyone greeting Brad and high-fiving Garvin as the rotors slow to a stop.

"Why are we all so excited?" I manage to ask Garvin as we trail back into the dining hall.

"We've been looking for a chopper for a while. And a pilot, of course."

"Where will you get fuel for it?"

"There's a full tank right here at the airstrip. Plus we boosted a tanker months ago. Good for a few dozen flights."

"Flights to where?"

I don't get an answer because a new wave of celebration greets us in the dining hall. It turns out that one of the boxes I schlepped across the park is a case of home brew, so soon a party is in full force. No one asks me how Dylan is doing—not even Garvin. I help myself to a beer and linger at the edges of the dining hall while Garvin and his minions seem to be congratulating one another. As the first case of beer is drunk and a second one opened, Garvin takes position at the front of the hall. The boys fall into a respectful silence, which Garvin leaves open for a moment, heightening the tension and the sense of excitement in the room.

"We're at a crossroads, boys," he begins. "The supporters of the treaty might see elevation as the defining feature of the surrendered territory, but we disagree, don't we?"

"Hell yeah!" someone says. The rest of the guys shout their agreement.

"And I think the Nahx view the web as the border. But our search on this side continues because we have a right to eradicate Nahx from human territory. The chopper extends our reach immeasurably. We can get to places we've long suspected to be Nahx hiding places. And what is our policy on killing Nahx?"

"KILL WHEN NECESSARY!" two dudes behind me shout in unison. I'm getting the feeling Garvin has given this speech before, or something like it.

"And it is always necessary to kill Nahx. They don't surrender. Do we surrender?"

"NO!" the whole room shouts it.

I can feel the bristle of energy as Garvin speaks, his voice firm and resonant. "We are not ignorant to the odds against us. We are not oblivious to the strength of the Nahx defense nor to their stranglehold on our planet, our governments, and our resources. But do we give up?"

"NO!" I shout along with everyone else this time, caught up in the moment.

"Do we lose hope?"

"NEVER!"

"Do we despair?

"DESPAIR IS DEATH!" Garvin's followers shout in unison.

The room erupts, everyone, arms around one another, jumping and chanting and toasting the air with their low-grade homemade beer. I jump and shout too, because the last thing I want anyone here to know is how scared I am.

And how I think I might betray them all.

RAVEN

We sent Blue off with a detailed description of August. After a lot of bobbing up and down, and guessing on my part, we confirmed that Blue knew who Tucker was. They'd been in the cell with us and followed when the Fifth dragged me off.

"And Tenth," I added as Blue prepared to zip away. "You remember Tenth. Try to find any or all of them," I instructed. "Bring them back here. Don't make a scene."

It was an hour before Mandy was even able to speak to me without making a face. I don't know which part of my story horrified her more. It's not lost on either of us that August very well could have been the same Nahx who darted her back in Calgary. Unbelievably, I never thought to ask him.

Blue comes back near the end of the next day, with Tenth trailing behind them. A group of nearby Nahx scatter and stride away at the sight of Blue, who follows them menacingly until they disappear into the crowd of Snowflakes.

You want to get inside? How? Tenth signs. He stands casually about ten feet away, not looking at us, pretending he's monitoring the crowd for any troublemakers.

If we break the rules? You could take us? I sign when he glances back at me.

He flicks his head back and nods.

"What are you saying?" Mandy whispers.

"Just go along with me. Do you remember the self-defense stuff Topher and I taught at the base?"

"Yes. Of course. To me it was less than two weeks ago, remember?"

"Right. Good. Well . . ." I grab her by the front of the coat, tugging her to the edge of the crowd. Before she can voice a protest, I shove her down onto the ice and snow. A couple of Snowflakes step out of the way as I leap down on top of her. She does exactly what I taught, going for my face and my throat as I fake punch and pull her hair. She even gets a thumb jammed nice and hard into my armpit, which tickles more than hurts but weakens me enough for her to shove me off. Then we're rolling in the snow, pathetically scrabbling at each other. It's the untidiest fight I think I've ever been in, but it does the trick. Less than thirty seconds after we start I feel the strong grip of a Nahx on the back of my neck. I struggle and squeal for effect, twisting enough to see that Tenth has Mandy gripped in his other hand as he drags us past the line of Nahx guards and along the high walls toward the nearest door. I turn my head to see Blue sailing along behind us.

Minutes later we're inside a dim cargo bay, Blue leading Tenth as he drags us across the hard steel floor. Other Nahx turn in our direction as Tenth tugs us up onto a platform, mashing us together and straddling us as he somehow manages to get shackles on our wrists. When he stands, Mandy and I are bound together, facing each other, wrists to wrists. Tenth presses some kind of control and the platform begins to descend. There's a second of darkness as the hatch closes above us, and then a dim yellow light activates. Tenth is looking down at us, his hands on his hips.

"I'm going to have trouble signing like this," I say, rattling the shackles.

No problem, he signs, flicking his head backward. *I can hear.* But he clicks the shackles open and tucks them away.

"What's the plan?" Mandy asks.

Find Eighth, he signs, which causes my heart to thump against my ribs.

"You think he's here?"

Tenth shrugs. *If Eighth is on the ship, he would be here.* I translate for Mandy.

"What about Tucker?" she asks.

"One thing at a time. Don't look at me like that."

"I didn't say anything."

"No, but you thought it. If August is here, if he's . . . functional, he will make getting off the ship a lot easier. He'll make finding Tucker easier. Tenth, do you know where Tucker is?"

He shakes his head, stepping back as Blue zips between us. They flicker excitedly.

There's a loud groan of metal on metal and the platform rumbles to a stop. A heavy gray door hisses open, revealing endless inky darkness. In the weak light oozing out from the platform shaft I can make out some shadowy shapes, motionless at the edges of my perception.

Nahx.

Hundreds, thousands of Nahx standing motionless in messy rows, extending as far as the light reaches into the dark.

Blue floats out and the rest of us step off the platform, following them. It is as though we have stepped into the underworld version of the arena on the surface. The Nahx are lined up, roughly organized into groups and formations, but those formations are broken. Some Nahx are kneeling, staring at the floor. A few are totally prone, lying as though dead. The rest stand, practically motionless.

And the *sound*, the characteristic buzzing of their breathing as we pass, some of it wheezing and labored like Tenth's, some of it gentle like sleepy bees, more of it weak and intermittent. Some of them don't seem to be breathing at all.

Two very tall Nahx turn their heads to us as we pass, but Blue drifts up and they step back deferentially.

"What's wrong with them?" I whisper.

Broken, Tenth signs. *If Eighth helped humans, Eighth is broken. Eighth could be here.*

I turn away. If August is here . . . is he one of the silent ones, the ones lying dead on the floor?

"AUGUST!" I yell it impulsively and listen as my voice echoes, rolling over what seems like a great distance. How large is this . . . place, this holding pen? I remember something the First said in the cell after Tucker killed one of his guards.

Take her down to cold storage . . .

It *is* cold in here, though I barely notice cold anymore. Some of the Nahx radiate heat, as August used to. But some, as we pass them, I can see are crusted with ice, like something left in the freezer too long.

"Are they dead?" I whisper to Tenth. "Are some of them dead?"

I think so, he says. Blue bobs up and down in agreement.

I swallow, but the lump in my throat remains.

"AUGUST!" I yell again. "IT'S ME! IT'S RAVEN!"

"Is that wise?" Mandy says. Some of the Nahx around us begin to stir. Tenth steers us away, down another row and across until we are out of sight. But as the murmur of movement seems to follow us, Tenth runs, pulling us along, his boots clanking on the steel floor. There are thousands and thousands of Nahx in here. How would I ever find August?

Before I can think more on that question, a wailing alarm

begins to sound. I don't want to leave yet. I know it will take days, but I want to search for August in here. I feel like I owe it to him.

The sleeping Nahx around us ripple as though brought to life by our trespass on their slumber.

"We should move," Mandy says. "Blue, which way?"

Blue sails off and we hurry after them, Tenth's metallic footsteps echoing behind us. As we push through denser formations, some of the Nahx reach for us, listlessly at first, but then with more determination. One of them gets Mandy by the neck and shoves her down. Several others surge at her.

"Mandy!"

Blue shoots into the fray, and the Nahx scatter backward as though thrown by the force of an explosion. Some of them put their hands on the backs of their heads as they recoil and crawl away.

Tenth helps Mandy to her feet. There's a streak of silver blood dripping out one nostril, but apart from that she is uninjured.

"Let's get out of here," she says.

Blue bobs up and down. We stick close to them as we continue through the seemingly endless chamber. Blue and Tenth manage to stave off any further harassment, though I can tell the Nahx are agitated by our presence.

At last we reach a kind of doorway, though one blocked by

some kind of glowing force field. I reach forward and touch it experimentally, only to have my arm jerk back from an electric shock.

"Can we disable it?" Mandy asks.

Tenth clicks on one of his shoulder lights and examines the control panel, but Blue just kind of dashes at him, making him stumble backward as they fly right into the panel, disappearing.

"Blue?"

Seconds later the force field dissolves.

We waste no time stepping through into the dark passageway beyond. As I turn back, I see some of the Nahx are moving again, advancing on the open doorway.

"Blue? Now might be a good time to reactivate the field."

One of the Nahx reaches through the doorway just as the field crackles to life. The Nahx goes flying back, spiderwebs of electricity lighting up its armor as it lands in a heap. The other Nahx seem to lose interest immediately, turning away to trail back into the dark.

"Everybody have all their limbs?" Mandy says.

Tenth turns, arcing his light down the long passageway.

"Did Blue come out?" I search for them. "Tenth, turn your light off so I can see."

He obeys; darkness falls around us like a blanket.

"Blue?"

Nothing but a small amount of flickering light from the force field.

"Blue, where are you?"

A minute goes past, steeped in my silent dread that Blue has sacrificed their life for us. But just when it looks like it might be safest to carry on without them, I notice a dim flare far down the passage.

"Blue? Is that you?"

They bob up and down.

We tiptoe to join them, trailing our hands along the wall to find our way in the dark.

"How did you get all the way along here?" I ask.

Blue draws a circle in the air, which isn't very reassuring.

"Do you know where we're going?"

A little too much time passes before Blue bobs up and down again. Tenth turns one light back on as Blue leads us along the narrow passage. The vague shapes of doors are occasionally visible but Blue ignores them, picking up speed until we're jogging to keep up. At last we come to a T junction, opening onto another dark passageway, this one not as narrow. Tenth shines his light down either way, where the passage seems to disappear around a curve.

"Which way?" I ask.

Blue drifts up around the ceiling, bouncing along as though searching for something. After a few seconds their light flares and they spin in a frantic circle.

"What's up there?" Mandy asks. "Tenth, can you reach?"

Tenth reaches up, turning so his light illuminates what looks like a manual release lever. With Blue demonstrating, Tenth turns the lever to the left until something somewhere makes a low, deep clang, like an atonal church bell.

The wall in front of us begins to move—first a thin sliver of light cracking where it meets the ceiling, then slowly descending, grinding metal on metal as it goes. Instinctively we all creep back into the corridor, pressing against the wall, ready to fight whoever awaits, but there's no need.

There's no one beyond the wall. No one alive, at least.

In front of us, spreading the length of the wide passageway, bodies are suspended on some kind of framework or machinery, hanging like carcasses in a butcher's freezer. They appear to be joined to tubing via their ears, noses, mouths, and even genitals. A glowing gray sludge is moving slowly through the tubes.

"Oh my God . . ." Mandy says.

Horrifyingly, the bodies closest to us *have* been butchered, sliced crossways at their ankles, calves, knees, and upward until they resemble a block toy waiting to be put back together. But as I gingerly step closer I realize the reality is even more gruesome. The nearest body, a young male probably no older than Mandy, has been *separated*, the slices of his body divided into two sets, each one 50 percent of the boy he was. Down the row, either way along the corridor, we can see that other boys have met the same fate, or are about to. Some seem to be further into the process than others. In some the gaps between the slices are narrower. In others they seem to be joined together by a kind of matrix of light, over which globules of flesh and tissue are growing. Behind the first row, disappearing into the distance, are other rows, one after the other. Hundreds, maybe thousands of bodies.

"Okay," Mandy says shakily. "I see what they're doing here."

Whatever protective systems my body now has go into full crisis mode. My vision becomes so enhanced that even the dim light from the machinery behind the boys looks bright; my muscles tense, my heart rate shoots up, and my whole body tingles with energy as that strange shimmer resonates through my cells again. It's like being adjusted or reoriented to some new objective still unclear to me. If we find Tucker here, sliced apart like this, I don't know what I'll do.

"What are they doing?" I ask. I've figured it out too, but I don't want to say it out loud.

"They've . . . bisected each one. And somehow, splitting them into two sets, they are regrowing the missing tissue. Turning one human, or whatever these are, into two complete beings—each of them half of the original."

Repeat, Tenth says. He taps my shoulder to get my full attention. *Repeat twelve times.*

"Twelve times? Like the Nahx?" I stare back into the rows and rows of bodies. "This is how they made you, Tenth? How they made all the Nahx?"

"If they did this twelve times, then the twelfth one would be barely human. Just around two ten-thousandths."

Repeat me, Tenth says. *Tenth is a tiny bit human.*

"But it would turn one soldier into twelve soldiers," Mandy says ruefully. "Pretty good way of making an army."

These are not Nahx, Tenth says. I've never seen a Nahx make this sign before, but he does it in the most obvious way: *Walk Night.*

Not Walk Night, he repeats. *Snowflakes.*

"These ones were taken from the crowd upstairs?" I ask. "From the arena?"

"But it's the same process that made the Nahx, right?" Mandy asks.

Different, Tenth says. *Nahx are copied first, then changed.* He waves his hands up and down his armor. *These Snowflakes have been changed already. Now they are trying to copy them. I've never seen that before.* I translate for Mandy.

"So this is a new technique? An experiment?"

Tenth nods, and Blue bobs up and down.

"We need to find Tucker," I say. "Now."

Blue zips off into the rows as Mandy, Tenth, and I check along the length of the corridor.

"He's not here!" Mandy shouts back from one end of the row.

When we reach the other end of the row, my relief at not having found Tucker all sliced up turns the panic in my body down a single notch. Still raging panic, but slightly more manageable.

Blue suddenly pops out of the rows, bouncing manically, their light reflecting off the machinery and its victims.

"Did you find him?"

They bob up and down. *Yes.*

"Alive?"

Yes.

"Show us."

As Blue leads us into the dense machinery, it becomes clear that whatever is happening here is not as extensive a project as it could be. Most of the machinery, most of the framework scaffolding, is empty. Eventually we reach a clear passage though the machines and follow Blue into an open chamber. Lining the walls of the chamber, laid out on slabs like bodies in a morgue, are several dozen humans—Snowflakes, from the metallic sheen of their skin. I'm slightly mortified to see that they are all completely naked. And, as is embarrassingly obvious, all male.

I push every thought about that aside as Blue leads us through the chamber. We find Tucker on the second-to-last slab before the wall. As we get closer I see the small smattering of blood on the slab under his head, his brown hair matted in it.

Mandy must sense my panic flaring.

"He's alive," she says, taking his wrist. "He's breathing; his pulse is steady." She shakes him gently and gives his face a couple of light slaps. "Wake up, Tucker."

He doesn't move or react.

"Help me roll him over," Mandy says. I stand back as Tenth helps her roll Tucker onto his front. The source of the blood under his head becomes apparent. Imbedded in the base of his skull, just above where his head meets his neck, is a small device, almost like a headphone jack.

"God. Is that where they plug them in?"

Don't worry, Tenth says. *I have one too.* He taps the back of his head. *It's for repeat mind rules.*

Before I can ask him to elaborate, part of the wall in front of us suddenly dissolves like smoke, revealing a blinding glare behind it. A First is silhouetted there, flanked by two huge Nahx. They raise their weapons.

"Run and you will be discarded," the First calmly says.

When he steps forward, I recognize him. His face is distorted—a misshapen nose, one eye socket seems off-kilter, silver scars bisect his upper and lower lips. This is the boy the Nahx beat to a pulp up in the arena. Not a copy, or a tall, armorless Nahx like the First I met in the cell with Tucker. His clothes are still stained with gray blood. This *is* that boy.

And not. He has the same vacant look as the other First and a cloud of lights operating him like a marionette.

While I try to think of something to do, something hits me hard on the back of the head, making me see stars. As my vision clears I see Mandy has gone down too, and Tenth is clutching us by our necks, pressing us into the floor.

"Shackle them," First says.

I'm still too dazed to resist as Tenth obeys, shackling me and Mandy together again, face-to-face.

"Well done, Tenth."

Lying, treacherous little shit. I glare up at him, but he is pointedly looking away. Blue is nowhere to be found, but strangely, on the table next to Tucker's sleeping form, is Tenth's knife. I dart my eyes away quickly, not wanting to draw any attention. Something is going on; I'm just not sure what. Or who is in on it. Or who to trust.

The First steps closer to me, staring down with bruised and bloodshot eyes.

"What did you do to him?" I ask. "This human being you're wearing like a suit?"

The First tilts his head to the side until his neck cracks, fixing his eyes on me.

"Human curiosity is certainly tenacious," he says. "Here you are with no guarantee of living for another minute, and what you ask for is answers."

I bite my tongue, because suddenly the idea of spending my last moments being surly is unappealing.

"This boy asked questions at the end too," the First says, waving his hands vaguely down in front of his chest and abdomen. *What's happening? Am I dying? What are you doing to m—"*

The First twitches suddenly, and before my eyes, the floating cloud around his head changes color, from pale yellow to a kind of soft pink. As I watch, I realize the lights haven't changed color so much as position. Pink ones have taken the outer positions in the cloud, becoming more visible.

"Forgive us," the First says unexpectedly. "That was cruel."

"God . . ." Mandy whispers. While I try to plot a way out of this, I can't help filing away this new observation of the First. Do the color changes signify a change of mood? That knowledge might prove useful if I live past the next minute. If not for the still unnoticed knife on the slab, it wouldn't be looking good.

"Unfortunately this *snezjinka* was being disruptive," the First says. "The ones you call the Nahx have been instructed to cast out disruptors, but . . . they . . ." He looks disappointed suddenly, almost ashamed. "They are unpredictable. What are you—" The cloud changes again, shimmering back to yellow. "This one is incompletely processed. She should be discarded."

The First steps back, as though he's been startled by his own change of heart. I watch in astonishment as the cloud then changes again. Not back to pink, but to a shade of Creamsicle orange, an optical illusion caused by the yellow and pink lights mingling together. Finally he releases a theatrical sigh.

"Being among humans for so many years has made consensus impossible for us." The First shakes his head in what is maybe the most sincerely human gesture I've see it make. It's disappointed—with us, with itself. "Your ways are so . . . juvenile. So petty and selfish. It's no wonder, really, that . . ." The cloud shimmers again, splitting into two colors before remerging.

"What? What is no wonder? What does 'incomplete' mean?"

The First takes another step toward us. Mandy clutches my hand, but before I have the chance to choke out some choice last words, one of the First's Nahx guards suddenly collapses in a clattering heap, as though dead.

"What—" the First says. Then I have to hyper-focus my visual processing to even see what happens next. In a blur Tenth lunges forward, grabbing the remaining guard by the neck, and they go crashing down together. At the same time Tucker springs up from the table with a wild growl, landing on the First and slicing his throat open with the knife as they both crash to the floor.

Well. That explains that.

Tucker leaps up, naked and bloody, as the First writhes, his life pouring out of a gaping wound in his neck.

"Raven," Tucker says. "Raven, what the fuck?" His eyes dash around wildly. "Where are we?"

He lurches back as Tenth steps over the chaos and clicks the shackles open. Mandy and I clamber to our feet.

"What now?" Mandy says.

"Where are we?!" Tucker repeats.

"It's okay, Tuck," I say, trying to stay calm. "Let's get you out of here and I'll explain." I have no idea how much of the last few days he remembers. He seems completely lost, which is only about 10 percent more lost than I am.

Blue reappears, drifting out from under the Nahx who collapsed. They fly in a rolling motion as though urging us to follow.

"Did you see where the First's cloud of lights went?"

Don't worry, Tenth signs.

We have to run to keep up with Blue as they sail along another dark corridor. Finally a wall slides back, revealing a platform like the one we descended on.

"Back up?"

Blue bobs. *Yes.*

We jostle together as the platform begins to rise.

"Tucker needs clothes," I say, my voice coming out smaller than I intended.

"You think?" Mandy laughs. She begins to strip. "He can have my khakis. I've got leggings underneath."

As Tucker dresses in Mandy's khakis and one of her sweaters, I notice how he's breathing—hard and fast, as though panicked. He turns to me, and I feel like time has finally slowed down enough for me to get a good look at him. I'm shocked by his expression. He looks dazed, haunted.

"Raven," he says, his voice breaking. "What happened? Where's Topher?"

Mandy spins around. "Oh . . . shit."

His memories are back, Tenth says, pointing to Blue. *The Firefly did it. Here.* He taps the back of his head again.

Something about the thing they implanted in Tucker's skull? I don't know what to do with this new information, but my brain files it away along with a million other things. Who knows what facts might be useful anymore?

The platform crunches to a stop and the doors hiss open, revealing another wide cargo bay. This one is dimmer than the one I know, and less populated, with only a few scrappy-looking Nahx, and there don't appear to be any guards. The Nahx are working silently, pulling bits off half-assembled transports and installing them on others, carrying tools and equipment around. It has the air of a large auto repair shop, only alien.

Blue floats down into the bay and accosts one of the Nahx, pinging into its forehead. It snaps to attention as Blue flickers at it. The Nahx points to a transport near the bright cargo bay door. Blue rolls again, beckoning us to follow.

The working Nahx step back deferentially as we pass. I wonder if they think we are Tenth's prisoners or if they've got some other idea of what is going on. It's clear they don't want trouble with Blue, though. One Nahx literally jumps out of the way as we approach the transport. There is no ramp, but the hatch is open so we hop up, finding the transport's hold to be nearly empty and in a state of disrepair.

"What's going on? Someone tell me," Tucker says, staring down at his forearms. "What's wrong with my skin?"

I take his hands and tug him down into a corner, sitting across from him as Mandy, Blue, and Tenth head into the cockpit. We hang on to each other as the transport lifts off. It rumbles and shakes, and I can barely hear Mandy yelp with fear as we suddenly bank hard, one flank apparently not quite clearing the bay doors.

I go rolling away before Tucker gets a hand around my wrist. He clings to one of the handholds.

"Veer right!" Mandy screams. "Hard right!"

I slide back into Tucker, and he wraps his free arm around my waist. "Hold on to me," he says.

I pull myself into his chest, breathing in his still strangely human smell, his warmth, feeling the familiar landscape of his athletic body.

"Climb!" Mandy yells. "Take us up!"

My ears pop as the transport shoots up, the wall of the ship blurring outside the hatch until it's swallowed by night sky. As soon as we're over the wall, Tenth slams us into reverse, wedging the transport against the ship, and then, yanking some levers, he jerks us sideways and suddenly we're flat against the exterior wall, cowering like a bug on a leaf.

"What—" I start.

"Quiet!" Mandy says.

Tucker tightens his grip on me, and we watch through the hatch, now above our heads, as three Nahx transports fly right by us. After another tense minute goes past, and then Tenth releases something and the transport drifts down, straightening out. We coast away from the giant ship, flying only meters above the ice until we reach the edge of the lake. Tenth takes us up then, my ears popping again as we breach the clouds and Tenth finally closes the hatch.

We made it, somehow. We're free.

I pull back from Tucker's arms, looking into his frantic eyes. He lifts one hand up to touch my face, his eyes desperate, as though he's searching.

Then he leans forward and kisses me.

XANDER

I pack carefully for my next journey up to the transmitter, discreetly raiding the stores for a miniature electric lantern, a few extra batteries, matches, and a thin tarp, which I roll up as tightly as I can inside my sleeping bag. In my cabin I grab only those personal items I can't live without. I need to find a balance between looking like I'm packing for a few days and actually packing for the rest of my life, which is challenging. I check and double-check my pocket for the key pieces of equipment I spent all night searching for—a handful of paper clips, finally found in the bottom drawer of an old desk someone had dumped in the recycling depot.

Garvin's pistol, which I've been hiding from the others, I conceal in a slit I've made in the lining of my coat.

Mobbs and Logan have been assigned to relieve whoever is at the transmitter. They grumble about the cold and mostly ignore me, letting me trail behind as we skirt the town and head up the mountain track. Logan smokes again, this time long, thin, minty-smelling cigarettes that Mobbs calls "girl smokes."

"Offer Xander one," he says.

"I don't smoke."

"Not even *girl* smokes?"

They guffaw until Logan has a coughing fit so bad he nearly falls over. I just keep walking, ignoring them.

When we reach the camp the two sentries Logan and Mobbs are relieving have little to report about the Nahx.

"She was quiet. I heard her moving around just after sunrise."

I have to shrug off my pack to get through the narrow entrance to the cave, and drag it along the damp ground behind me. Inside I flick on my flashlight.

The Nahx girl looks up at me, straightening her back and shuffling a bit on her knees. I dig the lantern out of my pack and light it on its lowest setting, flicking my flashlight off. The cave dims around us and I wait for my eyes to adjust, wondering how she has sat alone in the dark up here for more than three weeks without going mad. The Nahx aren't solitary; they almost never travel alone, and I got the feeling from August that he didn't like being alone. It was always a struggle for him whether he would crawl into a shelter with me or linger outside. Claustrophobia versus loneliness. Some choice.

"I'm supposed to ask you some questions," I say. She doesn't react, instead watching me as I set the lantern down out of her reach. "You do understand me, don't you?"

After a few seconds go past, she nods.

I could get a lot of information out of her with just yes/no answers, and Garvin has given me a list of questions to get me started, but I hesitate. I haven't made a final decision about going along with this. As much as I'd like answers too, I don't want to be part of how this is going to end. The Nahx girl seems to sense my conflict. She huffs a sigh and rests back on her heels as though she's waiting.

Digging in my backpack, I come up with my harmonica.

"Do you like music?" I ask. She tilts her head to the side. I blow a few notes, which seem to flutter around in the cave like happy butterflies. The Nahx girl rises up onto her knees.

"Yes? You like music?"

She nods slowly.

I sit cross-legged, starting with some improvised blues that for whatever reason morphs into "Amazing Grace," a sad melody at the best of times. In here it feels like encroaching doom, inevitable and dire. As I play, the girl sits back again, looking at me for the first verse, but as I start the second, she looks away. I keep playing because the music loosens the knots in my brain, letting me think about what I'm going to do next. When the song finishes, I start another, "Moon River." I had a booklet of songs that came with my harmonica, and it was sort of typical for me that I learned them all, even though they were so old-fashioned and sad. But I'm glad of it now. I work my way through that repertoire, taking breaks between each song to sit and think while the silence settles in around us. After four songs, the girl breaks the silence with a little hiss. I look up at her.

Please, she signs. It's a very distinctive sign, and although she can't quite do it properly because of her chains, it's unmistakable.

"Please what? More music?"

Yes. Please.

This goes on for over an hour, until sunset is not far off. Finally after a particularly sad song I announce I'm going to leave the cave to get some boiling water for tea. The girl merely nods.

Mobbs and Logan smirk at me as I emerge.

"Music?" Mobbs says as I set a snow-filled pot on the fire.

"I'm trying to build a rapport," I answer. "It's standard interrogation procedure."

"Maybe you just like hanging around with her," Logan says with a smirk. "They do say chicks put out for musicians. Is that what you're trying for?"

"You're disgusting."

Logan leans back on his pack, lighting another cigarette as though that makes him look cool.

"I'm not the one making friends with a Nahx."

"I'm not making friends with her." I stare down at the pot, wishing it would just boil so I could have my tea and get away from these creeps. "I'm interrogating her, like I've been ordered to."

"For an interrogator you don't seem to be getting many answers," Mobbs says.

"Maybe you'd like to have a go." I regret it as soon as I've said it. Mobbs wriggles out of his sleeping bag eagerly, goading me.

"Maybe I will. Maybe she'll warm up to me better than you. You're a bit weedy."

Logan hoots with laughter at this, but Mobbs isn't done messing with me. He clambers right over the fire, nearly spilling the pot of boiling water, and heads for the cave entrance.

"Hey! Don't!" I leap after him, pulling him back by the arm.

"I just want to talk to her."

I grab the collar of his coat, and with a quick forward kick, sending both his legs flying out from under him. He lands on his ass with a satisfying grunt of shock.

"Whoa," Logan says. "Xander, calm down."

"I'm perfectly calm."

But I miscalculated, because Mobbs still has his rifle and he wrenches it around, smashing the butt into my forearm, not quite hard enough to break a bone but hard enough for me to feel it in my balls and make me let go of his coat. He jumps up and shoves me backward, and I contort myself to not fall right into the fire. I end up smacking my forehead on the icy rock. By the time I shake the stars from my eyes, Mobbs is disappearing into the cave.

I stagger after him, pushing Logan out of my way. When I get into the cave Mobbs has taken position over the Nahx girl, the barrel of his rifle pressed into her neck. She kneels, hunched over with her hands up.

"Not so tough, are you, Nahx bitch?" Mobbs says, jabbing her with his rifle. "I got the badass bullets in here too. Take your head clean off if I pulled the trigger."

Logan lurches in, flicking on his flashlight.

"Mobbs, Garvin said . . ."

"I'm just playing, bro. Chill."

In the light of the flashlight I can see what the Nahx girl is doing, extending her free leg behind her, straightening it out.

"Mobbs, you need to move back," I tell him evenly. "Now."

"You don't give orders, kid."

This time, because I know what she's going to do, it's like I'm seeing it in slow motion. The Nahx girl rears up, swinging her good leg around while somehow also catching the rifle barrel between her chin and her shoulder. Mobbs goes down as her leg sweeps his feet out from under him. His rifle is wrenched from his hand and goes clattering to the stone.

Logan swears, arcing his flashlight around wildly so it's like watching through strobe lights. I vaguely see him raise his own rifle, and I frantically reach for the pistol under my coat.

"Let him go! LET HIM GO!" Logan screams.

I spin back to see the Nahx with her leg wrapped around Mobbs's neck. His eyes are rolling back in his head as he writhes beneath her.

"No! Stop!" I shout.

But it's too late. There's a sickening crack, and Mobbs goes limp.

Logan fires his rifle, sending chunks of rock flying everywhere, and the next thing I know I have my pistol in his face, safety pulled back, finger on the trigger, barely able to see anything but the pulsing red of my blood boiling in my eyeballs. His flashlight has rolled away and stopped, wedged against the wall, emitting a weak light.

An eternity goes past.

"Drop it," I say. I don't even know where his weapon is pointed. Not in my face, so I guess that puts me at an advantage.

"I always knew you were shit," Logan says. I feel the barrel of his rifle press into my thigh. "Femoral artery," he says calmly. "You'll bleed out before you even get out of this cave."

"Cerebellum," I say, pressing the pistol's muzzle right on his forehead. "You'll die before you hit the ground."

I don't know where the Nahx girl is or whether she's even

alive, but when there's a small noise behind me, Logan moves fast, lunging into me with his whole body until I tumble backward. All I can see is him raise his rifle. All I can hear is the Nahx girl's hiss and the explosion of the rifle and the ringing of chains against the rock. All I can feel is the pistol still in my hand, still pointed right at Logan's head.

God help me, I pull the trigger.

I shoot him.

When my ears stop ringing, the Nahx girl is growling, not in a threatening way, more as though she's trying to soothe me.

"I killed him."

Her growl is like the purring of a cat, vibrating on both the inhale and exhale as she breathes. Something happened to the flashlight. My lantern dies and it's now pitch-dark in here, the only faint illumination from the narrow exit to the twilight outside. I think Mobbs is a dead shape near the overhang where the Nahx cowered all this time. Logan is a dead shape on the dirt floor. The Nahx girl is a trembling shadow under the low rock ceiling.

My mouth is so dry, I have to peel my tongue from my teeth to talk. "Did you get shot?"

If she moves, I can't see it. I get down onto my hands and knees, searching the dirt and rock, feeling around for the flashlight or the lantern. There's a loud snap and a spark of light flares up, glowing for a moment in the air before it snuffs out in the dirt. She snaps her fingers again. This time the spark illuminates her corner well enough for me to see she is kneeling favoring her left side; her arm hangs limp.

She snaps her fingers again and again, sending a dozen sparks into the space between us, each one reminding me of August setting himself on fire. At last my eyes fall on the lantern overturned near Mobbs's body. I snatch it away from him as though he might try to take it from me in his condition. As I click the light on, the rest of my senses come back with my vision. The metallic smell of blood, so familiar to me after that terrible day on the mountain when Raven and Liam died. The cold of the cave fractured by the intense heat radiating off the Nahx girl's body. The silence but for her soft purring and my gasping, trying to catch my breath, and the chattering of my teeth. A bitter taste in my mouth.

I set the lantern down in the center of the cave and take two shaky breaths before reaching over to gingerly close Mobbs's staring dead eyes. I have to resist the urge to correct the unnatural angle of his head and neck.

Promise, the Nahx girl says. *Promise you.*

"How do I know you're not going to kill me, too?"

She just shakes her head, turning her palms to face me.

I could conceivably get out of this. I could shove things around a bit, make it look like she grabbed Mobbs's gun after throttling him and shot Logan before I could stop her. No one is going to do ballistics tests or anything. I could leave the Nahx girl chained up and run back down to the mill, throw the pistol into a crevasse, and rehearse my story. *Omigod omigod she got Mobbs she got his rifle and shot Logan I don't know how it happened I only left the cave for a few minutes to take a piss omigod they're dead she killed them both omigod . . .*

I mean, that's what I *should* do. But instead I shuffle over to Logan's slumped shape and check him for life signs. There are none. His blood spray has left a shadow on the cave wall behind him, like graffiti: *Logan died here.* I drag myself away from him, digging in my pockets for the paper clips.

"Can you break your chains?"

She shakes her head. Getting closer to her, I can see her posture is contorted; she's curled to the left, and blood drips from her wrist and elbow. Maybe if she wasn't injured and weakened she could break these chains. I saw August break chains nearly this heavy once. That seems like years ago now.

"I'm going to try to pick this lock, okay? It will help if you hold very still."

She's a master at that, kneeling like a statue but for the shallow movement of her breathing.

The bar through her right wrist is bolted at one end with a heavy padlock attached to the length of chain, which is in turn bolted to the stone wall. How they managed to rig this up without power tools is beyond imagining, but I suppose if you want to hurt someone badly enough, you find a way. Pushing that thought aside, I concentrate on the padlock, bending the paper clips into the required shapes. Tucker and I looked up lock picking on YouTube years ago because we wanted to use the warming hut when we played night hockey on the lake. All well and good until we got caught smoking weed in there.

My hands are trembling so bad, I wish I *had* some weed. I focus on time instead, start a clock in my head, counting down the seconds, the minutes, the hours until the relief shift turns up here around noon tomorrow. I want to be long gone by then. The bent paper clip wedges into the padlock nice and tight as I fumble for the other one, the straight one with the end shaped into a shallow W.

The Nahx watches me silently, while I'm hyperaware of all the ways she could kill me right now. A sharp downward head butt would crack my skull or break my neck. There's enough give in her chains that if she got me in the crook of her elbow she could strangle me. Hell, she could crush my throat with one hand. Or she could wipe me out with her leg the way she did to Mobbs, and then, I don't know, stomp on me, crushing my ribs?

I close my eyes for a second, feeling the pins in the lock slide up one by one until the sixth pin grinds into place. I twist the bent paper clip and hear the bolt click up. The lock falls to the floor with a clang.

I consider the metal bar skewering the Nahx girl's wrist. There's a congealed film of gray gunk surrounding the hole in her armor—blood or something. Her body has been trying to reject the spike, building up a layer of tissue and pus just like a human would with any foreign object.

"Do you want me to pull the bar out?"

Please. Yes.

"I think it might hurt." Understatement of the century.

Please.

I grip her arm just under the elbow and wrench the bar upward. It comes out, dripping thick blood and slime.

The girl yanks her arm back, and when I turn, she is tearing at the other lock. Before I can even offer to help, she has crushed it, flinging it down with the chain and yanking the bar out with a spray of gray blood. The last lock, on the spike through her knee, won't need my help either. She hooks her fingers through the shackle and tears it apart with a violent growl. She wrenches the last spike out and throws it away so forcefully that it ricochets off the cave wall and I have to duck to avoid it smacking into my face.

Now that she's free, the Nahx girl's demeanor changes from helpless to furious in a millisecond. Growling and hissing, she

lunges for me, her hands dripping oily blood like some creature from a nightmare. Standing, she's at least a foot taller
than me. I turn and try to scramble for the cave exit, but she
grabs hold of my coat and I go crashing down, twisting away
as she releases me. I spin in the dirt, pressed up against the
rock with the pistol somehow miraculously in my hand and
pointing in the right direction, at her neck. She stops there,
poised, hands raised like great claws, back curved like a frightened cat. Shiny metal blades flick out from her mask like fangs;
I'm sure if I could see her face, her teeth would be bared too.
But then something happens as we wait there, both frozen in
place by the impossibility of any kind of resolution between
us. She softens; first her fingers unbend until her palms are
flat, facing me in a gesture of appeasement. Then she slowly
lowers herself to her knees. Her right hand, still dripping
blood, moves to press side-on into her abdomen. The blades
on her face retract with a hiss.

Sorry. Broken. Sorry. Repeat.

I witnessed August lose himself like this once, when he
thought Raven was threatened; he was also probably mad with
pain at the time. There's a lesson twice learned that I'm not
likely to forget. The Nahx are dangerous and unpredictable if
they're threatened or injured. Why should this surprise me?
Humans are no different.

"You understand what is happening, right?"

She nods, sitting back on her feet. Her breathing is improving. Unbelievably, I think she's already healing.

"I can't go back to . . . the other humans now. They'll kill me or . . . something." I struggle to keep my voice even as I go on. "I want to get back through the web. Do you know a way?"

She lets a few seconds go by before she nods.

"I want to look for someone. Another human I left behind. If you could help me get through the web, I can find him."

Help, she signs. It's one of the ones I learned from August. *Help you promise.*

"Okay, good. We have a much better chance if we stay together."

I shove everything that's not soaked with blood back into my pack and drag the whole thing out into the basin. She emerges after me, stretching her long arms up before bending to gather a handful of snow, which she rubs on her head and face. Another handful she presses on her wounded wrists and knee as I scavenge the camp for anything useful. There's a rifle, some ammunition, a bit of food, a hatchet. I pack and tie them all tightly into Logan's pack along with his sleeping bag and the tarp they were using as a windbreak. The Nahx girl takes this pack from me and slings it over her back.

She limps slightly as we cross the basin. The night is moonlit, but I still need the flashlight to find the slash through the rocks.

"You go through," I say. "You'll have to squeeze and take off your pack. I'll be right behind you. I just need to do one thing."

When she's out of sight in the rock-and-ice crevasse, I turn back to the campsite, bend over, and let myself vomit up everything in my stomach, taking care not to get any of it on my boots. Then I follow her into the dark.

PART THREE

AIR

"It is true, we shall be monsters, cut off from all the world; but on that account we shall be more attached to one another."
—MARY SHELLEY, *FRANKENSTEIN*

RAVEN

The transport, limping along on apparently only reserve power, keeps us in the air for just under twenty-four hours before Tenth has to set it down on a frozen lake outside a small town.

"Grande Prairie?" The snow-dusted welcome sign on the highway seems to mock us. "We're barely halfway to the base. We could have driven faster."

"Except there's no road from where we were," Mandy snaps at me.

We're all a little tense after a day and night in a cramped and rattling Nahx transport, wondering whether at any moment engine failure might send us careening into the ground.

These transports are made for short trips, Tenth says. *Sorry.*

"It's not your fault."

Tucker is still clinging to me; though seemingly unbothered to be walking barefoot through the snow in freezing temperatures, he is silent, almost dazed. He hasn't said more than a few words since we escaped. I'm worried that however Blue managed to zap his human mind back has damaged him in some way.

I tried asking Blue, but of course all I got was bobs up and down and the occasional circle. Not the easiest way to get medical detail.

The town looks deserted, so we risk taking the highway down onto the main business street, in the hopes that we might find a working vehicle. But after trying a dozen as we trail along the road and finding them all dead, we give up, resigned to the fact that we'll have to walk the rest of the way. Turning east, we discover the town is indeed as empty as it looks. Tucker slows as we pass a sports supply store and, without saying a word, lets go of my hand and runs across the parking lot, kicking up snow with his bare feet.

We chase him and find him inside, stripping and redressing in proper winter clothes and boots.

"Were you cold?"

He doesn't answer.

Though none of us needs to sleep, we decide to spend the night in the store, spreading out sleeping bags, with puffy winter coats for pillows. Blue floats by the door as Tenth stands guard. His wheezing had improved a bit on the transport, but now it's gotten worse and I'm worried about him. But mainly I'm worried about Tucker, whose stunned silence has hardly changed since we escaped the Nahx ship. He scooches his sleeping bag up next to mine, pressing against me.

"Say something," I try for the hundredth time.

"Topher is alive, right?" This is the same thing he's repeated periodically since we rescued him. The only thing.

"He was last time I saw him," I say. "We're going to go look for him." I reach up and stroke his face, and when he pulls me into his arms and closes his eyes, a fraction of the tension seems to leave him at last.

"What's the last thing you remember?" I ask.

He doesn't answer for several long seconds, but finally he speaks.

"Camp," he says. One word. But I've become an expert at waiting, and a few minutes later he speaks again.

"Something is wrong with my brain," he says. I hold my breath. He's whispering now. "It's like there's a wall in my head, or like one of those toxic waste silos, but it's been smashed to pieces and everything is coming out. Everything before . . . I got darted, didn't I?"

"Yes. Last September."

He nods, frowning, and I can almost see the chaos behind his eyes as I wait for him to say more. But that's all I get. A few minutes later his breathing changes, and it's clear he's fallen asleep. I can only hope his dreams aren't the terrifying ordeal that mine have been.

So the last thing Tucker remembers is being with me at the camp, with Topher and Xander and the rest of our crew, most of whom are now either dead or darted. He wouldn't know anything of what we learned about the Nahx since then. He certainly wouldn't know what happened after he got darted and we buried him. And he doesn't seem to remember what has happened since we woke up on the dunes, as though that little pocket of memory has been exchanged for the much more complete set of the rest of his life. Now he remembers us together, a doomed couple in love at the end of the world. I feel like I finally have what I wanted, what I dreamed of after August's dart snatched Tucker away from me so abruptly—I have him back, alive, next to me. We're together again at last.

Why, then, do I feel so sick? When I close my eyes I see those rows and rows of dormant Nahx, frosted with ice, slumped and staring. What if August was one of them? What if he heard me calling out to him but he couldn't move? What if he watched me run off and leave him?

Suddenly being so close to Tucker seems wrong. I untangle myself from his arms.

"He's in shock," Mandy whispers when I sit up. "Sleep will do him good."

I carefully slide out of my sleeping bag, trying not to disturb him.

"Be honest," I say to Mandy. "How bad does my hair look?"

She stifles a laugh.

"There's a drugstore right next door. I'm going to see if they have anything to fix it."

"Want me to come?"

I shake my head. "Keep an eye on Tucker." I lower my voice. "And Tenth." We both look over to where he's guarding the door like a faithful sergeant at arms. "I don't like the way he's breathing. We need to get him up to higher ground."

"A couple of hours," Mandy says. "Or we'll all lose our minds and be of no use to anyone."

"I don't know what use we'll be anyway." I look around the empty store as I stand. Dimly lit with some travel lanterns we propped on the top of displays, it's like a museum exhibit now—a relic of all the strange things humans used to do. There are fiberglass canoes strung up above us, and snowboards lining the walls. There's a locked rack of hunting rifles and knives, an aisle of hockey sticks and skates. Are we fighting to get this back? For whom? Everyone is gone.

Mandy smiles grimly, as though she knows what I'm thinking. "Let's concentrate on getting back to the base. See if we can rescue anyone there. We can worry about what to do next later."

She's right. And it helps me to have a direction, a plan, at least for the next few days.

Tenth greets me with a nod as I approach him by the door.

"Are you feeling okay?" I notice he is leaning on the wall with his left hand.

Don't worry, he signs.

I am worried. His wheezing breath now sounds wet and tubercular. But when I stare at him a little too long, he waves me away, and ducks backward as Blue tries to inspect him.

I'm good, he insists. *Strong. Take the Firefly with you?*

"No, it's okay. They can stay here."

Tenth huffs a bit but doesn't argue. I don't think he likes Blue much, but the truth is, I want to be alone.

The drugstore looks like it's already been looted. The door is smashed in, the aisle strewn with tumbled products. I find a grim scene in the center aisle—the remains of a Mountie. There's not enough of him left to see how he died, but the desiccated bones of his fingers still cling to his sidearm. I extract it delicately and pocket it, leaving the Mountie and his bony stare.

I find what I need in the hair aisle and spend nearly an hour in front of a small mirror trying to brush out my matted curls and tug them into six tight braids, which I smooth with cocoa butter cream and argan oil. I smell like a tropical cocktail when I'm done, but anything is better than stale lake water and dirty sand.

Feeling a bit more at peace, I wash my face with some wipes and try a very expensive moisturizing sunscreen I've always coveted. In the low light of a pair of flashlights, I examine my skin. My color hasn't changed much; it's still a light golden brown, but it's glossier, as though I've gone a bit overboard with the highlighter. There is also a dark spiderweb of bronze lines starting from my neck just under my ear, where August stuck the dart into me. It spreads down one shoulder and just peeks out into the décolletage revealed by the low-cut green dress. It's not ugly, exactly—in fact it's almost like avant-garde jewelry, sort of delicate and lacy. But looking at it, I realize I've been marked for something, branded against my will. I'm tempted to look for a good concealer to cover it up, but that seems . . . well, pointless. I smear on some frosty lip gloss instead, and pocket it.

A noise coming from the back of the store distracts me from further theft.

"Hello?" I say stupidly. "Mandy?"

There's no answer.

If there are humans hiding back there, how will they react to me? And how will I react to them? I feel the shape of the Mountie's pistol in my pocket. It's unlikely that humans are a real threat to my life, but they could hurt me enough to slow me down, to slow us all down, and that's the last thing I need.

But maybe I could help them. If there are humans, maybe I could help them get out of here, to safety.

The impulse that drove me from the moment the Nahx attacked, more than a year ago now, to head west, to get away from them and their ships and their soldiers, to get as many humans away from them as possible, flickers for a moment in the dark expanse of my mind; flickers and dies. That's not my mission anymore. I try to drag it back from the abyss, try to commit the shape of that last dying light in my memory, but it's gone, leaving something hard in its place, like stone.

I don't know why yet, but this is bigger than human life, bigger than me and my friends and my family. In karate, we sometimes talked about eastern spirituality and the idea of being connected to everything. It made me feel small then, but now it's as though I've zoomed back and can see the full picture, and that's all that matters. The fine details aren't as important. I almost walk away from the possibility that there are humans nearby, but curiosity gets the better of me.

Hearing the noise in the back of the store again, I move without thinking, running the length of the aisle, past the dead Mountie and toward the staff-only doors next to the pharmacy.

Three raccoons dash away as I enter, leaving behind their scene of destruction. Torn-open boxes of food are scattered across the storeroom, shelves are overturned, and in the center of it all is a dark shape splayed out on the floor. I focus my flashlight on it and take a step toward the shape before realizing.

It's a Nahx. The Mountie's pistol is in my other hand, aimed and cocked without my even needing to think about it.

But there's no need; the Nahx is obviously dead. Nahx never

lie down in their armor, or even sit. They rarely kneel. This one is spread-eagled, arms and legs wide, his head slumped to the side, with detritus strewn all around him, even on top of him, like the raccoons have been using him as a dinner table.

I crouch down to brush some crumbs off his chest, just to make sure. There's no star-shaped scar there or on his shoulder. Sitting back on my heels, I exhale heavily, scanning the dark corners of the storeroom, letting my brain record and collate everything I see. I'm starting to get used to it now.

The Nahx's armor is icy cold. Bending down over his face, I notice silvery gray fluid dripping through the grill in the front of his mask and dab my fingers in it, taking a tentative sniff.

It smells like ordinary death, oddly—ordinary human death, rancid and sour. I'm strangely comforted by this. At least in death this Nahx returned to his human form, mortal, fragile, and impermanent. I have a sudden impulse to drag him out into the field behind the store and leave him to finish decomposing there, returning to the earth as all humans should. Thinking back to the dead woman Tenth and I found on the dunes, an altered human like me, a Snowflake, who decayed into a fine metallic sand, I wonder if this is something else stolen from me—a messy, organic death with all the rot and ruin that entails. Maybe I'll return to the molten metal at the planet's core when I die, rather than to the loamy earth itself.

Maybe that's what awaits all of us—Mandy, Tucker, and the rest. The longer I live with my upgraded body, the less fragile I feel. Death used to frighten and nauseate me; now I just find it a little sad.

I fill two shopping bags with antibiotics from the pharmacy, thinking that if anyone is still alive at the base, they will be able to use them, but that makes me feel weird too, as though the weakness of human disease is another relic, almost quaint.

When I get back to the sports store, all hell has suddenly broken loose. Tucker is sitting tangled in a pile of hiking boots, screaming his lungs out.

"What is it?! WHAT IS IT?!"

Mandy and Tenth circle him, trying to get him to calm down. Tucker launches a boot at Tenth's head.

"Whoa, Tuck." I pull Tenth away, stepping in front of him as Tucker scrambles backward. "What's going on?"

"He saw the rift," Mandy says behind me. "He saw it in his sleep, like we did."

"WHAT DID YOU DO TO ME?!" Tucker's face is streaked with gray tears and twisted with terror.

"Nothing, Tuck." I hold my hands up, palms out. "It's okay. It was just a dream. Calm down."

"Raven?"

"Yes, it's me. Everything is okay." I kneel down and crawl through the tumbled boxes. He must have run into a display stack as he tried to escape. He reaches for me as I get close, pulling me into his arms again.

"Rave, Rave," he says into my shoulder. "Are you okay?"

"I'm fine. Everything's fine. It was a dream." I can feel his heart pounding even through his layers of sweater and coat. Glancing back, I see Mandy giving me a puzzled look.

"Can you tell me what you saw, Tucker?" I ask. "What was in your dream?"

He takes a couple of shuddering breaths before answering.

"It wasn't the Nahx. It was something else. Like a . . . black hole or something. It split everything open."

Mandy nods at me knowingly.

Tucker presses his lips into the side of my face. "It split *you* open, Rave. It killed you. It killed Topher." Then he clings to me tightly, as though he's trying to meld us into one or crawl inside me. "It was so real. It wasn't like a dream."

I sense more than see Mandy and Tenth drift away. Blue floats up by the ceiling as if they too want to give us some space and privacy. Pulling back, I take Tuck's face in my hands, holding him, trying to still the chattering of his teeth.

"We've had the dream too," I say. "Mandy and I. It's something to do with the Nahx dart's toxin."

"What does it mean?"

"I don't know. They've made us into . . ." I pause here. If he's completely ignorant of what little Mandy and I know, do

245

I want to share it with him? Maybe it would be better to keep him in the dark. But then I think about how my brain has been churning since I woke up, recording every new piece of information and putting it together, trying to construct a final picture of what is going on. I can't deny him that.

"They made us a kind of army. Blue's people, those tiny Firefly creatures." I look up at Blue swirling around the light fittings. "They call us sentinels or Snowflakes. And we're supposed to be guarding what they call fissures."

"And that's what I saw in the dream? A fissure?"

"I think so."

"Where is it?"

"Back where we woke up, on the dunes, I think. Not far from the ship."

He appears to think about this for a few seconds.

"And we're supposed be there? To go back there?"

"I don't think we were supposed to leave in the first place," I say. "Do you want to go back?"

"Fuck no. I want to find Topher and get him as far away from it as I can."

Something about the way he says this fills me with relief so palpable it's almost euphoric. This is the real Tucker. Not the insensible automaton who woke with me on the dunes, and not the crazed and terrified boy we rescued from the ship, but Tucker, stubborn, reckless, foul-mouthed, and determined.

Like the force of nature who blew my life apart within months of meeting me. I can't help but smile. I know we were always a disaster. But at least we were *our* disaster. Tucker made me feel like an insider for the first time in my life, a founding member of a two-person club of destruction and chaos. I've missed that. A bit of the sickness I felt earlier subsides.

I can do this if I'm not alone, if we're in it together. Once we reunite Tucker and Topher, I can decide what to do next. It's better if I try not to think of August, and I'm used to that anyway, after all those months of trying to forget him.

"We should go," I say, standing up.

Mandy and Tenth don't argue. They pack up a few items while Tucker smashes and raids the gun cabinet, loading two rifles and slinging them across his back, stuffing the pockets of his coat with ammunition. The last thing he takes is a crossbow and a quiver of arrows. He grins as he slings that over his shoulder. As he strides past me, bending to tuck a hunting knife into the top of his boot, I'm suddenly reminded of the last time Tucker strode off with a crossbow and arrows, and what happened. And why he did it.

Who he did it for.

Ah well, I had a good minute of feeling okay about things. I should be grateful for that, I suppose.

"What's wrong?" Mandy says when I join her and Tenth, following Tucker out into the snow.

"Nothing."

Blue drifts down and settles on my shoulder like a microscopic parrot.

Having a firm and settled goal makes the walk through a dark and nearly featureless landscape a little less soul destroying. At least none of us seems to tire. I'd like to take a nap just so I can get away from the superprocessor in my head. It's still churning away, filing things, pulling things out and reclassifying them. I can't seem to stop it, so instead I try to pull something out of my thoughts that will entertain me, at least. I start with music and find I can play whole songs as clearly as if I have headphones in. That's kind of neat. I switch to episodes of TV shows but keep getting distracted and losing my place. Music seems to be able to play in the background while the rest of the thinking continues.

I try something new. Selecting a song like a DJ, I set it playing in my mind while I dig up scenes from various karate tournaments I competed in. I used to like doing this before everything changed; I would redo fights in my head, especially ones that I lost, and try to figure out how I could win next time. My coaches encouraged it. But this time it's so vivid that at one point I actually veer back, trying to dodge an imagined straight jab.

"Are you okay?" Mandy asks, alarmed.

"Fine." I can't help smiling. It must have looked pretty

funny. "I don't know about you, but now when I remember things they're supervivid, like a 3-D movie. I was remembering a fight I lost."

"I heard that didn't happen very often."

"Who did you hear that from?" I expect her to say Tucker or maybe Topher.

"Xander," she says instead. "He was in awe of you."

"Are you sure it was awe and not fear?"

Mandy shakes her head, squinting ahead to where Tucker trudges determinedly, with Blue floating behind him.

"*I* was a little scared of you at first," Mandy says. "But Xander told me you never threw the first punch."

I'm about to laugh and argue, but my analytical brain has to confirm that detail, and when it does I discover she's right. I even check my data twice, and it's true—every fight I got into, outside of a legal spar in a karate competition, I was just defending myself. They line up in my head like one of those surveillance systems with multiple screens showing different events.

Every time I got into trouble for fighting it was because someone else started it, took a swing at me or shoved me or, on at least a couple of memorable occasions, tried to grab my ass or boob. And yeah, all of them ended up either bloodied or on the floor, sometimes both. And I always ended up the one in trouble, because . . .

I shake my head, my good mood dissipating like mist. I want to ask why Mandy was scared of me before she even knew me, but I'm afraid the answer will make me dislike her, and I need a friend right now. And I'm not sure that with my new superpowers, my old superpower of being able to forgive people of pretty egregious infractions still works.

I look at Tucker and think of him fooling around with Emily in the woods while I was oblivious. Without being too obvious about it, I slow down until I'm walking side by side with Tenth, taking up the rear of our little band of travelers.

All good? he asks.

"Yes. What about you?" I ask.

He points forward. *Mountains*, he says. *I will feel better in the mountains.*

"Do you think we'll find any other humans there? I mean . . . real humans? Do you think many people survived? Not darted like me and not . . . killed in other ways? Survived? Got away?"

He hangs his head, giving it a little shake.

No.

"What about farther west? Did many humans survive? Do you know?"

Past the sky prison light, yes.

"Sky prison light? What's that? You mean the drone web? The border web west of the mountains?"

He nods again.

So the web is real. Kim talked about it when we got to the base. That was her excuse for not trying to lead us all out of there. Privately I'd had some doubts that it even existed. I thought she was lying to us for her own purposes. Maybe that was unfair, in retrospect.

I let my thoughts drift back into their game, but before I can continue my review of my sporting accomplishments, I find my mind focusing on August instead, maybe because the conversation with Tenth reminded me of him. I suppose I could redirect my brain onto something else, but the memories of the weeks I spent with August are so vivid that I just let them play behind my eyes like a movie. It's a sad movie, I discover, and by the end of it, by the time I get to my death scene on the side of the mountain, I have to look down at my feet so I can be miserable in private.

When I look back up, Blue is hovering there, buzzing inquisitively.

"I'm fine. I'm just thinking." They buzz away, placated by my gormless lie.

Why did August leave me? That's what haunts me. He must have known I was going to be revived. Why did he shackle me to Tucker's body? The only thing I can think of is that he thought that's what I wanted—to be with Tucker?

You'd think my last moments as a human might be lost to

me, given how my brain was shutting down from blood loss, but no, I remember everything clearly. I said "Tucker." That was my last word. August must have thought . . . after everything he did for me, that I wanted Tucker. And not him.

Not August. Who I would give anything to see again.

We arrive at the web just before dawn, and I have a backward déjà vu moment on top of being half frozen. The web rises above us, as glowing and foreboding as it was when I was trying to get through it the other way. If I'd known then the stupid choices I was going to make, I might not have bothered.

The Nahx girl turns north, clambering easily over the steep and rocky terrain as I slow down, joints locking up, face numb. I can't feel anything below my knees. She turns back every few minutes, urging me on. I suppose there's a reason why the Nahx are so loyal once they've settled on a traveling partner. It's part of their programming or something. I'm grateful for it, anyway. If she gives up on me, I really am dead this time. Dead for good in the remote mountains of British Columbia. No one will ever find me.

We reach a frozen pond as the sky begins to turn pink, the blue glow of the web competing with the rising sun, turning the snow around us into a rainbow of pastel colors. The tendrils of light seem to pierce into the ice crust of the pond, though there's no evidence of melting. The drones that infest the web like vigilant spiders hum above us, watchful but for now uninterested. All my obsessive journeys to the web outside Prince George taught me enough to know that if you stay out of the narrow expanse of light tendrils, the drones ignore you.

If not, they try to kill you. Not likely to forget that.

"H-h-how do we get across?" Now that we're not moving, the cold becomes even more dire. I wrapped Logan's sleeping bag around me, and over that the tarp, tying them with bungee cords. I must look like a creature from Mars, but I suppose next to the Nahx girl that's not saying much.

Under, she signs. I remember this sign from August.

"Under the ice? I don't . . . I'm not sure I can do that."

I'll help you. Promise.

I jump on the spot to stay warm as she steps carefully onto the ice, lowering herself to one knee, and draws her fist back.

BANG!

She punches the ice with such force that the ground shakes. Whatever pain was troubling her a few hours ago has clearly abated. She draws back and pounds the ice again and again, until cracks begin to form beneath her. Edging back, she motions to me, miming a knife. I creep forward gingerly and hand her mine.

She leans down and picks at the cracks in the ice until a nice-size hole has formed. Flipping the knife over, she hands it back to me.

In, she signs.

I would be insane to go along with this. I stare through the web to the other side, about thirty meters along the pond. The surface is black there, which could mean that it's not frozen, or it could mean that it is frozen but not frosted. Door number one, I live. Door number two, I die.

"Are you sure we can get out on the other side?"

I'll break it. When I hesitate, she signs again. *Break it. Repeat past. Repeat today.*

"You've done it before?"

She nods and seems to be satisfied that she's got my agreement. I strip off the tarp and sleeping bag and try to wrap them together in a way that will keep the bag dry. Making a loop with a bungee cord, I attach them to my foot so I can drag them along like a trailer.

The Nahx girl slips off the pack and lays it on the ice next to the hole. Then she beckons me.

Me one. You two.

"Okay . . ."

She slides into the hole as naturally as a seal, disappearing for a moment before popping back up to wind one hand around the strap of the pack. She holds her other hand out to me.

I get down onto my knees, lowering myself until I'm crawling across the ice. I take a deep breath and grab on to her. With a firm tug we both slither into the dark water.

The cold knocks me so close to unconsciousness that the journey across the pond seems to take forever and no time at all. Before I even know what's happening, she's pushing me through a narrow opening in the ice and shoving me toward the shore as I gasp for air. I can't move, instead lying there like a fish until she clambers after me and drags me up into the trees. I turn back, focus returning to my eyes.

And there it is: the web, with freedom and the human race on the other side.

We did it.

I need to get out of these wet clothes or I'll die. Fast rather than slow, which is how I'll die once I get them off. The Nahx girl disappears from my field of vision for a moment while I struggle to tug off my gloves. They're already starting to freeze. My brain is frozen. I try to form my lips to call out to the girl, but I can't think of how to address her. She doesn't have a name.

It's darker than it should be, and I realize that I'm starting to lose consciousness. My fingers are too numb to work the zipper of my coat or the laces of my boots.

"H-h-hey . . . ," I manage. "C-c-can you . . . ?"

There's a flash of light and a wisp of smoke drifts across my face. When I cough, a splash of cold water comes out. With intense effort I turn and see the Nahx girl crouching by a pile of pine boughs and twigs, snapping her fingers, sending sparks into the tinder as it begins to glow. The thought of a fire enlivens me, and I finally get my frozen fingers around the zipper of my coat, drawing it down. I peel it off painfully.

The girl leaps over the fire, landing next to me.

"I n-n-need t-t-to get undressed."

She nods solemnly, tugging my arms out of my sleeves. I go limp as she pulls two soaked sweaters over my head. Behind her the fire blazes up.

I'm not going to die. Not here, anyway.

When she has me stripped down to boxers and an only slightly damp T-shirt, she helps me shuffle forward until I'm practically sitting in the fire. I untangle the bundle of tarp and sleeping bag, finding the bag to be nearly dry when I sling it over my shoulders. Then I lie down, facing the fire, my back covered with the sleeping bag. Vaguely I feel her tucking the tarp around my back too. After a few seconds, she lays her hand over my ear and I feel the heat of her armor—warm at first, then hot. She moves her hand to the top of my head as my eyes drift shut.

When I open my eyes again I'm so warm that I get confused for a second. Maybe this was all a dream. But I blink a few times and the roaring fire comes into focus, along with an array of branches over which my clothes are festooned like festival decorations. And sitting a few feet away is a human girl.

I sit up so fast, I nearly launch myself into the fire.

"Who . . ."

The girl turns to me, her irises reflective metal, her skin practically glowing white. She hisses and flicks her head back a few times, revealing a tangle of metal implants on her throat and chin. When she lowers her head I see that her eyelashes are as pale and opalescent as cobwebs, and her hair, slicked back and hanging limp down her shoulders, is silver.

"Oh . . . it's you." I turn my eyes away instinctively, slightly worried her unearthly beauty might burn my corneas. Instead of her armor she's wearing a dark gray body-hugging suit that looks a bit like motorcycle leathers, with panels and intricate-looking seams, and some of the weapons we took from the transmitter camp strapped over it. The whole effect is disconcertingly badass. I feel like I'm camping out with Lara Croft.

Cold? she signs. She is taking deep gulps of the mountain air.

"I'm fine, actually." I snake one hand out of the sleeping back and rub some feeling back into my nose. "Are you okay? Can you breath here?"

Yes. You understand?

"I know you prefer higher elevations, yes. A . . . friend explained it to me. How high are we?"

Five. Zero. Zero. Zero.

5,000 feet. A comfortable elevation for Nahx. I look around uneasily as my brain continues to thaw out. The freezing swim shook a few things loose. Now I can't for the life of me think of what I had in mind coming back through the web, leaving a relatively comfortable and safe situation with Garvin and his crew. Would it have been so hard to do what Garvin asked?

The Nahx girl squats by the fire, poking at the flames with a long stick. Behind her, her armor is carefully laid out, glistening a bit, reflecting the gold and orange flames and glowing coals. Has she been polishing it? For some reason this gives me a chill, as though I caught a glimpse inside her head for a moment. She must have been dirty and uncomfortable in that cave for all that time. Another surreptitious glance at her tells me she has probably washed her face too, and her hands. Her skin has that freshly scrubbed look, and her hair is damp around her ears.

Ignoring me, she unfastens something on her jacket and unzips it, revealing a sleeveless silver garment, like a tank top. Shrugging the jacket off, she slides it underneath herself and lowers down to sit cross-legged on it. Her muscular bare arms are as pale as the rest of her, but the scars from the bolts in her forearms are conspicuous, and though they appear to be healing, they are surrounded by a fine spiderweb of pewter lines. I can feel my stare turning into a gape. She's both beautiful and frightening, and there's something else. Wounded? Sad? August was like that too; even without taking his armor off he exuded heartbreak, well beyond his obvious grief for Raven.

She hisses suddenly, swiping at me with the smoldering stick still in her hand. I roll away from her, wrapping the tarp and sleeping bag around me protectively.

Stop staring! she signs, baring her teeth with a low growl. At least that's how I interpret it. Maybe that's optimistic, because what it actually looked like was *dead eyes*.

"I'm sorry," I splutter. "I haven't seen one of you without armor before. I'm just curious. I'll stop." I roll over, my back to the fire, and kind of burrow into the sleeping bag.

Moments later she makes another noise, a kind of snuffle. I ignore it at first, because she probably just wants privacy, but after a few minutes when the snuffling intensifies, I turn, peeking out from under the tarp.

She's crying.

Not just a few tears either, but hunched, the back of one hand pressed over her mouth, the other holding the top of her head, clutching a handful of her silver hair. And shaking with deep, body-racking sobs made even more devastating by their voicelessness. If she had a voice, I'm sure she would be wailing, but as it is, it's as though she's gasping for breath, each almost silent sob releasing a cloud of mist around her head. Her contorted face is stained with dark tears and snot.

"Hey," I try. "Hey . . . what's wrong?" Instinctively I reach for her.

Her response is swift and brutal. She bares her teeth and lunges at me, snarling. I scuttle backward, tumbling into one of the sticks where my clothes are hanging. My damp sweater and jeans fall over me as she signs, her hands sharp, her words punctuated by angry hisses. I don't know all the signs, but the meaning is clear enough.

You don't look at me! You don't touch me! I'll kill you!

"I'm not. I won't!" I pile the sleeping bag, tarp, and my damp clothes over me as though I could just burrow down and hide like a spider. "I wouldn't dare touch you," I say, keeping my eyes on the ground by the fire. "I'm sorry. I won't look at you."

Her anger seems to melt away then and she slumps, practically prostrate, sobbing. It's so visceral I have to clench my fists, stomach, and brain to not start crying with her, because I think I know where it's coming from and it's sickening. The replay of me shooting Logan stops playing back in my head for a brief instant and changes to *her* shooting him. I know that's not right, but it feels right.

Out of the corner of my eye I can see her repeating a very familiar sign.

Sorry. Sorry. Sorry.

"You don't need to apologize." I speak into the sleeping

bag, which forms a cave around me. "None of those creeps will ever touch you again."

Now I can't get *that* thought out of my head.

As quietly as I can, I pull on my clothes—they'll dry faster on me now anyway—and stand up, tiptoeing to the other side of the fire to collect my boots, socks, and mittens. I leave my coat. It's still pretty wet, so I turn it inside out and move the makeshift clothes hanger a bit closer to the fire. Finding some dry branches and logs piled nearby, I add a few to the flames and watch it blaze up; the snaps and pops, the smell of smoke, the warm glow fill my mind and calm it, infusing me with comfort and nostalgia. For the first time in months I feel free, like I can breathe.

I discover my backpack propped against another set of branches, its contents carefully laid out to dry. Grabbing my steel camping cup, I fill it with snow and set it on the coals at the edge of the fire. In seconds it's steaming, and soon it's filled with simmering water. With my mittens on I fish it out of the embers and approach the Nahx girl, setting it down within her reach.

"Are you thirsty?" I ask. I don't even know if they need to drink. August never did in the time we spent together. "I have tea bags too, somewhere, if you prefer tea. But this is just water. It might make you feel better. It's hot, though, so be careful."

I step back, out of her personal space, as she looks up. She frowns at me until I lower my eyes to the cup. But she picks it up delicately, the heat of the metal not seeming to bother her, and sniffs the water suspiciously.

"You can add some snow if it's too hot."

She sips a few times before gulping the whole cup practically in one deep draft.

Repeat, she says with a sniff, handing the cup back to me.

We do this five times, and though she's still crying when we start, by the fifth cup her tears have stopped. I search through my things for the small amount of food I was able to sneak out of Garvin's stores. She rejects everything but some moose jerky, which she devours while I reclaim the metal cup and brew myself some tea. When she's finished eating, she washes her face again, wiping away the gray streaks of tears.

I sip my tea and eat some dried peaches, along with a boiled egg I snuck out of breakfast. The tea bag and eggshells hiss on the fire when I discard them.

As the morning mist dissipates, the sky clears, shining blue above us with the crown of craggy snow-tipped mountains all around, and the day warms enough for me to emerge from the sleeping bag and spread it out to dry fully, along with my coat and snow pants. While I'm busy with this, I hear the Nahx girl drag her armor over the rocks until she's partly concealed behind some scrub. I keep my eyes averted. I saw August remove his mask once, and that was disturbing enough. Nahx armor is organic somehow and integrated into their bodies via tentacle-like tubes that penetrate through their mouth, nose, valves in their neck, and God knows where else. I don't care to watch her put hers back on, and I doubt she wants me to see. It feels private, intimate, like a bodily function. The noises alone make me blush.

By the time she's done, I've determined my coat and snow pants are dry enough to put on, which I do while she stokes the fire.

"We'll have to put the fire out before it gets dark, right?"

Yes.

"Are there still Nahx around here? Your people?"

She shrugs.

"I suppose we should talk about where we're going. Now that we're here in Nahx territory."

Find your friend.

"It's a long way. Where I left him."

She signs quickly, and all I catch are *broken* and *think.*

"I'm sorry, I don't understand. . . ."

She sighs impatiently. *Promise,* she signs. *Trust.*

I suppose she has reasons to trust me, since I killed one of my own people right in front of her. But me? Would I be a fool to trust her?

Maybe she let me see her cry on purpose. She didn't need to

take her armor off. And she didn't need to drag me out of that pond or build a fire or help me get out of those wet clothes. She could have killed me in the cave for that matter, as soon as she was free of the chains.

Apparently satisfied with the fire, she sets down her stick and reaches for me as I sit, touching my shoulder. Even through my coat I can feel how hot her hand is.

I am with you, she signs.

I just shake my head because none of this makes sense. But she's right. I have to trust her. What choice do I have now? I watch the fire for a moment, feeling that freedom bubble up in me again, my mind leaping around, into the flames, into the sky, over the snowy mountains. It's almost intoxicating.

"I should know what your name is," I say, and it occurs to me as the words leave my mouth that maybe this is a really personal question to the Nahx. "Unless you don't want to tell me, of course."

She seems to think about it for a moment, her head slowly tilting to the side.

Six repeat, she signs, before doing another sign I don't understand.

"I'm sorry, I . . ."

She mimes firing a rifle and marching.

"Soldier? Soldier twelve? Oh! Rank? That's your rank? Twelve? Twelfth?"

She nods.

"Is that what you want me to call you?"

She sighs again and appends this one with a growl no bigger than a kitten's purr. Then she shakes her head, lowering herself to her knees and resting back on her heels. The fire crackles, and we both watch it for a few seconds.

She points at the sky, then at me, making a *Z* with her finger before repeating herself.

"Xander. That's right. Your name is Sky?"

No. Sky. Fire. Night. She does a waving motion and repeats those three signs, blending them together.

"Fire wave in the night sky? Oh! Northern lights? Like the colored lights in the sky at night?" I try mimicking the way she signed it, but all that accomplishes is to make her laugh until she nearly loses her balance.

"Aurora," I say. "They're called aurora borealis in English. In French too, more or less. I could call you Aurora. Would that be okay? Since I'm sure I mangled the sign?"

Yes. Aurora.

"I'm Xander." I hold my hand out. "Xander Liu."

She tilts her head, reaching forward a little warily, and we shake like comrades.

"It's nice to meet you, Aurora. I'm sorry it wasn't . . . under better circumstances."

She pulls her hand back, resting it on top of her head and

tapping her helmet nervously. I busy myself with relacing my boots to diffuse the awkward silence. After a few seconds she reaches over and touches my knee to get my attention.

You are broken. I am broken. Together we are unbroken.

I can only nod, looking down at my boots again, as my vision blurs.

RAVEN

The night is already profound when we reach the deserted helipad above the path down to the base, at the end of the third day.

"Should there be a guard here?" Tucker asks.

"No," Mandy says. "We always left it unguarded to draw less attention to the base."

"We might encounter sentries, though," I point out. "Tenth, you should take the rear. Leave your lights off. Mandy, you have the best night vision. You lead us. Me first after you, then Tucker. Blue, can you stay with us and out of sight?"

Yes. They disappear somewhere in Tenth's armor.

"All right. Everyone stay together."

The steep canyon path has always been quiet, but tonight it seems *too* quiet. The farther we descend, the more nervous I get. Liam's policy was to not post guards on the top of the path or the helipad because that would draw attention to the hidden base. But by the time we get to the bottom of the path and halfway across the canyon to the main entrance, we should have been challenged by someone. Or heard someone. Even if they are sneaking around planning to ambush us, there's no way the five of us with our preternatural hearing wouldn't detect them, but there's nothing.

"This isn't right," Mandy says.

I turn to Tucker but he's just frowning, silent and thoughtful. None of this would be familiar to him anyway. He got darted before the rest of us set foot in this place.

Behind Tucker, Tenth stumbles, steadying himself on the rock face to the side of the path. I let Tucker pass me and slow to talk to Tenth. His wheezing has gotten worse still.

"Do you want to wait for us on the helipad? It's higher up."

Don't worry, he signs.

"I am worried, Tenth. You don't sound good."

He lets out a low growl as we walk a few more paces, taking care to not slip off the narrow path.

Raven, he signs when we reach an easier section. *You are my Offsides, my team. I will stay with you.* If sign language can have a scolding tone, Tenth manages it. He's annoyed at me for even suggesting he stay behind, even though it's clear he's struggling to breathe, and God only knows what dangers await him when we reach the base. If there are humans still alive there, the most likely scenario is that they will try to kill him, maybe all of us.

When we get to the main entrance my anxiety only increases. Inside the entrance, which is carefully camouflaged to look like an abandoned mine, there's a wide storage bay.

It lights up as we enter and trigger the motion sensors. But there are no guards to greet us. Mandy and I lock eyes.

"Hello?" I yell out. There's no answer. The heavy, blast-proof door is a few inches ajar, the corridor behind it dark.

"Would they leave it open? Unguarded?" I ask Mandy. "If they were having a meeting or something that everyone needed to attend?"

"No. No way."

Tenth lingers in the entranceway, a shadow outlined by the night sky.

"You should wait here," I tell him. "If you see or hear anything, run. Don't worry about us. Nahx won't hurt us, and humans can't hurt us. You understand? Don't try to be a hero."

He nods solemnly.

"Blue, can you come with me?" They might be useful as a light in the dark. And I've gotten used to their company.

Tenth disappears into the shadows outside the entrance as we cross the bay, passing one of the Humvees as well as some piles of weapons and supplies. Now I'm really worried. Before going any farther, we open a few of the crates, Mandy and I helping ourselves to two rifles we find in there, as well as some ammo. Tucker makes do with a loaded pistol he pulls out of the Humvee.

More automatic lights activate as we squeeze past the heavy blast door, entering the long main corridor, which is empty and silent. We close ranks, Blue leading us as I tell them where to go, Tucker and I following, with Mandy walking backward behind us.

The first place we check is the dining hall and common room, and there's enough evidence in there to get a good idea of what happened. Tables are overturned, dishes broken and scattered with food still crusted on them. Blue hovers above a broken chair until I bend to inspect it. There's a Nahx dart embedded in the plastic seat. Instinctively we raise our weapons, but only silence greets us.

"They got attacked," Mandy says.

My eyes start to burn. This is everything I was fighting to avoid for everyone here, and most of the reason I wanted to come back. But I'm too late.

"When, though?" I have a faint hope that it might have just been some holdouts, that Topher and the rest had already gone, maybe inspired by my attempt. It's pretty fanciful. Topher knew better than anyone that I was dead less than a day after I left.

Well, he likely *thought* I was dead.

We head into another corridor. This one remains dark as we pass, guided only by Blue's light, until we reach the apex of the residential wings. The men's wing is also dark, but the lights in the women's flick on when we enter.

"Hello?"

There's no answer. When we check, we find the quarters empty, some of them with belongings strewn around, as though people tried to grab things in a hurry.

"Do you think they got away?" Mandy says.

Tucker speaks up so assertively that for a moment it feels like he's been replaced by his twin.

"Of course they got away," he says. "Wouldn't their bodies be here if they didn't? The Nahx just leave the bodies where they fall, remember?"

Mandy and I look at each other.

"But Tucker," I start, "they would have gotten up, like us. That's where we come from. We got darted, and we got up."

He looks confused for a second, but it doesn't last.

Mandy looks around. "So the Nahx came, darted everyone whenever, then came back to revive them? Is that how it works?"

"Or they moved them. You woke up on the dunes, didn't you?"

"Yeah."

We check the men's wing but find that deserted too.

"There's no one here," Mandy says as we head back to the common room. "Unless they're hiding down in the lower levels or in the thermal vents. That's what I would have done if the Nahx came."

"Let's split up. You and Tucker check down below. I want

to go up to the command level and see what's there. Blue can come with me."

Mandy and Tucker head down to the lower levels while I start the long climb up to the command level, Blue lighting my way, my apprehension increasing with every step. Before I even reach the top, I stop in my tracks when I spot something in Blue's dim circle of light on the landing above me.

"Stop." They pause, hovering at eye level on the landing. I take the remaining stairs three at a time.

There on the floor is a body, facedown, so bundled in winter clothes, I can't even tell if it's a boy or a girl. There are papers and files strewn around them.

I have to stop and give myself a little pep talk then. This person is dead, properly dead, for whatever reason. Sometimes the Nahx broke necks or crushed skulls instead of darting people.

"Blue, come down here. I need more light." They drift down, and sure enough, the extra light reveals a pool of dried blood under the person's face. A boy, I'm thinking now, from the shape of his shoulders and his size. And if it's Topher . . .

I don't know what I'll do.

I take a breath and flip the body over.

His face is desiccated, skin dried so tight over his bones that his lips are pulled into a sneer. I think his eyes were closed when he died, apparently from the obvious and brutal skull fracture just below his hairline, but death and time have opened them slightly into narrow slits, as though he doesn't trust me. Even with the decay of death and the sunken, distorted skull, one thing is certain: It's not Topher.

It's one of his friends, a boy called Chris that I didn't know well, though I recognize him from his distinctive black ear gauges. He was one of Liam's favored inner circle. I'm sorry he's dead, but my relief that it's not Topher is so powerful that I almost laugh.

Blue drifts down and floats over some of the spilled files on the floor.

"They must have been important, huh? He came back up here to get them, to take them somewhere?"

Yes. Blue's light dances up and down on the walls.

The red LED emergency lights are still on in the command center, but the bitter cold tells me a bit more about what transpired here. The observation windows are smashed inward, and snow has gathered in thick drifts over the computers. On the floor a sheet of ice nearly makes me slip. There are ruined papers and maps strewn everywhere here too. I leaf through them quickly, folding the ones that look important and stuffing them into my pockets.

"The Nahx busted in here, from the plateau. But they must have come in through the blast door at the main entrance too. Why else would that be left open?"

Blue flies in a circle. It occurs to me how much simpler it is to communicate with someone who only ever says "yes," "no," and "I don't know."

"Pretty efficient raid. I only hope some people got out via the lower exits."

On the way back down the stairs I stop to gather the files Chris dropped when he died, rolling them up and tucking them into my jacket with the rest.

I meet Mandy back down on the main level as she emerges from the lower stairwell.

"Where's Tucker?"

"You better come down," she says.

The lighting is fully functional in the lower level, where we find Tucker standing silently in the open doorway of one of the detention cells. He seems to be frozen in place. When I reach his side and turn to look at what he's staring at, I see why.

Emily. Emily's body is right where it was the day I left, now as withered as the boy on the stairs. Her one-eyed death grimace is even more macabre; the dry, cold air has twisted her mouth into an open, silent scream.

I don't know how long I stand there next to Tucker—it seems like only seconds—but Mandy comes back with a sheet, which she throws over Emily's body. Only then does Tucker seem to stir, turning to me, his eyes wild.

"Did you kill her?" he says.

"What? No!"

"Who did, then?"

"Why would I kill Emily?!"

Tucker looks like he's a microsecond away from answering truthfully. Maybe whatever they did to his brain has made him less able to spit out lies like they are cherry pits. Maybe he'll just admit that he cheated on me with her. It hardly makes a difference anymore, but for some reason I want him to, at least so I can have the satisfaction of being the injured party. But he just presses his lips together, and everything I'd shoved away while occupied with trying to rescue him from the Nahx ship comes rushing back. Why did I do it? I should have left him there to get sliced up.

Tucker grabs my arm and pulls me out of the cell.

"You're still not going to tell me, are you?" I say as he continues to glare at me. "I risked my life for you."

Mandy joins us, closing the door behind her, sealing Emily's tomb.

"We are *not* doing this now," she says.

Tucker lets go of my arm and stomps down the hallway.

"Blue, go after him," I say. Blue drifts away, leaving a streak of light behind them.

I turn on Mandy. "You knew too, didn't you?"

Mandy rolls her eyes. "Yes, of course I knew. Everybody did."

"*I* didn't know! You could have told me."

"We don't have time to argue about this."

"But—"

"Raven." Mandy takes me by the shoulders. "According to what's left of Tucker's memory, Emily died basically *yesterday*. And he just found out. I'm sorry that it hurts you to know that he cared about her, but we don't have time to turn that into some kind of crisis. Do you understand? You have to set it aside. Save it for peacetime."

I allow myself about three seconds of fuming. But Mandy's right. Now is not the time. I gaze past her to where Tucker disappeared around a corner.

"Here's the thing," I say, lowering my voice. "Emily died the day I left with August. She died right there in that room."

"How . . . who?"

"It's a long story. It wasn't me, though, okay? But her still being there means that the Nahx must have attacked that same day. Because otherwise someone would have moved her. Even buried her. It was spring. We'd actually been digging graves that morning."

"Does that mean that your friend August brought the Nahx with him?" Mandy asks.

I close my eyes. "It's complicated," I say. "But no, I don't think August brought the Nahx. I think he knew they were coming and came to warn us, to get me away."

Mandy crosses her arms, not even trying to conceal her skepticism.

"Look, it doesn't matter right now," I say, because I have an inkling of doubt too. August's affection for me was indisputable, but he cared very little for other humans. I push that thought aside and find that it easily slots away, as though it's been filed in a "deal with later" folder. "Let's check the lower walkways to the northwest exits. If they got out, it would have been that way."

Before we even get down to the walkways, Tucker's voice rings out.

"You guys! Down here!"

We find him staring at the door to the walkways, and a message scrawled in red pen. The desperation and trembling hand of its writer is evident in the shaky handwriting:

The Nahx are here.
> *We're going to run for it.*
> *Xander, I hope you made it out.*
> *—Toph*

"Topher," Tucker says. "So he didn't get darted? He's not like me?"

I can't tell whether Tucker is happy about this or disappointed.

We find the hatch door firmly jammed, and rather than waste time trying to force it open, I send Blue through the narrow crack around the door frame.

"Check both the walkways to the exits. See if there is anyone down there."

They disappear into the crack while Mandy and Tucker check the rest of the level. A few minutes later, Blue pops back out from behind the door and traces a big zero in the air.

"Nothing?"

Yes.

"Were the exits closed?"

Yes.

"That's good news. Thanks. Mandy! Tuck! Time to go!"

They join me at the bottom of the stairs. Blue leads us up through the dark.

"Where would Topher go, do you think?" Mandy asks.

"Calgary," Tucker says. "We said . . . after the . . . we said if we got separated, we would meet back in Calgary."

"But Topher thinks you're dead, Tuck. He wouldn't go looking for you."

As we cross the deserted dining hall I can't help but picture the scene right after the Nahx raid—inert darted bodies everywhere. And the scene months later, when they all got collected or stood up and walked out on their own or whatever happened. It's like something out of a zombie movie.

"He would look for our parents, then," Tucker says.

"But—" Mandy touches my arm to stop me.

"It can't hurt," Mandy says. "I'm not sure about going into the human territory, even if we could get through the web. Wouldn't they shoot at us? So where else can we go? Everyone is gone."

"We could take a Humvee," Tucker suggests. "I saw fuel in the entrance bay."

We decide not to activate the bolts on the blast door but close it to keep scavengers out. Maybe one day Emily and Chris can have a proper burial. They might even have family alive somewhere. It seems the least we can do. And the most. I don't think it's wise to linger long enough to bury them.

When we emerge from the main exit onto the dark canyon floor, Tenth is not in sight. We hear him before we see him; his wheezing, rattling breath is audible even over the wind. We find him kneeling in the shadows behind one of the old mining carts.

"Tenth! Are you all right?"

Good. Yes.

Tucker has to help him to his feet, supporting him under one arm.

"You're not all right. It's still too low for him here." I slide under his other arm. "We need to get him back to higher ground. Quickly."

Tenth tries to sign so weakly that it's as though his words are slurred.

Find and *friend* are the only two words I can discern.

"Don't worry about that. Just try to hang on."

But it's pointless. In the moonlight reflecting off the fresh snow I can see he's dripping with dark gray blood from the grill around his mouth and nose, from his ears, even from under his arms. His breathing is labored and wet, as though he's drowning.

"What happened?" Mandy asks, tugging us awkwardly up the narrow path.

"He spent too much time at low elevations. The air pressure damages their lungs or something. Just hurry. He'll feel better higher up."

Blue floats up and leads us, while Mandy helps hold Tenth upright.

After an eternity of climbing in silence but for Tenth's labored breathing, we finally reach the plateau and the helicopter pad. He shakes us off.

I can walk, he signs.

But before we've taken two steps he starts to cough, bending at the waist and gasping, in between heaving wet coughs, each one pushing streams of gray blood onto the snow.

"Tenth!" I rush to his side. "Just try to breathe. Help me!"

Mandy and Tucker take an arm each, and we try to haul

him upward while Blue zips around frantically.

We drag him ten feet but suddenly he wrestles away from us with surprising vigor, his signing slurred, almost nonsensical.

Leave me. Feel broken. Thank you. Sorry. Please.

His coughing has been replaced with a wet whooshing sound, as though a river of blood is flowing out of him.

Sorry. Repeat forever.

He falls to his knees. I fall down with him, putting my arms around his waist.

"You haven't done anything but help me, Tenth. You don't need to apologize."

One of his hands wraps around my shoulders as I look up at his face. Blood is leaking out of his helmet in a torrent now, as he signs weakly with his other hand.

Raven. You fix . . .

But his body slumps until I can't hold his weight. He pitches forward into the snow.

"Blue! Help!"

They zip over Tenth's body, disappearing for a moment into the armor at the back of his neck while my heart pounds hard enough to hurt. But seconds later they reappear and trace a slow sad circle around Tenth's head.

I lean down on Tenth's back but can no longer hear his breath at all, nor a heartbeat.

"Is he dead?"

Yes.

"Like *dead* dead? He won't get up?"

No.

"Are you sure?"

Yes.

I look down at his shape, my vision blurring with gray, and angrily pinch away the tears. Why did he stay with us? He could have climbed up to higher ground hours ago. Maybe that would have saved him.

"Help me flip him over."

Tucker and Mandy kneel with me, and we heave him over. His weight seems to have doubled somehow, though the snow under him is stained with his gray blood. I feel around his helmet, over his ears, and find something like a latch, which I tug on until it gives and lets out a loud crack like a gunshot. The latch on the other side is easier to find. It clicks open loudly.

With two hands I yank up on the front of Tenth's helmet and the whole thing splits open, revealing the mass of tentacle-like tubes that snake into his mouth and nose. His face is covered in gray goo. Mandy helps me tug the tubes out, and I let his helmet roll away.

"Oh gosh," she says. "He looks young."

She's not wrong. He looks young and *dead*, and if there was ever a more apt metaphor for war, I don't know what it is. I use the long folds of the green satin dress to clean away some of the gray gunk, revealing a soft, hairless face with lips so plump, they look swollen, a long freckled nose, and wide gray, staring eyes wet with silvery tears. His hair, when I wipe away more of the oily fluid, is almost like rose gold, as though he might have been a redhead in his normal human form. Or the boy he was copied from was a redhead.

Tucker takes one of his hands and Mandy takes the other, while I can't help but be reminded of how many times we've done this since the invasion. Me and Topher, crying over Tucker's body. Sawyer sobbing in Emily's lap when Felix died. Liam hanging his head over Britney's grave. And so many others—too many to name. I know now that half those people aren't actually dead. Or at least they are only half dead, walking, talking shells who barely remember themselves, destined for some purpose as yet unrevealed.

Poor Tenth has been spared it, whatever it is. I reach over to close his eyes, but hesitate. Above us, the sky is alive with northern lights and stars, the moon still peeking out from behind the craggy mountains. In daylight, I remember, it's beautiful up here too, with a bright blue or cool gray sky framed by the rocks and cliffs. The mornings are misty and fresh, the twilights velvety and soft, and the nights, like this one, often almost magical. The colorful sky seems to be singing to us. No one argues with me when I decide to leave Tenth's eyes open.

"Good-bye, Tenth," I say.

Tucker actually lifts one of Tenth's hands to his mouth and kisses it, a painfully familiar gesture. It's exactly what Topher did to Tucker before we buried him, never thinking for a moment that we would see him again.

Blue lingers for a moment over Tenth's body, grieving, I suppose, in their own way.

Tucker moves Tenth's body into a more dignified position, pushing his legs together and resting his hands on his chest. After a few seconds he retrieves Tenth's knife from its holster and tucks it into his hand, adding a kind of sci-fi Viking effect to the scene.

"Why do you think he helped us?" Tucker asks, stepping back.

"He was just a nice person. Some of them can't help being nice, I suppose."

Blue buzzes around my head as Mandy joins us. We hold hands and look down on Tenth where he lies. It doesn't feel right to pray—I don't believe in God, and anyway, wouldn't the Nahx have a different god? A song might be okay, but I'm not much of a singer, and no one else starts one. Instead we let the sky sing for a while, until by some unspoken agreement we determine that enough time has passed. We leave Tenth there to stare at the sky.

"It's sad," Tucker says, unexpectedly, as we step back down

onto the steep path. "When someone's nature is so contrary to their . . . expectations."

He could be speaking of any of us. I look back to the plateau before we get too low to see it, where Tenth is just a wisp of gray in white snow and moonlight.

XANDER

After hiking south for days, we have fallen into a pattern that feels so familiar, it's as though it's carved into my bones or written in the blood that fills up my socks. At night Aurora carefully washes them in a puddle of melted snow while I wriggle my blistered toes over the fire. When she gives back my socks, they are toasty warm. It occurs to me that when a Nahx decides to take you into their care, there is very little they won't do for you.

Aurora stands guard while I poop behind bushes. She digs a hibernating squirrel out of its den and roasts it on a stick for me to eat. She melts snow in the metal cup, heating it in her hand until it's steaming, then watches me drink, making sure I finish every drop.

It's like having a terrifying robot mom.

One night I wake up in the dark, blanketed in snow, with her hanging over me. Bitter cold has set in, along with a snowstorm so dense, I can barely see past the remnants of our campfire.

Go now, Aurora says, urging me upward. She shakes out my sleeping bag and tarp, rolling them up and stringing them over her shoulder with the bungee cords. We trudge off through the storm, her walking behind, guiding me with gentle pressure on my shoulder.

I'm starting to think I might die out here. Cold does that to you. Growing up where I did, I'm familiar enough with the sensation. You stop caring about it. If it wasn't for Auror, I probably would have stayed in my sleeping bag, let the fire die down, the snow bury me, my heart trickle to a stop. She seems to have a destination in mind, though, and whatever it is, it is probably something I wouldn't want to miss.

We keep the glowing web to our right, never straying farther than about a kilometer away from it, though sometimes that requires difficult climbs or clambering over frozen rock falls or squeezing through dense forest. When I ask where we're going Aurora simply signs *friend*. I don't know whether this means she's my friend so I should trust her or that we're looking for my human friends. She says other things to me sometimes, as though she's trying to explain, but I can't understand. I think her sign language might be slightly different to the way August spoke, as though they use different dialects. And I never had time to learn his words anyway.

For the past year and a half I've had too much time to do nothing and not enough time to do everything else.

Just as the rising sun crests the eastern peaks, Aurora slows by a frozen stream, pointing to the opposite side. I have to strain to see in the low dawn light, but finally spot what she's trying to show me. Tracks—and by their size and the distinctive triangular tread, I recognize them. *Nahx.* My insides curdle.

She turns us away from the web to follow the stream, careful to step only on the stones and not leave footprints in the fresh snow up the bank. I do the same. About twenty minutes later she stops, holding a finger up to silence me, and then points into the scraggly trees.

I don't see anything. I shake my head.

Drawing me closer, she redirects my attention, pointing emphatically at a section of forest that seems thinner than the rest, light streaming through from the reflective icy terrain behind it. Finally I see what she's pointing at—hacked-off stumps of slim saplings. The stumps bear the easily recognizable wedge-shaped marks of a hatchet. Humans did this.

"Someone building a shelter?" I whisper.

Aurora nods. We proceed carefully, silently, as the frozen creek carves a gully through the rock. Soon we are creeping along the edge of a steep cliff a good twenty feet above the creek bed. Ten minutes farther along, she stops me again, this time pointing at a clearing in the trees and a mound of dirty snow.

Aurora points to her nose.

Human, she signs.

"You can smell them?"

As I stare into the clearing, my impression of the mound of dirty snow suddenly changes. It's not just a mound, and the "dirt" is actually thatch made of twigs and forest debris.

It's a shelter.

"Wait here," I say. "Stay out of sight."

I look down at my feet to find a safe way of climbing up the slippery bank, and when I look up again, Aurora is gone, as though she vanished into thin air. Turning in a circle, I search for her, just to have an idea of where she is, but I can't see any trace at all. I know Nahx do this, disappear like this—I've seen it before—but it's still disconcerting.

I step carefully through the undergrowth, hyperaware of the loaded pistol at my hip, the rifle slung over my back. This is a human shelter, but there's nothing to guarantee it's a friendly human. I'm not even sure such a thing exists anymore. I stumble and have to shuffle around dozens of large stones that look as though someone has scattered them among the trees like marbles. I wonder if whoever made the shelter left them here, and why. Some kind of early warning system? It would be easy to trip over them in the dark.

The shelter is empty when I reach it. Under the blanket of snow, I can see it's a beautifully made conical wickiup, a kind of tepee made from the slender trunks of young trees, layered with pine boughs and needles. It's the type of winter shelter Sawyer taught us to make right after the invasion, to pass time at the nearly empty camp; one of the activities he had planned for the campers who never arrived.

Topher excelled at it. It's a lengthy, tedious, and precise task that suited his meticulous personality.

Inside the shelter, I remove one glove and bend to feel the embers of the round hearth. They are cool but not cold, as though the fire has been out for hours maybe, but not days. Army green sleeping bags are folded up neatly and stacked on top of a tarp to keep them dry. There is evidence of meals eaten in here, animal bones and an empty can, but no weapons or tools.

I step back into the bright clearing.

"Topher?" It seems crazy to hope, but Aurora brought me right here. She obviously knew about this camp, knew where the humans were. And Topher knows how to build a shelter like this. Those sleeping bags are just like the ones they issued us at the base, and according to where I think we are, we're mere miles from the path I mapped out—just south of the Yellowhead Pass. If Topher was anywhere, he could be here. He might have seen Aurora. He might be hiding.

"TOPHER!" I yell it so loud, it seems to disturb the trees. "It's me, Xander!"

I wait for a minute, bleeding hope as though from a lethal

wound. But nothing happens. The wind rustles the scrub around the camp. I spin when I hear a small noise, but it's just Aurora, delicately picking her way up from the stream.

"No one here."

She nods, bending to look into the empty shelter.

"The hearth is not completely cold. There might have been someone here last night or yesterday. Maybe we should look for tracks."

As I turn, she grabs me, hand over my mouth, and holds me there, her head flicking from side to side.

I use one of her signs, wriggling my fingers in front of my face.

What is it?

She takes her hand off my mouth and taps her ear.

I heard something.

A second later I hear it too—a creak, followed by the distinctive twang of an arrow being loosed from a crossbow. Aurora shoves me down into the snow, spinning away as the arrow glances off her shoulder.

"Wait!" I shout. "I'm human!"

The next thing I hear is gunfire, a loud crack of a rifle. The force of the bullet sends Aurora flying backward, skidding along ground.

"No!" I dive for her, yanking her back milliseconds before she sails over the edge and down to the creek.

"Are you hurt?"

No.

"Get out of here, then. They won't hurt me."

She hesitates, her hand on my shoulder. Another bullet zips over our heads and cracks into the rocks on the other side of the creek.

"Go!" I shove her. She flicks her head back once and leaps over the creek to the sheer slope on the other side, scrambling up it like a spider and disappearing over the top.

I clamber to my knees, hands raised above me just as a hooded figure appears from the dense trees.

"Get your hands up. Keep them there!"

He looks like a yeti, swathed in a dark coat, crusted with snow and ice. He's armed to the teeth with a rifle, a crossbow, and knives in holsters strapped over filthy jeans. The only visible parts of him are his watery brown eyes in a thin slit between a knitted hat and a thick scarf.

"Where did the Nahx go?" he says. His voice is heavy and raspy.

"What Nahx?"

He jams the barrel of his rifle right into my solar plexus, knocking the wind out of me. I sway backward.

"There was a Nahx with you!" he says. "Where did they go?"

"I . . . I'm not sure . . . I—"

He reaches forward and tears my scarf down. I watch those glassy eyes widen with shock as he steps back. Almost as an afterthought he raises his rifle again, aiming it at my head.

"What are you doing here?"

"I'm—"

"Where's Raven?"

Up to this moment I had thought the cold was making me hallucinate, but now I struggle to speak. Even though I've imagined this moment a million times, it never looked like this.

"She's dead, Topher. She died."

"Was that him? Raven's Nahx? August?"

"No. He's . . . dead too." We stare at each other over the rifle, which I note is cocked and ready to fire a bullet right into my forehead. "Topher . . . come on."

The frigid air freezes the tears in my eyes. What has happened to him? The coat he's wearing hangs off him, his eyes are sunken and haunted, his skin parched and red. Even his voice sounds like an old man's, as though he's aged a hundred years since I last saw him. I try to piece it together. He left the base? Maybe with some of the other guys? And they've been out here in the wild, in the winter, for God knows how long? Why is he alone?

"Topher . . . what happened? What happened at the base?"

"Shut up!" He pulls his scarf down, revealing his gaunt,

windburned face, his lips drawn back, practically growling at me. "My friends got darted over the summer. Know anything about that?"

"No! We only got here a few minutes ago."

The sudden pressure of the rifle on my neck makes me tumble backward, sitting and slipping on the ice. I have to fight to keep from sliding closer to the edge of the creek bank.

"You admit there was a Nahx with you?" He plants his feet on either side of my legs, looming over me, the rifle now aimed at my heart.

"She doesn't even have a dart rifle," I say. "All we have is human weapons."

As though saying it makes it real, the unmistakable red dot of Aurora's rifle laser sight appears on Topher's chest. My eyes draw Topher's attention down, and as he lurches back, the laser moves up to his face

"No! Aurora, don't!"

The red dot flicks off—a warning. I scan the other side of the creek, the sparse edges of the tree line, the high drifts of snow, but I can't see her anywhere. I have to gasp a few times to catch my breath enough to speak.

"Nahx aim is flawless," I tell Topher. "She could take you before you even spotted her. You know this."

"What are you doing with her? What are you doing here?"

"I came back to look for you," I say. It sounds ridiculous now it's out in the open.

"You led the Nahx right here."

"I didn't! How would I even know where you were?"

Topher sneers at me again. "You found me, though, didn't you? Explain that."

"I can't." My arms are starting to ache from holding them up. All the blood has drained out of my hands, leaving them numb and tingling. "Aurora . . . the Nahx. She knew I was looking for you. I've just been following her. She must have known you were here."

I see him hesitate, but it's as though someone else is thinking for him, as though his mind is possessed or decayed. He re-aims the rifle.

"You know what they do in wars to collaborators?" he snarls. "They shoot them."

"Have you done that?" I wonder now how many humans have been adopted by rebellious Nahx, if Topher has encountered such a thing before. Is it common? "Toph?"

His eyes widen, staring at me, and I see an eternity of grief in them, as though he's witnessed every death that ever was since the beginning of time. Or maybe it's just Tucker's death that broke him in a way that can never be fixed.

It seems to go on for so long that I start to think maybe I'm dreaming. Maybe this is one of those nightmares that feels real and not real at the same time. Topher has never said or done anything to hurt me for as long as I've known him. He and I clung to each other those weeks Raven was missing. Most nights I would wake up and find him curled up at the end of my bed, like a faithful dog. Eventually he would just crawl under the covers with me, and . . .

"Crying is not going to help you," he says, blinking. How could I have not seen how damaged he was? All that time I was lost in the chaos in my head, but he was beyond lost. He was dying inside.

"Don't, Toph," I try. "We . . . we're friends."

"I . . . I thought you were dead," he says. "You never came back. I thought that Nahx killed you. Raven's Nahx."

"He didn't. He helped me. This one, Aurora, is helping me too. You have to believe—"

We both hear it, a sound that makes the blood drain out of my head—the distinctive whine of a Nahx dart rifle charging.

There's a loud crack and a flash of red, and suddenly all hell breaks loose and I'm falling with Topher on top of me and a mouthful of snow and being crushed by something *hot*. We crack down onto the creek and slide, and then we're flying, hard cliffs and a frozen waterfall rushing past us.

Every breath in my body is expelled by force when we hit, as Aurora lands on her back in the deep snow, both Topher and me cradled protectively in her arms. Before either of us can catch our breath, she has wrenched away Topher's rifle and sent it sailing into the distance. Topher moans, stunned, and rolls over onto his face as Aurora leaps up, aiming her rifle precisely into the mountain above us.

My head spins, but I have the presence of mind at least to drag Topher across the ice and under cover of the looming rocks. The snow is hip deep in the shade, and I have to dig around us to keep Topher's head aboveground. His eyes are rolling around, his mouth working like a dying fish's. I hold his chin, shaking him gently. As he regains consciousness he starts to squirm away from me, which I take as a good sign. At least nothing seems broken. Aurora broke our fall over a fifty-foot waterfall with her own body.

I look up to see Aurora with her rifle still raised, scanning the cliff.

"Do you see them?"

She lowers her rifle with a huff. *No.*

"We should move. Hide somewhere."

Topher suddenly gasps behind me, launching himself upward only to fall face-first into the snow.

"Easy, Toph," I say, helping him to sit.

He glares at me before turning his head to spit blood onto the snow. Aurora sucks in her breath.

"Are you hurt?" I ask. He pulls away from me.

"I bit my tongue!" He scoops a handful of snow into his mouth and tries to stand again. I tug him down, but he shoves me roughly away.

Aurora drops to one knee, slinging the rifle over her back. She looks around uneasily as she hauls me upright by the back of the coat. *Walk yes?*

I test my limbs. They all seem to be working.

Good, she signs, before turning to Topher. *Good-bye, mud head.*

"We can't leave him here!" She shoves me, pinching my shoulder hard enough to hurt. I push her hand away. "No! This is the friend I've been looking for! I'm not going to leave him now."

She replies with a stream of signs I don't understand, apart from the acute clarity of her fury and impatience. Before I can ask for further explanation, she pulls the rifle from behind her back and aims it at Topher. He raises his hands above his head with a sigh of resignation. He lost one of his gloves somewhere in the tussle. I notice two of his fingertips are blistered and peeling from frostbite.

Walk, Aurora signs with one hand.

Topher stands slowly, steadying himself on the rocks, but before we can move, Aurora leaps on us, pushing us back with the barrel of her rifle.

Quiet!

I clamp my hand over Topher's mouth as Aurora spins, rifle raised. I can't see anything or hear anything, but something spooked her. I press us both back into the rocks, sliding down into the deep snow.

Suddenly dark shapes are falling from the sky. But rather than crashing to their deaths, they land gracefully around us, one after another, until we're surrounded.

Nahx. But not like any Nahx I've seen before. Their armor is mottled as though it's been painted or broken, and some of them seem to be wearing scraps of human clothes. One of them is festooned with strands of metal chain; another wears what looks like a wolf skin as a stole. In addition to Nahx rifles they have an array of human weapons—guns, bows and arrows, knives. I glance at Topher, whose eyes are wide with horrified fascination.

Aurora kneels in front of us, growling protectively, her rifle raised, but we're hopelessly outnumbered. There must be twenty of these strange Nahx now circling us, pinning us against the cliff face. Finally one of them steps forward, signing. I catch only a few words.

Lost. Broken. Together?

Aurora nods, and there's a collective sigh of relief like a gust of wind over the ice. She steps away from the cliff face, signing too fast for me to see. Four of the Nahx descend on us, hauling Topher and me up over Topher's protests. I strain my head around as we're dragged off, trying to see where Aurora is in the crowd of Nahx that surrounds us as we begin a slow ascent back up the cliff.

When I finally catch sight of her, she signs at me, short and sharp but distinctive.

Promise.

RAVEN

Our journey to Calgary is endless. Even the normally windswept highways are deep with snow in places, and our passage is punctuated with frequent breaks to dig out drifts enough to drive through. After four thousand years of this, stuck in the Humvee either staring at the back of Tucker's head or listening to him tunelessly humming behind me, I'm ready to kill someone. Finally, about an hour outside the city, Mandy, who has taken over driving for the day, slows. My eyes, which have been drowsily gazing at the mountains to the west, are drawn back to the road.

"What the . . ."

I open the passenger door and leap out before Mandy has even fully come to a stop.

"Raven, wait!"

Ahead of us, blocking the road, are a pair of Nahx, kneeling, motionless. One of them has dropped their rifle beside them, the other still has theirs slung over their back. Neither of them moves or reacts as I approach.

"Hey!"

I don't turn as I hear Mandy and Tucker get out of the

Humvee behind me. The sun beats down on the road and the snow around us, creating a harsh glare that turns the two Nahx into dark gaps in the blinding light. Are they even breathing? As I get closer I see that their only movement is a slight sway in the strong wind.

"What happened?" Tucker asks as he joins me. "Are they dead?"

"Where's Blue?" I shield my eyes, trying to see Blue's light against the glare. "Blue!"

The Nahx are dusted with snow and ice, as though they've been here for days or weeks. I brush some away from the taller one's chest, the male. His armor is pristine, almost polished-looking. The female is a bit more scuffed, and she has a dent in the armor of her mask, over her jaw, that makes her face look lopsided. The male has his hand on her shoulder.

Blue appears in front of me, dimly visible with the bright snow behind them.

"Are they dead? Can you tell?"

They hover in front of the male's face for a moment before circling around to the back of his head. Moments later, they do the same to the female. The slow death circle they do this time is large, encompassing both the motionless Nahx.

The cold wind stings my eyes as I turn, surveying the featureless landscape. There is nothing to indicate any kind of battle, no evidence of a Nahx transport landing here, and the

Nahx don't appear injured, apart from the female's jaw. I bend down to dig at the snow that has drifted up around their knees.

There's a frozen black puddle under each of them, as though their blood dripped down their bodies inside their armor and drained out their knees.

"What caused this?"

Mandy takes her hat off and scratches her head. "I mean, it looks a little like what happened to Tenth, but . . . I don't know anything about Nahx physiology."

"Maybe they're just dying," Tucker says. I had forgotten he was even there.

"What?"

"Maybe they're programmed to die or something. Since those glowing bugs made us, they don't need the Nahx anymore. Maybe they're all going to die soon."

Mandy glances at me before turning on him.

"Shut up, Tucker," she snaps.

"What? Tenth just dropped dead, and—"

"Shut up about the Nahx. You don't know anything either."

In the uncomfortable silence that follows, Blue drifts down into my pocket.

"Raven." Mandy nudges me, and I tear my eyes away from the dead Nahx. "We should go. It will be dark soon."

I don't answer, instead turning and striding back to the Humvee, wishing I could express one or two of the millions of thoughts in my head into words, just so I could get them out, even for an instant.

Mandy lets me drive, which gives me something to focus on at least.

We enter Calgary from the north and too quickly can eliminate one possible place Topher might be hiding. Tucker's suburb—the one I bused to from our rambling character house in the cool downtown neighborhood so I could attend "the good high school"—has been razed to the ground, the wide boulevards scorched and the cookie-cutter houses burned to cinders. We manage to navigate to Tucker's exclusive street, but there's nothing left of his house save a black splotch on the flat white lot. I park the Humvee and we tramp up through the snowdrifts to see if there is anything recognizable left. Blue floats over the charred remains of Tucker's house as we examine it.

"Do you think there are bodies under there?" I ask them in a whisper, while Tucker walks farther away, into the backyard.

Blue makes another slow, sad circle in the air before coming back to perch on my shoulder.

Tucker's house could be anyone's ruined history. The demolished street spreads out on either side, telling the same cataclysmic story over and over. Behind the ruins, the pleasant suburban lake shines white and pristine, as though inviting us to tramp across it. If we had skates and sticks, we might clear a neat square and play a quick game of hockey. As it is, we trudge back to the Humvee in silence.

"Maybe he would go to the school," Tucker says tightly. It's so strange to see Tucker keeping himself contained; that's normally more Topher's style. But I know his mind is buzzing like mine. I recognize the way his eyes flick around, observing everything, analyzing it. Mandy does it too. It's as though we're all compiling giant databases, for what I don't know. The devastation around us, the ruined houses, the burned-out cars, should be horrifying, evidence that everyone we ever knew or loved here is gone. But instead of mourning, I simply record it, estimating, inferring from the ruins how many of my friends and neighbors were not outright killed but darted and turned into Snowflakes like us.

The large number I come up with is almost satisfying to me. The more of us there are, the more likely we are to win whatever battle is coming.

I take the driver's seat again and slowly drive the Humvee through the winding streets to our high school. Unlike the surrounding houses, it's miraculously intact, as though the passing tornado of doom took pity and spared it. When we get out, we find the doors drifted with snow and as firmly locked as they were on the last day of school—two days before Tucker, Topher, Xander, and I got on the bus to camp, the bus that saved our lives.

Tucker kicks the front door open easily. The school is deserted and quiet, and even with the changes in my life of the past year and a half, I still get that weird sensation you get visiting a school after hours. It's almost like being able to walk through another dimension, as though the school and its students might be buzzing with activity somewhere just out of your view. It's like being dead, I suppose, but we are the living ones now. Everyone else is a ghost.

On the lower level we find a broken window in the staff room, and the couches and tables dusted with a fine layer of snow. There's a human-shaped dent in the snow by the window, almost as though someone made a snow angel. But I know that's not what happened. Someone was darted here— maybe the security guard who patrolled the school once a day in the summer. He might have been darted during the first siege and lay there as though asleep for all these months, waiting to be revived with the rest of us, to shake the snow off his uniform and join our zombie army. I wonder if he was there on the dunes or at the giant ship.

We trail down the hall, away from the staff room, trying the gym, the boys' locker rooms, the science lab where Tucker liked to set things on fire, the music room where we met, when I found him inexpertly plucking out a Pink Floyd song on a badly tuned guitar and thought he was the most beautiful boy I had ever seen.

But no one is here.

Mandy walks ahead of us into one of the social studies classrooms. When Tucker and I join her, she's staring at a large globe. Blue floats off my shoulder, drifting curiously around the globe as we study it.

"Remember that globe back at the ship?" I ask. "What do you think the bright white spots were?"

"No idea," Mandy says. "But I'm pretty sure this is where the dunes were. And there was a bright spot there, remember?" She points to a spot in far-north Saskatchewan.

"Lake Athabasca?" Tucker says. "There are sand dunes there?"

"A huge dune sea, nearly the whole length of the lake."

The three of us stare at the globe in silence for a few seconds. Behind the superprocessor humming away in my head, something else is growing. It's almost as though the rift I saw in my dream is now in my waking mind too, like a new kind of gravity pulling my thoughts toward a vortex to the northeast. I should say something, but I don't want to be the one to bring it up. I don't want to be the one to push us into confronting whatever it is we need to confront. I definitely don't want to look at this globe anymore and remember all the other bright lights. Are *all* of them fissures like the ones we dreamed of, or vortexes pulling the sentinels, locking them into place for their battles? There were *dozens*.

"Let's go," I say. "Maybe we could try downtown. The dojo maybe? Downtown wasn't bombed."

The day has cleared when we get outside and a bright blue sky shines around us, outlining the gray silhouette of the distant foothills and the downtown high-rises to the west and south.

We head back down to the Humvee and I drive us into town, relishing the lack of traffic on the freeway. When I was learning to drive I dreaded getting on and off the freeways, which were usually packed with traffic at all hours of the day and night. Now, of course, we are the only moving vehicle as far as we can see, though there are quite a few abandoned cars and trucks, some of them with the telltale dart holes in their windows.

Tucker sits in the back of the Humvee, silent and impassive, staring out the window as if we are taking a scenic drive on a summer day. I pull up outside the dojo and Mandy and I wait while Tucker breaks in. He reappears a few minutes later.

"Anything?"

He shakes his head. "Darts," he says. "In the walls of the changing room. I think some people might have been hiding there. But they're gone."

I feel something like grief. I knew those people. We were all close at the dojo. If it was them hiding, our teachers and classmates, all of them were darted. All of them got up and walked away with the rest of the zombies. Most of them don't know who they are.

Yeah. I feel that. It makes me angry.

This whole exercise is starting to seem like a giant waste of time, but I suppose we just needed some kind of destination when we busted out of the ship. We can't head west—likely the drone web would stop us, and anyway, if the reaction of the Métis girl by the lake is anything to go on, I don't think we'll be very welcome among humans. So where can we go?

Looking out the Humvee's front window, I can see the concrete skyscraper condos rising on either side of the freeway like towering monuments. There won't be answers inside, but there will be beds, clothes. We might be able to clean up a bit, or even find something to eat—if we even need to eat. And in one of them . . .

"What?" Mandy says.

"What, what?"

"You gasped," she says. "What are you thinking?"

I put the Humvee in gear and pull away from the curb.

"When you lose something, how do you look for it?" I ask.

"You retrace your steps. But we've done that already, kind of." She lowers her voice, glancing back at Tucker, who has returned to staring out the window. "The chances of finding Topher were always practically nil."

"Not him," I say. "Someone else."

The high-rise looks much the same as when I left it that night all those months ago with August. And there *is* a dead body there on the concrete entry courtyard, partially concealed in snow, but it's a Nahx, the one I pushed off the balcony—it must be a year ago now. I kick some of the snow away and bend to inspect her. There's a pool of congealed black sludge spreading out under her body.

Definitely dead.

She deserved it—she was trying to dart me—but I can't help feeling a pang of guilt. Her bloodthirst was probably not her fault, and I suppose in that moment it was her or me.

"What are we doing here?" Mandy asks. The sun is setting, and though we haven't seen anyone, there could be humans around, if they're good at hiding. I have no desire to encounter them.

"This is where I stayed when I was injured," I explain. "I left a whole bunch of useful stuff behind." I stare up at the top of the building, forty stories above us. "I mean, what else do we have to do? It's not like we have to be anywhere."

As one, the three of us flick our eyes to the northeastern sky, as though tugged by invisible puppet strings. But whatever it is, it's not quite enough to pull us back in that direction yet. It's more like a dull ache, or an itch that can't quite be scratched.

I unholster my weapons as we enter the lobby, and Mandy

and Tucker wordlessly do the same. The lobby and the entry to the stairwell are just as deserted as the last time I was here, but the clarity of my memory ensures that I recall the dead Nahx August and I passed on the stairs. We tiptoe up the first three flights, the only light coming from the thin strip of windows that runs the full height of the building and Blue drifting ahead of us, their light dancing on the walls.

The dead Nahx boy should be on the third landing, but all that is there is a tiny pile of crushed metal, wire, and glass. Blue hovers over it, vibrating, their light glowing brighter and throbbing as though they are angry.

"What is that?" Mandy bends down to examine it closer, closing her human eye. "Huh. It's radioactive. Nahx technology?"

Blue bobs up and down curtly before whizzing up the center of the stairwell and out of sight.

"Whatever it is, I don't think Blue likes it."

We follow their flicker up ten flights, twenty, then thirty. The exertion doesn't affect me the way it might have once, though my heart thuds more and more heavily the closer we get to the penthouse level. I don't know what I expect to find. It's true that some of the stuff I left behind might be useful— clean clothes, a few weapons, food. I reach up and feel the bulky braids I made in the drugstore. There's a king's ransom of hair products upstairs that will help me improve on them.

And maybe . . . would he go back there if we got separated somehow? Would he think that I would go back there? It does seem sort of logical, but August was not very logical. And there's my suspicion that he left me on purpose, that he was done with me at last.

It's not like I didn't tell him a million times that we didn't belong together.

We reach the fortieth floor. The door from the stairwell has been torn from its hinges, a reminder that makes me smile despite my unease. In the communal hallway, four open doors lead into four penthouse apartments. I'm drawn to the most familiar one, of course, but as though by prior plan, Mandy, Tucker, and Blue each disappear one by one into the others. Maybe they sense I want to be alone.

I linger in the doorway. Outside, through the western windows, the sun is setting, casting a golden glow over the modern furnishings, and the bright glare nearly conceals the mess we left, so for a moment I can remember the time I spent here as an idyllic retreat rather than the den of domestic indolence it really is. My eyes adjust to the light and travel over the mess—piles of clothes, discarded magazines and food packaging, different knickknacks and trinkets August brought me over the weeks.

I step slowly into the living area, afraid to disturb the quiet, afraid to touch anything, just letting my eyes drift over the familiar chaos and mess. Memories play in my mind as clear as a movie—August standing out on the balcony with the sun shining on him, August emerging from the kitchen with a steaming bowl of soup, August carrying me, kicking and screaming, down the hallway as I tore mirrors and pictures from the wall and smashed them on the floor.

August's shadow in the dark, sweeping up the mess I made.

My eyes fall on the coffee table, and something glitches in my photographic recall. The coffee table is not where it's supposed to be. Just before we left the apartment, when I fought with the female Nahx who is now dead out in the snow, the coffee table got turned over and kicked to the side. The books and dishes that were on it are still tumbled on the floor, but the table itself is back where it's supposed to be, in front of the couch.

"August?" I call out. He's been here. He might still be here. "August?" But I only hear the whistling of the winter wind through the balcony doors. I poke my head into the kitchen, grimly taking in the unspeakable mess we left in there. It's not unsanitary, at least; August was very sensitive to bad smells and would quickly throw away any leftover food, usually off the balcony. But there are clean dishes stacked everywhere and unopened boxes and cans of food, as well as books and medicine and clothes on the counters, the floor, on top of the stove. It's as though a hoarder was living here.

But there's no sign of August. At least, it doesn't look any different from when I last saw it. I leave the kitchen through the other door, emerging into the long hallway to the bedrooms and the second bathroom. All the doors are open except for one. At the end of the long hallway, the door to the master bedroom, where August nursed me back to life, is shut. This is different. While we stayed here, this door was rarely closed because the walls of windows in the bedrooms would let light into the hall.

I move toward the door with trepidation, glancing into the guest bedroom and bathroom but finding them empty. I don't know why I'm so reluctant to open that door. It's true that even when we stayed here, after I had recovered enough to move onto the sofa, I didn't like going into that room. It smelled of sickness and reminded me of things I couldn't remember. I didn't like thinking of how vulnerable I had been, delirious with fever, weak with nausea, with a giant alien hanging over me, at his mercy.

Even with the changes in my heart, the changes to my feelings about August, there are parts of me that think I should reexamine those days I lost, just to confirm there was nothing . . . untoward. But I know he would never do anything to hurt me, never, indeed, do anything self-serving. The fact that Tucker is with me is proof enough of that.

I open the door.

And he's there, kneeling by the bed, just as he did those long days and nights when he tried to stop my life from slipping away. His hands rest on the box spring in front of him.

"August." I whisper it, because of course he would have heard me yelling and come to me if he could.

I don't want to move. I don't want to cross into the world where August is . . . where I have to learn that he's . . .

I don't even want to think the word.

Dead. I think he's dead.

I'm not surprised or shocked, not really. I've known all along that this is what I'd find. The only reason August wouldn't be with me is if he were dead. It's the only thing that makes sense. I don't know where he went after he left me, but I know enough about him to know he wouldn't stay away forever. August has tried to stay away from me before, and it never worked.

I move slowly, as though I'm walking in the thickness of a nightmare, and sit on the bed, nudging his hands to the side so I can face him. His head is hanging, almost as though he nodded off here, just lowered his head to rest and never lifted it up again. I take one of his hands and hold it in mine, trailing my other hand over the star-shaped scars on his chest and shoulder. His armor feels icy cold.

"August . . ." I start, and then, despite myself: "Wake up."

He doesn't move, of course.

I don't believe in fairy tales, but I lean forward and kiss the armor of his mask, where his mouth would be.

"Wake up, please. I don't think I can do this without you."

And the reality of what "this" is cascades over me like an avalanche. There's going to be a battle of some kind, a battle in which I'm a soldier, along with Tucker and Mandy and the other Snowflakes, both those who know enough to resist their roles and those who don't.

"I'm so tired, August. I'm tired of fighting."

I take his other hand and hold both in my lap, touching my forehead to his. He still smells the same as he did, almost. His smoky charcoal smell has cooled to damp ash. And there is no buzzing breath, no creak of armor as his shoulders move up and down. I wonder if I stay here long enough, I might join him in his silent stillness, and we might become a monument to the infinite capacities of . . .

I don't want to think that word either.

Love.

I love him.

"Raven?" Mandy's voice breaks me out of my nihilistic day-dream.

"I'm in here!" I call out, still watching August, despite

every piece of evidence, for any sign of life, for any reaction.

I look up to see her skid to a stop in the doorway.

"Oh. Is that . . . ?"

I nod.

"Is he . . . ?"

I don't nod this time. I can't move.

After two hours of slippery, awkward ascent we reach an ice wall, where a narrow glacier bisects the mountains. The Nahx ahead of us start to disappear, and as we catch up to them I realize they're jumping into a shallow crevasse. The four Nahx who are acting as our guards and escorts ease us down carefully, one at a time. The bottom of the crevasse is slick ice that I struggle to find my footing on, on either side of a trickling stream. One of the Nahx steadies me as I watch Topher being tugged down. I search along the crevasse to where the water disappears in the dark, while the rest of the Nahx gather, adjusting their gear and signing among themselves.

"They're like punks," I say to Topher, in a vain attempt to start a conversation. He ignores me. "Topher, you need to talk to me. Tell me what happened to you. Help me understand."

Suddenly, the dark end of the crevasse is infused with a golden glow, and seconds later the source of the glow appears—two Nahx, toting burning torches, emerge as though from within the ice.

Our escorts urge us forward, and rounding a curve, I see

that the crevasse leads into a long tunnel in the ice, its glistening walls now dancing with reflections of the torches and the Nahx's lights as they flick them on.

"What the hell . . ." Topher says, the first words he's spoken in hours.

The river tunnel seems to go on forever, meandering and narrowing in places before widening to small caverns where the water has pooled in slushy puddles. When Topher slips and crashes to his knees, one of the Nahx gently helps him back to his feet. Topher shoves the Nahx away, brushing ice and snow off his hands. They haven't even bothered to shackle us, because I suppose they don't think two exhausted humans are much of a flight risk.

Nearly an hour has passed in the ice when the illumination changes and the Nahx start flicking off their lights one by one. Ahead of us the two Nahx with the torches round a corner and disappear. Our escorts hurry us along behind them, helping us jump over a wide swath of flowing water and through a gap in the high cave walls, toward glowing a blue light. Large hands reach down from a bright hole above us and haul us up, one by one.

We clamber out of the hole into a wonderland of frost and mist, delivered into a wide craggy basin sheltered by looming rock faces and gnarled pine trees. To one side of the basin, another waterfall has been frozen in its tracks, creating a fantastical castle of ice out of the rolling cascade of rushing water locked in time. The tiny amount of water still trickling down is what formed the river that led us through the tunnel in the glacier, what carved it open, no doubt, over decades or even centuries.

Toward the center of the basin, surrounded by craggy, snow-covered rocks, a rippling pool of water glows like a milky blue opal, the steam rising from it infusing the surrounding air with the unmistakable sulfurous smell of a geothermal spring. Fat, fluffy snowflakes drift down, softly landing on the surface of the water, where they disappear, sucked into the pool as though by some magic.

"Is that . . ." Topher starts, but when I turn to him he bites his lip and falls silent, though I can see the longing in his face. *Hot* water. My frozen fingers and toes tingle at the thought of it as we tentatively approach. I pull off one of my gloves and feel the water. It's actually not very hot, but certainly warm enough to bathe in comfortably. When I look up, Topher is turning slowly on the spot, his eyes scanning the basin, and I know he's looking for escape routes, trying to formulate a plan of attack. His posture is guarded and tense, like a cat preparing to pounce or to defend himself. Attack seems unlikely, but Topher clearly can't see that.

The Nahx, who are ignoring us, milling about the landscape, crouching up on rock overhangs, kneeling in groups in the trees, or trailing toward us, weapons hanging loosely at their sides, seem to be so integrated with the landscape it's as though they have been here for centuries too. Everything— the rocks, the trees, even the Nahx—is coated with frost as though the whole scene has been carved from alabaster. Topher's pale, chiseled face fits right in.

"If they wanted to hurt us, they would have done it already," I say.

He presses his lips together and turns back to gaze up into the mountain peaks.

Out of the haze, a Nahx approaches us as our escorts drift away.

"Aurora?"

Good Xander?

"Yes, we're fine. Cold."

Yes. Angry Boy wash. Smell mud death.

I cover my laugh by pretending to cough.

"We need towels or something, and dry clothes, or we'll get too cold."

Aurora starts to answer, but we're interrupted by a commotion in the trees above us, which seem to explode in a cloud of snow and ice as a very tall Nahx plows through them. Topher yanks me back, startled, but the Nahx hurls a pile of clothes and blankets at us before crash-tackling Aurora and sending them both sliding off into the mist. Seconds later the tall Nahx has picked Aurora up and is swinging her around as they cling to each other. Now that the tall Nahx is not moving at breakneck speed I can see that they aren't wearing a helmet—their long hair swings around as they spin.

"I think they're friends," Topher says in a dry voice.

I turn back to Aurora and her companion, who is now tearing at Aurora's helmet. When it finally comes away with a slurp of gray sludge, they fall down together into the soft snow, kissing and laughing and touching their faces, arms and legs intertwined. It starts to feel rude to watch, so I look away.

"More than friends, apparently," Topher says. We stare at each other. "I don't know how you found me," he says at last, and I can see his composure start to crumble.

"I have a theory." But now is obviously not the time, because I'm too struck by how bad he looks, how thin, how pale, scarred by frostbite, hollow-eyed. "Topher, I . . ."

He sighs, a long slow sigh that conjures up a cloud of mist around his head as though he's already becoming a ghost.

"Did you ever tell Raven about us?" he asks, and it's so unexpected that I have to cough again before I can answer.

"No. Did you?"

"Of course not," he answers almost irritably.

"Probably one of us should have."

He nods, and I can see that he's about to cry, and there are still Nahx surrounding us, not watching us, exactly, but not ignoring us either. And because we're both human males, even when it's probably totally reasonable, maybe even healthy, I doubt Topher wants anyone to see him break down, so I do the only thing I can think of.

I put my arms around him and tumble both of us into the hot pool.

We sink in our layers of winter gear and boots, but the floor of the pool is only a few feet deep. Topher surfaces, dripping, red-faced, and gasping. I expect him to get angry, but all he does is start peeling off his scarf, hat, and coat, pitching them and the rest of his clothes onto the shore in wet piles. I join him, and soon I'm trying not to laugh, the pleasure of getting out of those fetid, itchy winter layers making me almost giddy. Topher sinks down under the water again, scrubbing at his disheveled hair and beard with his fingers.

The Nahx leave us in the pool but linger nearby, keeping watch. One of them gathers up the piles of clothes the tall Nahx threw at us and folds them neatly on a dry rock nearby, presumably so we can get dressed when we finish our bath. Aurora and her companion seem to have disappeared for the time being.

"I think that other Nahx was a girl too," Topher says, breaking his long silence. "The one who was kissing your friend."

"Really?" I didn't get a good look. "Have you seen Nahx out of their armor before?"

He doesn't answer for a few seconds. "Only dead ones," he says at last.

I hesitate to ask for any details, but it seems he's ready to share them anyway.

"The Nahx were already there at the base," he says, pausing for a moment to rub the warm water on his face again. "After I left you and Raven on the mountain, by the time I got back, the Nahx were already there. Half the base was dead out in the snow. They'd made a run for it but the Nahx took them out. Darted them. They left a couple of the kids, though. They were just standing around crying."

"Fuck . . ."

"Yeah. I grabbed them and went down into the canyon and back through the thermal vents. I stashed the kids behind one of the generators and went looking for other survivors. The sentries were dead. Jayden was one of them. I can't remember the other one's name. It was an older woman."

"Why did you go back into the base? If you'd come back up to the plateau where you left us, you could have caught up to us. You could have come with me."

He looks at me like I'm crazy. Or stupid. Or both.

"That would have led the Nahx right to you. I figured you still had a chance to get away. I didn't want to . . ." He stops, his face pained, and I know he's thinking about watching Raven die and not being able to do anything about it. Maybe he's even doing what I've been doing for months, obsessing about the choices that if one of us had made differently, everything would have been better.

If I had stopped Topher from going after Raven.

If Liam had let August surrender peacefully.

If we hadn't gone to Calgary in the first place, because that was stupid.

If we'd never left camp.

If Tucker hadn't been so reckless as to go hunting alone at night.

If one of us had had the guts to tell Raven about Tucker and Emily before it was too late.

If . . . so many ifs.

"Anyway," Topher continues at last. "I found Dinesh, Chris, and Mason hiding with a few girls and another kid. You remember that one whose great-grandmother died in his bed?"

"Oh God, yeah."

"We waited for hours, hiding down in the vents. We were going to sneak away, but Chris wanted to get the intel files from the command level."

"Why?"

"I never found out. He went up there to get them but never came back. When we thought it was safe, we bailed."

He falls silent for a moment, staring at the swirling water between us.

"I left a note for you."

The pool is suddenly a bit too hot for me. I move over to sit on a rock so I'm out in the cold air from the waist up.

"Do you know what I thought?" Topher asks. "I imagined maybe in years, after we had defeated"—he looks around; none of the Nahx appear very interested in us, but he lowers his voice anyway—"these guys, I thought you might come back to the base, almost like a historian or something, to see where it all happened, and you would find the note. And know that I didn't forget about you."

"You didn't think you could tell me this one day?"

He shakes his head. "I was pretty sure I would die out here."

"But you didn't."

His face twists. "Everybody else did, though. The kids, the girls. I was hunting, and when I got back to the shelter everyone was dead. Darted."

"That shelter where I found you?"

He nods, rocking back and forth in the water, as though he's trying to comfort himself.

"It was over the summer."

"I didn't see any graves. Did you—"

"You don't believe me? I don't even know why I'm telling you this."

I decide silence is probably the best response to that. When I try to see our current situation from his point of view, I can't make sense of it. It barely makes sense to me, but at least I've seen that the Nahx can be benevolent to humans sometimes.

"The ground is too hard up there. I put them in cairns." He looks away, and then continues so quietly, I barely hear him. "The Nahx came back and took them."

"The bodies?"

He nods.

"When?"

He shrugs. "A few days ago . . . or weeks. I . . ." He trails off for a moment. "I hid in the creek. It was still running then. I heard the transports so I jumped down into the creek and hid in the water."

"That must have been cold," I say, though I'm thinking more of the fact that Topher lived surrounded by his dead friends in cairns in the trees for months and what that would be like. No wonder he seems so haunted.

I look down at the dark water as he climbs out of the pool and wraps himself in one of the blankets the Nahx left on the rocks. As he digs through the pile of clothes, pulling on a pair of way-too-big sweatpants, I glance up, struck by the way his rib and shoulder bones protrude from his papery skin. He has been dying of starvation. I take a breath to speak to him, to reason with him, but he turns on me.

"That Nahx who took Raven—he timed it well, didn't he?

Kidnapped her just in time for the rest of us to get slaughtered by his friends."

"That's not what happened."

"How do you know, Xander? How do you *know*?"

"Because he helped me. After Liam killed her, he helped me get out of the Nahx-controlled zone. Through the web."

He's in a frayed sweater now and mismatched socks. A silent Nahx approaches gingerly with our coats and boots, laying them carefully on the rocks as Topher glares. They steam there, as though they've just come out of the dryer. Topher pulls his boots on, frowning.

"So it was a coincidence that the Nahx arrived just after Raven left? Only an idiot would believe that. And also there's no way through the web."

"But . . ." I try.

"We searched up and down for months. Hiked hundreds of miles. There's no way through. So you're either lying or you've lost the plot. Probably both."

I scramble out of the pool as he stomps away. The Nahx wander after him, stepping in his way as he approaches a gap in the trees, stopping him again as he tries to go back into the ice tunnel. I'm struggling into a pair of jeans as he shouts back at me.

"If they're so friendly, why won't they just let me leave?"

"Because you'd die of cold!"

I pull my coat on, jamming my feet into my boots, and clomp over the snow to join him by the tunnel. Three Nahx watch from nearby, silent, almost deferential.

"You're starving, Topher. You're covered in frostbite. You wouldn't make it."

His demeanor hardens so fast, I can almost see it crack, and I start to worry he might literally fall apart, bones and skin and organs all tumbling into the trickling stream to be washed down the mountain and back to his camp in pieces.

His voice is barely audible when he speaks again, barely a whisper. "How did you find me?"

But before I can answer, his knees give out and he slumps forward. I catch him, and one of the Nahx grabs him under the arms from behind, holding him upright.

"He's starving," I say. "I think I had some food left in my pack." I lost track of what happened to my pack and weapons somewhere on the glacier.

The Nahx drags Topher back to the pool, propping him up on the warm rocks. He mimes bending over the pool to drink. I cup some of the warm water in my hand and hold it up to Topher's mouth. He coughs out the first sip but manages to swallow a few sips after that. The water is silty but probably safe to drink—spring water usually is.

Then my pack appears, and I dig out some of the roasted squirrel I saved. Topher is weak suddenly—I think the soak in the pool drained him. I have to break pieces of meat off and feed him the first few bites like a baby. When he starts to eat by himself I look up and see that it's Aurora who has brought me my pack. Her tall companion, who does appear to be female, stands with her arm around Aurora's shoulders. They are both out of their armor, wearing gunmetal gray suits and looking like two very tall and intimidating motorcycle racers.

The tall Nahx has dark skin, long dreadlocked silver hair, and large expressive eyes with irises the color and sheen of a copper pot. Her nose is pierced through the septum with a small padlock, which makes her look like an old-school punk. Without the Nahx armor, her shape is rounded and feminine, with a small waist and rather large boobs. I flick my eyes back to Aurora, who is grinning at me.

Xander, she signs, pointing at me. Then she points to her lover. *Night Sky Light.* I don't understand the fourth sign.

"Star? Something?"

Aurora mimes it, bunching both hands into fists and then flinging them open, fingers splayed out, hands flying apart.

"Star exploding?"

She points up to the sky, nodding.

"Oh! Supernova! That's your name? Nova?"

The tall Nahx nods, but as I reach out to shake hands she simply steps forward and crushes me in a bear hug, lifting me up and shaking me until my teeth rattle.

Thank you thank you thank you, she says as she sets me down.

"You're welcome, Nova," I say, trying to subtly check that all my bones are still working. "This is Topher." He doesn't look up from his eating.

Angry Boy strong walk? Aurora asks.

"I . . ." I have to bite my lip again to keep from laughing at the name they've given Topher. *Angry Boy*. It's so fitting.

"Can you walk, Toph?"

He grumbles but follows as Aurora and Nova lead us up to the trees and through a kind of fairyland gate created by the frosted branches. The new clothes are warm and dry, and we both discover mittens and knitted hats carefully tucked into the pockets. Everything is too big for me, though, and I have to keep hitching the insulated pants up. It makes me wonder why they had the clothes in the first place, where they got them, who died in them.

The walk is steep, and I keep a close eye on Topher for any signs of flagging, but the meager meal seems to have restored some of his strength. At least his stubborn silence has returned. I try to reason with him as the trees begin to thin.

"They want to help us. Why else would they have clothes? They don't need clothes."

He ignores me, but I forge ahead. He needs to hear this.

"Okay. So you asked how I found you. I think Aurora knew where you were. Where your camp is."

"How would she know?"

"You said you were looking for a way through the web. She knew a way through. She was probably looking for a long time too before she found it. She probably saw you."

"If she saw me, why didn't she dart me? Or maybe she *was* the one who darted everyone that day. Maybe that's how she knew where I was."

That makes me pause, but only for a second. "I don't think that's what happened."

"You don't think at all. What's new?"

I hitch up my pants again and hope Topher can't see the heat rising in my face. After a minute goes by, I try a different tack.

"They might be able to get us back through the web," I say. "We can get out of here, Toph. Go out to the coast like Raven wanted us to."

He turns to look at me with such disdain in his eyes that it feels like being slapped across the face.

"You're insane if you think they'll help us do that," he says, and pointedly strides forward, overtaking me, making it clear this conversation is over.

We emerge from the trees onto a plateau gently sloping up to a flat summit, the thick, fresh snow coating the surface like cake frosting. To the west of us, above the distant mountain peaks, I can see the drone web, just a faint outline against the bright sky. From the forest edge a wide path has been carved through the snow, tramped flat by Nahx boots, leading to a clearing at the far edge of the plateau. A Nahx transport is parked there.

"What's that?"

Aurora takes my shoulder, signing with her other hand.

Look. Listen.

She beckons me to follow her.

The transport looks as though it has been salvaged and cannibalized for parts. Its door is missing; thick cable conduits have been pulled from its innards and spread out across the plateau. Most perplexingly, the conduits seem to be connected to decidedly human technology—solar panels. Some of them are clearly emblazoned with company logos, companies that I've heard of—Alberta Clean Power and BC OffGrid Living. Apparently these Nahx have been pilfering solar panels from cabins and cottages across two provinces.

I turn to Topher, who is frowning, looking around at the arrangement of wires and panels. Aurora takes us past the transport, following another bundle of conduits over some boulders until we are looking down onto a lower plateau. There are more solar panels there, dozens of them, and, in the center, another transport, this one even more pulled apart, its whole hull splayed open like a surgery patient. Its innards have been reconfigured somehow too, panels and shielding and conduits laid out in a circular shape like . . .

"I think I know what this is!"

Just then three Nahx emerge from the transport below us, signing to Nova and Aurora, who turn and relay the signs to more Nahx back at the first transport.

Look. Listen, Aurora signs, tugging me back. I have to run to keep up with her long stride. Topher follows me silently as Aurora and Nova usher us up the ramp.

The inside of the transport has been torn apart too—wires everywhere, discarded circuitry and valves in piles on the floor, wall panels missing. Cables spill out of display screens, both those that seem part of the original design and some that look like they've been rigged in after the fact.

"Does your watch still work?"

Topher looks at me like I'm crazy. "What?"

"What time is it?"

He glares but pulls back his coat sleeve and looks at his expensive watch. "Nearly noon," he says.

Just then the transport starts to hum, and the display screens light up one by one. Then the humming changes to a low-frequency rumble, soon getting so low that I feel it in my rib bones, and deeper, in my stomach. I stop being able to hear it as it seems to travel down my body until I can only feel it in my feet, as a vibration in the transport's metal floor.

The static on the screens coalesces into images.

"What the hell?" Topher says.

On one display screen is the familiar logo of the emergency broadcast system, appended with "Day 494" and the date. Another screen shows a list of refugee centers and information on how to get to them. Yet another shows a video I thought I'd never have to watch again: the chase through Garvin's compound that culminated with Dylan's hand being amputated.

"Is that you?" Topher says, astonished.

"Yeah. Long story."

We turn to another screen; this one has a soundtrack. A gray-haired and pinch-faced man is talking, a defeated tone in his voice, almost as though he's reciting a prayer to a god he no longer believes in.

". . . revised count is now at just over eleven thousand. Stockpiles are low. We are burning wood salvaged from empty homes for heat. Gasoline is completely gone. With this snow we have ample water, which we will store more extensively in the . . . in case . . ." The man takes a breath and swallows painfully. "In the unlikely event that we survive another winter, we will need water to make it through the summer. If the Nahx continue to ignore us." The screen crackles with static before resolving again. ". . . here in Edmonton. If anyone is hearing this, please send help. Please, please send help. We can't—" The screen abruptly switches to another image, something violent, just for a few seconds, before returning to static.

"Was that eleven thousand people?" Topher says. "In Edmonton? Eleven thousand survivors?"

He turns in a circle to look more at the other screens, some of them showing Nahx killing stuff, some of them pleas for help from the looks of them; some of them are static, but over the low vibration and other noises I can hear murmuring human voices, like voices from the grave. These are survivors, wherever they are, desperately using any means they have to call for help.

I feel a bizarre rush of pride that there are still human voices out there among the devastation. The Nahx surely were trying to eradicate us, in the high ground at least. But they couldn't, not with their murderous soldiers, not with their advanced technology. It's been eighteen months, and the humans here hung on through all that.

"We've got to help them," Topher says.

"Yeah. Do you understand what this is?" I wave around at the wires and screens.

Topher shakes his head.

"Remember how Kim told us back at the base that they would only pick up radio or video signals at around midday? And more likely on sunny days? And how it was the same for us at camp?"

"Yeah."

"Kim thought something, or someone, was jamming the microwave scrambler the Nahx were using to disrupt any communications. She was never able to figure out how."

"Right." Topher frowns darkly as he looks around the transport again. Aurora, Nova, and another Nahx stand watching us patiently, as though waiting for Topher to figure it out. "So?"

"So this is how the scrambler was being jammed. These Nahx were jamming it."

"Wait." He turns to Aurora. "On purpose?"

She nods.

"Why?"

Help you, Aurora signs. *Help humans.*

"To help us," I translate.

"But . . ." He reaches out to steady himself on the back of a console. "Why? Why are they helping humans?"

Aurora and Nova flick their heads back. I guess they think it's funny.

"Because they're traitors, Topher," I say. "They're traitors and they're on our side."

Though the cold doesn't bother me, Mandy brings a blanket, which she tucks around me in silence before leaving. I turn my eyes away from August for a moment and watch as she departs down the long hallway, bathed in the pink light of the rising sun, the second sunrise since I found August here. I've been sitting with him in the dark bedroom all this time, unsure of what to do, unable to make a decision one way or another.

Tucker has disappeared. I heard him arguing with Mandy, and her, ever the peacemaker, pleading with him to not make a scene. But later Mandy told me that he figured out that August was the one who darted him, that she had to restrain him, to reason with him.

"I told him he couldn't kill what was already dead," she said simply.

I find that I can't stay mad at him. I even understand why he would feel betrayed. As far as his memories of the world go, I'm still his girlfriend. His devoted, clueless girlfriend.

Blue drifted in not long after Tucker left, apparently mildly interested in August's still form. They hovered at the back of his neck for a few seconds, their light flaring, before zipping away down the hall and, I think, over the balcony. God knows where they've gotten to now.

I know I can't stay here forever—the dark rift in my mind is expanding and solidifying so that I can almost see it now, even with my eyes open, its gravity tugging at me with increasing strength—but I also feel like my quest is complete, at least this part of it. I wouldn't have been able to go on without knowing what became of August. Now I do.

When Tenth found me on the dunes, we were surrounded by immobile Nahx soldiers, kneeling with their heads hanging just like August is now. And in the cold storage on the giant ship there were more, also seemingly dead, still, silent, so cold that they were dusted with frost. Some of them had obvious injuries, but the others? I think they just wore out.

Did August know his end was near? Is that why he came back to this place? I suppose I'll never know exactly what he did after my non-death. And he'll never know . . .

I run my memories again, like a video screen in my head. Did I ever really tell him how I felt? I screamed at him and spit on him, smashed a glass vase over his head and held a knife to his throat. Despite that, could he see what he meant to me? How his patience restored me? How his unfaltering forgiveness rebuilt me? How lost I was without him all those months?

How lost I am now?

"I don't know what to do, August." It feels good to say his name out loud. I keep my voice low because I don't want Mandy to think I've lost my mind. "I know you didn't mean it to turn out this way. I know you only did it to help me, but my plan, to go to the coast and try to find my parents, doesn't work anymore. I've . . . we're different now. I don't think we would fit in with humans. I don't think the Nahx are fans of ours, either."

Even in his silence, in his death, August indulges me. He listens. He doesn't judge.

"I guess you know how that feels, don't you? To not fit in anywhere?"

I close my eyes, and the image of him nodding, agreeing with some silly thing that I said, appears in my mind as clearly as if he were standing alive in front of me. But when I open my eyes he hasn't moved. I wonder for a moment whether I should take his mask off but decide I'd rather remember him like this, armored and regal, along with the brief glimpse I got of his living face the last time I saw him alive.

As I reach for him, the blanket slips off my shoulders and onto the floor. I lift it and drape it over his back like a cape. It's a Hudson's Bay blanket, so it makes him look a bit like a Canadian superhero, which makes me smile.

"I think we have to go back to the dunes," I say. "I don't

know where else to look for Topher. Maybe I'll just have to hope that he made it out somehow. Maybe . . . maybe he followed Xander's map? I hope he did." I pause before I say the next words, because I don't want them to be true. "We might be able to stop whatever is coming. Stop it from hurting anyone else. Maybe that's my destiny."

In August's signs, the word "maybe" is a combination of the word "almost" and the word "hope." The word "almost" is very obvious. In fact, it's exactly the way a human would mime "almost," by holding a thumb and forefinger close together. But "hope" resembles "flying dream" or something like that, a fluttering hand drawn up the forehead. I was never sure my signing was accurate, but I try it now. It feels . . . respectful to speak to August in his own language, with his own unique grammar.

I hope not pain you, I sign. "I hope it wasn't painful, whatever happened to you."

I hope you weren't sad.

My hands make shadows in the pink light seeping in from the hallway.

I hope you know you walk in my dreams. You fly in my dreams.

Then I can't resist him anymore. I slide down to kneel between him and the bed and wrap my arms around him, laying my head on his chest, his arms draped over my shoulders. Every time I've done this before his armor has been nearly too hot to touch, but this time it's icy cold.

"Raven?" Mandy stands silhouetted in the doorway.

"I know he's dead," I say. "I'm not crazy."

"Okay." Her voice is gentle. "Tucker came back. He's sulking on the couch."

"Oh." I'm actually relieved. "Good."

I turn my head away from her to lay my other cheek on the cold metal. Morning light is peeking around the edges of the heavy velvet curtains.

"We could move him, if you want. Make a grave or something."

"No. I think a forty-story building is quite good as a tomb, don't you?"

Mandy huffs a little laugh. "Sure. Like a pharaoh."

"Exactly."

"Do you want to go somewhere else? We could go to your house."

I shake my head. I don't want to be reminded of everything else I lost. Not now.

There's a noise from the main room, and Tucker's voice.

"Raven?"

I slide out from under August's arms and back up onto the bed.

"Uh, Raven?"

Suddenly Blue zips down the hallway so fast they leave a streak of light behind them like a slipstream.

"Raven . . . shit!"

Three Nahx appear at the end of the hallway, marching toward us with Tucker stumbling behind them.

"Weapons! Weapons!" I hiss.

"They're in the other room," Mandy says.

I reach for the closest thing at hand, a broken lamp from the bedside table, and wield it over my head like a battle-ax, ready to smash my way out of here.

Two of the Nahx stay in the hallway, their weapons hanging loosely at their sides, while the middle one steps through the door.

Mandy has armed herself with a small desk chair. We stand on either side of August's immobile form, as though he needs protecting.

"What do you want? Go away," I say.

The Nahx, a stocky male, tilts his head to the side with a low growl. His weapon is hanging over his back. He raises his hands slowly, palms out, holding them there for a moment, before making a familiar sign.

Help?

"We don't need any help. Leave us alone."

Blue zips around the room, bouncing on the curtains like a fly trying to escape. The Nahx watches them, his head flicking back and forth.

Not you. Him. He points to August.

"He's beyond help. He's dead."

Blue comes to rest on the top of August's head, like a tiny crown. Their color softens as they make a vibration on the metal of August's helmet.

Not dead, the stocky Nahx says.

A shiver goes up my spine so fast, I nearly drop the lamp.

"What?"

Help him. Yes?

I toss the lamp on the bed and step back as the other Nahx enter. One of them strides smartly over to the curtains, tearing them open, letting the dawn light stream in. The other puts his hands over August's body as though feeling for life signs.

"He's d–dead," I stammer. "He's cold. He's not breathing."

Stupid Snowflakes, one of the Nahx says. The other two actually laugh, flicking their heads back with amused little hisses.

Then they start to talk to each other, quickly, and I can make out only a few words as their hands fly.

Awake

Sun

Eat

Move

Broken

Two of them take an arm each and hoist August up,

dragging him away from the bed. I stand dumbly in their way. How could I have been so stupid? There's no evidence of what I know of Nahx death, no puddle of gray blood—no sign of blood at all. I don't think he's . . .

Up, the third one says as they push past me.

"What's happening?" Tucker follows us as the Nahx drag August out into the communal hallway and toward the stairs.

"Where are you taking him?" They ignore me, letting August's knees clatter against the concrete stairs as they climb up to the roof exit, one flight up. As Mandy, Tucker, and I emerge onto the rooftop behind them, the bright sky is rent with the screeching of a Nahx transport's engines. Mandy and Tucker have armed themselves somehow. They raise their rifles, protectively turning their backs to us.

"Where is it?" The blue sky is clear and innocent-looking.

A dark shape rises from behind the other side of the building and hovers there, its engines blowing snow in every direction as it lands and powers down. The door hisses open and a ramp inches out to the roof surface.

More Nahx appear in the doorway.

"Don't let them take him!" I clutch August's arm. "Blue! Do something!"

Blue hovers between us, their light pulsing. One of the Nahx signs, too quickly for me to understand anything but a few words.

Lost

Broken

Dark

Blue bobs up and down. *Yes.*

"No! We're not going with them. They'll take him back to that cold storage place."

The Nahx ignore me, one of them shoving me out of the way so hard, I go sliding across the roof. Tucker leaps on her and somehow has a Nahx knife in his hand before I have time to stand.

"Tucker, no!" Mandy yanks him back, twisting his arm until the knife drops into a snowdrift and disappears. The fallen Nahx jumps to her feet, hissing, while the other two raise their weapons, and it looks like we might be about to have a brawl right here until Blue pops up between us, flickering angrily.

In the silence that follows we all hear August take a strained breath.

It's sudden and small and barely audible, but his chest pushes out fractionally, and a second later he exhales.

"Did he just breathe?"

The stocky Nahx signs at me slowly and sharply. *Yes, stupid human Snowflake. The sun woke him up.*

"The sun?"

Yes, mud head. The armor eats the sun. He needs to eat and go to the mountains.

"Mountains? Where he can breathe better?" Mandy seems to be the only one who can think rationally at the moment.

Yes. Mountains. Where he can breathe.

"Can I . . . can we come with you?" I'm not leaving August. Not now.

Yes. He points at Tucker. *No fighting.*

"I'm not going with them. I—"

Blue flicks him in the forehead, making him yelp, but beyond that he holds his tongue.

The female Nahx drags August up the ramp by one arm, letting him fall in a heap on the floor of the cargo bay. The rest of us follow. I sit cross-legged next to August and pull his head into my lap as Mandy shoves Tucker down to sit against the opposite wall. I know neither of them is happy to be back on board a Nahx ship, but we've formed an unbreakable team. If we're going to figure this out and survive whatever battles are coming, we need to stick together. Trust each other. I cradle August's head, stroking his mask as the transport lifts off, making his armor rattle on the metal floor. Maybe he moves, or his shallow, barely there breathing changes somehow. I'm able to process and measure so much detail now about my surroundings that I'm still getting used to it. It takes a moment to interpret the change, to figure out exactly what is different.

Tension. Muscle tension. Where previously August's body

has been loose and pliable, now there's a growing tautness, as though he is slowly coiling up, preparing to flee. It's happening at a glacial pace, but my new perceptual acuity detects it, interprets it, files it away.

He's frightened.

"Don't be scared," I whisper, making his signs as I speak. "I'm staying with you."

And saying this seems to awaken something in me. It's as though the human girl inside this cold, hard facade, the tiny wisp of softness that I hid away even before all this started, finally escapes, peeking out and taking its own shaky breath. And the next thing I know is only my own tears and sobbing; the rest of this catastrophe disappears. It's just me and August and tears.

Dimly I hear Tucker murmur something and Mandy hiss a curt reply. Maybe she recognizes that I need this moment. I need to wash away the metal and fire and find the flesh underneath. But as my tears drip onto August's armor and my dress, I see that they are metallic, like molten silver, and that just makes me cry even more. How can I go on like this? Can I ever go back? If my parents are alive somewhere, how can I face them like this, as a monster?

A hissing sound distracts me, and I feel the air pressure in the transport rapidly change, making my ears pop. August takes another weak breath. Bending to lay my head on his chest, I listen for his pulse. It's there but barely, just a low ticking under the noise of the transport, and slow, probably no more than fifteen or twenty beats per minute.

The first time I heard August's heartbeat was a shocking, almost frightening change of perspective. Before that, despite his kindness, I had persisted in thinking of him as a machine, soulless and insensible. Companionship with him was a means to an end, but when I heard his heart . . .

Does it matter? Animals have beating hearts, even insects. Maybe there is something in a human heartbeat that feels familiar, or *familial*, something another human heart recognizes without even knowing why. I suppose this is why August didn't kill me when he could have multiple times. The human in him recognized the human in me. And maybe why I dreamed of killing him for far longer than was reasonable. My heart hadn't recognized his.

It doesn't seem that much time has passed, me watching August's breathing improve, his body seeming to awaken inch by inch, before the transport begins to descend. I slide out from under August's head, standing so I can see into the cockpit and through the window.

Outside, everything is white, and as the transport slows I see that we are flying through a heavy snowstorm, seemingly only a few hundred meters over the top of the mountains. The Nahx at the controls is clearly a good pilot, but I'm still dubious about landing in these conditions. I sit back down, pulling August's head and shoulders into my lap and wrapping one arm around his chest. With my other hand I cling to one of the metal rings on the cargo bay wall.

"Hold on to something," I tell Mandy and Tucker. Even Blue seems a bit nervous as the transport begins to jostle. They float down and slip into the front pocket of Mandy's coat.

"Are you okay?" she asks me, her brows knitted.

"Yes." I let go of the handhold long enough to wipe the last silver tears from my eyes. "I just needed to let it out."

"I know what that's like."

There's a sudden loud noise and the transport banks sharply, wrenching my arm as I cling to the ring. After another loud bang, I lean over and see the pilot struggling with the controls as two other Nahx stumble back into the hold. They take positions on either side of the hatch, weapons raised. There's another, louder noise, which makes the metal of the transport ring.

"Someone is shooting at us," Tucker says, so offhandedly that I have to bite my lip to keep from snapping at him.

"Humans?" Mandy says over the increasing noise. "Who else would shoot at us?"

The transport lands hard, and despite my best efforts I lose grip of the handhold and go sliding across the metal floor.

One of the Nahx by the hatch shoves me away with her foot as the hatch hisses open.

The glare of the landing lights on the heavy snow blinds me for a moment as I clamber to my feet. Mandy and Tucker join me and we take positions behind the Nahx in the open hatch, August still splayed out on the floor at our feet.

Something in the transport's engine vents, releasing gusts of cold air that blow the falling snow away enough for me to see more clearly what's outside. At first I think some very foolish humans have gathered to challenge us, but as the air clears more I realize it's Nahx—twenty or thirty of them, armed, with weapons raised, in a defensive circle. Behind them I can see frost-covered trees and steep rock cliffs. We've landed on some kind of sheltered plateau.

The pilot makes a few signs that I don't catch, and one of the Nahx on the plateau nods curtly. The female Nahx turns and pushes past me, bending to grab August by the foot and dragging him down the ramp.

The other two Nahx don't stop us as we follow.

The female leaves August in a heap and marches smartly back up the ramp, the hatch hissing closed before I even have a chance to say thank you. And what am I thanking them for, anyway? The armed Nahx around us creep forward warily, not lowering their weapons as the transport takes off. I kneel, rolling August over onto his back.

"He's sick," I say. "He's breathing, but really slowly, and he wasn't breathing at all for . . . I don't know how long. We found him—"

I'm interrupted by two dark shapes bursting out of the trees in a cloud of snow and ice. They're bundled up to the eyeballs but they appear to be human. Tucker, next to me, stands protectively, his fingers gripping his rifle as the humans skid to a stop a few meters away. One of them says something, but the words are muffled by his heavy scarf.

"He's sick. We need help," I say. Part of me knows asking a human for help with a Nahx is probably futile, but I'm desperate. And I don't understand what's going on. My eyes are flicking around, gathering data, trying to process, but what I'm seeing doesn't make sense.

These Nahx don't look like Nahx. Half of them are missing parts of their armor, and a couple of them aren't wearing any armor at all but rather some kind of fitted jumpsuit. A few of them are wearing items of human clothes too, and they are armed with human weapons. Where are we?

One of the humans pulls down his scarf.

"Raven?" he says.

His face is ruddy with cold, and more chiseled than I remember. And he has a wispy black beard. But apart from those changes I recognize his twinkly eyes and cheeky grin easily.

"Xander?"

"Oh my God, I was right." He stares at me for a moment before looking down. "Is that August?"

I'm about to answer, but the plateau, which was noisy with the roar of the departing transport, the crunch of fifty feet on the ice, the wind rustling the trees, suddenly falls silent. My eyes are drawn to the other human, who seems frozen in place. Tucker makes a small noise and tosses his weapon down. He takes a step toward the other human. Whoever it is, they move at last, taking a stumbling step backward.

"You don't need to be scared."

The human doesn't reply, but I can see them tense up as Tucker reaches forward and tugs down their scarf.

Oh . . . God.

It's Topher.

Tucker touches his face gently, drawing his fingers over the familiar shape of his cheekbone and jaw.

Topher speaks at last. "It can't . . . it can't be you. It isn't you." His eyes are wild, terrified and horrified and overjoyed and despondent all at once. "Tucker, you're dead."

"Not quite," Tucker says, and they throw their arms around each other.

PART FOUR

WATER

*"Life, although it may only be an accumulation of
anguish, is dear to me, and I will defend it."*
—MARY SHELLEY, *FRANKENSTEIN*

S ixth.

Sixth?

I look down, watching her feet kick up spring shoots and the snow-soaked leaves and damp earth.

Where are we going?

I don't dare look back. Dandelion lies dead . . . or asleep or . . . something under the budding tree, her human boy, Tucker, dirt-crusted and stale, and cold and gray, next to her. Shackled to her. I couldn't think of anything else to do.

Sixth didn't see them. She only saw me.

Follow, she commanded, and I did, as though no time had passed at all. We're not far from the place Tucker shot an arrow into her, the place where I darted him and left him where he lay, as instructed.

Maybe everything else was a dream. Maybe Sixth got up after all.

"Wake up, August."

That's Dandelion's voice. She was wearing the green dress, spread out under the tree, the turned earth all around.

Eighth, Sixth signs sharply. *Follow!*

It's raining and cold and approaching dark, and yet somehow I feel the warm sun on me and the tingle of my armor converting sunlight into energy. That can't be right. I'm malfunctioning again. I put my feet into Sixth's footprints, happy that Dandelion gets farther away from us with each step. Sixth would kill her, tear her limb from limb, if she knew, and care nothing for rules and directives.

"What's wrong with him? Should you take his armor off?"

No, Dandelion. Stop speaking. Be quiet. Hide.

"But I want to help him. I should be with him when he wakes up."

Is this a dream?

Where are we going, Sixth?

She turns and shoves me so hard, I stumble over a tree stump.

You don't need answers! Follow!

I could try to kill her, but if I failed, she would search and find Dandelion and rip her to pieces.

"What's happening? Why is he shaking? You're hurting him!"

Her voice is getting farther away. I would touch her if I could. If she's talking, she's alive. She would be warm again. I think we've split into two worlds somehow. Or two times. Time is getting mixed up in my head.

Sixth draws me on, my fingers curled around her shoulder. But I can't feel anything. It's as though we're ghosts.

Where are we going, Sixth?

She turns back this time, slowly, fluidly. The soft twilight behind her like a halo soothes my troubled mind and seems to draw the gaping hole in time closed. I reach through it, not knowing which side is right. I can see Sixth's silhouette outlined by the gray light as she answers.

We're going home, Eighth, she says. *We're going home.*

My lungs fill so quickly, it's like my spine is snapping and twisting me in half. The darkness is sucked away, bright light blinding me, and I'm wide-awake, staring up from where I lie on the floor.

One of us is there, just a dark break in the light at first, but gradually he comes into focus as he helps me sit up.

What is your rank? Part of his mask is missing, and his armor is covered in swirling designs, like eddies in rivers. He takes my wrists, moving my hands together in my lap.

Rank? he repeats.

Somehow I manage to move one finger enough to touch my other hand.

Eighth is the sign, but when my mind speaks it, I hear *August.*

August. What the girl called me.

She swims in my thoughts in silver and gold, her hair like a crown made from clouds. I must be dreaming again.

359

Breathe. Obey.

The breath I take is like swallowing ice. I take another and another, and slowly I stop fighting. My mind searches for directives to follow, but there is nothing there but . . .

The girl, protect the girl. Dandelion.

Human girl? The signs are weak and sloppy, one-handed and vague.

The human girl is safe, the other one says. *I am Ash.*

Ashes? Are we dead? Why is his mask broken? Where am I? Where is my armor?

Rank? I try.

He sighs, and I see the eye visible through his broken mask crinkle into a smile. *Eleventh*, he signs. *But call me Ash.*

My hips hurt. My back hurts. It takes all my concentration to roll over and lift myself to my knees to sit back on my heels.

You need to eat, Eighth, Ash says.

It seems I blink and the next thing that happens is that I'm cramming meat into my mouth and cracking open a large bone to slurp away the raw marrow and blood. My vision seems to expand as I eat. I'm in a stone cave or . . . no, a small stone hut, by a cold fireplace with a slaughtered sheep flayed open in front of me. My hands and arms are bloodied up to the elbows. A low growl forms in the back of my throat. I can't seem to help it.

There is another one of us here now. A female, not in her armor, her skin so white she glows. She stands over me.

Summer King, she says. I don't know what that means so I just nod.

I am Sky.

I nod again. I know where I am now. These are the Rogues, the defective Elevenths and Twelfths Sixth told me to avoid. I look around for her by habit, the fingers on my left hand twitching.

But Sixth is dead.

I'm sure of that now.

Sky? I try. My hands are clumsy and sticky with blood and wool.

Yes. She drops to one knee, placing a hand on my shoulder. *You are with the Rogues now. Will you stay with us?*

Where is Dandelion?

Sky looks confused. *I don't know who Dandelion is. Your Offside? One of us?*

I close my eyes, trying to think. It seems half my words are gone, and I have to search for her name. It comes to me at last.

Raven. The human girl.

Sky appears to think about it for a moment before answering. *She is with the other humans.*

I don't know what happens. I seem to drop out of time. The black gate opens and sucks me through.

361

Put your armor back on, Sixth says. We are by the side of a burbling creek.

No, I say. *I don't know where it is.*

She grabs me by the neck and flings me into the creek before I can fight back. The water is icy, cold as death.

You don't say no to me, stupid mud for brains! Your armor is right there!

But my vision goes dark and I can't see. All I can feel is the frigid stream flowing over me. Then a warm hand on my cheek. I open my eyes. The real world stacks up like the stone walls around me—the dead sheep, the fireplace, Sky.

Summer King? Sky says. *Why are you shivering?*

I flick my head away from her. *I don't know.*

Sky watches me, not moving, as though she is waiting for me to say something more.

I didn't mean to hurt her, I say at last, because I can't help it.

Was it you, then? she asks. *You darted these humans? The two girls and the boy?*

I didn't mean to. I was lost.

Sky's face tightens. *Where is your Offside?*

Behind my closed eyes Sixth glares at me accusingly. I open them, fixing my gaze on the stone floor.

Dead, I say.

Sky huffs disapprovingly. It is a terrible failure to let your Offside die. I know this.

The humans are better now, stronger. You didn't harm them.

It takes me a long time to find the words to say next.

But they didn't choose it, I say. *They had no choice.*

No, Sky agrees with me. *None of us had any choice.* She touches my face. *Rest now, Summer King. You are safe. You are with friends.*

RAVEN

The leader of the Rogue Nahx, Sky, finds me on the steps of the large climber's hut she and her followers have colonized up here in the clouds. Xander and Topher are inside, warmed by a blazing fire in the potbellied stove. Tucker and Mandy have been updating them on what happened to us and what we've learned, but I've been frozen in time and space, awaiting news of August, who Sky and some others spirited away soon after we arrived. Sky stopped me from following.

He needs to rest, she signed sternly as they disappeared into the trees, dragging August up a steep path. That was hours ago. I've barely moved from this spot, despite occasional exhortations from Mandy and Blue. Now as Sky strides toward me, her long legs swishing away the powdery new snow, my chest tightens and all my muscles tense, as though I might need to flee. If the news is bad . . .

I stand as Sky reaches the bottom of the steps. She doesn't bother with polite greetings.

He is strong, she signs. *His heart is strong*.

"Is he awake? Should I come see him?"

Sky sniffs and flicks her head back a few times. She towers over me and glistens in the sunlight like an ice sculpture. She's not wearing her armor, and with her bald, nearly white head and sparkling silver eyes, she looks the least human of all the Rogue Nahx I've met so far, but her manner is measured and patient, almost motherly.

He's eating, she signs calmly, and I think she's about to leave me, but instead she puts one hand on my shoulder, signing with the other.

Summer King is strong, she says. *Repeat strong.*

Summer King is the way she signs his name. In the minutes after we arrived I told her it was August and showed her the way he signed it, but it seems his sign was simply *Eighth*, his rank, and these Rogues disapprove of ranks. When we briefly explained what August means, Sky came up with Summer King. It suits August so well, I'm annoyed I didn't think of it.

Give Summer King time, Raven. His mind is in pieces.

"Why? What happened to him?"

Sky smiles at me. Most of her teeth are silver, some as though they were broken in a fight and grew back the missing pieces. It's surprisingly beautiful.

Don't worry, Raven, she signs, studying me for a moment. *We have other things to discuss. The humans cannot stay here.*

"I know."

You Snowflakes cannot stay here either.

I edge backward, letting her hand fall from my shoulder. "Are you going to send us away?"

She continues to watch me, her silver eyes thoughtful. *You're very strong too,* she says after a moment.

"Yes. Made that way. I wish I knew why."

A fight, she says. *Repeat fight.*

"A battle? I figured that. With who?"

I don't know. But I know where.

"Northeast of here, right?"

North. East. South. West. Across the water. Across the mountains. Many battles.

"Are you going to fight in these battles?"

Her face hardens and becomes grim. *No. The Rogues have chosen not to fight.* She says it like it should be printed on T-shirts.

"Could I do that? Just choose not to fight?"

Sky tilts her head to the side, a little smile curling her lips up at the corners.

We will speak in the future, she says, and abruptly turns and strides away. Before she disappears into the trees she is joined by her two companions—"Offside" seems to be the word they use—a male named Ash, whose broken helmet reveals burnt, mottled skin on one side of his face, and Thorn, a female who is missing one hand and has replaced it with a tangle of barbed wire.

Ash and Thorn are what made me realize these Rogue Nahx name themselves, based on aspects of their lives or things they love. They choose mostly nature names, and of course only use the sign versions with each other.

They have built a community, led by Sky and her Offsides, an enclave of rebels and deserters here in the remote mountains. If the Nahx who brought us here are anything to go by, this is not a secret community. Perhaps it's more a tolerated one. There only seem to be a few hundred here, and what is a few hundred compared to the thousands, the millions that obediently took our world? Who would even notice if we joined them?

When I can no longer hear Sky and her Offsides in the trees I turn and climb the stairs into the cabin.

Sky's cabin is a mountain climber's refuge, with a large central hall flanked by two rooms, all three spaces heated by large woodstoves. Topher, Xander, Mandy, and Tucker sit on the floor in front of one, the files I took from the base spread around them. Xander looks up as I close the door behind me.

"Is August okay?"

"He's alive." I shrug. "Sky seems to think he'll recover, but . . . I don't think he's ready to face . . ." I wave my hand around. "All this. All of us."

Tucker huffs, pointedly ignoring me, but I forge ahead.

"Sky says you can't stay here."

"Who can't?" Mandy asks. I notice Blue hovering above her, near the beamed ceiling.

"Topher and Xander, I guess. But us too." I don't like putting us into different categories; I especially don't like putting Topher and Tucker into different categories, but those are the facts.

Xander scoots aside as I join their circle.

"Before we go anywhere, we need to figure out how to get back through the web," he says.

"Couldn't Aurora take you back the way you came?" I ask.

"Oh, so you're ready to talk about this now? Now that your boyfriend is breathing again?"

"Don't be a dick, Tucker," Mandy says.

"I'm Topher."

She looks up, frowning.

"How about *none* of us be dicks?" Xander says cheerfully. Both Tucker and Topher scowl at me but keep their pretty mouths shut.

I look down at the papers and maps laid out on the floor. One of them is a plain sheet on which someone—Xander, I assume—has doodled a rough map of the world.

"What's this?" I note an X marking the map on the spot where Mandy, Tucker, and I were revived on the dunes.

"I was telling Xander about the globe on the ship," Mandy says.

"And?"

Xander brightens. "I noticed something weird." He sketches on the map, adding a penciled outline the length of the Rocky Mountains as he talks. "So this is the border web, roughly. Apparently there are webs like it elsewhere in the world. Mandy says Nahx occupation areas were marked too, along with bright lights—maybe those were the giant ships like the one you were in."

"Okay . . ."

Mandy points to the map, taking over. "When we first heard about the invasion, they listed Bogotá as one of the cities hit especially hard." She puts her finger on the northwest corner of South America. "I remember it because it was one of the places I could have volunteered last year, before I decided on Nunavut."

"But we know why now," I say. "The ground invasions were in high-elevation cities because the Nahx have trouble breathing at low elevation." I have a sudden urge to tell Tenth's story, in memory of everything he did for us, but I resist.

"Right," Xander continues. "Except the bright lights denoting the ships aren't all at high elevations. In fact, most of them aren't. Mandy says there aren't any in South America at all, for instance."

I can see the globe from the ship very clearly in my mind; I can even make it spin and slow it down or speed it up as though I'm operating it by remote control. And they're right.

"I didn't get that good a look at it," Mandy confesses. "I was mostly searching the crowd, looking for you and the others."

"I don't see how this matters," Tucker says.

Mandy flicks him a look. "Remember before how Xander suggested not being a dick?"

Tucker presses his lips together, crossing his arms like a sulking child. I ignore him. I don't have time to deal with butt-hurt boys right now.

Xander sighs like he's a little tired of it too. He bends over his rough map, pencil in hand. "So where were the other bright lights? Raven?"

I turn the globe in my mind, remembering the details as I point down to the map. "There were several in Russia . . . here and farther north, around here. And there were two in North Africa. Like in the Sahara or something. And some in Australia, here in the center and then to the west, like here." I lean back and look at the places Xander is marking. "I think they're just remote places, away from populated areas. That makes sense, doesn't it?"

"Wait," Xander says, holding up one hand while he finishes marking the map with the other. "There were some lights over the oceans, too, right?"

"Yes. A bunch here, sort of, in the Pacific. Also there were some here. Is this India or China?"

Xander marks the map without answering.

"Okay," he says, suddenly very grave. "I want you to think carefully. Were there any in Japan?"

"Yes."

Xander takes a breath and pauses a second too long.

"How many?"

"Two."

Snatching another paper from the collection strewn in front of us, Xander flips it over and quickly sketches the distinct seahorse shape of Japan. He hesitates before sliding the paper and pencil over to me. I lean down and make two marks in southern Japan.

The five of us stare at the map as though by making the marks I have cast some kind of freezing spell.

"Oh God," Mandy says.

"Is that . . . ?" Topher, suddenly interested, leans over to get a closer look.

Xander taps the two new marks on the map, one after the other. "This is Hiroshima. And this is Nagasaki."

"Oh GOD."

"So these are all nuclear detonations?" Topher says, pointing at places on the first map. "This would be the first test in New Mexico. And these ones are the Bikini Atoll tests. What do the Nahx want with nuclear detonation sites?"

"Maybe some kind of energy they can use?" Xander suggests. "The radiation?"

"Wait." Tucker puts his hands flat on the two maps as though to cover them. "This makes no sense. Where we were in Saskatchewan is not a nuclear detonation site. There has never been a nuclear bomb detonated in Canada."

"Unless . . ." Xander says.

A silence follows, one infused with a vague sense that everything we were ever taught was a lie.

"Well, shit," I say.

"Right?" Xander says. "If you were Canada during the Cold War, would you trust the Americans to protect us? And if you didn't, and you wanted to test a nuclear device, wouldn't you do it in a desert in remote Northern Saskatchewan, less than fifty miles away from Canada's biggest uranium mine? And wouldn't you keep it a big ol' secret?"

"I bet it was Trudeau," Topher says.

"Senior or Junior?"

"Either. Both."

Xander and Topher snort with laughter, but Mandy, Tucker, and I lock eyes, exchanging a moment of shared dread. There aren't just Nahx ships at these sites, there are "fissures" and a future battle none of us yet understand. And I'm pretty sure I'm not the only one who doesn't care for the added detail of nuclear radiation. Are we going to war with some kind of mutants? In a second, as though by telepathy, we three come to a silent consensus to not let Topher and Xander in on these details. Not now, anyway. I glance up at Blue, who flickers and seems somehow to agree with us.

I'm about to say something to change the subject, but Sky does it for me, throwing open the door and striding in, flanked by her Offsides. It becomes immediately clear that she has called some kind of meeting, because soon the hall fills up with Rogues. Xander silently shuffles the papers into a bundle and he and Topher take seats by the fire. Mandy, Tucker, and I hop up and sit on the kitchen table.

When the room is full, Sky calls attention by clapping her hands together, making a sharp smack that resonates in the high-ceilinged hall.

Now we must decide what to do with the humans, she signs.

As I translate, the Rogues shuffle a bit, but none have any suggestions.

"We can go back down to my camp," Topher says after a moment.

No, Sky signs sharply. *You will die.*

"No we won't," Topher says. "We can—"

Sky interrupts him with a hiss. *Mud brain humans can't see death when it is staring into their eyes. Nahx soldiers will come. You will die.*

I only translate the last part.

"The Nahx are still darting people?" Mandy asks. "Even now?" I notice that Blue is now sitting on her shoulder, twinkling like a tiny diamond brooch.

Some have orders to stop. Many do not. They follow orders until they die, Sky says. In the brief, thoughtful silence that follows, the door creaks open and August comes in, fully armored and dusted with snow. He looks around, facing me for a second before moving to join the crowd of Rogues. I want to follow him, to tug him away so we can have the proper conversation we obviously need to, but Mandy interrupts me.

"What's she saying?"

Sky is talking again. I try to catch up, ignoring my growing awareness that Tucker has decided to crunch a handful of my green satin skirt in his fist.

. . . back over the mountains and through the drone web. Aurora, can you get them back through?

Aurora, with her tall Offside's arm slung around her shoulders, nods.

If it's ice, yes. If not, no.

"So we need to go now," Xander says. "Not wait for spring."

"I'm not leaving my brother."

Beside me, Tucker sighs. I take the opportunity to yank my skirt away from him.

Sky's Offsides, who flank her like stoic bodyguards, suddenly speak, with Aurora and Nova joining them in a flurry of signs too fast for me to interpret. Sky claps her hands together again after a moment.

Snowflakes will not be safe with the humans, she says.

"We can defend ourselves," Tucker says.

Snowflakes should not harm humans, she snaps, shaking her head dismissively. *Humans would not be safe with you.*

"These three aren't going to hurt anyone," Topher says. "And we can find someplace where we won't have to see other humans. Away from Nahx, away from humans. It's a big country."

Raven will not want to leave Summer King, Sky says. *I will not allow Summer King back among humans. It is not safe.*

"What did she say?" Mandy asks.

"I don't know," I lie. "She was talking too fast." Tucker tugs at my dress again, this time sliding his hand around until it's almost touching my butt. I know he is doing this for August's benefit, because whatever affection for me reawakened after his memories came back has been trickling away since he discovered Emily's body. And since we found August, he has barely looked at me. So now his intrusions into my physical space just piss me off. And even though I could very easily elbow him in the face, he knows I don't want to make a scene.

"Can I ask a question?" Xander asks.

Sky nods in his direction.

"Is the web what is keeping you and the other Nahx on this side of the mountains? Like, if it wasn't there, do you think Nahx would trail down into BC or down to the coast?"

No, Sky says. *It's very uncomfortable to leave the high ground. We don't do it unless ordered.*

Not even then, Nova says. *If we can avoid it.*

"So if the web wasn't there, that wouldn't endanger the humans outside the occupied zones, in the low-lying areas? They'd still be safe?"

Sky nods slowly, as do several of the other Rogues.

The web is for keeping humans in, Sky says. *To let us finish the preparations.*

"Why is it still up, though?" Mandy asks. "Aren't all the humans dead? Or darted?"

"There are over ten thousand still alive in Edmonton," Topher says. "We heard their distress call."

"Ten thousand?" I knew from the Métis girl that there are survivors in remote places, but Edmonton? That surprises me. "A recent distress call?"

"Day before yesterday."

There are other humans, Sky says. *In a place called Red Animal.*

"Red Animal? Red Deer? South of Edmonton? There are survivors there, too?"

She nods. *Many.*

Topher and Xander whisper to each other for a few seconds. Finally Xander speaks.

"I think we should take down the web. Destroy it."

The room becomes so quiet and still, it's like being in a museum. Sky moves at last.

Go on, she says, wriggling her fingers in front of her mouth.

Xander stands nervously. He's at least a foot shorter than any of the Nahx here, and almost looks like a child about to give a school report.

"When we were all living in a military base north of here," he starts. "It's maybe about three or four days' walk—"

Sky nods and wriggles her fingers again. *Continue.*

"We were gathering intel. We had these drones, and we sent them out on recon flights to take photographs. The commander of the base, and later her son, Liam, were both very cagey about what they found out. I don't think they trusted me. Or Topher, for that matter."

Topher nods, giving Xander an encouraging smile. Xander picks up the map we've been doodling on, as well as a few of the printouts.

"When Topher left the base it was under attack, but one of his friends went back to get some files. He never made it out, nor did the files, but Raven was just there and she found Topher's friend—dead, unfortunately. But he still had the files with him. Raven was smart enough to think that if he risked his life to get them, they must be worth something. So she took them."

Riffling through the printouts, Xander chooses one and holds it up, what looks like a map of Alberta and BC.

"See this? This is Bennett Dam. It's about a hundred and fifty miles north of here. There were a bunch of pictures of it in the file, along with some other stuff, probably from the pirate transmissions. It's . . . well, like I said. They were all very cagey, but I know this territory really well, and from what I can tell, Liam and maybe even his mother before him were planning on attacking Bennett Dam."

"Why on earth . . . ?" Mandy says.

Xander holds up some of the printed photographs. I scoot forward to get a better look, and to get away from Tucker's creeping hand.

"The plan is not specified in any of the notes. But it makes sense. Look. This is an aerial shot of the dam. You can see there's a fair bit of Nahx activity there. All those dark triangular shapes are transports, for example. So the Nahx are occupying the facility. Well, we knew this. Even in the human territory we know the Nahx have taken control of a lot of things—power stations, transmitters. But this image . . ." Xander holds up another photograph. "This is the same view, only this one is taken at night. And see this?" Across the page, a bright line meanders west from the dam site. "That's the drone web."

Sky bends to inspect the image. *Light prison?* she signs.

"Yes. Much easier to see at night. Topher and his friends have searched up and down the web and not found any gaps or weaknesses. No way to get through. Aurora and I got through, though, coming the other way. And maybe we could take a few people back that way. But it depends on a fluke, a frozen pond, basically, that was too small for the Nahx to be guarding but just big enough to get across under the ice. Who knows how long until that catches their attention? And the way I got across the first time, with August, that's been destroyed too."

Xander is in his element now, talking about maps and escape routes. I can feel his enthusiasm.

"Sky, you said the Nahx will follow directives until they die, right? One of the directives is obviously to maintain the territory, maintain the drone web to keep humans in. If we pick at little weaknesses, they will just come along and close them up. But if we could take down the whole web . . ."

"Surely the dam can't be powering the whole web?" I say. "It's thousands of miles long."

"You'd be surprised," Xander says. "Bennett Dam pumped out millions of megawatts. And anyway, even if we take out only this one power source, there's a chance it could cause a cascading failure and bring down the whole thing. That's how power grids work. That's where those massive blackouts down east came from."

Sky taps her hands together to get our attention. *How long would the web stay down?* she signs.

"How long? I don't know," Xander says. "Normally in a blackout it's just a malfunction they can fix in a few days. If you totally destroy a power station, they can't fix it. So unless the Nahx have some other easy power source to take its place, it might stay down a long time."

"Long enough to get all those survivors out?" I ask.

"Maybe. If they have vehicles and fuel. Or if rescuers could get in."

I turn to Mandy, who doesn't seem convinced. As for Tucker, he flicks his eyes away from me and crosses his arms again.

"Sky, how do you think the Nahx would react to an attack like this?" Mandy asks. "Would they retaliate?"

Sky makes some signs.

"She says the Nahx will think it was the Rogues and come after them."

"Would they, though?" Xander asks. "If the Nahx wanted to dart these survivors, they would have done it. I think they just don't care. So why would they care if we try to rescue them? And anyway, they must know that you disrupt their jammer every day. They've never tried to stop you."

Different, Sky says.

"We could do it without any violence. No casualties. A bit of careful sabotage and we can shut it down more or less permanently. They might not even know we were there."

"Sneak in?" Topher says. "I thought we were talking about blowing it up."

I notice some of the assembled Rogues are fidgeting, shuffling their feet back and forth impatiently.

"You can't just blow it up if there are hundreds of Nahx there," I say.

"Why not?" Topher says, his voice rising. "They've murdered thousands of us. Millions. And anyway, Nahx don't even die."

"If you blow us up, we die!" I shout it, though I didn't mean to. "This room is full of Nahx," I say, gathering myself. "Are you counting on their help? But you don't care how many you kill?"

Topher turns his head to look at the flickering fire in the stove for a moment, and when he turns back it's as though the flames have transferred to his eyes.

"Do you know what we're talking about here, Raven? We're talking about trying to figure out a way that I can avoid being separated from my brother again. My *undead* brother. I pretty much have to give up any hope of ever living a normal human life because of that. Because of what the Nahx turned you into. So forgive me if I'm not sensitive enough to casualties among the things that did this to us."

The assembled Nahx shuffle again and "whisper" among themselves, their signs small and discreet. I see a few words I recognize—*humans, fight, dead, falling*. None of it seems very promising.

Sky claps her hands again. *Look, listen*, she says, and signs slowly. *The Rogues chose not to fight in the past. Now they will choose again. Understand?*

"Yes," I say. "She's opening it up for a vote."

Sky turns to the Rogues, getting their attention with another loud clap. *Join the fight? Yes or no?*

Ash and Thorn nod immediately, but the other Rogues begin to trail out of the cabin. Some of them sign quickly to Sky as they leave. One very familiar word.

Sorry.

I suppose I can't blame them for not joining our fight. If I were in their position, I'd probably bow out too.

A few stay back. Aurora looks at Xander as she signs, *Promise*, with a wink. Nova stays by her side. As more Rogues depart, I notice August is still down on one knee, staring at the floor.

In the end, there are eight Rogues left with us: Sky and her two Offsides, Aurora, Nova, August, and another pair we met right after we arrived. Xander determined their sign names to be *Sun* and *Moon*. For some reason they objected to the spoken English but accepted Topher's suggestions, Sol and Luna.

Eight Nahx, two humans, and three of whatever Tucker and Mandy and I are. Thirteen doesn't seem like enough to storm a heavily guarded base, but maybe it's the perfect number to sneak in like cat burglars.

Sky scrutinizes the team as they assemble around her.

Thirteen, she signs. *We'll all fit into one transport.*

"We'll have to land pretty far away, or they'll know something's up, surely," Mandy says.

Sky nods. *What's the plan?*

"Okay." Xander flips one of the printouts over to the blank side, pulling a pencil from his pocket. "Come closer. It's easier if I draw a diagram."

As I slide off the table, Tucker follows behind me, his hand straying up to rest on the back of my neck. I move to twist away from him but his fingers—by accident or on purpose—get tangled in one of my unraveling braids, tugging it painfully. I barely make a noise bigger than a kitten's squeak, but it's enough.

August dives across the room, and he and Tucker go flying over the kitchen table, upending a shelf full of tin cups as they land.

"August!" I yell over the clatter. "Stop!"

August hesitates enough for Tucker to roll away, but as he leaps up he gets August's fingers in a lock. Bending them backward, he spins and stomp kicks August in the side of the head. The sickening sound of August's fingers breaking is as shocking as a gunshot. Sky flies at them, tearing Tucker back and slamming him against the wall, pinning him there by his neck.

"Did you break his fingers?!" I scream at him. "What the fuck did you do that for?"

383

Tucker spits silver blood. "He jumped me!"

August lunges at him again, growling.

"Stop it!"

Sky smacks August solidly in the forehead with the heel of her free hand. He stumbles back, tripping on the fallen shelf and landing on his ass with crash.

All eyes are on me as a million different mortifying thoughts stream through my head, highlighted by the idea that I should let them kill each other. I also think of a thousand ways to react and things to say, but I decide to go with the simplest.

"Both of you, just stay away from me!"

Mandy and Xander call after me as I push the door open and stomp outside, but I ignore them.

Tucker and August's fight has become a popular topic of gossip among the Rogues. In the morning, when I emerge from Sky's cabin, warm, well rested, and fed on the large hoard of survival food we found in the kitchen, I catch Sol and Luna chatting about it as they tramp across the open basin. I recognize a few signs: *human, broken, hand, cold.* They laugh in the silent breathy way Nahx do, clutching each other as they trail into the dense trees. I see the last signs Sol makes, and recognize them too.

Summer King. Mud head.

I'm tempted to shout after them in August's defense. He saved my life. He saved Raven's life. He deserves respect for that, surely. And I don't think there's anything wrong with his mind. He's hurting because he loves Raven and thinks she doesn't love him back. Whether he's right or not I don't know, but I know what that feels like.

Plus, Tucker *was* being an ass.

I turn as the door creaks behind me. Topher pokes his head out, squinting in the bright sunlight, his face looking pained.

"How do you feel?" I ask.

He walks delicately across the porch and eases himself into one of the wooden chairs.

"Not going to lie. Kind of fragile. That second can of condensed milk was a mistake."

"I did try to tell you."

He rubs his stomach, grimacing.

"Has Tucker come back yet?"

Tucker had a brief but intense screaming match with Raven out in the snow late last night, after which he disappeared, literally up a tree. Mandy dragged Raven away to help Sky and her Offsides refit one of the two partially working transports. As for August, he is nowhere to be found. So we're all kind of a mess. Not a very promising attack team, I've got to say.

I take Topher by the shoulders and turn his body, pointing to the top of a pine tree, where Tucker is a dark smudge.

"For God's sake," Topher says, standing and stomping down the stairs and across the clearing. I leave them to it.

Raven and Mandy are still working on the transport when I find them up on the plateau. The bright morning sun reflecting off the ice and snow makes the whole setting sparkle as though it's electrified.

"Hey," Raven says as I hoist myself through the open hatch. She barely glances up from her work, which seems to be the reconnecting of hundreds of tiny wires into the back of an impossibly complicated circuit board. She's moving at an incredible speed, her hand blurring as the wires click into place.

"Topher and I are going to head out pretty soon."

"Is Aurora going with you?"

I lean on a half-dismantled console. "Yeah. And Nova. We'll be fine."

"And Topher is sure he has enough explosives?"

Despite the disruption, we did manage to discuss the attack on Bennett Dam last night. The only missing link was explosives to blow up the power transformers. The Rogues, having sworn off violence, only have enough weapons to defend themselves, so they don't have any. But Topher, as usual, planned for the worst.

"He says he took about a dozen C-13 grenades from the base. It's going to have to be enough."

Raven looks up from her circuit board finally, fixing me in a frank stare. Her eyes sparkle as the light from the open hatch hits them.

"What?"

"I never thought you and I would be having conversations about grenades," she says.

"We've changed."

She laughs. I notice the tiny creature she arrived with, the one she calls Blue, is hovering over her left shoulder. They bob up and down as though acknowledging me. I nod back, feeling a bit stupid.

"Have you talked to August yet?" I ask.

Raven sighs. "I don't know where he is. Sky told me not to worry about it. She says his hand will be fine in a few hours."

Blue draws a big, slow circle in the air, but I don't think Raven notices. She connects a few more wires before speaking again.

"Sky says August has gotten it into his head that I'm his Offside, because his original Offside is dead and . . ." She shrugs.

"*Are* you his Offside?" I ask.

"I'm not a Nahx, you know." She stands back from her work, staring at the tangle of wires. "You should get going. You want to be back before dark."

I lean into the cockpit, where Mandy is half submerged in a torn-apart dashboard. "See you later, Mandy!"

She grunts her reply, waving a wrench. I don't know when these two learned how to repair Nahx transports. Mandy says their minds are working at a thousand times normal speed, so I suppose that helps.

"Hey," Raven calls out to me as I jump down from the hatch.

I turn back. "What?"

"You haven't changed, Xander. Not like me."

Tugging my tuque out of my pocket, I pull it over my ears.

"You haven't changed much either, Raven."

I jog back down the hill before she can argue.

Topher, Nova, and Aurora are waiting for me outside Sky's cabin. I notice Tucker is no longer up the tree, but he's nowhere to be seen either.

"He's not coming with us," Topher says, anticipating my question.

"I hope he's planning on staying away from August." I say it offhandedly, without much thought, but Topher snaps back at me.

"Why do you care so much?"

"About August? Because he saved my life. Multiple times."

"Yeah, and he killed my brother."

I take a cool breath. "Tucker told you." I've been wondering when this would happen.

"Of course he told me. I'd like to know why you didn't, though."

"Because if you decided to try some revenge fantasy with August, he would snap you like a twig. Anyway, Tucker's not dead. You were just talking to him."

If Aurora and Nova could whistle nervously, they probably would. Topher frowns at me, slinging a rifle over his shoulder.

"Whatever. Let's go."

The sun beats down on us until we reach the tunnel through the glacier, and is still shining brightly when we emerge. Though it's cold, by midday when we climb up to Topher's camp, we've both unzipped our coats and tucked our mittens and hats into the pockets. Topher looks brighter with every hour in the sun. I suspect he's been literally hiding under rocks for months. Who could blame him?

His camp looks the same as we left it, and since we have two Rogue Nahx to keep watch, Topher and I decide to make a fire in the shelter so we can have a hot lunch. It's just soup we brought from Sky's cabin, heated right in the can and eaten that way too, with two spoons, but it tastes like a gourmet meal.

Outside, Nova and Aurora carefully dig up Topher's cache of weapons, insisting we rest while they work. I still can't get Aurora to stop babying me, even after more than a week of trying.

Topher swigs from a canteen and hands it to me, lying back on the pile of sleeping bags.

"I want you to reason with Tucker," he says. "He thinks that once we get the web down he's going back with Raven for some great battle up north."

"Tucker is no more likely to listen to me than you."

I silently wish that my mind could work a thousand times faster than normal too, even just for a few hours. The last couple of days have been too much to take in. Tucker, Mandy, and Raven still alive. *August* still alive. I poke at the fire, thinking of those weeks after I was rescued and taken to the refugee camp, how I mourned him secretly, never able to tell anyone, never able to get the image of him on fire out of my head. Now here he is. Back in my life like a phantom, though he has barely looked in my direction.

Since the invasion I've gotten used to people dying. Now, bizarrely, it seems I have to get used to them *undying*.

And Topher—everything I thought was finished is obviously unfinished. There is certainly no lingering tenderness between him and Raven. It's almost like, with Tucker back, they have no need for each other anymore. That gives me a strange feeling. I have so much need for all these people—Topher, Raven, August, Nova and Aurora, even Tucker—that it makes me a bit sick.

"It doesn't sound like the kind of battle that will have many survivors," Topher says, breaking my defeatist reverie.

Outside, Nova's shovel goes *chuff, chuff, chuff* into the frozen ground.

"How deep did you bury this stuff, anyway?"

Topher slides over, patting the sleeping bags beside him. "Deep. And the ground is frozen solid. We'll be here awhile."

"Should we help them?"

"Hell no. I think I'll take a nap."

I lie beside him, and we both stare up at the neatly entwined boughs that make up the curved roof of the wickiup.

"Raven's parents are alive," I say.

Topher sighs and doesn't answer for a while. I explained

the register to him the day we found each other and told him that none of my family or his family were on it. But I think we've been avoiding talking about Raven—for a whole bunch of reasons.

"That's what she always believed," he says at last. "Never shut up about it, in fact. She was sure they made it to the coast."

"Well . . . they did."

"Have you told her?"

"No. I thought it might be better to wait until the web is down and she could get back to them. If that's what she wants."

The question of what happens when this mission is over, of who goes where and with whom, I leave unspoken. I'm thinking about how to bring up the topic of Jack's offer for me to live with them when Topher rolls over to face me. He has the same dark and moody look on his face that always made me stupid.

"Raven and I never slept together," he says.

"I . . . okay." Like I said. Stupid.

"I know what it looked like from the outside. But it wasn't that. We were just . . . I was trying to . . ."

I roll onto my side, and when he closes his eyes, like he can't find a way to go on, I reach forward and put my hand on his face. He lifts his own hand to cover mine and we lie like that for a few seconds, taking deep breaths of the warm, smoky air of the shelter.

Topher speaks without opening his eyes. "I shouldn't have dropped you like that when Raven came back. I don't know why I did. It was just such a shock to see her alive, and she was so . . . traumatized that I was sure something had happened to her out there, something terrible. I felt like I needed to protect her. At least until she could tell me about it. Or tell someone."

"But she never did."

"No. Because . . ."

He opens his eyes, and there is something sharp in his gaze that's both beautiful and a little frightening.

"Something did happen to her?"

"The Nahx happened to her," he says bitterly.

"August never hurt her, Toph. Honestly, he's not like that."

"He never hurt her? He turned her into a zombie!"

From what I've seen, Raven, Mandy, and Tucker are far from zombies, but one of them is not my twin brother, so I don't think I can argue. I know what it feels like to live without a sibling you love. If what Mandy says is right, Topher will grow old and die, and Tucker will have to live without him for hundreds, maybe thousands of years. Or there's the other possibility.

"Do you think they know things they're not telling us?" Topher asks.

"About what?"

"The whole thing with the nuclear bomb sites and whatever it is that Tucker wants to go back to."

"I think they know as much as we do. Why would they keep secrets?"

Topher moves my hand off his face and scratches his beard.

"I suppose because their plan is for us to go west and them to go east."

Something changes, and whatever moment we were having is suddenly a different moment. We both roll back and face the ceiling again.

"When we get the web down, I'm going with them," Topher says.

"With who?" I ask. "With Raven?"

"With Tucker."

"With *Raven*." I repeat it as I sit up, brushing dirt and pine needles from my snow pants. "She doesn't need you, Toph. None of them need us. We can get out of here. Go live on the coast. Be humans again."

"Tucker needs me," he says. I don't turn around, but I hear him stand and start to fold up the sleeping bags. "Tucker can't be a human again."

"We don't know that." I stand and kick dirt onto the fire, because it's starting to look like we're done here. "Maybe there's . . . a cure or something."

"Why would he want to be cured?"

"Is that what this is? You're jealous? Why don't you ask one of the Nahx to dart you?"

When I turn, the way he's looking at me makes me want to crawl under a rock myself. "I'm s-sorry," I splutter. "I didn't mean that."

He shakes his head, leaning down to push the door flap open and look out into the clearing. Nova and Aurora are now hip deep in the hole they've dug and are scooping dirt out with their hands.

"That's what I hoped for, you know," Topher says, letting the canvas flap fall. With the fire nearly out, the shelter darkens until I can barely see him. "After the Nahx killed . . . darted everyone else, I hoped they would come back and get me. Sitting up here in the dark, bodies all around me? I *prayed* for it."

"I'm sorry, Topher."

"What are you sorry for?"

"I'm sorry I said that." When he doesn't seem satisfied with my answer, I go on. "I'm sorry I went with August that day. I'm sorry I didn't come back for you sooner. I'm sorry I . . . surrendered so easily, when Raven came back. I should have fought for you."

Even in the dark I can see his eyebrows creep up. "Why would you fight for me then? I was being a world-class dick."

He's still being kind of a dick, but since when has that ever stopped me? Or anyone? I put my hand on his shoulder and, after a second, slide it around to the back of his neck.

There's a moment, an instant really, where he tenses and a look crosses his face like he might, just shove me away and dive out the flap to run off like a startled animal. But I wait, and the moment passes.

Then I pull him forward and kiss him on the lips.

When we part I give him time to take a single breath before saying anything.

"Don't freak out," I whisper.

"Why would I freak out?" He slides one hand, then the other, into my coat and around my back.

"You did the first time we kissed."

He chuckles, pulling me close. "I got over it, though, didn't I?"

We kiss again. He tastes of soup and smells like sweat, and his lips are chapped with cold, and the skin is peeling off the tip of his nose from frostbite, and his beard itches. Also the world has come to an end and most of the people I love are either dead or zombie soldiers.

But apart from that, this is perfect. A glorious five minutes pass before we're interrupted, five minutes where my mind empties of all the garbage that's been building up in there and refills with melted chocolate and homemade dumplings and clean warm towels fresh out of the dryer.

It's Nova who pokes through the flap. She waits for us to untangle before speaking, but her curt signs are easy to interpret.

Time to go, mud brains.

Nova and Aurora simply jump off the steep cliff down from Topher's camp, landing gracefully at the bottom, where they wait for us to clamber awkwardly after them.

"Wouldn't you like to be able to do that?" Topher says, steadying me as I dislodge my toe from a root.

"Jump off cliffs? We can cliff dive on the coast if you want."

He falls silent and stays that way until we reach the bottom, where the trickling waterfall has frozen into glistening spindles and swirls.

Some parts of the hike back to Sky's cabin are like a pleasant winter stroll, marred only by the fact that Nova is carrying a pack with twelve live grenades inside it. Topher checked them all before we set out, making sure the pins were tightly in place and the safety clips securely fastened to the levers, but it still makes me uneasy. Garvin had grenades too, and I hated it when he showed them off. I don't know why they bother me more than guns. I've gotten used to carrying a gun again, but I suppose grenades remind me that this is really a *war*, not just some kids fooling around with their dads' hunting rifles.

Topher holds my hand for the easy parts, where we stroll across flat plateaus, crunching through the crust of ice that has settled on top of a foot of snow. Nova and Aurora hold hands too, or they walk with Nova slightly behind, her hand on Aurora's shoulder. It's sweet and quiet and peaceful, and I could almost pretend, if I turned my face away and looked up at the mountains and the puffs of clouds in the blue sky beyond, that life was normal. And safe.

But as we get closer to Sky's cabin, Topher lets go and keeps lagging back, letting me get ahead of him. Finally, when we're in sight of the small glacier that marks the entry into the Rogues' territory, I stop.

"Breather," I say. Nova and Aurora wander a few yards farther up toward the ice while I turn back to Topher, who crouches down to retie his boot.

"It's not that I don't want anyone to know," he says, not even looking up at me. "I'm not closeted or anything."

"Okay . . ."

"You didn't tell Raven either."

"I guess I assumed you would."

He stands, pulling his mittens back on. "I just don't want complications. Not now."

My face gets hot, and I turn away so he won't see me blush. Am I being dumped again? Already? That's got to be some kind of record.

He crunches up behind me, pressing against my back, his forehead on my shoulder. "It's not that I . . ." He exhales, and a little cloud of his breath puffs around my neck. "I always knew there was something wrong with me."

"Jesus, Toph. There's nothing wrong with being gay."

He snuffles against my coat, and at first I think he might be crying, but when he steps back and I turn, I see he's laughing.

"What's so funny?"

"You!" He laughs until he has to bend over and catch his breath. Glancing back, I see Nova and Aurora watching us, their heads tilted quizzically to the side. Topher straightens up, wiping tears of mirth away with his scarf.

"I meant I'm so . . . stitched up. It always made me so uncomfortable for people to notice me. And identical twins get so much attention, it drove me crazy. I used to hide in our room at our birthday parties. Tucker would eat all the cake."

"That sounds right." I'm not that different. I don't mind attention, but I definitely want it on my own terms. "That's probably why things were so hard for you . . . without him. No diversionary tactics. No one to hide behind."

"Yeah . . . God."

His mirth dissipates. I put my hand on his shoulder and leave it there. It feels surprisingly good. Solid. I can see why the Nahx like to walk this way.

"Listen, Toph. We're about to attempt a literally insane attack on a Nahx stronghold. If we survive that, we have to figure out how to travel a thousand miles across Canada in the middle of winter—whether we go east or west. And one way or another, some sort of zombie alien apocalyptic battle is looming. I'm pretty sure no one is going to notice anything different about you or me or anyone. And if they do, they're not going to care. The Rogues certainly aren't going to."

As though to demonstrate this, Aurora and Nova have started throwing snowballs into the trees.

Topher shakes his head, looking down, kicking at our footprints. "You're right. I just . . . want you to know it's nothing personal. If I act cool around you. It's just because I'm weird. It doesn't mean I don't like you." He leans forward and gives me a quick kiss.

I momentarily lose my ability to speak. I'm not exactly happy with where we've landed, but I understand at least. "Let's get these grenades on the road again."

He slings his arm around me as we head up to the glacier and rejoin Nova and Aurora.

"Grenades," Topher says with a snort. "People will probably notice *that*."

There's a tapping noise on the door of the stone hut. I stare at it, trying to latch onto the familiarity and let it lead me. To move. To do something.

Tap tap tap.

Answer it. I need to answer the door. Muddy death, that is so simple. How could I have struggled with that?

Sky is behind the door when I open it. She is in her armor except for her helmet, which hangs over her shoulder, the long breathing tentacles looped and clinging to her, as though waiting to be fully connected.

You're in your armor, she signs. *Good.*

I was sleeping.

She nods.

Now I'm not sleeping.

Sky smiles, reaching forward and touching my arm gently.

Yes, Summer King. I can see that.

My body heats up, and I try to think cold thoughts to cool myself down, but it doesn't work very well. So I look out at the snow over Sky's shoulder and imagine rolling in it.

I'm sorry, I say after a moment. *I'm still a little confused.*

That will improve with time, Sky says. She has explained this to me before. She says some of the other Rogues were brought to her after they'd let themselves run down, and it took them a while to be able to function again, to think and talk and make decisions without getting stuck in a loop of muddled thoughts.

We are preparing to go, she says. *Will you come with us?*

Yes. Yes.

I have no rifle or any other supplies, so I simply join her on the small porch of the hut, pulling the door closed behind me. According to Sky, there were darted humans in this hut when she found it. Their packs are still piled in one corner. Though I've been bored up here by myself, and I like to look at human objects, I haven't touched them. The darted humans were taken away by other Nahx about a month ago, Sky says. It feels wrong to disturb their things, as though maybe they might come back for them when it's all over, whatever this is.

Sky lets me walk with my hand on her shoulder as we pick our way down the path to her cabin. Her Offsides meet us at the tree line. Ash greets me with a nod, but the girl, Thorn, pointedly turns in the other direction. I don't think she likes me. It's possible she's jealous—Ash and Sky have been spending a lot of time with me, bringing me food and making me eat and drink water and reminding me to put my armor back on when I start to wheeze. I'm not a baby. I know I can take care of myself, but it's as though thoughts that should come naturally need some force to be drawn out, like a blade rusted into its . . . I can't think of the word. My mind is sharpening, but it's happening too slowly.

When the trees clear again and Sky's cabin becomes visible in the distance, she stops me, letting her Offsides trail ahead.

The humans are coming with us, she says.

Yes, I know.

The changed humans too. The Snowflakes.

Yes.

And Raven.

Yes.

She leans back, studying me, frowning.

Scabbard, I think, the word coming to me at last. I'm like a disused rifle that needs to be cleaned and oiled and reloaded. But all my weapons are as lost as my thoughts.

Raven has a bond with the Snowflake Tucker, Sky says. She signs his name as *Hard Boy.* I know she means impermeable or tough, but when she says it I think the word "unkillable." I would never tell her that, though.

You are not to harm him, she says. Her hands snap together sharply.

I won't.

You should stay away from him. From both of them.

I'm grateful for my mask then. I wouldn't want Sky to see the expression on my face. I flick my shoulder away from her and bend, pretending to dislodge a piece of ice from my boot. When I stand, I glance back up the path we've left, into the trees, beyond which is the wide steep plain up to the stone hut. There is only one thing in the world I want more than to go back up there and fall asleep again—to help Dandelion and her friends, even though I'm on the outside of her circle now.

That's my own fault. I can't blame her.

I'm worried, I say to Sky. *Won't I be a . . . ?* But then I can't think of the word. Not the sound of it or the sign. My mind rolls over like a boulder in mud.

Burden? Sky suggests.

Yes. I will be too slow. I will put the others in . . .

Danger?

Yes, danger. Sometimes the Rogues use signs I don't know, but this is one I should never have forgotten. It's a sign we used in training, for battles. A sign Sixth and I used often.

Sixth. I don't like to think about her. It's as though sometimes I can see her shadow in the corner of my vision, lingering just out of sight, watching me. I twitch as the shadow moves.

Sky puts her hand on my arm again.

Would you want Raven to go without you?

My skin gets hot under my armor.

No. I would not.

And could you stop her? Sky is smiling now, which makes me want to smile. I flick my head back.

No.

She squeezes my arm, which I feel through the sensors in my armor as tingling warmth.

You are unusually sensitive for an Eighth. I wonder if that's really your rank.

Bizarrely, I take this as an insult and have to fight the urge to defend myself. But then I'm not sure why. Is it good or bad to be sensitive? Once I would have been ashamed to be seen as a lower rank, and fantasized about pretending to be a Fourth so I could be above . . .

Mud. Sixth appears before me like magic, in armor but for her helmet. She bares her teeth. I lurch back and . . .

Sky is holding my wrist, keeping me upright. She signs with her other hand.

Your mind is playing with you. Ignore it.

Yes. Yes. But my heart is galloping, making me want to cough.

Past the cabin, on the plateau, the engines of the repaired transport rumble. I try to shake off the vision, following Sky and her Offsides as we head in that direction. Sol and Luna emerge from the ice tunnel and join us.

You are strong, Summer King, Sky says to me as we board the transport. *Your body is strong and fast. Use your mind to watch me and do as I say.*

She makes it seem so simple. But then, that has always been my main directive, the whole scope of my first mission.

Follow orders.

Do what Sixth tells me.

I don't know why I'm thinking of her so much. I wish that would stop.

Raven boards with her friends and the tiny glowing creature who constantly hovers around them. It seems ridiculous to be afraid of them—Blue, Raven calls them—but they make me uneasy. I remember these creatures from the big ship. As friendly as Blue seems, others like them I have encountered have been . . .

Something. Worse than unfriendly.

Toxic. Like poison. It's reassuring to know the others like me feel the same way. Sky, Ash, Nova, and the rest. They avoid Blue too.

When everyone is aboard and the hatch is closed, a sudden lull overtakes us. The past two days have been a hum of activity, which I spent most of either clenched with anxiety or fast asleep, senseless in a dark void or running from nightmares. Now that we're on our way to the dam, every preparation in place, there is time to rest. The others like me stand in the hold, clinging to the metal loops on the wall. We are all in complete armor, and I wonder if the others are doing as I do, replaying certain thoughts and words to help keep me focused, to prevent me from sinking into the mind-dulling sludge.

Once I thought of Raven when I felt myself slipping away, of her strong shoulders and firm jaw, the way she tilted her head back defiantly even though I could see how scared she was. Her eyes would blaze; the sun would light up her hair. It was so . . . magical. She was magical, like some kind of medicine.

But now when I look at her, she's different. And though my feelings for her haven't changed, the way she makes me feel has, if that makes sense.

Maybe because she needed me, because my people were so hostile to her and I could protect her, that made it so I was . . .

Something. I can't find the word.

Not a monster. Not monstrous. What is the opposite of "monstrous"?

Sky joins me in the hold, looking over my shoulder to where Raven and her friends are sitting between the weapons racks.

I know what you're thinking, she says.

You do? I reply. *That's good, because I don't.*

Sky and the Rogues flick their heads back to laugh like I do, but they also huff out little breaths as they do it. There is a lot of laughter in the mountains where they live. They are so happy. It makes me wonder that any of them agreed to come on this mission at all.

We met long ago, you and I, Sky says.

Yes, I remember now. I wish I had joined them then as she asked. But if I had, and other things had gone as they did, then Raven would have been killed in the city and I never would have known. I wonder if I would have continued to dream of her.

Did you know Raven then? Sky asks.

Muddy death, she *does* know what I'm thinking.

Yes. I didn't know her name.

She nods with another huff of breath. *You are not the first of us to become entranced with a human. Likely not the last, either.*

I turn to look back at them, because Raven can understand our language. But she and the boy clones are deep in conversation. I don't . . . I can't . . . I shouldn't feel the way I do about that. The fluid of the armor flows through my veins, washing away the softness Raven created in me. Normally I might resist it, but this time I just let it happen, let the gray sludge sharpen my insides, turning me back into a hard, cold machine. Softness doesn't destroy dams. It doesn't win battles.

I don't want her to be harmed, I say, because I find I can't help it. The way my memory works, some images fix themselves like photographs, and one of them haunts me—Raven, Dandelion, in my arms, broken and nearly dead, covered in blood—my body gets so hot, it's painful. I have to clench down on the mouthpiece of my breathing tube to make it stop.

It would be very hard to harm her the way she is now, Sky says.

And maybe the one thing that makes me not a monster or machine is gone now too. I don't say this, of course. I doubt Sky would understand.

When I glance back, Topher, the human twin, is laughing, and strangely I feel a sudden . . .

I can't think of the word.

Connection? Sympathy?

Affinity. Understanding. I feel like I can understand him, because I would like to blow up the dam too.

And I don't care how many of my kind are killed.

RAVEN

Blue, you have to wait with the transport."

They zip angrily from side to side. *No!*

"Why can't they come with us?" Mandy asks. "They could be useful if we run into trouble. The Nahx are scared of them."

Blue bobs excitedly. But Topher, thinking logically as usual, backs me up.

"If we do things properly, we won't need to encounter any Nahx. And even if we do, we can fight back. Yes, we're going to try to steal another transport, but if that doesn't work and we lose this one, we're screwed."

The transport is partially concealed by some scrubby trees outside a deserted town east of the dam. But Topher's right. We can't take chances.

"Please, Blue," I say. "It's important, and I don't want you to get hurt."

They flare for a moment before flicking into Topher's forehead, making him stumble back. He recovers as Blue disappears back into the transport.

"Your friend is a real asshole," Topher says.

"Well, I'm used to that," I say.

We hike from the town up to an elevation high enough for some of the Rogues to take their armor off. The plan is to rest here overnight and infiltrate the dam at dawn.

When Topher and Xander bed down, with the Nahx surrounding them for warmth, they are soon asleep, exhausted from the long, steep hike. Mandy checks on them and quickly draws me aside, with Tucker following. I've been expecting it.

"Did you feel it?" she whispers, glancing back to make sure the Nahx aren't listening.

About halfway into our voyage, Tucker stumbled in the transport. Topher caught him before he fell, and Tucker claimed he tripped on the corner of the rifle rack and lost his balance. But Mandy and I knew the truth. If not for the fact that we were sitting down at the time, we would have stumbled too.

"It's because we're farther north now? Closer to the fissures?"

It was like being cut open with an ax, or a dark swath of night suddenly erasing every thought in my head. It lasted only a second and I don't think anyone else noticed, but it was enough.

"The dart toxin programmed us somehow," I say. "It wasn't real. It was just in our mind, trying to get us to go back to fight."

"Maybe," Mandy says. "But it felt like a migraine or a stroke. What if the next one is worse? Maybe they build in strength until they kill you."

"That seems . . . extreme," Tucker says. I have to remind myself that Tucker hasn't seen half the things I have.

"Comparatively, it's not," I say. I don't elaborate. What Tucker doesn't know can't hurt him. Or send him careening into insanity the way I sometimes feel I am.

"We'll just do this and then we can head back to the dunes," Mandy says. Her strange eyes have grown slightly wild-looking. They flick around like a trapped animal's.

"What about Xander?" I ask. "Or Topher?"

Tucker stands. "I'm not leaving him!" he says, loud enough for one of the Nahx to turn and look at us. It's August, I realize. After a second, as he turns away, he bends to adjust Xander's blankets, tucking them carefully around his feet.

August barely acknowledged me when I got onto the transport and has ignored me for the whole journey. I don't know why I thought things would go back to the way they were when he regained consciousness, back to our kind of easy companionship that defies description. Things are different now. I'm not even human anymore. But Xander is. Maybe the protective affection August had for me has simply transferred. It shouldn't hurt as much as it does. With the computer churning in my head, I should be able to focus away from the pain or archive it or delete it. But the pain remains.

"So we'll do this, then we'll talk properly about it," Mandy says tightly.

Tucker ignores her and, moving over to where the boys are sleeping, shoves one of the Nahx out of the way so he can sit next to his brother. The Nahx, Sol, simply takes a new position, standing behind him like a bodyguard.

"What are you thinking?" Mandy asks.

I'm actually thinking of how much I miss being first on someone's list, how intoxicating that was—before Jack came along and it was just me and Mom, when Tucker and I first got together and were so obsessed with each other. And August. Those weeks with August when it seemed like he would do anything for me, that I was the center of his universe. It feels selfish to think that now, though, when thousands of lives are at stake, millions. I'm certainly not going to share it with Mandy.

"I'm wondering whether any of this is worth saving," I say instead.

"That's the question, isn't it?"

Reaching down, I take a handful of snow and pine needles and let it sprinkle into the space between us.

"Have you ever seen whales in the wild?" Mandy asks. It's a non sequitur, but I'm quite happy to have the subject changed. She stretches her legs out and crosses them, leaning back to look up at the dark sky.

"Yeah." I imitate her posture and, through the treetops, watch the dense blanket of stars as they move. Imperceptible to normal human eyes, of course, but I can see it. "I have an aunt who lives on Quadra Island. There are a ton of orcas around there."

"Nice," Mandy says. "I saw belugas when I was in Nunavut."

"Like in the song?"

She laughs. "Yeah. Remember when we sang that at the base?"

I can't help but laugh too. It's a nice memory. One of the few I've made in the past two years.

We stare at the stars for a long while, the forest around us quiet but for the Nahx and their buzzy breathing. A thin cloud wisps across the sky as Mandy breaks the silence.

"This thing that's coming, this fissure or whatever it is, I don't think it's just a threat to humans. Or Nahx. Or us."

Ah. Not a non sequitur after all. Mandy was planning to be a nurse, but I think she would have made a good shrink.

"No. In my visions it tore everything apart. Like, even at a molecular level. If that's what it is, how can we fight that?"

"I don't know," Mandy says. "It might not be that. Maybe it's like . . . dreaming. Maybe that's just how our minds interpret something we can't understand."

"I don't see how that's better."

"No. Me neither. But this is worth saving, don't you think?"

She waves her hand around at the trees, the sky and stars, the Nahx and the boys. "All this?"

I take a cleansing breath of the cold night air. "It is worth trying to save. I don't know what chance we have. But yes, it's definitely worth it."

I flick my eyes back to August and wish that I could curl up and sleep beside him too, warmed by him, guarded by his shadow. He is worth saving above all, at least to me, even if his feelings for me have changed.

Sky rouses the boys at the first sign of light on the eastern horizon. We pack up in total silence in the near dark, waiting while Topher and Xander bundle into a few extra layers of clothing. It's dangerously cold, and even though I know the cold won't harm me, it's annoying—just another thing to think about.

August and Aurora stay close to them as we approach the summit, the morning sun now shining on our backs. We lie down in the snow, passing binoculars along the line so we can get an idea of what we're up against.

The dam is still at least a mile away, but luckily, though the day is clear, there's enough tree cover to enable us to approach stealthily, maybe even not be seen until we are literally breaching the perimeter.

"Will we climb the fence?" Topher asks.

Sky shakes her head. *Human fence. Easy to cut.*

I think she's probably worried that Topher and Xander couldn't make it over, bundled up as they are.

The power station itself is contained within the Nahx web, as is the landing field where the transports are parked. We suspected that would be the case and planned for it, but it is disappointing. If it had turned out we were wrong about that, this whole plan would be easier to pull off.

Single file, we creep along the ridge of the summit until we can disappear under the safety of the trees. There's a rutted track to our south but we keep off it, veering back north along a steeper descent. It's a more difficult path, and Xander and Topher have to be helped down some inclines the rest of us can easily jump, but it's safer. We're less visible. If the Nahx realize we're coming, they could launch a full-scale counter-attack, and that would be the end of our mission.

We approach the dam grounds via the southwest, where the craggy riverbank provides some cover. After we wait in the trees for a few minutes, it becomes clear that the sentries neglect this part of the perimeter.

Sky was right about the fence; it's a surprisingly flimsy chain-link embarrassment that the Nahx and Tucker simply leap right over. Mandy and I wait with the boys while Sky easily unravels the wire enough to create a narrow opening.

"You're not too cold?" Mandy asks. Being made super-human hasn't dulled her motherly instincts.

"No." Xander jumps on the spot, lifting his scarf to cover his nose.

"Tucker says you guys don't feel cold," Topher says.

"We feel it, but it doesn't hurt us. Like, we can't get frost-bite or anything," I say.

"Must be nice."

This is the longest conversation I've had with Topher since we were reunited. Whatever there was between us, before my almost death on the mountain above the base, is so absent now, it's like something from a dream. Or a nightmare.

I pick August out easily from the group of Rogues on the other side of the fence. Not just by the scars on his chest; his posture is different from theirs—both more formal and more human, if that makes sense. When my eyes aren't being drawn to the northeastern sky, they are drawn to him, and I remember the feeling I had when I knew he had come back for me; he was there to rescue me from Topher, and the ice and lies that were growing inside us both like cancer.

Half the changes in my brain aren't from the Nahx venom but from time and wisdom. Tucker and Topher were nothing but trouble for me from the start. I see that now.

When we're inside the fence we split into the teams we set up when our plans were finalized. Topher, Mandy, Ash, and I are going to breach the dam facility via the lower portal and disable the turbines at the head of the tailrace. This all means something to Topher, who was always a bit of an engineering nerd—a quality I used to find annoying, but annoying qualities so often turn out to be useful; that's another thing I've learned. The lower portal and tailrace tunnel are outside the web—that's what matters—and once the turbines are disabled, the web should lose power.

August and some of the other Rogues are going to commandeer a transport so we can make a hasty exit when the shit hits the fan.

And that proverbial shit hitting that proverbial fan is going to be Tucker, Xander, and the rest of the Rogues planting Topher's grenades in the transformers of the power station. The Nahx could repair the turbines fairly easily, but rebuilding an entire power station would take time. And in that time, we're hoping the outside world can launch a rescue mission for the humans left inside the occupation zone.

I don't like to hang anything on hope anymore, but at least Topher and Xander could get out.

When the power station goes up in smoke, we'll have mere minutes before the Nahx around the dam get very, very mad.

Sky has explained that it would be some time before any reinforcements arrive, if at all. Nahx are trained to be self-reliant, whether singly, in the pairs, or in platoons like the one guarding the dam. There is very little communication with a centralized command beyond what she called "repeat mind rules." Xander translated that as "mission directives," and that seemed to fit. Apparently they are fed into Nahx consciousness via a transponder in their armor. All the Rogues, including August, disabled their transponders long ago. But the Nahx on the dam will be operating on mission directives to protect the dam, along with the directives all Nahx have, which is to dart humans on sight.

Sky has made protecting Topher and Xander a top priority. She reiterates this in sharp signs as she does one last check of everyone's weapons. I notice that August stands completely still, staring at the human pistol in each of his hands, before Sky chooses for him, taking one pistol away so he can holster the remaining one.

She promised me she would stay with him and keep him safe, but part of me wants to grab his hand and drag him away from here, away from this. How many more times will we two have to endure finding each other only to face losing each other? Will it ever end? Maybe that's why August has been ignoring me. I *hope* that's why.

His team heads off first, and as I watch them disappearing into the trees, August does turn back to me, signing quickly.

Stay safe, Dandelion.

Repeat you, I sign. *Safe repeat forever.*

I don't know how three words can change a whole outlook, but they do.

"What are you smiling about?" Mandy asks.

"Nothing."

I turn away. I've never liked watching people leave, and with August . . . well . . . his leaving me usually presages catastrophe, so I'm reluctant to bear witness to it. Under a snow-drooping tree, Topher and Xander are talking in low tones. I try not to listen, but with my improved hearing it's hard not to.

"I can't go through that again," Topher says.

"He's practically indestructible, Toph. It'll be fine."

"I know, but you know how he is. So . . . reckless."

I flick my eyes around to try to locate their subject, and sure enough, Tucker is halfway up a nearby tree, scanning the dam through binoculars.

When I turn back, Topher and Xander are kissing.

Kissing. Like, *really* kissing. Topher tugs one glove off and tenderly lays his hand on Xander's face as they part, and I barely believe I'm looking at the Topher I know and not some hero of a swoony romantic novel. Every time he ever touched my face like that, it was about as tender as being slapped by a frozen fish fillet. They press their foreheads together and he whispers something I can't hear through the blood rushing in my ears.

When Tucker jumps down from the tree, Xander follows him back up into the dense forest with Aurora, Sol, and Luna behind them. I know their packs are sagging with Topher's grenades. They'll lie in wait until the web surrounding the power transformers comes down, and then they'll blow them up.

Easy, right?

Topher's cheeks are bright red when he joins Mandy and me by the river.

"Well. That certainly explains a few things," I say.

Topher becomes officious again, like he's flicked a switch. "Can we talk about it later?"

"Or never, maybe."

"Play nice, children," Mandy says.

Ash, who chose not to replace his damaged helmet, rolls his one visible eye at me. Easy for him; he's only in a love triangle. I've lost track of what shape we're up to in my life now. Is it a pentagram?

We clamber down the riverbank to the winding path up to the dam's lower portal. Ash takes the lead. Mandy and Topher walk side by side. I walk behind them and look at Topher's feet and think about Tucker and think about August and wonder if I shouldn't just throw myself into the river to make things simpler.

It's not that complicated in the end. I have to go back to the dunes with Tucker and Mandy, and August can't follow me because the low elevation would kill him. Topher and

Xander will head out to the coast if things go as we planned.

Ash calls us to a halt with a raised fist, taking two steps backward until he's pressed us against the rocky face of the riverbank.

One guard, he says.

Let us go, I answer in signs, indicating myself and Mandy. *Nahx aren't permitted to harm Snowflakes.*

Topher remains silent but nods his agreement.

Mandy and I draw our weapons and march down the path to where it curves. There are three steps up to a long concrete platform and, down at the end, one Nahx standing guard by a very unassuming metal door. As we approach, the Nahx doesn't move, and I wonder if he's even awake. Maybe he's dormant, like August was. There's even some snow accumulation on his shoulders. But when we're about ten yards away he suddenly springs to life, sweeping his rifle from his back and firing it. I watch the Nahx dart sailing toward me with mild interest, as though it's traveling in slow motion, and easily pluck it out of the air before tossing it into the river.

The Nahx fires another, which we both dodge, letting it lodge in the stone retaining wall behind us.

"Those darts don't do anything to us," Mandy says. "Stand down."

The Nahx lets his rifle fall and, in the same motion, unholsters his knife. Mandy and I have rifles, but bullets sometimes don't even slow Nahx down, and though he probably couldn't kill either of us, we don't have time to recover from any possible injuries either. I take a step toward him, speaking as firmly as I can, trying not to be distracted by a squirrel or something scrabbling in the trees above us.

"Stand down. You have orders not to harm us."

Human, he says, then changes the sign slightly. *Vermin.*

"He doesn't know what we are," Mandy says.

"We are not humans. We are sentinels. Snowflakes. *Snezjinka.*"

He hesitates, his head tilting slightly, but that's enough time for the source of the noise in the trees to make itself known. In a flash of metal and snow, Ash falls on the Nahx guard, sending him crashing to the concrete. The knife flies out of his hand and slides down the riverbank.

"Ash, no!" Mandy yells as Ash pins the guard down, twisting his head with both hands and one knee. There's a sickening crack, and the guard falls limp. Ash leaps to his feet and shoves the body over the edge of the platform and into the river below. I watch, struck dumb, as it sinks like a stone in the frosty water. There's a gleam in Ash's eye when he looks back at us.

Topher slides down out of the forest a few seconds later.

"That was noisy," he says. "We should get moving."

Noisy? My mind is screaming at me, wondering why these boys find killing so unremarkable.

Ash kicks the door in before I can stop him; the tear and crash of metal rings across the river loud enough to make the trees shake. Inside the door we enter a narrow, dark corridor, but the noise of the tailrace is easy enough to follow. It rushes and rumbles evenly in a low thrum, like a bath being filled. After a few twists and turns the corridor opens onto the brightly lit tailrace chamber, an endlessly long concrete-and-steel tunnel with a river channel churning with water in its center. The air is full of cool spray, the walls slick with condensation.

"There could be more guards in here," Mandy says. "So keep an eye out."

It doesn't take long for Mandy's prediction to come true. Another Nahx appears, approaching from the far end of the tunnel and on the other side of the river's flow. This one is a female, and she's mad as hell. She barrels toward us, her boots clanging on the hard floor.

"Stay on this side!" I say. There's a catwalk across the river, but I don't relish the idea of being stuck on the other side with a furious Nahx. But catwalk or no, she's out to get us. With a graceful leap she's over the rushing water, landing hard a hundred feet ahead of us, making the whole tunnel vibrate. Her rifle whines, and I have to dive to pluck another dart out of the air before it hits Topher.

"Cover him!" I shout. Ash is already charging at the female.

I follow him as Mandy rolls on top of Topher, shoving him against the tunnel wall. The female turns and runs to the catwalk, slinging her rifle back as she grabs the metal railings and pulls.

"No!" The catwalk is the only way across the water, the only way to reach the turbine assembly at the end of the tunnel. I raise my rifle and fire round after round as I rush the Nahx. The bullets bounce off her armor plates and ping around the tunnel, ricocheting off concrete and steel. With an animalistic growl she tears the catwalk from its moorings and flings it down into the river, where it is borne away by the current. Ash dives for her before she can raise her dart rifle again. They slide along the concrete, flailing at each other, until finally they tumble down over the edge of the tailrace trench and into the water.

"Ash!" All I can see are limbs occasionally surfacing in the froth as I chase them back down the tunnel. "Ash!"

Where the water exits the tunnel into the river is a large grate, probably used to catch any debris. The remains of the catwalk are mashed up against it, water churning over the bent metal. There's a loud clang and the mangled catwalk rattles, and suddenly Ash and the female Nahx surface, her hands tightly wrapped around Ash's throat. Before I can raise my rifle there's a loud pop by my right ear, and the female's head flicks back, black fluid spraying out of her neck.

POP. POP. POP.

Topher holds his pistol out straight and steady, pulling on the trigger over and over, until finally the female loosens her grip and goes slack. Ash shoves her body away and, hoisting himself out of the water by a railing above the grate, kicks at it until part of it gives way. The mangled catwalk and the dead Nahx slip through the gap and are washed out into the river.

"Are you okay?" I ask as Ash clambers across the grate.

Cross here, he signs with one hand. *On this rail.*

We clamber across in silence, trying to stay clear of the burbling water.

Topher checks the clip on his pistol as we hurry up the other platform to the turbine.

"Are you all right?" I ask him. His face is as white as the foam on the river.

"Fine," he says through clenched teeth.

Ash and Mandy have reached the turbine assembly chamber. Ash gets to work on the bolted gate as Topher and I catch up with them.

"I'm not bothered about you and Xander," I try. "I was just a bit surprised."

He reholsters his gun, tossing the empty clip into the water. "I don't care if you're bothered," he says, his voice cold.

I have to keep reminding myself that half my friends have lived a virtual lifetime since I saw them last. For me it's only been a week or so, but Topher has been hiding and starving and freezing for months. And he sees me as one of the Nahx now, I suppose. And probably still blames me for everything too, including turning his brother into a monster.

Ash deals with the locks on the gate to the machinery surprisingly delicately. Three padlocks clink to the floor and we're inside, with the turbines roaring around us.

"We need to be fast!" Mandy shouts over the noise.

Topher examines the complicated tangle of cables and valves, shining his flashlight into the machinery. "Ideally we would destroy the turbines!"

"Why don't we?"

"That could cause the dam itself to fail! And if we block the flow, the reservoir could breach! If there are any survivors downstream, they'd be washed away!"

"So what do we do, then?" My ears are picking out individual noises in the thunderous rumble—the whine of the turbines, the clanking of pistons, the whoosh of the rushing river, even the hum of electricity. It's perfectly parsed in my mind, almost musical, and hearing it in such detail gives me insight into how the dam works and what we need to do.

"Cut the cables to the power inverter!" I say. Topher turns back, looking as surprised as I feel. He even smiles a little.

"And?" he says.

"And the turbines will keep generating power, but it won't

go anywhere. Once the backup battery wears out, the power station will shut down."

A grade-nine science unit on electricity and hydropower. I remember it in precise detail, including the fact that I got a C on the quiz because I barely slept the night before.

Topher shines his flashlight up the wall and to the ceiling of the tunnel, where a huge bundle of cables disappears up a dark shaft. Following the cables back, we can see that they originated at the top of the assembly above the turbines.

"Ash, can you get up there and pull them out?"

He doesn't bother answering before leaping easily up to the top of the machinery and across it until he reaches the cables. They pop out with a bit of force, each one connected to the machine by a heavy, multipronged plug. There are dozens of them in the bundle, though, and Ash has to tug them out one by one. After the tenth cable comes out, the tunnel is suddenly plunged into darkness.

"Fuck," Topher says. "That one must be a direct circuit."

"What does that mean?" Mandy asks.

"It means other things in the station might be powered directly from the turbines," I say. "Which means that the Nahx might know we're here."

Topher nervously shines his flashlight back down the tunnel.

"Ash!" I shout over the machinery. "Hurry up!"

He swings down from the ceiling just as I spot some movement at the other end of the tunnel.

"Shit!" Topher says.

Four Nahx barrel up the tunnel.

Quick, Ash signs. *Up there. Up the cables.*

He hoists Topher up to the access ladder before he can protest. We clamber up behind him, diving over the rumbling turbines to the cable outlet by the back of the tunnel wall. Above us in the ceiling is a narrow shaft, and another access ladder snakes up into the dark along with the now dead cables.

Up, Ash says. *I will stop them.*

"Stop" in Nahx signs is very similar to "kill," but I suppose right now it doesn't really matter which it is.

We don't have time to argue. Mandy scrambles up the ladder first.

"Topher, you follow me. Raven, if he can't keep up—carry him!" She leaps up the ladder, taking the rungs two at a time. The flashlight clenched in Topher's teeth is our only light apart from Ash's lights, which swing across the shaft entrance below us. I can't hear anything over the rumble of the turbines, but now there are multiple lights flashing in the tunnel, and faintly I can feel things vibrating. Then something happens to the steady noise of the rushing water. It changes briefly, as though . . .

"Ash!" I yell back down the shaft. "ASH!"

The flashing lights have stopped. The rushing water has returned to normal.

"Ash?!"

We wait there in the shaft, frozen, the darkness pressing down on us, but nothing happens. The Nahx appear to be gone.

But Ash is gone too.

S o. You and Topher are an item," Tucker says. He's perched halfway up a tree, a pair of Nahx binoculars slung around his neck.

"Keep your voice down," I whisper.

He licks his lips and lifts the binoculars, gazing out at the dam.

"That wasn't an answer," he says after a moment.

I don't know how to answer him. I could tell him a long story or a short story or only part of the story, but whichever way I choose, it will be hard to gloss over the part where Topher and Raven were involved when they thought Tucker was dead. That's incredibly awkward.

"I figured he had a thing for you," he says unexpectedly.

"You did? Why didn't you tell me?"

"I prefer to keep the attention on myself." I can never tell if Tucker is being ironic. If he's not, this is about the most self-reflective thing he's ever said.

I try to rub some feeling back into my face. Aurora, who is lingering by me like a giant shadow, reaches over and pinches my nose with her warm, armored fingers. I wriggle away from her after a second and look back up to Tucker, who has broken an icicle off the tree and is sucking it suggestively, waggling his eyebrows at me.

So much for self-reflection.

"I thought you were into Raven," he says.

I was, in truth; briefly, anyway. But there's no way I'd tell Tucker that. Not now. I try to scoff convincingly.

"You tried to grab her ass that time, remember?" he says, undeterred.

"And she nearly killed me? Yes, I remember. I only did it because you dared me to."

Aurora turns to me and, if it wasn't for her mask, I'd be sure she was glaring disapprovingly.

"Oh yeah." Tucker chuckles. "That was funny."

My face is plenty warm now. I turn away from Aurora to find Luna also probably glaring at me, signing something I easily translate.

I don't think Raven found it funny.

"No. You're right," I mutter. I suddenly want to punch Tucker in the face. Why was I so eager to impress him back then? I cross my arms and try to burrow into my coat a bit, to stay warm and to hide. I can't remember now why Topher and I ended up on different teams on this suicide mission. And I'm about to get really annoyed with the person who dreamed it up until I remember it was me.

"Topher's coming with me when we finish here. Back up north," Tucker says. Now it's almost like he's trying to piss me off.

I slam my hand against the tree, making snow drift down from the branches. "He is NOT!"

Tucker shrugs, unmoved by my outrage. "You can come too."

"That's not . . . you're crazy. That's not our problem. Let the Nahx fight their own battles." Behind me, Aurora lets out a low hiss, but I ignore her.

"You don't know what you're talking about, Xander. It's everyone's problem. Believe me."

"Topher is still human, Tuck. He can't fight an extraterrestrial battle with you."

Tucker slings the binoculars over his shoulder and shimmies farther up the tree. It takes a few minutes for him to get comfortable in his new perch as I watch, waiting for him say something.

"Topher won't let me go!" he finally shouts down. "Not without him!"

Aurora hisses loudly this time, clapping her hands together.

"Be quiet, Tuck." I say it at normal volume and know he heard when he makes a face at me. "Just because you can't be killed doesn't mean I can't."

It's obvious this is a stupid time to be discussing this,

and it's just like Tucker to start something that can't be finished. I tap the tree again, and when he looks I mime holding the binoculars. He unhooks them from his neck and drops them down through the branches. I have to dive, but I catch them.

Creeping forward, I stay low to check on the power station itself. Not only is it enclosed within the web but it's also contained by a tall razor-wire-topped fence that crackles with high-voltage electricity. We're hoping that one or both of them will go down once Raven and the rest disable the generator, but so far nothing has changed.

Inside the fence and the drone web, patrolling the power station on foot, are two Nahx guards. I've noted that they are armed with ordinary Nahx dart rifles, which means any incursions they anticipate would be from humans. That gives us the element of surprise, at least, since we have Sol, Luna, and Aurora with us, and Tucker, whatever he is. The darts in the rifles are for me, basically. I need to keep that in mind.

I'm trying to focus on our specific goal, getting into the power station and getting the explosives planted, but all I can think about is what Topher is doing at the generator site and whether he'll get out of that alive.

Why did I agree to be on this team? I should have gone with him.

I jump when I feel a hand on my shoulder.

Me, Aurora signs when I spin around. *Friend.*

"What's going on?"

Zero. Good you?

"Is Tucker still up the tree?"

She nods.

I watch the Nahx guards in the distance. They march back and forth along the fence like robots, never stopping or slowing or acknowledging each other. I know there are living, thinking beings inside the armor, but it's hard to remember that sometimes.

Aurora draws my attention with another light touch.

Are you frightened? she signs.

"No. Yes."

She flicks her head. *I'll keep you safe.*

I look back at the Nahx sentries coldly marching and wonder what it took for Aurora to escape that. Was it Nova? Maybe it was a mistake for the makers of the Nahx, whoever they are, to make them so devoted to their partners. Maybe it made them irrational and prone to impulsivity and rebellion.

I shake my head. I've got to stop thinking like a poet and go back to thinking like a soldier.

Aurora hoists me up and we creep back to the others as quietly as we can, but just as we arrive there's a commotion above us as Tucker untangles himself from the branches.

"Topher!" he shouts. He swings down a few feet, then dives

headfirst out of the tree. He flips in the air at the last minute and lands gracefully in a patch of snow.

"Dude, be quiet!" I snap.

He grins at me and stomps off toward the fence. I catch up to him just as Topher, Raven, and Mandy appear, popping up through a manhole *inside* the power station.

"Oh f . . . That's not good."

I scan the station for the sentry guards, who are just rounding the corner and will see us in seconds.

Raven spots us first and, with wild recognition dawning, seems to realize where they are. I have no earthly idea how they got to that manhole, but it has just screwed everything up.

"TOPHER!" I yell it impulsively. He turns toward me just as Mandy dives down on him, sliding him across the ice until they both tumble back down through the manhole. Raven spins and kicks the manhole cover precisely, and it clanks back into place just as the Nahx guards come into full view.

They raise their rifles and fire without a second's hesitation. Raven dodges two darts easily, but a third slams into her shoulder. She tears it out, furious.

"Stand down! I'm a sentinel! You are not permitted to harm me!"

The Nahx don't seem to care. They shoulder their weapons and break into a run, wielding their knives.

"Stand down, goddamn it! We're on the same side!"

Suddenly Tucker is flying through the air. There's a blinding flash as he breaches the drone web and clears the electric fence easily.

The hovering drones converge on his exit point and arc out like lightning bolts, remaining connected to the web with thin filaments of electricity. The stream of light targets Tucker as he runs for the charging Nahx. I raise my rifle and fire at the Nahx, right through the web, because it's all I can think to do. I'm only vaguely aware that Aurora, Sol, and Luna are beside me as we bolt down the perimeter of the web, trying to get a better vantage point.

The arcs of light home in on Tucker as he dives onto one of the Nahx guards, but at the last second he rolls away and the bolt of light cracks into the Nahx, sending him flying through the air. Another bolt curves back toward Tucker. He swings at it with his rifle, and the force of the charge shoots the rifle right out of his hand, sending it spinning away.

"Tucker!" Raven yells. The other guard leaps at him. Tucker curls into a ball, letting the Nahx press him down into the snow as the drone bolt zeroes in.

There's another blinding flash and the bolt lights up the Nahx like a firework, sparks flying everywhere.

Everything stops. The low hum of the power station and the web sputters and wanes before surging. The arcs of light crackle, flailing around as though confused, and suddenly flare out, drifting slowly to the ground like dying embers. There's a loud thump and the drone web begins to snuff out, grid by grid, around the power station and back along the reservoir. I pray the whole thing comes down like we hoped. The hovering drones, disconnected from the web, drift up and away, shooting across the sky as though they are finally free.

The Nahx on top of Tucker moves. I train my rifle on it but it just flops over, seemingly dead, as Tucker shoves it off.

"Tuck!" Raven rushes toward him, pulling him upright.

The Rogues and I run back along the fence to the gate, which Sol tears open easily. Tucker grins up at me as I stomp toward him.

"You jumped over without the explosives, you tool!"

"I was trying to save my brother!"

"Oh my God, Tucker. Can you try to stop being so impulsive? Just for the rest of the day before you get us all killed?"

Raven levers the manhole cover open with her knife. "You can come out now."

Mandy and Topher pop their heads up. I reach down and hoist Topher out, letting his momentum propel him into me. We wrap our arms around each other and linger there, breathing, letting silence blanket us for a few precious seconds. We made it this far. We can do this. We can get out of here.

After a moment, Tucker leaps on us, shaking us with excitement.

"Did you see that? The drones nearly roasted me!" He seems pretty happy for someone who so narrowly escaped death.

"Explosives!" Raven says sharply. "We don't have much time. Xander, come with me. Topher and Tucker, you take the transformers to the south. Mandy, go with the Rogues back to the gate. Kill anyone who tries to get in."

I'm not sure when Raven took charge, but her orders make sense, so I don't see the point of challenging her right now.

"Where's Ash?" I ask as we hurry around the station to the giant transformer units along the north fence.

Raven presses her lips together. "He . . . I don't know. I think he's probably dead. He saved our lives."

I can't think of anything to say. Raven and I have been through this before—an absolute clusterfuck of a mission where people we relied on didn't make it out alive. We both know no amount of crying about it brings them back. No one knows that better than us.

But Raven did come back. And so did Mandy and Tucker. For all I know, every other person I thought I lost to a Nahx dart has come back too. It's too much to process.

I pull out the grenades when we get to the transformers. Topher came up with a makeshift fuse idea using tightly packed snow under the detonator pin. As the snow melts on the warm transformers it releases the pin, and BOOM.

That's the theory, anyway. It's a stupidly dangerous premise, but what choice do we have?

Raven gathers loose snow with her bare hands, making it into a hard-packed ball.

"So you and Topher were a thing while he and I . . . ?"

"Are we going to discuss this now?" I ask, incredulous.

"We might not have another time."

I tuck the first grenade into the snow under the transformer. We're going to plant them from coolest to warmest in different positions over the six transformers. That will ensure we have time to set them up before the first one's snow fuse melts. Once they're planted we'll run back and pull the pins. We will have to be fast.

"It started when you were in Calgary, with August," I say. "Topher thought you were dead. He was pretty messed up about it."

"So you were brought together by grief?" Her tone is sharp as she slaps the snow into a ball. "Did everyone know but me again?"

"Raven. Don't be like that."

"I don't think I get to choose what I'm like anymore."

She waits as I place the next grenade.

"I just wish . . ." Her voice trails off as I turn back to her. Her face is shining, with sun reflecting off her metallic skin, her blazing eyes. It's not frightening, exactly, but it does feel alien. As though the girl I knew from school and karate and camp has been replaced by an almost convincing machine.

I take a breath. We don't have time to talk about this, but I figure I owe her one moment after everything she's been through. One wish.

"What do you wish?"

"I wish people had been honest with me. Told me about Tucker and Emily. Told me about you and Topher. I feel like everyone was afraid to tell me the truth because they thought I'd lose it and beat them up or something."

"Wouldn't you? You nearly choked me once."

She hands me another grenade with the packed snow fuse.

"Because you tried to grab my ass! Someone tries to grab me, yes, I'll take them out. But if someone tells me something unpleasant or . . . unexpected, why would I hurt them? I feel like you all thought I was some kind of insane monster."

I tuck the last grenade into place, hiding behind the hair that flops over my eyes.

"I'm sorry, Rave, I—"

"Whatever. Now I *am* some kind of insane monster, so it doesn't matter anymore."

She steps back out toward the fence and whistles. "Topher? We're good?"

So much for discretion, I guess.

"All good!" Topher shouts back. "On three! One! Two!"

"Three!" Raven shouts. She sprints past me to the end of the row of transformers, pulling the pin, on the grenades as she doubles back.

"Do the last one!" she yells as she activates the grenade in the transformer next to me.

I reach into the hot coils and yank out the grenade pin.

"Run! Run!" Raven screams.

Topher and Tucker catch up to us by the gate, where Mandy and the Rogues await.

"How are we doing?" I ask as we barrel away from the power station. We have no real way of knowing when the first grenade will detonate, only that we should be as far away as possible when it happens.

"We'll be great if Sky and the rest have managed to get a transport," Mandy says, leaping over a snowbank.

I don't bother asking what happens if they haven't.

The plan was to wait until the first explosion, but when Sky hears yelling, it is time to act. None of the soldiers take much notice of us as we march down from the trees onto the icy landing strip. Sky, Thorn, and Nova have reverted to their hard, stern posture. Despite being lower ranked than me, they are females, so their role is to lead me. It's frightening how easily we fall back into our patterns. There are racks of munitions and other supplies laid out along the ice. We could arm ourselves, resupply the missing bits of our armor and equipment and rejoin these Nahx, and no one would know that we were ever Rogues.

It's not tempting, exactly, but there's something soothing about the idea, as though I could drift off into a kind of trance and never think for myself again. If I did that, the pain and struggle inside me might dissipate too. I might become numb again, and not remember anything from day to day. Not remember . . .

Another vision dances at the edge of my consciousness but I manage to shove it away with something else, something real. Dandelion.

I'm so worried about her, it is like being stabbed in the throat. My breathing tube is contracting in painful spasms, which no amount of concentration seems to stop. I know I'm not fully restored yet. I can't control my limbs without supreme effort. All I can do is fix my eyes on Sky and try to mimic her. This is a survival skill we were trained in. If for some reason our thinking was impaired or we were confused or distressed, we would simply latch onto another, our Offside or a member of our team, and do as they did. It was supposed to be almost automatic, though I was never very good at it and needed to put supreme effort into that as well.

I was never very good at any of this, but I watch the Rogues and the other soldiers around the landing field and try to do as they do.

Thorn has removed the brambly wire from her wrist, and hides her missing hand behind the barrel of her rifle as she walks. If no one looks too closely, we could be mistaken for any other small patrol, rejoining our unit after receiving a revised mission transmission. Sky impersonates a high rank with envy-inducing ease.

The transports are parked along the bank of the reservoir, lined up in rows of two, their cargo ports splayed open. Some of them are being fueled by lines originating at a bulbous black tank higher up the bank. Sky leads us past those to two transports at the head of the line.

Fully fueled, she signs discreetly. *Thorn with me, Nova with Summer King.*

As we split up, I transfer my mimicking effort to Nova, who has a quirk in her mask that makes her breathing chirp and click like a grasshopper. At first it was distracting, but now I focus on it, letting it hypnotize me into becoming her mirror. If I do what she does, I have a smaller chance of screwing this up.

There are three others in the transport Nova and I board. One of them, a high-ranking female, accosts us at the top of the ramp.

Rank? she signs.

Sixth, Nova lies, then points to me. *Eighth.*

Ah, muddy death; that makes my blood run cold.

The high rank hisses, but before she can reprimand us or kick us off her transport, there's a flash of light outside, and seconds later the air around us cracks and roars with the sound of the first explosion.

And then I lock my eyes on Nova, because everything is confusion as six more explosions make the ground shake and I'm standing in the open hatch with a dart rifle in my hands as though I will shoot at any humans I saw, which is the opposite of what the plan is. The high rank and the other two soldiers barrel past us, weapons raised, and by some miracle the high rank spins back and gives us an order.

Hold this position.

That I can do. I can stand perfectly still and never move again. Nova yanks me back into the transport by my neck.

Look at me. Obey, she signs.

Yes. Yes.

Breathe.

I take a breath, feeling the tube expand and release. A burst of numbing fluid washes through me and my focus improves.

The explosions are part of the plan. I can do this. I just need to watch Nova and breathe.

Leave the hatch open, Nova signs. *And hold on.*

I sling my rifle back and grasp a handhold above the hatch. The transport vibrates as it lifts off, blowing snow and ice over me. I have to wipe my mask with my free hand and hang on as Nova banks us away from the chaos below. Across the field I can see another transport lifting off and veering toward us. I lean back to see into the cockpit as Nova flicks switches and dials. Suddenly, over the rumble of the engines, the crackle of radio transmissions buzzes out of the bay speakers.

There are dozens of voices at first, human voices talking over each other, as Nova searches for the right channel.

". . . also deactivated all the way to the south, at least to the hub north of Salt Lake. Fairchild has launched a squa—"

". . . jamming signal has been disabled, too. We are reading multiple distress—"

". . . er jets from Chilliwack. ETA is—"

I don't know what any of that means. I've never heard human radio transmissions before. It gives me a strange feeling. Like somehow we've tuned into a different time, a time before my people destroyed this world.

The radio crackles again, and the human voices are replaced by a series of beeps in various tones. I've never understood this communication code. It is for pilots only, and almost all the pilots are female.

Trust. I make the word with my free hand, trying to rise above the disorientation that threatens to overwhelm me. I need to trust Nova. I need to trust these Rogues, but there is so much betrayal among my kind that the urge to simply jump from the hatch and run off, find Dandelion, and whisk her away into the darkness and shelter of the trees is . . .

The word . . . the word is . . . confusion.

Confusing. Think. I need to think.

I really should not have come.

Nova banks the transport hard, and suddenly we are flying in tandem with another transport whose hull is so close above us that I could nearly reach up and touch it.

Some kind of alarm goes off, ringing out of the cockpit into the hold. Nova drives her fist into the display panel and the blaring alarm stops. Below us, on the surface, some of the soldiers have noticed that what we're doing doesn't seem quite right. They fire at us with the heavy cannon I've seen used against human aircraft. Nova banks again, sharply, and the transport above us suddenly brakes, allowing us to overtake it. I lean out of the hatch and watch them descend like a falling stone until they are nearly on top of the cannon position. I can see Thorn hanging out of the hatch as I am.

Sky spins the transport only a few feet above the ground. Adjusting her pitch upward, she activates the boosters and roasts the cannon and its two Nahx operators in a blazing fireball. The whole position sinks into the lake as the ice melts, and Sky's transport rockets upward, disappearing into the clouds.

I close my eyes, just for a second, and try to blink away the afterimage of the fireball.

Nova dives back down toward the dam. Now I can see the rest of our team running along the crest road, back toward us. We're still too far away for me to pick out who is who, but I can count. Eight running that should be nine. I scan the surroundings for any stragglers, anyone left behind.

Get closer, I sign to Nova when she glances back. She accelerates past the crest and doubles back until we are behind them. Now I can see three of the Rogues running backward behind the humans, firing at the soldiers chasing them.

Eight. Less three. Five. There are five humans. We started with five.

Dandelion made it.

Nova descends until she's practically on top of the thin ice on the west side of the crest. The hovering thrusters blow up clouds of snow and mist until I can barely see, and the turbulence buffets us against the concrete dam.

"August!" I can barely hear Raven's voice over the noise of the wind. "August! Take the boys! Take them!"

Nova slows down so we match the pace at which Raven and the rest are still running. Nudging ahead, she veers to the side until we are across the crest about a hundred feet in front of them. Two Rogues stop and drop to one knee, raising their rifles and firing back at their pursuers. When Mandy and Raven reach us they practically throw Xander through the hatch. I have to step out of the way as he rolls into the hold. Aurora dives in after him. Behind them Tucker pulls Topher along as the Nahx soldiers gain on them.

"Get inside!" Topher yells at Raven, like an idiot. As though we would leave a human behind after all this.

Suddenly another transport is firing on us. Charges hit the water, sending up huge geysers, making the air roar and shriek around us. A massive explosion on the crest sends rock and concrete flying everywhere. Nova steadies the transport as I leap out blindly into the cloud of dust and debris and by memory alone manage to get hands on Mandy and Raven.

"Get Topher!" Raven screams, trying to squirm away from me. I dive back to the transport hatch, dragging them both with me as the dust of the explosion clears.

"Where are they?" someone says. I grab Xander by the coat to stop him jumping out as we take off.

"TOPHER!"

There's a huge gap in the crest of the dam. Ice and water are pouring through it in a torrent, and beyond that the two boys have turned and run straight toward the Nahx soldiers, emptying their guns, screaming like animals. Sol and Luna are nowhere to be seen.

"Nova!" I realize I've been holding on to Raven's wrist this whole time. She shoves me away when I let her go. "Get between them!"

Nova banks us hard, sending Xander rolling away from the hatch and into the ammunitions rack. Darts and rifles and other supplies crash down and slide across the floor.

"Strap him in!" Raven yells. She and Mandy take positions by the hatch while I do something useful for a change and yank Xander to the back of the hold. There are no safety straps of any kind on transports, so I snatch a set of wrist restraints from the pile of tumbled equipment on the floor.

"You are not—" Xander tries to protest, but before he has finished his sentence he's cuffed to the rifle rack and yelling obscenities at me. I stumble back to the hatch just as Nova brings us down on top of the crest again. There's another blinding explosion and the dam dissolves under and around us until we're hovering over a rushing river. The boys keep running, and at the last second Tucker grabs his twin around the waist and jumps.

"No!" Raven screams. Before I can stop her she launches herself out through the hatch. I feel my limbs seize up for as long as it takes to see that she is attached to the transport by a winching cable. Then I'm able to move. I slide down on my knees, hooking one hand to a grip by the hatch, scooping up the cable with the other. Leaning out of the hatch, I can see Raven hanging below, holding on to one of the twins by his wrist. The other one hangs below that, perilously close to the churning torrent of the escaping lake.

Raven looks up at me and for just an instant she grins, as if this is all part of some grand adventure. And as much as I'd like to live in this moment forever, repeat forever, my shoulders feel like they're about to pop out of their sockets and everyone behind me is screaming for me to pull them up. I yank on the winch cable and Raven and the twins come flying up toward me, limbs flailing.

"Give me your hand!" Mandy yells. The formless shouting from the back of the hold takes shape at last.

"Do you have Topher?!" Xander has slid across toward the hatch as far as he can, vainly stretching out the restraints. "Do you have him? Aurora? Is he there?!"

Aurora reaches down and grabs Topher by the ankle, flinging him back into the hold. Raven crashes right into me, and Tucker rolls on top of us, sending us splaying in a heap on the floor. Above us Mandy shouts her head count.

"Raven, Topher, Tucker, Xander, Aurora, Nova, August!"

There's another explosion somewhere. The transport rocks violently.

"Get us out of here!" Raven yells. "Everyone hang on!"

Nova steers us straight upward, the rapid change of pressure making the breathing tube inflate in my sinuses. My ears pop. Raven untangles from me and leaps to her feet, steadying herself as we careen into the clouds.

"Where are Sol and Luna?" she says, spinning around.

There's a beat, a break in time that empties like a broken blood vessel.

"They didn't make it," one of the twins says. The fully human one. Topher. "They were right under the first explosion."

I fix my eyes on Nova because I suddenly forget a whole set of words again. I didn't know Sol and Luna very well. It was

hard to talk to the Rogues. They used words I didn't understand and talked so fast, and I can't even think of the word.
Stopped? It's like stopped.

Dead? I finally manage when the word comes to me. It's an
obvious one.

"Yes."

"August, are you okay?" Raven asks.

Yes.

Where are Sky and Thorn? Aurora asks.

Yes. Wait. I search for the words. *They took another transport.*

Aurora joins Nova in the cockpit, signing quickly. I turn
away because I don't want to see what they are saying about
me.

"August?" Raven reaches for me. "You're shaking."

I'm good. Don't worry. But she takes my hand. Behind her,
the others are distracted with the humans. Topher's nose is
bleeding and he's yelling at his brother to leave him alone,
and Xander is complaining about still being shackled to the
weapons locker, and Mandy is shouting at them to shut up. I
look down as Raven gives me a small smile.

"Too many humans?" she says.

One is a good number, I say, but I'm not sure she understands.

A dark shadow crosses the open hatch. Instinctively I
mash Raven to the floor, covering her, but when I look up I

can see Thorn standing in the open hatch of the other transport, waving, flicking her head back like she's laughing at me.

"Get off," Raven says, shoving me again. She raises her hand to wave back at Thorn.

There's a flash of light, an earsplitting screech, and the other transport suddenly explodes in a fireball.

"NO!" someone screams.

"What was that?!"

Raven and I are on the other side of the hold, her pressed against the wall behind my back.

"Nova, get us out of here!"

"What is it?!" Topher yells.

Mandy has staggered into the cockpit. Over the noise and the ringing in my ears I can barely hear what they're saying. I watch Nova and Aurora instead as they sign quickly, frantically.

Humans. Firing on us.

Through the hatch in the distance I see a human jet shoot past.

"Dive down, Nova!" Topher shouts. "That's a Hornet! They can't maneuver for shit at low altitudes!"

Nova dives, sending us all sprawling again and trying not to roll out of the hatch. I manage to get my hand on the emergency lock button and the heavy blast panel comes down, plunging the hold into darkness, the only light now from the narrow window in the cockpit. After a moment I flick on one of my shoulder lights.

"August, you're crushing me."

Somehow I still have Raven tightly clasped in one arm. I release her and she stumbles into the cockpit just as an alarm starts blaring.

"What's that?"

I've lost track of who is talking. That might have been Tucker.

"It's locked on to us!"

"What has?"

"A fucking air-to-air missile!" Raven screams back from the cockpit. "Jesus Christ, why can't this day be over?"

The pitch of the transport suddenly tilts and we dive so fast that the change in pressure fills my nose and throat with fluid. I can feel my breathing apparatus trying to suck it away, my armor trying to adjust the pressure in my lungs and blood so I don't pop like a bubble of snot. My head throbs with pain and my armor washes my insides with something numbing that makes me lose my senses. Dimly, I see someone straining up in the cockpit to pull a lever. There's a loud hiss and the pressure stabilizes. The pain in my head dissipates mercifully, though I'm still trying to cough away the fluid in my throat. I can see Nova and Aurora also convulsing as they try to control the transport's steep dive.

"Nova!" Raven screams.

"Whoa, is that a good idea? Oh shit. Hold on to something!"

I dive down and gather the twins into my arms, sliding across the floor to where Xander is still shackled to the gun locker.

"BRACE FOR IMPACT!"

We hit something, hard. The sounds of the engines change, becoming muffled. Then there's a low rumble coming from above us and we're slowly shaken as though by rolling . . .

Water, I sign.

"We're under*water*?" Xander says. "Now you need to unhook me, dude. You really do. I don't want to drown in here."

I press my thumb onto the latch sensor of the shackles and they snap open.

The transport rocks gently as we crowd into the cockpit. Outside the window everything is a dark greenish gray, with sediment and small things floating around us. Nova flicks something on a screen and it lights up with a radar image of the surface above us. The remains of the missile show up as a ripple on the water, the single fighter jet a distant spot circling around as we all hold our breath. Finally, after descending and doing a slow loop around the reservoir, the fighter peels off eastward and disappears from the scope.

"It was probably a scout," a twin says. I turn to look properly at him. It's the human one. Topher. "They would have been permanently scrambled to take out the power station as soon as the web came down. A single pilot with a full load would have been plenty. If they knew, that is."

"They obviously knew," Tucker says. "What about the other Nahx transports?"

Sky took them out, Nova signs. Raven translates and we all breathe in and out together as though from relief and recognition that Sky and Thorn just died on a mission they could have very well refused. I suddenly realize something I hadn't noticed.

Where is Ash?

"He's dead too, I think," Raven says. "We got attacked under the dam and he was washed away."

Nova's fingers just touch the back of my hand. I don't know if I can even grieve for any of these Rogues. I know they helped me, but I don't feel like I'm one of them, or one of anything, really. And yet when Nova's clicky breathing catches softly and she reaches for Aurora, I think I must still be mirroring her because my own hand rises up to rest on Raven's shoulder.

"Uh, Nova?" Xander says, turning back toward the hold. "Nova? This isn't good."

Murky water is pouring out of the floor vents.

Nova spins back to the control panel, throwing switches and levers so fast, her hands blur. The transport engines gurgle and rumble, and more water sloshes in.

"I don't think these are amphibious," someone says, unhelpfully.

The transport tilts, sending us sliding back into the hold, now up to our knees in water.

Lift? I say to Raven, but she waves me away.

"I'm fine."

The transport banks to the side, creating a wave that soaks Topher and Xander up to the shoulders. I pull them up until they can grab on to handholds above the hatch and hang there, the water still swirling around their feet.

"Nova, can you get us out of this?" Topher says.

Wait, wait, she signs without turning back.

Finally we seem to move, but the pressure regulator fails at the same moment because my ears suddenly burn as though I'm being stabbed. The transport shakes violently, churning the water into a froth around our feet. After what seems an eternity, the deep dark outside the cockpit window changes to dull green, then glowing pale gray, and finally bright white light as we nose out of the water, lingering there, still gripped by the surface, until finally Aurora smashes her hand down on a switch and the distinct roar of the afterburners rings so loud, my teeth ache.

We limp upward as Nova and Aurora struggle to get the hovering engines engaged enough to keep us airborne.

Open the hatch, Nova signs at me.

I slosh over and activate the hatch control, but of course it doesn't respond. All the console lights are flickering madly and short-circuiting. The manual release is below the hatch and now under thigh-deep water. It's hard to think with my head throbbing and my ears on fire and my breathing tube pulsing and writhing around, but I drop to my knees and dive under the water, feeling around blindly for the access panel.

My armor engages a protocol I've never felt before. I stop breathing and something switches, as though a backup system has engaged, and I feel myself fill up with thick, syrupy dullness, like I could sink to the bottom of the lake and just wait there forever for someone to rescue me. This is a bad design, I manage to think, on a planet with so much water, to shut down like this, but somehow, as though guided by instructions I don't remember anything about, my fingers close on the latch of the access panel.

Above me, through the heaviness of the water and the blood filling my ears, I can hear Raven's voice.

"August? August!"

The panel pops open; a spring function shoots the manual release lever into my hand. The water makes the lever slippery but I yank on it with both hands, and nearly get washed out into the lake when the hatch shoots open and the water cascades out.

Raven is looking down at me when I roll away from the hatch. "Are you okay?"

Perfect, I sign. *Perfect forever.*

The bright sky behind her outlines her head like a gold-and-silver halo as I clamber up onto my knees. Everyone appears to be standing, wet but alive.

"We should get out of here, Nova," Raven says. "We're literally sitting ducks out on the lake like this."

Nova signs back at her too fast for me to understand most of it, but I recognize *engine* and *restart* and *water, repeat water*, so that gives me a fair idea. We hover there, a few feet above the surface, rumbling as the air vents rattle and gurgle and Nova tilts us so the rest of the water can sluice out of the hold.

The engines cough and judder and die.

"Nova?"

We drop down before the reserve hovering thrusters engage, leaving us mere inches above the rippling waves. Nova's hands fly over the controls and finally the engines groan back to life, rumbling and whining loudly, frothing the water beneath us, but over that sound . . .

"What is that?"

A low rhythmic thumping mixes in with the noise of the engines.

"Where's it coming from?"

I lean out of the hatch again and look up. Above us a dark shape descends, silhouetted against the bright blue sky.

The hatch suddenly fills with light and sounds as the electrical systems restart. Nova shoves the throttle forward and we rise, engines still coughing, water pouring out of the chassis and hull. We're badly crippled, and whatever that is above us can see it now.

When I lean out again, a bullet pings off my shoulder.

"Is someone shooting at us now?"

I don't have a sign for "helicopter," but my impression seems to get the picture across when I duck back inside.

"Ah shit!"

Nova manages to veer us up and away until we are level with the helicopter, now about a hundred yards off the open hatch.

"Maybe if they see we're humans—" Mandy steps into view before I can stop her. The force of gunfire sends her flying back into the hold.

"Mandy!"

She lies slumped against the far wall, her chest and neck streaked in silvery blood. "I'm okay," she says, rolling over. "Fuck, that hurt." Aurora drags her back into the cockpit.

The helicopter swerves toward us. Nova struggles with the controls, trying to get the sickly engines to respond. We sway and shake, every system fighting gravity and the inundation of its critical parts.

"Wait," Xander says. "I know that helicopter!"

But I push him back as more gunfire peppers the hull. I smack the emergency lock panel again but nothing happens—only a spray of sparks shooting in my face.

"Nova!" Raven yells. "We can't get the hatch closed! Can you turn us!?"

I flick my eyes back to the helicopter, now slightly above us, because something is not right. There's a flash of light and a crack and a dark blur hurtles toward us. I reach out without thinking, and when I look down, I'm holding it, my hand burning inside my glove.

It's a . . . I don't know the word. It's a human word.

There's another flash and I'm plunged into darkness and Sixth is above me, blurred from the blood in my eyes.

You scared me, Eighth, she signs. And the pain. The pain is so . . .

"Xander!"

I blink back, fighting against the vision, pushing on it until it cracks and shatters like a window.

One of the twins dives onto Xander, flattening them both against the floor. The other twin leaps at me, flying across the hold and wrenching the thing out of my hand. His feet hit the edge of the hatch, and then he's sailing out into the sky and water spray, arcing up as though lifted by invisible wings until he slams into the helicopter gunner, tumbling him backward and out of sight.

A second passes that seems to stretch out forever, and then the helicopter explodes, flames erupting, the air shaking and blurring as though it's about to break open. All I can do is stand there, dumb and immovable, as the shock wave buffets us and we're showered in fire. And metal.

And blood.

PART FIVE

BLOOD

"Heavy misfortunes have befallen us, but let us only cling closer to what remains and transfer our love for those whom we have lost to those who yet live."
—MARY SHELLEY, *FRANKENSTEIN*

My brain spins at a million miles an hour, desperately trying to file away what I just saw, what I know to be true.

Tucker.

That was Tucker. I'm covered in particles of Tucker's blood. The air is full of Tucker's life, his spirit, his body, as though all that's left of him is a wisp of acrid smoke, and screaming. The sound of his brother screaming.

August kneels hunched over by the open hatch, clutching his head with both hands, hissing and choking. He falls forward to rest his elbows on the steel floor. I drop to my knees beside him.

"Are you injured? August?! Are you injured?!"

He shakes his head finally, curling away from me. Topher's formless screaming seems to leave bright flashing lights in my vision that mix with the afterimage of the explosion. I saw everything. My supersonic brain processed every frame like a high-resolution film. Tucker's body flew back and then . . . just seemed to fragment, as though he was being broken down to his component parts, his molecules and atoms. The disembodied voice on the Nahx mother ship comes back to me.

Explosive disintegration is terminal . . .

Tucker has been disintegrated. Disembodied.

He's dead. This time he's really dead.

"God, help me . . ." It comes out as a whimper. I don't even believe in God, but I need help. I can't process it. It's too much. I'm in danger of being disembodied myself. I feel as though I might fly apart or dissolve like a cloud or be caught by a gust of wind and scattered.

Like a dandelion.

Only when I feel August's fingers curl around my ankle do I come back, and my thoughts coalesce into something at least partially stable. I put my hand on his head, to steady myself, before turning to take stock of our condition.

Topher is a screaming mess collapsed against the wall, writhing as Xander desperately tries to contain the immensity of his grief and rage. He presses their faces together as Topher claws at him and wails loud enough to wake every sleeping creature under the frozen earth. Mandy is slumped in the cockpit, her silver-bloodied hands clamped over a wound in her belly. But her eyes are bright and alert as she yells back at me.

"I'm okay!"

Aurora is bent over into the cockpit console, pulling wires apart, lights flashing around her, while Nova struggles with the throttle and controls. August is at my feet. I'm in one piece.

At last the clamoring of the engines settles into a healthy roar of steady power and we rise up, away from the ice and water, away from the carnage of the disintegrated helicopter and its dead occupants. Nova steers the transport along the river, skirting around the mountain to avoid the need for more altitude. Even with those precautions, the damaged engines crap out at the edge of the desolate town where we started this mission.

It's not a crash landing, exactly, but when we finally skid to a stop after smashing through the trees for a hundred feet, we're rattled but all still breathing. August leaps through the open hatch without turning back. I half expect him to run off into the forest and never be seen again, but instead he strides down toward the river, and following him, marching to the rhythm of Topher's endless, wrenching sobs, we arrive at the hidden clearing where we left our original transport.

Blue confronts us before we reach it, just as they were instructed, and their buzzing excitement is soon explained when we follow them into the hold and find Ash standing there. He looks regal and proud and a bit damp, but very much alive. He slings his rifles back and signs to us.

What happened?

I find even with my relief about his survival, I can't get my mouth to work. Aurora ushers him on board, signing discreetly. Nova carries Mandy, whose strength is returning slowly. By the time Xander gets Topher aboard and sits him safely in the corner by the weapons racks, Ash has obviously been told about the loss of his two Offsides. He stands just outside the cockpit, staring at the floor, both of his hands on his head. His one visible eye is streaming with silver tears. Between his grief and Topher's anguish, and Xander's distress and Mandy's pain, I don't know what to do or how to help any of them.

Surprisingly, it is August who seems able to console Ash. He faces him, resting his left hand on Ash's right shoulder. After a moment, Ash mirrors his posture and they lean into each other until the tops of their heads are touching. It is somehow so much more intimate than a proper hug that even their breathing is synchronized. They stay like this as Nova lifts us off, and remain there, in silence and stillness, as we journey back to the Rogue settlement.

For my part, I crouch in a dark corner of the hold, trying to let my brain suck away what I saw. But it doesn't work. Tucker's obliteration replays over and over until I feel like my sanity might just drip out of my ears. I press my fists into my eyes, which makes colored lights flash behind my eyelids, but all that accomplishes is to make Tucker's death seem like part of a fireworks display. I didn't realize until right this moment how much I was hanging on him still being alive. Somehow, his life made everything that has happened seem worth it; it made what's *going* to happen seem bearable. Now that's gone, and the only thing left is Topher's endless, crushing grief, now amplified by a few glorious days of having his twin back only to lose him again, permanently this time.

And it's my fault. Everything is my fault again.

When I open my eyes, Blue is floating in front of my face.

"Oh." My throat is so dry, I croak it out. "How was *your* day?"

They just flicker colorfully and drift down to perch on the tip of my nose. I put out my hand and nudge them into my palm.

When I started high school, and the "clever little black girl" image started to morph into a little girl who was too clever for her own good, I went to the first of many perplexed therapists. This one hardly said a word. She just sat there and waited until I got bored enough to open my mouth and spew out random, confused thoughts and feelings. And she listened. And though sometimes the silence seemed like judgment, I remember feeling relaxed after those sessions. Refreshed, almost cleansed. There were things said there that I would never say to Mom or Jack or any of my friends.

"Sometimes I feel like there's a monster inside me," I whisper into my palm. Blue flickers softly but doesn't move. "Or a curse," I continue. "Everything around me gets twisted up. People end up dead."

It's ridiculous to blame myself. I see that now. The only mistake I ever made was letting Tucker and his dreamy eyes get to me.

"I wanted to protect them. But all I did was lead them into shit."

I'm actually relieved, I realize. The first time Tucker "died" he was still attached to me, still anchoring me to this peculiar, mistaken impression of myself. This time, the tether is broken. He's gone. The menace of his misbehavior was never really part of me. *He* was cursed, not me.

"Sometimes I wish I'd never been born."

I don't know why I'm saying the opposite of what I'm thinking. It's as though the two sides of my brain are ignoring each other. Or my new brain is letting my old brain have a few last illogical words before shutting up forever.

"You're a good listener, Blue."

They flicker again, vibrating gently against my skin, as though recognizing that I've finally spoken some truth.

"This thing that has happened to my mind," I whisper. "It's just, like . . . an amplification of what was already there, right? I never could think less than three thoughts at once. It used to drive me up the wall. Now it's like thinking a hundred thoughts at once, but they're lined up like soldiers. Is that by design?"

Blue bobs up and down once. *Yes.*

"Do you think I'll ever get the answers to what is really happening here?"

Their light dims for a second until they almost disappear before flaring back. Then they bob up and down again.

Yes. Yes.

"Oh. Well, good, I guess."

The transport rumbles and dips, and through the open hatch I can see that we are descending into the mountains. The sky has turned a soft, moody lavender, which gives the sleeping trees a purple tinge and makes the deep snow look like cake frosting. As we bank down to the landing plateau, about a dozen Rogues emerge from the surrounding cliffs, somewhat spoiling the impressionistic effect.

August and Ash join them as soon as we land, jumping out the hatch without lowering the ramp. Half the group disappears back into the trees before I've even stood up.

We'll take the human boys to the cabin, Aurora says.

That seems wisest. It's bitterly cold, and Topher and Xander are both showing signs of physical exhaustion on top of their fragile emotional state. They need rest and warmth. Blue and I follow with Mandy, who has recovered enough to walk. She shows me the healing bullet holes in her abdomen and shoulder.

"Does it still hurt?" I ask. I have some experience with the healing process, after all.

"Like Christ," Mandy says. "Burning, cramping pain. Does that go away?"

"Eventually, yes."

Xander puts Topher to bed, bundling him with blankets as Aurora builds a fire in the stove. Topher still hasn't spoken. He probably won't sleep, and as I watch from the doorway while Xander goes in search of food, he turns his back to me. In Topher's mind, the worst thing I ever did was separate him from his twin, first by taking up space as Tucker's girlfriend, then by causing his "death." This time there will be no forgiveness. It's not fair. It's not logical.

Once I thought I might die in front of him to get to the bottom of his emotional repertoire, but I guess that was wrong. It was Tucker who had to die. And now it's clear that we've hit rock bottom. It's over.

When Mandy limps over to join my vigil, I just shake my head at her and walk away, Blue drifting behind me.

"I still can't get used to that," Xander says when I find him in the kitchen, pointing to Blue. He empties canned soup into a pot while I hop up to sit on the table.

"It's kind of rude to talk about someone as 'that.'"

Xander pauses over the soup, and I can tell from looking at him that he has a million possible things to say. I decide to rescue him.

"I suppose you won't have to get used to it. Are you and Topher going to head out soon?"

"Tomorrow, if we can. Aurora doesn't think the Nahx will bother putting the web back up, but I don't want to take the risk. And she says she saw trucks on the roads heading through the pass when we flew over it."

"Heading east? Rescue trucks?"

He shrugs. "You're not going to come with us, are you?"

Blue does a large slow circle in the air, as if to say *Wow, he's pretty clueless.*

"No. Of course not. Mandy and I are going back north."

"To wherever the thing is going to happen?"

I nod. Xander lights a can of Sterno and props the pot of soup above it on a metal stand. These refuge cabins are so well provisioned, it makes me laugh. It's so Canadian. Like a country run by Boy Scouts.

"You still don't know what the thing is?"

"Some kind of battle," I say. "Sky seemed to know about it, but no details."

"August never told you about it?"

"I don't think he knew."

Satisfied that the soup is simmering, he turns back to me. The kitchen is lit only by faint blue twilight seeping in through the window and a row of candles set up on the sill.

But even in the dim light I can see that Xander is barely pushing through a state of mental, if not physical, shock. He's pale, his eyes are twitching back and forth, and his hand, as he sets down the spoon, shakes enough to rattle it against the counter.

"I never thought I'd see him again," he says.

"Tucker?"

"Topher." He shakes his head, laughing a little. "I *knew* I wouldn't see Tucker again. He was dead. Buried. You don't see dead and buried people again."

"No. Do you know how I ended up handcuffed to him on the Athabasca Dunes?"

"Last time I saw you . . . your body, I mean, or whatever. August left you in a hotel room in Jasper. That's where . . ." He waves his hands at my jacket and dress.

"He undressed me and put me in this?"

"Mmm."

"And you were there for that? Watching him undress me?"

"I averted my eyes."

I let that sit there for a few seconds.

"Your clothes stank of death, Rave. I kept suggesting to August that we bury you, but he wouldn't. And it got to the point that I thought he'd kill me if I suggested it again, so I just followed what . . . he wanted to do."

"Which was leave me in a hotel?"

"I thought he meant to come back for you. Didn't he?"

I shrug. "The parts between dying and waking up on the dunes are a bit murky."

"You haven't talked to him about it? August?"

It's an obvious question, and one that doesn't surprise me. I know he's been avoiding me. And I'm pretty sure the reason was blown to smithereens a few hours ago. The guilt about that is difficult to catch and sort away. It keeps flaring up, like the unruly embers of a forest fire.

When I look back at Xander, he's stirring the soup and crying. Not like heaving sobs or anything—in fact, he's quieter than he usually is, and I don't know if it's because he doesn't want me to see or if he's too exhausted for anything more or if this is just how it is. Sometimes quiet crying hurts the most, because it's like everything is packed into a few little tears and it feels like you're crying hydrochloric acid. I could go and put my arm around him, but something tells me not to. It's not a sense of threat, exactly; it's more like I can read Xander's aversion to me, and I don't want to cause him any more stress than I already have.

And that's when I realize that Xander is done with me too. I can tell just by looking at him that he's popping with anxiety, PTSD, lack of sleep, lack of sunlight, lack of food, and all the stuff he started out with. Xander got sent to the principal's office nearly as much as I did. He confessed to me once that he was failing everything but gym.

He's run out of bandwidth. How do you process that all your friends are either dead or have been turned into alien hybrid soldiers? At least he has Topher. If they can just keep each other from falling apart, maybe they'll be okay.

Xander turns back to me with a large mug of soup in each hand.

"I should have told you this, but I guess I didn't know how to say it." He looks at me for a moment before setting his cups down and taking my hands. "Your parents are alive, Rave. They're on Quadra Island."

The sudden rush of joy is so powerful that my cells do their weird thing again, trying to contain the joy as though it is some kind of attack. But all that accomplishes is to spread the feeling around so my skin is happy, my toes are happy, my eyelashes are happy.

"How . . . how do you know?"

"Jack wrote to me. He wants me to go out there to live with them."

I have never loved and hated Xander as much as I do at this moment. He's going to get what I've been searching for this whole time. What I can never have now. But he'll also be there for them. He can watch over them, take care of them. Xander can be flaky sometimes, but if he puts his mind to it, he's a good soldier, a good hunter. And if . . .

"Are you taking Topher with you?"

"Of course."

I let that sit there for a while.

"Keep him away from the battle, Xander," I say when I work up the strength. "Keep him away from anything to do with the Nahx."

Xander nods and picks up his cups of soup.

"You should find August," he says.

"Why?"

He sighs, staring down at the mugs for a few seconds before answering.

"Do you remember that moment when August took his mask off? On the plateau above the base—you know, when we thought you were dying?"

"Yeah. I remember."

He nods thoughtfully. "When you two looked at each other finally, face-to-face? I've never seen anything like that in my life." He doesn't elaborate. "I don't want this to get cold," he says, raising the mugs. "I'll see you later, Raven."

I wait for him to disappear back into the bedroom before venturing out of the kitchen. Following a golden glow outside the cabin, I find Mandy with a large group of Rogues gathered around a bonfire. Most of them are out of their armor, sitting cross-legged and staring into the flames. Nova and Aurora flank Ash, their arms around him. It seems to me that they are mourning in the silent way Nahx can mourn. Ash is not crying anymore, nor are any of the others, but there is a somber, introspective mood. I could join them, I suppose. Tucker is dead too—I have every right to grieve—but looking around the group, I can't see August. He's not an unfeeling person. His abject horror at Tucker's death is evidence enough of that. He's a loner, though. There are so many things still to learn about him, but I know he doesn't like crowds.

Blue drifts away from me. I watch them settle on Mandy's shoulder. It's almost as though they know I need to do this alone.

Skirting the fire, and staying out of sight in case anyone thinks I should be drawn in, I follow the path up into the trees, the one I saw Sky and Ash use when they were coming and going from nursing August back to health.

Finding his tracks is easy enough: large, striding footprints in the fresh snow lead up through the dense trees. I follow them for a long time, settling into a rhythm of my own, letting the silence and darkness lull me. Walking alone at night in a Canadian forest is stupid at the best of times, more so in the winter. There might be wolves up here, even a bear that's gotten bored or hungry in its winter den. And of course it's dark. I could easily step off a cliff.

But I'm not human anymore. As I let my eyes adjust, I can see quite well even though the dark is profound. And I can smell the sleeping wildlife around me, mixed with the smell of the dormant pine trees. There are squirrels in that tree, and an owl, and burrowed under a log . . . something . . . maybe mice? A bear has been by recently but didn't linger. The strongest smell is some kind of livestock or maybe deer, but it smells dead.

Even if there were a threat, I'm pretty sure I could defeat a bear, even a grizzly, as long as it didn't literally bite my head off. The thought of it shimmers along my nerves, and I feel my cells adapt slightly, as though preparing for an extremely unlikely attack. A few paces later, with no threat appearing, I shake it off. This is the first time I've felt this strange effect outside of a situation of real danger, so I can analyze it a bit. But even with a built-in database, I can't quite figure it out. I know it has something to do with the toxin, but I don't know what. How is it working on me? What is it doing?

The trees begin to thin until the ones I pass are gnarled and misshapen and clinging to rocks, eking their existence out of the paltry soil. Then I leave the tree line and gaze up a wide, white expanse, marred only by one set of steady footprints disappearing up into the dark cliffs. Has August decided to climb the mountain tonight? Does he have a cave up there? All I can do is follow.

Distances are distorted by night. Time draws out. It seems that twilight was ages ago now, but nights this time of year are so long. Have I been walking for hours? Or only minutes?

August's tracks continue to draw me on, oblivious to my uncertainty. I plod slowly, placing my feet in his prints.

Eventually the chill wind dies down and something changes. The clouds covering the moon grow heavy, and I sense snow will fall soon. I taste it. I hear it. I feel it in the thin mountain air around me. Turning in a circle, I stretch my arms out and let the feeling permeate through my clothes and into my skin as though to nourish me. When I turn back to the path made by August's footprints, I see I'm no longer alone up here. A dark shadow is trudging back toward me. Though the cold doesn't affect me, a shiver crawls up my spine. I know it's August and I know of course that he would never hurt me, but his presence is so impressive—like all the Nahx, he's so tall and graceful and intimidating that it's hard not to feel a tingle of fear when I see him, even after so much time.

He stops a few feet away, his head tilted to the side.

I heard you, he says. *I came outside because it's going to snow.*

I think I've finally cracked the use of verb tense in Nahx language. It has to do with the direction the signs are aimed in.

He takes a tentative step toward me. *Are you cold?*

"I am, but it's not going to hurt me. My ears are cold."

Think warm, he says.

Maybe my hinting at wanting one of his warm hugs wasn't

obvious enough. I try his suggestion instead and consciously attempt to raise my temperature. It does bump upward a bit, with that familiar shimmer through my cells. I can see this skill being useful.

Yes? August says.

"It worked a little, I think." If I look straight forward, I'm staring at the middle of his abdomen. "How hot can it get?"

He shrugs.

Very hot, he signs. *Very cold.*

"Could I make my body hot enough to melt away? Or cold enough to freeze into ice?" I didn't mean to say this. It just came out, a small part of my emotional state put into words.

August waits a moment before answering, reaching forward to nudge my chin upward so I'm looking into his face.

I don't think you would like it.

I feel stupid for saying it. Maybe this is what August tried to do, more or less: to freeze himself into ice; silent, motionless, unfeeling ice. I think I'm starting to understand why.

A single snowflake falls between us, and we both look up as the air fills with them, falling around us like the ashes of a ruined world. August lets his hand rest on my shoulder and we stay like that, watching the snow, not speaking, for a long time, until the mesmerizing effect of the snow wears off and the nagging awareness of the battle in my future starts to seep back into my consciousness. The chaos of the past few hours pushed it aside temporarily, but it returns, if anything, stronger than ever.

August must sense my change of mood.

Feel broken? he signs. *Explain?*

"I'm just so tired, August."

I'll carry you.

"Not that kind of tired."

He steps back, tilting his head again.

I'll carry you.

Everything is so simple for him. I could argue, but the truth is, I want him to pick me up and carry me, if for no other reason so I can shirk responsibility for a while longer. I smile despite my miserable mood, looking back down at our fading tracks in the snow.

"All right, then."

He steps forward and scoops me up, lifting me under the butt so I'm facing him, our faces level. Tilting his head until our foreheads touch, he turns, trudging back along the way he came, this time with me wrapped around him. After a few minutes we reach a steep, rocky path that, though covered in thick snow, seems to be carved into a staircase. I lay my head on August's shoulder as he climbs it, and he moves one arm from under me to wrap around my back, pulling me close.

We reach another plateau, and there, set neatly into the middle like something out of a storybook, is a tiny cabin. Its windows glow orange and flicker, clearly from a fire inside. As we approach I take in details—stone walls, small sash windows, a heavy wooden door. This cabin is old, probably built nearly a hundred years ago, much older than the bigger one the Rogues have claimed. August sets me down on the stoop, stamping his feet, brushing snow from my shoulders.

You have snowflakes in your hair, he signs, flicking his head back, making some other signs that look a bit like his new sign name, but different.

"Winter Queen?" I laugh. "Is that what you said?"

Yes. Yes. Winter Queen.

I put my hand on the rough-hewn stones of the cabin, feeling their coldness.

"Is this our castle?"

Yes. He sighs, laying his hand on my shoulder again. His other hand pushes the wooden door open.

I feel something I haven't felt in a long time, that kind of thrill of losing control, but in a good way. For so long everything has been chaotic and terrifying and catastrophic, and there has been almost nothing I could do about it. And that's been so awful as to be sickening. But right now, this instant of uncertainty, this step into the unknown, is like an exhilarating leap off a cliff. I have no idea what August is doing up here or what he has in mind. And I don't care.

Dandelion stops just inside the door, looking around the dim hut. I haven't thought much of the furnishings while I've been here, but there are places for her to sit, a bed if she wants to sleep, a table, even food in the packs left by the humans. But both of us wait as the firelight flickers on the stone walls. I'm not sure what to do next.

Pitching all my strength into the effort, I finally unearth a memory of human manners and pull a chair out from the table.

Sit please, I sign.

Dandelion sits, arranging the tattered green dress around her, and unzips her jacket.

Are you hungry? Thirsty?

"I'm not sure I need to eat anymore." Her eyes fall on the fireplace and widen slightly. "You can eat, though, if you want to."

Of course. There is still a half-devoured sheep carcass there by the fire. I'm frozen for a moment, not sure of the . . . word.

Etiquette. It's a pretty word, but not one I would often need.

What is the etiquette in this situation?

I grab what's left of the sheep by its curved horn and drag it out the door.

When I come back in, Dandelion is smiling at me. The dead sheep has left a trail of blood on the floor. Her eyes flick toward the stain.

"It's fine," she says.

She must think I'm some kind of wild animal. This is already not going very well.

I want to take my armor off. Outside.

"Okay."

Outside, in the near dark, I move far away from the cabin so Dandelion can't hear the odd sounds removing my armor makes. The tentacles and tubes resist and pull at my insides as I tug them out of my nose and throat and the valves in my joints. I try not to gag too loudly, vomiting up the excess fluid from my stomach. I'm glad Dandelion agreed to stay inside. I wouldn't want her to see this. The process of taking off my armor has always been painful, but I've never been embarrassed about it before. It suddenly seems so . . . I can't think of the right word.

Washing my hands and face with fresh, fluffy snow soothes my discomfort somewhat. I scrub at my hair, trying to get some of the oily sludge out. It's surprisingly long, my hair. I think more time has passed than I realized.

Carnal. Carnal is the word.

I have no sign for that either. It's the opposite of etiquette, an ugly word that sounds like what it is, like raw wounded flesh.

The sensation of the gray fluid draining out of my mind makes me dizzy. I stop on the path back up to the hut and bend over, taking deep gulps of air and shoving handfuls of snow into my mouth. As the dizziness subsides, the events of the past day return to my thoughts.

What is Raven doing here? Why would she even want to talk to me after what I did? I could run off. These mountains go on forever. She would never find me. But when I look up, she is standing in the doorway, the pale orange firelight behind her.

I step up to the porch and let my armor clatter onto the stones there. We're not supposed to let it out of our sight, but I don't want to take it inside. I don't want her to see the way the tentacles slither around, looking to reconnect to me. It's gross.

"These are quite cool, the suits you wear under your armor," she says as I close the door. "Kind of like motorcycle leathers."

Taking a step toward me, Dandelion reaches out and touches my jacket just below my left shoulder, feeling the slightly raised star-shaped marks the twins left after shooting me with arrows.

"Are these scars? This suit is self-healing or something? Like your armor?"

Yes.

"That's kind of . . . interesting."

I don't want her to take her hand off me, but she does, turning to sit at the table again. I remain standing at first, unsure what to do.

I will clean up the blood, I say, out of desperation more than anything else.

She sighs, giving me a little smile. "It's fine, but okay."

A T-shirt from one of the human packs works as a cleaning cloth. When I'm done, I toss it outside. I know that's not quite right, but it will have to do. Being alone with Dandelion is making it hard to think. I unfasten the top of my suit because I'm getting hot.

She's still so . . . indescribable. Her skin is shining and her eyes are sparkling and the melted snow in her hair is making tiny little curls escape from her braids like puffs of mist. I feel dizzy again, and unpleasant memories scratch at the edge of my vision, threatening to steal me away, to hurl me back in time like . . . I kneel so I don't fall and close my eyes, breathing deeply until the dizziness passes.

"August? Are you okay?"

Good. Forever. Don't worry.

She moves her chair around, her face level with mine. Her

clothes smell of pine needles and campfire smoke and lake water. Under that, a bit like mine, there is a chemical smell like the oily sludge from my armor but more . . . refined, somehow, more pure. And under that she still smells human. Her color is better than mine too, more alive, more natural.

We were mistakes, the Nahx, as the humans call us, poorly designed, flawed and weak in so many ways. But she is perfect and immutable and immortal. Like a girl turned into a goddess. I wish they had done this to me—made me like her instead of what I am.

But I didn't exist before. The few memories I have of being human aren't really mine. I know that now. We were only tools, a step in the process that ended with Dandelion and the others, perfected.

She was always perfect, to me, even as a fragile, wounded little human. An *angry*, wounded little human. I can't help but smile as I remember.

"How did you get this scar on your face?" She reaches forward and traces down from my temple to my top lip.

Hit with a . . .

I still can't think of the word. An exploding thing. Like the one that killed . . . Tucker.

Suddenly I can't look at her. I can't look at anything. I hang my head and squeeze my eyes shut and try to think cold thoughts to put out the fire in my mind and keep Sixth from dragging me back in time again. She's dead.

She's dead. I know she's dead.

Please forgive me.

"There's nothing to forgive. It—"

Dandelion's voice anchors me. *Tucker—*

"That wasn't your fault. Open your eyes, August. Please."

Her face is inches from mine, her eyes bright and serious.

"That wasn't your fault."

I'm sorry for so many things.

"Me too, but it doesn't matter anymore."

I'm sorry I pulled your hair.

"I'm sorry I smashed a vase over your head." Her lips curve up. "I don't think we have time to go through everything we did, so maybe we should just let it go." She touches my face again. "How long can you keep your armor off?"

I shrug. *Sunrise, maybe. Until it becomes hard to breathe.*

Watching her think is like watching the stars moving in the sky as they spell out the mysteries that are so perplexing to us but so easy for them. I look into her eyes and can almost read the constant flow of information behind them. Whatever the dart did to her mind, it's so powerful, I can see it.

"It was Blue . . . creatures like Blue who made you, right? We saw a kind of cloning lab on the ship. That's how you were made?"

Yes. I think so. I don't remember.

"So the Firefly creatures, they came from another planet and used cloned humans to make an army?"

I don't know.

"You haven't been to their planet?"

No.

"But you've been on their ship? Those huge round ships?"

Yes. I don't remember very much.

Without even realizing it, I have lifted my left arm up to put my hand on her shoulder.

"We should have talked about this a long time ago, when we were together in Calgary."

Yes.

"I was too scared of you, I think. Too scared to have a proper conversation."

I would never hurt you.

"I know. I'm not scared of you anymore."

Unexpectedly, that fills me with warmth—not the uncomfortable heat of shame or embarrassment but the opposite, like the warmth of a campfire or sunlight or other things that have never actually happened to me but I remember anyway. Warm drinks, being held by someone, a bed with blankets.

I wish all that was real. It feels wrong to enjoy stolen memories.

"You look tired, August." She looks down at her hands, and the glittering spiderweb on her neck and chest darkens a little against the glossy copper skin behind it. It is as though she is made of precious metal and jewels, like a magical idol brought to life. "I'm tired too, though I think I've forgotten how to sleep."

Sleep on there, I say, pointing to the bed. *I will look at you.*

When she makes a face, I realize what I've said.

Guard you! I clarify, though the signs are very similar. *Keep you safe.*

"Just like old times, huh?"

Yes, I sign, and think how much I would like to revisit those times and live there forever. Not when she was sick; that was terrifying. And not when she was angry or scared, because I was so helpless to change that and it felt awful. But when she was fed and warm and asleep and safe, I became calm enough for the gray sludge to stop swirling around inside me. I could think.

That was when I woke up properly for the first time and started to understand who I was, what my purpose was, and how this happened to me. Little pictures would float into my head and hover there for seconds before popping like bubbles. If I put the pictures together in the right way, it almost makes sense, but it is not a nice story. It is a story of monsters, man-ufactured monsters filled with danger and malice.

"What if you went to sleep and I watched over you?" Dandelion says.

We could sleep together.

She laughs behind her hand. I have to hold my head for a moment to keep the dizziness from rattling my brain. Her laughter puts different pictures in my head.

I didn't mean to say that.

"It's okay. You're right, anyway. It's a big bed. Why don't you lie down and I'll sit next to you and keep watch?"

I don't normally sleep on beds. At least this version of me doesn't. I do remember beds and other normal human things, but they are faded, almost transparent memories, like twilight shadows. I've been sleeping on the floor in front of the fire here in the hut. I don't know why. It seemed wrong to sleep in the bed, but surely, if Dandelion wants to, if she gives her permission, it would be acceptable.

Yes, I sign. *I am tired.*

Dandelion digs in the humans' packs and comes up with some blankets, which she tucks around the bed, while I put more wood into the fire, blowing on it until it blazes up. The bed is too short, but if I curl up on my side, I fit. Dandelion sits cross-legged next to me. We stay like that, quiet, as I listen to her breathing and her steady heartbeat. If I close my eyes, I know I'll be asleep in seconds, but I don't want to leave her yet.

"It's strange," she says after a while. "Seeing you like this, without your armor. I thought it might feel like you were a different person from the one I know, but it doesn't."

I roll back to look at her and to free my hands so I can talk.

I thought you would be a different person too. But you're not.

"I've changed."

Not very much. Not to me.

She strokes my hair, gently untangling it strand by strand. I try to keep my eyes open so I can stay with her, but sleep stalks me like a persistent, hungry wolf and finally takes me.

XANDER

I sleep at last. Topher's trembling got so bad that I pulled him into my lap and cradled him there, buried under blankets that Aurora piled on top of us. One of the other Rogues warmed smooth stones they took from the outdoor fireplace, wrapped them in dish towels, and tucked them around us until it was like sitting in a cramped, private sauna. But Topher settled finally, exhausted by his grief, and while he slept, I must have nodded off too.

I dream of the drone web. It crackles with electricity and my family stands behind it, stepping forward one by one to be vaporized by bolts of lightning. When my sister takes her turn I wake up, looking down at Topher. He's awake too, frowning, his hand on my face.

"Are you okay?" he asks.

I almost feel like laughing, because of course I'm not and neither is he, but laughing about it is probably not the right response either. Instead I bend down and kiss him on the lips.

"Your breath smells," he says. Then he closes his eyes for a few seconds, his body tensing. "It wasn't a nightmare, was it?"

Wriggling out from under him, I slide down so we can lie

face-to-face, tangling our arms and legs together, as I wonder where exactly his nightmare started. Was it losing Tucker yesterday? Or does it go back to the invasion, that night by the lake when we thought we were watching a meteor shower? Or somewhere in the middle? When Tucker got darted? When August ran off with Raven? When Raven came back and that spelled the end for *us*?

"It wasn't a nightmare," I whisper. "But it's over now."

We hold each other for a few minutes before a low hiss makes me tunnel from under the blankets and poke my head out. The room is lit by candles and the glowing coals in the fire. Aurora stands in the doorway, in armor, her helmet under her arm as she signs with one hand.

Time to go.

"Now? It's the middle of the night."

Long walk, she says.

I don't see the point in arguing. The truth is the nightmare is not quite over. We still have to get back to Prince George somehow. If we have to walk, it will take two weeks at least. The closest a transport could safely get us would be maybe fifty miles out. That's a two- or three-day hike, probably more like a week in these snowy conditions.

Topher groans as he eases himself up, swinging his feet down to put on his boots. We dress in our layers of winter gear in silence, because the things that need to be said will have to wait until we've both recovered our strength. Somehow we're going to have to figure out a way to be enough for each other. In the meantime, I have to decide what to do with the volcano building up inside me. I hope they have therapists on the coast.

Some of the Rogues emerge into the moonlit clearing to see us off. Part of me wishes I could stay here to study them, like an anthropologist discovering a new tribe. Their peculiarities give me a strange feeling. It's almost as though they offer a peek into a lost branch of humanity, a direction we could have gone in a million years ago, or maybe one we'll take in the future.

Gender doesn't seem to matter to them, or sexuality, and certainly not race, though their unusual prejudices about rank still linger, even though that kind of thinking is discouraged here. They're not possessive of the few objects they keep around, but they can be very possessive of each other. The bonds they form are deep and all-encompassing, and though they can be coolish with the rest of their kind, their attachment to their mates and partners is profound. They know themselves. They accept themselves. I admire them for that.

Mostly I admire the way they have broken free of the expectations of their kind. I've encountered enough Nahx now to know how rigidly programmed they are. However they came to be, whether they were made or evolved or adapted themselves from some other form, the Nahx's single-mindedness is the reason their conquest of humanity was so successful. And yet these Rogues shook off that role as easily as washing away a smudge of dirt or blood. They are literally programmed to be killers of humans, but they seem to love and cherish Topher and me. It's almost like they see us as pets.

Ash embraces us in turn, as do a few of the others, before they wander back into the forest. The path down from the cabin is dark, and when I turn back for one last look at the Rogues who saved our lives, all I see in the moonlight are trees and rocks and the silent cabin with a thin wisp of smoke trailing up from its chimney.

Aurora and Nova stay close by us as we descend through the glacier. We hope to reach the highway before dawn and flag down one of the trucks or buses now rumbling slowly along the deep ruts in the snow. Nova has very sensibly filled a large pack with the rest of the canned food from the cabin—the Rogues eat only fresh meat, we've learned, mainly unfortunate raccoons or squirrels, so the canned peaches and applesauce are of no use to them. But they will prove invaluable to us as trade, maybe even ensure a place on one of the buses heading west. If I learned anything as a refugee for all those months, it's that human charity has strict limits, and everything has a price, even things that should be fundamental rights.

Topher is silent as we navigate the steep path. I don't think he actually believes what I've told him about life outside the occupation zones. I know conditions in the refugee camps were pretty dire, but for him what I described must have seemed idyllic. And the idea of us catching a bus and going to live with Raven's parents? He didn't argue with me, but he must have thought it pretty ludicrous. That's the thing about privation. You get used to it. And anything else seems implausible. *Hot* water? Out of a tap? Doesn't seem real. Bananas? Are they even a thing? Did we really all walk around with video screens in our pockets?

Once the invasion seemed like it might be a nightmare. Now the world before seems like *it* was the dream.

It's still dark when we reach the road. Nova and Aurora draw us to a stop out of sight in the dense trees while they shrug off the heavy packs. We can see quite far down the road in either direction, so we'll have some time to get down there and make our presence known. Hopefully they will stop. Hopefully they won't shoot at us.

Topher and I rehearse our story.

"We've been holed up in a climber's refuge this whole time," Topher recites.

"Uh-huh? And why didn't the Nahx find us?"

"We were hidden in a gully. Cut off by a glacier."

"And what did you eat?"

"Squirrels and applesauce."

We both burst out laughing. Aurora and Nova have their

helmets on, but when they turn to look at us I can tell that they are frowning disapprovingly. Our story is just as implausible as the fact that we used to eat bananas that were flown in from Guatemala.

"We're humans, Xander," Topher says. "They have to help us."

I just nod, staring at the road. Topher will learn as well as I did that the social contracts we once lived by have been torn up and used as kindling in the fires that stave off death. Maybe he'll fare a bit better than I did, being a white boy, but who knows?

We fall quiet, waiting as the sky begins to lighten. Nova and Aurora kneel on either side of us, radiating warmth. I'll actually miss them. It's nice to think that I might come back to visit one day, maybe when humans and the remaining Nahx have learned to get along better. But I know that's a fantasy. I only hope the Rogues at least can remain undetected.

As for me, Topher and his broken heart are a big enough task, but I also have to figure out how to explain to Raven's parents that she's actually still alive. I imagine word of what has happened to everyone who got darted will travel pretty fast in the human zones. And, knowing humans, terrible suspicion and hate will spread soon enough. Raven, Mandy, and the rest have some kind of battle looming, and lord only knows what that means for us mere humans. And lord knows whether Raven will even survive that. I wonder if I should just wait until she can tell them in person that she made it through.

Nova makes a noise and we all four turn to the east, where a faint light appears on the road. It's moving slowly, but Topher and I need to get down to the highway. Nova leaps to her feet and hauls him up, helping him sling one of the packs over his shoulder.

"Well," he says. "Bye Nova, bye Aurora." He gets their names mixed up and directs his farewell in the wrong directions. Neither of them seems to mind. They reach out and touch his shoulder gruffly.

"I'll catch up to you," I say, and he heads down the path out of the trees. Nova follows him, keeping her distance warily. For some reason this is the moment my brain decides to put it together that Nova was the one who darted Dylan. Of course—she came to Garvin's enclave looking for Aurora. I don't know why I haven't thought of it before. But as I watch her tall shadow following Topher through the trees, I realize it doesn't make any difference. I would have done the same, and worse probably, if our situations had been reversed.

Aurora tilts her head to the side and huffs when I turn back to her.

"I can never thank you enough," I say. It sounds like a line from a movie, but it fits so I go with it. "I would have died a hundred times if it wasn't for you."

Repeat me, she signs, putting one hand on my shoulder. That lasts only a second before she tugs me forward and hugs me properly.

Me. Want. Explain. You, she signs, leaning back.

"You want to explain something to me?" I'm getting much better with their language. I think the Rogues use a simplified version when they speak to humans. When they speak among themselves it's much too fast for me to understand.

Yes, Aurora says. *Look. Listen.* She sighs before she goes on, signing slowly as I roughly translate the grammar in my head. *When you try to make a human into a machine, you get a monster.*

"Oh. You're not a monster, Aurora."

Not me. Angry Boy.

"Topher's a monster?"

He will try to become a machine. Don't let him. It will make him a monster. Like the Nahx.

Her insight takes my breath away. Most of my anxiety about Topher comes from this very issue. How do I keep him away from the edge after everything he's seen? I'm not sure I have the strength to be human enough for both of us.

Aurora rumbles her breath in a low purr as she touches my shoulder again. I can only imagine the kind of monstrousness she has witnessed, among humans, among Nahx, maybe even in herself. I made a point of never asking her or August or any of the Rogues about the bad things they might have done in the course of their duties. I don't want to know.

The last few steps to the edge of the trees are slippery, and as I lose my footing, Aurora takes my hand, steadying me. Topher has already left Nova and is plowing through the thigh-high snow in the ditch up to the highway shoulder. Nova takes my other hand as we reach her, and the three of us stand in a circle for a few seconds.

Stay safe, Aurora says when we part. *Take care of your Offside.*

"You too." I shrug the pack on and turn a little abruptly so they won't see the look on my face. Nahx can be very perceptive about human facial expressions. I wouldn't mind them seeing my sadness so much, but I don't want them to see the equal measures of relief. As charming as the Rogues are, the forsaken world of the Nahx has fueled my nightmares for long enough. I'm going to spend the rest of my life trying to forget it.

Topher waves his arms madly as the headlights approach. The vehicle slows, and when it gets closer we see that it's an army truck, its large wheels fitted with snow chains. I glance back to the trees, but Aurora and Nova are doing that thing the Nahx do in the dark, letting their armor conceal them, turning them into shadows.

They drift backward until they are indistinguishable from the branches and trunks. Down on the road, the heavy truck rumbles to a stop, crunching over the drifted snow.

When the passenger-side window rolls down I'm surprised to see two middle-aged women in the cab. They don't look military—they're not in uniform, at least, but I suppose in these circumstances, who would be?

"Where the hell did you come from?" the passenger says.

"We've been hiding in a refuge cabin this whole time," Topher recites. I join him by the side of the road, resisting the urge to look backward for one more glimpse of Aurora and Nova. I didn't think I'd feel this torn. I didn't think I'd feel torn at all, but seeing other humans again has reminded me of life in the refugee camp and how callous our species can be. The women in the truck seem suspicious of us.

"We've only got women and children," the driver says, as though to reinforce my impression of her and her passenger.

"We have food," Topher says. It's then that I notice the rifle propped between them. I have a handgun, buried under layers of clothing. So does Topher, I think, but we left the rifles with the Rogues. Aurora and Nova have one each, but I can't look back at them. And anyway, would I really have a shoot-out with two middle-aged ladies and their truck full of women and children? I'm more likely to just let them kill me, though I doubt Aurora would allow that.

"Let's see," the passenger says.

Topher slips off his pack and opens it, revealing cans of peaches and beans, crackers, dried noodles—the usual survival food, the kind of thing I saw people beaten unconscious for back in Prince George.

"Weapons?"

Topher and I exchange a look.

"I don't want weapons in the back," the woman clarifies. "There are kids back there, and it's a long ride."

She opens the door and slides out, sinking in snow up to her knees. Her partner, the driver, curls her fingers around the rifle, as though to warn us.

"Julia," the passenger says, holding out her hand. We shake without bothering to remove our mittens. I notice that under her open coat she's packing a gun in a holster too.

"I'm Xander," I say. "This is Topher."

Julia leads us around the back of the truck before pulling down the step board and popping open the canvas flaps.

"Shove your bags in," she says.

It's dark inside the truck but I can almost make out some small faces turning to us as we load our packs. Someone flicks on a flashlight for a few seconds and the rest come into view.

The truck is already way overloaded. Crammed into seating for twenty and splayed out on the floor, there must be forty women and kids in here, all of them looking like they are wearing every item of clothing they own.

"I meant it about the weapons," Julia says. Her smile is

friendly but firm, like a schoolteacher who is not taking any more of your crap.

Topher and I dig into our layers of clothes and hand over our guns. Julia unloads them expertly, also checking the chambers. She pockets the clips and tucks the pistols under her arm.

"It's a long ride yet. Try to get comfortable. If I hear a whisper of any macho bullshit, I will dump you in a gully and keep your food and guns. Got it?"

"Where are we going?" I ask as we climb into the truck.

"Does that matter?" Julia asks with another smile. "West. Past the border web. Beyond that, we'll know when we get there. And share that food around."

She closes the flap, plunging us into darkness. Topher has a small LED flashlight, which he clicks on as we shuffle on board, trying not to stand on any of the half-dozen children asleep on the floor. Just as the truck starts to move, a couple of moms pull their sleeping toddlers into their laps, clearing a small space for me and Topher to stash our packs and sit on them.

We pull out a bag of crackers and pass it around, whispering introductions. The moms relax a bit as we share the food. I kind of want to get their stories, but that would mean we have to share ours, and I'm already starting to forget what it's supposed to be. Better to let the silence and the rocking of the slow-moving truck settle us. Topher flicks off his flashlight and lets his head fall onto my shoulder.

A few minutes pass like that, and we drift off until a child yelping in a nightmare startles us both to full wakefulness.

"This is really happening, right?" Topher whispers, his lips almost touching my ear. I nod. It's quite warm in here, so I slip off my mitten and somehow find his hand in the dark, lacing our fingers together.

Once we get past the border I still have to figure out how to get up to Prince George to get the bus to the coast. I'm going to have to be discreet about it too, because if anyone from Garvin's camp is still alive and gets wind of me, it could get very ugly. I'm counting on the fact that Garvin himself was on that helicopter and is therefore dead. Doesn't seem like the kind of stupid thing he'd want to miss. I'm hoping some of the food will buy us somewhere to stay in Prince George until our travel passes arrive, at least. I'll deliver the medicine Raven gave me to the hospital. Maybe there's something that will help Dylan get better. If he's still alive.

Topher squirms, adjusting his position and snaking one arm behind my back to squeeze me around the waist.

"I knew you'd come back for me," he says.

I almost laugh out loud, because that's about the most preposterous thing I've ever heard. The idea of my even being alive after the last time we saw each other, the idea of my making it through the web that he had repeatedly confirmed was impassible, the thought that by some bizarre impulse I would seek to get through it again, come the other way, and look for him? After he had unceremoniously dumped me in favor of his doomed attachment to Raven? Only a crazy person would do that.

He knows me so well.

RAVEN

August's color changes as he sleeps. At first I think it's just the warmth of the candlelight and the faint orange glow from the fire enlivening his gray tone. But as dawn seeps in through the small windows I see a faint pink tinge in his cheeks, his slightly parted lips, and the tips of his ears. As I watch, it grows, until his coloring is almost like that of a human. A very tall, slightly odd-looking human, and one who is maybe a little short on vitamins, but human nonetheless.

He's just as beautiful as he was the first time I properly saw him, though now, being a bit more conscious and with time to let my eyes linger, I notice details I haven't before. The scar that traverses from his temple to his mouth has drawn both one eyebrow and his upper lip slightly askew, as though fixing him in a permanent state of wariness, even while asleep. His hair is longer than I thought, and now that I've detangled it somewhat, it's drying into soft black waves that fall over his ears and the nape of his neck. His skin is smooth, with just a shadow of a wispy mustache. There's a thin sheen of glitter over not only his eyelashes but also his lips and teeth, as though his saliva also has a silver tinge. Do I look like this? I'm suddenly taken by an urge to examine myself in a mirror. Not much time has passed since I did my hair in the drugstore in Grande Prairie, but it feels like fundamentals about me have changed. I wonder if my appearance has too.

Moving quietly so as not to disturb him, I slip off the bed and kneel to snoop in the piles of human backpacks in the corner. There are other signs in this cabin that a group of humans was cornered and attacked—a crushed lock on the stones outside the door, parts of a broken chair piled by the fireplace. There's even a dart embedded in one of the window frames.

I didn't mention this to August. I doubt he was involved, and anyway, if he was, this isn't the kind of thing that outrages me anymore, knowing what I now know. Maybe the people who attempted to take refuge here have been turned into mindless automatons; maybe they're like me. Maybe they're dead. It all seems small in comparison to what I know is coming. And the things these humans chose to bring with them on their attempted escape perplex me. There are obvious things like food and medicine, tampons and condoms, but there are also jewelry and money and *phones*, so many phones. It seems as though each person brought two or three. Who did they think they would call? All of them have dead batteries. They're just elegant silver bricks now.

There's a small makeup kit in the third pack I open. My

heart breaks a little bit then at the idea that someone brought makeup all the way up here, to their last stand in the high mountains. How is mascara going to help at a time like that? But I'm grateful for the compact mirror, and turning toward the light coming in from the window, I examine my face.

Well, it's embarrassingly dirty, for starters. In another pack I find baby wipes and set about scrubbing the grime off my face, hands, and ears. I slip the jacket off and use the wipes on my arms and neck. My week-old braids are still holding up quite well, but I unravel them, which leaves my hair nicely wavy and stretched so it hangs down over my ears. In another pack I find some moisturizing sunscreen, and that works to tamp down the frizz a bit. The final result pleases me, even though good hair isn't going to help anyone either.

As the daylight increases, the changes to my coloring become more apparent, and I find that I have a metallic sheen over not just my skin but also my eyes and teeth, my hair, my eyebrows, everything. It's as though I'm slightly gilded, like a girl caught halfway while transforming into a golden idol. Or transforming back. My freckles are like flecks of bronze. My fingernails, which were slightly ragged as a human, are now hard and glossy, as though painted with pearlized polish. The whole effect is preternatural but not hideous. More important, my attitude about it has changed. I kind of like it. I feel beautiful and strong.

Behind me, August sighs in his sleep, and I climb back up to sit on the bed next to him. His forearm is slung over his eyes as though to block out the morning light, and with his hand facing up like that, I notice that his palm is blistered and raw, as though it's been badly burned. I'm about to lean over to grab a first-aid kit from the pile of backpacks when he stirs and opens his eyes, blinking up at me.

Your hair, he signs. *Very pretty.*

"Thank you." Even after everything, everything I've seen and done and the war raging in my head, this makes my face hot.

August stretches and pulls himself upright, leaning against the wall behind the bed.

"Does that hurt?" I ask. "The burn on your hand?"

No. He closes his fist.

"It's from when you caught the grenade, right?"

I'm repeat sorry about Tucker, he starts, but I interrupt him.

"That wasn't your fault. You—"

No. No. I wanted to jump but I . . . forgot how. I forget things. Small things. Big things. My brain is half asleep. Half broken.

How can I tell him I'm glad he didn't jump without sounding like the worst person? Like I'm saying I'm glad Tucker died and not him? But that's the truth. And there's another truth there, one that should probably never be spoken out loud.

Tucker *knew*. The moment I realized August wasn't dead,

Tucker put together the facts and figured out that he was superfluous to my life. But the final part of it is worse even than that, so unspeakable that it should be locked in a box and buried deep under a mountain.

He could see that he was superfluous to *Topher's* life too.

The way my brain now works, I think all Snowflakes' brains work like that. Hyperobservant, analytical. Tucker knew I wanted August—anyone could see that. He knew Topher would only be harmed by any association with Nahx or Rogues or Snowflakes. And he knew we were in imminent danger of being killed by those unbelievably stupid humans.

Tucker's brain made a million calculations in a fraction of a second and came up with the only solution that made sense. So he tore the missile out of August's hand and dove for the helicopter, knowing the outcome would be his death.

His disintegration.

I look down to see that I have two handfuls of the tattered green dress clenched in my fists.

August covers one of my hands with his and we sit like that for several long minutes, while outside the day brightens. His touch instills me with momentary peace, enough to sort a few of the millions of thoughts in my head into a coherent idea about what I need to do, maybe not beyond the next few minutes but certainly in them. I need clarity—final answers about who I am.

"August," I say, turning to face him. "Do you love me?"

His wonky eyebrow creeps upward, and he squeezes my hand as he nods. Then he makes a low, voiceless purr in the back of his throat, and his lips curve into a smirk.

"I love you too."

He doesn't take his eyes off me, but I can feel the skin of his hand start to pulse hot and cold as he tugs me, gently, as though inviting me closer. I slide forward and clamber over him to straddle his legs. Once I'm there, facing him, our bodies touching, I lose my nerve somewhat. I think I was planning to make him a bold proposition that he couldn't refuse, but maybe he needs a gentler touch. He seems so innocent sometimes. And with me . . . well, aren't we the first girl and boy to ever try this?

"Is this how you want it to be?" I ask, my heart pounding. "How you want *us* to be?"

He continues to purr while he nods and his eyes sparkle, reflecting the bright light from the window. I move his hands up to the open lapels of my jacket. He slips it off my shoulders and down my arms, letting it fall to the floor beside the bed. The green dress, which I've been wearing for weeks, is torn and dirty in the skirt, but the bodice is still in relatively good shape. It's quite low cut, though, and shows more cleavage than I would normally choose to. August's eyes linger there for a few seconds before flicking back up to my face.

"Is this why you chose this dress?" I ask. I'm nervous now, and if I'm not careful, I'll start blathering overwrought nonsense. So I go with cheeky instead. "Because it shows off my tits?"

Thankfully he seems to get the joke. He flicks his head back and huffs his breathy laugh.

No. Repeat trees. Repeat earth. Repeat human. He lets his fingers trail in the folds of satin spread out on the bed around us. *Made you look alive. So I could see you alive.* He taps his forehead. *In here. In my dreams.*

I know exactly what he means. Images of dead people are fixed in my mind like they're carved from stone. If I could, I would dress them in green too, to make them seem alive.

He edges toward me, letting his hands move behind my back. One of them rests on the bare skin of my neck; the other pulls me forward until we're pressed together. I wrap my arms around him.

"Do you know what to do next?" I whisper.

No, he says, but then he kisses me.

I don't know what I'm expecting—maybe a quick, tentative kiss or a long, deep, passionate kiss. What happens is kind of halfway between the two. Our lips meet softly at first, then part; our tongues touch as he purrs again, making my teeth vibrate. When he draws back he presses the tip of his nose to mine and seems to inhale, as though he's trying to breathe me in.

It's neither an invitation for more nor an affirmation of our bond nor any kind of expression or clarification of feelings. It's deeper than that, as though the moment we kissed we were both opened up and laid bare as the people we really are. The same kind of people. Not human, exactly. Not Nahx. Not Snowflakes. Something older than that, something ancient and universal. Never enemies, more than friends, more than lovers, even. "Soul mates" isn't quite right either.

Intertwined. Two paths that cross and meet and split apart and come back together and get tangled and messy until no sense can be made of it anymore.

August's lack of experience makes everything seem new to me, too. When he removes his jacket and pulls off the silvery undershirt I feel as though I've never seen a boy's body before, and I want to touch every inch of him, to run my fingers over his pale, muscular arms and the scars on his smooth chest. And when I slip off the green dress, his enthralled reaction is so priceless, I can't help but laugh, and that makes him laugh. But as we wriggle under the covers and finish undressing, the mood changes and it starts to seem like we're carefully diffusing a complicated bomb together, achingly slowly and gently, as each step, each soft caress or kiss or each place where our bodies touch might spell catastrophe. We take time with that part, exploring and discovering each other. I'm no expert, but apart from a few metal implants on his neck and around his joints, his body seems to be just like that of a very fit human boy about my age might be, lanky and toned, with fine dark hair on his legs, under his arms, trailing down from his navel. And it responds just like you'd expect from having a naked girl in bed with him.

Though neither of us is exactly human, it feels natural to proceed cautiously, just as two humans would. I have to help him with the condom because he hasn't got a clue, and that makes me feel so strange that I pull back, both of us breathless, and take a moment.

"Are you sure you want to do this?" I ask.

He hisses a little when he nods. Then covers his mouth apologetically, his eyes smiling. But moments later he's serious again, his gaze fixed on mine, his hot hands resting on the curves of my hips as I move.

It doesn't last very long, but while it's happening my mind finally stops its incessant churning, and I float there, in a cloud of bliss and breathy silence—my silence, August's silence, the silence of a world that has temporarily laid its weapons down.

The calm before the storm.

After, as I pull my dress back on, August stares at the ceiling, lost in thought.

"Have you ever done that before?"

He chuckles softly. *No. It is forbidden.*

"Sex is forbidden? Even among yourselves?"

He nods.

"I'm not sure, but I think our Rogue friends are having quite a lot of sex."

He laughs then, shaking and huffing. I tentatively touch the implants on his neck.

"You don't have any vocal cords, do you?"

No.

"They removed them? So they could implant things here?"

Yes. For breathing with the armor.

"Do you remember it? Remember having a voice?"

No.

August is not much of a talker, but I get the sense that he has something else to say, so I let the hut become quiet but for the windows rattling in the wind.

I have two lives, he says finally. *One, a human, is not my true life, but I remember broken pieces of that.*

"What kinds of things?"

Being small, he says, but then he puts his hands over his eyes, as though it's painful to remember. *But that wasn't me,* he finishes. I think he doesn't want to talk about it anymore.

"And your other life?" I ask.

My other life was on one of the round ships. I don't remember much of that because the Fireflies stole . . . He stops, frowning. *Stole my thoughts. Some things have come back, but many are lost.*

"Sky said it has something to do with the transponders.

That's why Blue was able to fly in and reboot Tucker's memories. Because the Fireflies put a conduit for a transponder into his brain. Maybe Blue could do that to you, too."

August grimaces up at the ceiling. *No, thank you.*

The window rattles again, and a cold draft blows over the bed. Even though neither of us is likely to be harmed by cold, I climb back into the bed and we snuggle together, me tucked into the crook of his shoulder. His body is very warm but pulsing slightly, the temperature dipping and rising by a degree or two in a rhythmic pattern. I know he can control this, but it's also something he does during moments of high emotion, as he did after Liam shot me with an arrow. I don't know which it is now—whether he's doing it on purpose or just because of . . . everything. But I like it. It's relaxing, almost like being rocked in a train or car, and soon my eyes drift shut. I open them again and, looking up, see that August is watching me and breathing with me. He gives me a little smile, and I feel myself smile with him. His eyes close. My eyes close and I drift, floating down and dissolving into sleep like a snowflake on the surface of a thawing lake.

But then I sink. Into darkness, into density, deeper and deeper until nothing lives or feels and nothing can escape, not even a thought. Bolts of lightning pop in the depths, arcing around me, and something moves, something older and heavier than night that pulls at my insides, as though twisting the very atoms of me.

Then the pain starts, like nothing human, like something worse than fire, but before I have time to scream in agony or dream myself away, I bolt awake. A swath of my vision is still blacked out and crackling with lightning. Behind it, I catch glimpses of a Nahx holding me, pinning me down on the bed as I writhe. He has one hand over my mouth. I flail at him, tearing at his hands, twisting until we both go crashing off the bed, my head slamming hard on the stone floor. The lightning storm breaks apart, dashing across my vision like escaping animals before each dark fragment pops and disappears in a flash.

My vision returns—the stone hut, the pile of human things, and the Nahx now above me, grasping me, my head pressed against his chest, one hand still over my mouth. I growl behind his hand and he releases me, veering back as I lunge for him. But I stop myself just in time.

It's only August. He has his armor on but not his helmet, and he raises his hands, palms out, placating me.

I slam my hand over my mouth to stifle the moan I can't contain as the terror and pain of the dream wear off. I burn and sting like I've been flayed from the inside out, and feel around my body to make sure all my limbs are still there. I even count my fingers. I wriggle my toes.

Sorry. Sorry, August says. *You were . . . screaming.* His eyes are wide, and what little color he had has drained out of his face.

It wasn't real. I know that. But whatever Blue's people put into my brain, whatever diabolic lines of code can make me feel like that, could surely kill me. Why else would they do it? They want me to return to my post. To my *fissure*.

August moves forward, standing as he tentatively reaches for me, and I go limp, letting him pick me up again. I cling to him, wrapping my arms and legs around his body and pressing my face into his neck.

"I have to go, August," I whisper, my lips against his armor, which is now throbbing between ice-cold and burning hot.

He waits for a few seconds before shaking his head. I can feel him making the sign for *please* on my back.

No. Please.

"I have to. Whatever the Fireflies did to me, I'm worried it will kill me if I don't go back. It's getting worse."

August sets me down on the bed, kneeling in front of me. I notice that his helmet is on the floor a few feet away; the tentacle-like breathing tubes twitch and writhe around languidly, as though searching for him. I look away, pretending I didn't notice.

I will come with you, August says.

"No, you can't."

He growls harshly, baring his teeth. *Yes!* he signs sharply. *I will protect you.*

I take his face in my hands as his eyes fill with silvery tears.

"You can't come, August. The elevation is too low. It will kill you."

No. I'm strong.

"Not like this, you're not. I saw hundreds of dead Nahx there. The Fireflies don't care. You're dispensable to them."

Don't worry about me.

"I *am* worried about you!"

He hangs his head and lets himself fall forward until he's resting on my knees.

"I made a friend, up north where this battle is going to happen. He was a Nahx, a Tenth. He helped me a lot, helped me escape. But he spent too long at low altitudes, and even though we brought him back up to the mountains, he died."

August turns his head to the side to rest his cheek on the satin of my dress. I see that his face is streaked with gray tears. He signs with one hand.

You can't stop me.

August has hurt my feelings before, unintentionally sometimes or even intentionally. I've hurt him too. We're just two angry people in a desperate and terrifying situation. Someone is bound to get hurt. But somehow his willfulness on this hurts more than anything else has, especially after what we just shared. My brain clicks into gear again, analyzing, cataloguing, and I realize what the pain really is. It's just my own pride.

I don't own him. I don't control him. He has a whole other life outside mine. And he's right. I *can't* stop him. But the thought of losing him the way I did Tenth is like feeling Liam's arrow go through my spine again. I lift a corner of the green dress to crush against my mouth. It doesn't work, and before I can stop it, I'm sobbing uncontrollably, streams of silver tears staining the green satin.

August's head shoots up and he holds me, making the sign for *sorry* on my back with gentle chopping touches. He edges away so he can look into my face and sign properly.

I'm sorry. I'm sorry.

But that doesn't help. It just makes me cry harder. Because if I can convince him to stay behind, what would he stay for? My ruined body coming back in a coffin? I wallow in it for a few more seconds before I realize the only way to break down this horror that is consuming me is to get it out, to say things I've been trying to forget.

"Sky . . . Sky . . ." I have to gather myself before I can go on. "Sky told me you must have done it on purpose!"

Then I'm sobbing again, as August tries to hold me. I push him away.

"When we were living in the penthouse, the curtains were

never closed in that room! I didn't even notice they were there!"

I don't understand.

"Yes you do! Don't lie to me! You went in there and closed the door and the curtains so there wouldn't be any sun. So even your solar backup wouldn't keep your armor charged. Sky explained all of it to me!" I'm howling now, like a lost child.

Explain please, Dandelion. I don't understand.

"You were trying to kill yourself! You promised you wouldn't! You promised!"

It was so long ago, it's like another universe, but I remember it in precise detail. The two of us standing at the top of the path down to the base in the mountains. And me asking him to promise he wouldn't harm himself because I couldn't bring myself to say the word "suicide." And I couldn't bear to think of a world without him in it, even if I never saw him again.

And his reply, a sign I'd learned only the day before.

Promise.

He sits back on his heels, his hands curled into fists and pressed over his mouth, his eyes haunted and streaming with tears. And he tries to sign to me, but he's now shaking so badly, his words are mangled, and through the blur of my own tears I can barely translate them into any kind of sense.

I was lost. I was broken. I wanted to rest. Repeat rest. I'm sorry.
I'm sorry.

We stare at each other for a few long seconds that feel like a timer ticking away our last moments together. There's a low tap on the door. And Mandy's voice.

"Raven?"

Standing, I leave August by the bed and open the door.

Mandy doesn't bother with pleasantries.

"Did you feel it? It knocked me clean off my feet."

"I felt it," I say dully.

Behind her Ash trails through the snow from the transport parked at the edge of the plateau.

"We need to go," Mandy says.

Behind us, August hisses, and I turn just in time to see him stand up. He takes one step toward me before his eyes suddenly flicker and he falls forward.

"August!" I rush to him, turning him over just as Ash arrives. "Help me!"

If sign language can have a bored tone, Ash manages it. *He left his armor off too long*, he says. Bending to retrieve August's helmet, he kneels and straddles his chest, sliding the helmet into place.

The tubes flail around for a second before finding August's face, his nose and mouth, and starting to slither in. Smaller, very fine tubes emerge from the goo inside the helmet to wriggle into his ears and the metallic conduits in his throat. Finally the tubes constrict and seem to suck the two pieces of the helmet together. It snaps shut with a click so loud, I jump.

August's armor ripples, and after a few seconds the defensive blades in his face mask flick out before disappearing again. Then his whole body jerks, making the armor plates clatter against the stones. Finally, with a sharp, tortured gasp, August abruptly sits up, sending Ash sprawling. Mandy and I have to practically jump out of the way.

Ash huffs as he gets up. Slinging his rifle behind his back, he backs out of the hut, shaking his head.

August moves slowly, raising his hands to hold his head, and I think I must emit some kind of toxic-fury force field, because Mandy practically tiptoes out of the hut and closes the door behind her.

"August," I say through clenched teeth. "Don't *ever* do that again."

Sorry.

"I want you to stop apologizing and start being a bit more careful."

He holds his head, armored fingers clicking against the metal of his helmet as he awkwardly bends his legs around and struggles to his knees. I stand and am only a little taller than him kneeling. Putting my hand on his shoulder, I soften, like I always do, because sure, August is a mess, but he's *my* mess. That much is clear. After a few seconds he speaks.

I'm a soldier, he says. *I can fight.*

"You can't. Not this time. Not this battle."

Outside the hut, the distinctive rumble of the transport echoes across the plateau.

"I have to go," I say

No.

"Yes. You can't come with me. You can't follow me. Or come looking for me. No matter what."

He jerks away from my hand and stands, looming over me.

"You have to promise, August. I mean it."

He growls a low crackling growl, and now I feel like we're back where we started. Maybe this can never be resolved. I turn, suppressing an urge to punch him in his stubborn head. That clearly won't help anything.

Outside the hut, Mandy and Ash wait in the bright glare, while another Rogue clanks up the ramp into the transport. Apparently she's going to be our pilot. I stomp through the snow and don't acknowledge that August is following me, silent and sulky.

"Ash," I say, pointedly ignoring August, who is sighing petulantly behind me. "Under no circumstances is August to come after me. Seriously. I would rather you kill him."

Through the broken gap in his mask I see Ash's eyebrow

creep up, but as he reaches to put his hand on August's shoulder, August hisses and shoves him away. Ash calmly grabs August by the neck and kicks his feet out from under him. They both go *cloomph* as they fall in the deep snow.

"I'm going now, August," I say, a little louder than I need to.

He twists away from Ash and lunges at me, hissing. Ash yanks him back and holds him down, mashed into his own body print, looking miserable.

Mandy tugs my arm toward the transport as the engines whine up to full power. I'm lost as to what to do about August. This isn't how I pictured our farewell scene. This isn't how I thought he would be acting toward me now of all times, after everything we shared. I'm inches away from blaming myself for his bad behavior, which is exactly where I started and everything I've been trying to unlearn.

My eyes burn, and not just from the cold wind. I turn away from him.

"Let's go." I push past Mandy and climb up the ramp in three long strides.

Mandy follows me, and mercifully, our pilot, who I now recognize as the one Xander called Ember, activates the hatch door. It slides closed as the transport ascends. Blue appears, drifting out of the cockpit.

"Men can be a lot sometimes," Mandy says as the interior lights reactivate.

I don't answer. I'm clenching my teeth so hard, my whole head aches.

Ember sets the altitude thruster to auto and steps back into the hold, entering some numbers into a panel by the cockpit door.

"What happened between you and August? Did you have some kind of fight?" Mandy asks.

"No," I snap. "It was nothing."

Ember finishes whatever it is she's doing and turns to us, flicking her head back.

Sometimes when you put the armor back on it makes you a little up and down, she says.

"Up and down?" Mandy says. "What does that mean?"

For a short time, Ember signs, *the armor makes you crazy. While you're putting it on. After you put it on.*

"That's not really an excuse for—"

"Oh, shush," I say. I'm not in the mood. Moving into the cockpit, I scan the mountainside, now a hundred feet below us, through the window. August is running across the plateau, waving. A sniff behind me makes me turn. Ember flicks her head back in what I'm going to assume is the Nahx equivalent of a smirk.

"Can we go back down?" I ignore Mandy, who is standing behind Ember with her arms crossed. "Just for a minute."

Ember hisses softly, but she tugs the hovering throttle

down and we start to descend. By the time we reach the plateau, August is standing on the edge of a steep cliff above a ravine, with Ash running to catch up with him. Ember hovers the transport over the ravine. She turns us to the side and I jump back into the hold to activate the hatch. The thrusters and the mountain wind blow snow everywhere, but August stands firm on the cliff edge, with both of his hands in the air.

I hang from a handhold and look at him, trying not to smile.

I'm sorry, Dandelion, he says, making his signs big, as though he's shouting.

It's much too noisy for him to hear me, so I sign back, one-handed.

Stop saying sorry.

No, he says.

I give up trying to keep a stern expression. That makes me laugh.

I will wait for you, he says. *Right here.*

In the small house I hope. Not out in the snow.

Yes. I will wait. You will come back?

Promise, I say. The wind buffets the transport and Ember adjusts the thrusters again, nudging us upward.

Promise? August says as we rise.

"I promise!" I shout and sign at the same time.

Repeat me, he says. *I promise! I PROMISE I'LL WAIT! PROMISE!*

A gust of blowing snow obscures him momentarily, and when he reappears Ash is standing behind him with his hand on his shoulder.

PROMISE, August says again, then he waves. Then he puts both hands on his head and Ember turns the transport away and shoots us up into the clouds before I have time to answer.

PART SIX

TIME

"Beware; for I am fearless, and therefore powerful."
—MARY SHELLEY, *FRANKENSTEIN*

D o you want to talk about it?"

"No."

"Raven—"

"We're really not people who talk about things anymore. Look at me. Look at yourself. We've changed."

Anyone else would sulk, but Mandy laughs at me, which only makes me less in the mood to talk.

Even for a Nahx, Ember is aloof. She has barely made two signs in our direction since we left the mountains. Suits me. Something about slotting the answers I got from August into the information I've already gathered has started a frenzy of processing in my thoughts, and I'm just trying to keep up. If I can get a complete picture of what's going on here, I can make a decision about my role in it one way or another.

Ember flies us above the clouds for most of the way, but while we're still heading east, before we turn north to the unpopulated areas, I ask her to dip down so I can see some of the towns and highways.

Most of them look deserted. One highway is lined with

cars, abandoned as though they just parked there and let the snow drift around them.

"Can we land here?" I ask. "Just for a few minutes? I want to look around."

Ember nods once and sets us down in the center strip of the divided highway. Both sides of the highway are full of stationary cars facing west. They're empty, most with at least one door hanging open.

"Darted," Mandy says grimly. "I guess they got up and walked away."

"Or were taken away."

We come upon a truck. The cab is empty, the driver's-side door hanging open, but the back is laden with supplies—canned food, a plastic tub full of medicine, and fuel cannisters. Full ones.

"Let's take these."

Mandy runs her fingers through her short hair and sighs, but she doesn't argue. Ember begrudgingly helps us as we spend twenty minutes pilfering fuel and supplies from the truck and several of the cars.

"And our plans for this are . . . ?" Mandy asks as Ember lifts us off again.

"North of the dunes, on the other side of the lake. There are survivors there."

"Human survivors?" She makes a face. "I don't like their chances with whatever is coming."

"It's our job to protect them, isn't it?"

Mandy looks down at her hands, letting the light play on her metallic skin.

"Is that why they did this to us? So we can protect other humans? Why would they care?"

"I don't know. But I want some answers before I join in any battle."

Mandy just scoffs. I suppose she knows we aren't likely to get answers. And that we won't have any choice about fighting.

"Do you think we'll be in trouble for disabling their drone web?" Mandy asks.

That actually makes me laugh, though I'm not in a laughing mood. "Do you think we should tell them?"

That makes Mandy laugh, and soon the two of us are falling back on the floor of the transport among the fuel canisters and boxes of food, shaking with laughter until silver tears are streaming down our faces.

It drowns out the incessant calculations in my head for a moment and almost makes me feel human. Eventually reality creeps in, but we stay there, staring up at the metal ceiling of the hold. I wonder if Mandy feels what I feel—that weird shimmering sense of my cells moving around, adjusting with every mile we travel, as though they know what's coming and are preparing.

Ember takes the transport into a shallow dive when we reach the dunes. Mandy and I watch through the cockpit window as Ember skims over the crowd of hundreds, thousands of Snowflakes. Some of them turn up to look at us, but most of them barely seem to notice. Even at this distance, I can see the dull expressions on their faces. Maybe their cells are preparing too, but they just don't care.

"There's a human camp on the other side of the lake," I tell Ember. "Can you land near there? Not too near, though."

Ember huffs but does what I ask, turning the transport north over the frozen water. A few minutes later we set down on a scraggly peninsula. I scan the landscape, recognizing the spot where I encountered the human girl about a quarter mile to our west. We unload the boxes and canisters as quickly as we can, and just as Ember lays out the last of the supplies on the icy ground, I spot the girl, flanked by two men, about a hundred yards away in the trees. They have their rifles raised.

"Fuel!" I shout. "There's food and medicine too!"

I don't know what kind of reply I expect, but what I get is glares. Not very long ago I might not have cared—I've always been a bit of a misanthrope and made a point of not bothering with what people thought of me—but now that I've been pushed out of the human race, I crave their approval. Why would they approve of me, though? After all the Nahx have done, everything associated with them is tainted. The fading, irritated human girl, who is nothing more than a shallow impression inside me, like a footprint on a thin layer of snow, wants to argue. But instead I turn and follow Mandy and Ember back onto the transport. As we coast away, a hundred feet above the lake, I look down from the open hatch. The girl and her friends are running for our pile of supplies.

When we arrive at Black Lake, Ember sets us down at the edge of the ice. The ominous ship still rises into the sky like some ancient monster. I don't expect a prolonged farewell from our Rogue pilot. She doesn't even look back from the cockpit as we disembark, and the transport lifts off practically as soon as our feet hit the ground. I prepare myself for a long wait, but almost as soon as Ember's transport disappears into the clouds a heavy rumbling from the mother ship begins. Through the haze we watch a thin, dark strip appear in the smooth gray metal, extending the full height of the curved wall, as though it is splitting apart. I lead Mandy forward cautiously as the dark strip widens. Soon we can see that in fact the wall *has* split open, in a way, sliding back to reveal all the levels: the lowest level at the surface of the lake—its impressive height suggests some kind of hangar—and the upper levels, which are lower ceilinged. Sparks of light hover and drift across the opening, slowing as though turning to look at us.

Movement on the surface draws my eyes down to a team

of Nahx marching smartly toward us. I have a story prepared about getting lost and finding an outpost and convincing them to bring us back here, but as the Nahx approach I see that won't be necessary. I recognize the damaged face blade on one of them, the thin silver line that seems to draw the Fifth's expressionless mask into a sneer. Before I can even open my mouth to protest, he's grabbed me by the neck and wiped my feet out from under me. I could fight. It seems the last year of my life has been a constant stream of decisions about whether or not to fight. But the Nahx soldiers still have an edge on us in strength and size, and if I'm ever to get the answers I want, I have to learn to get along with them better.

One of Fifth's colleagues hisses sharply, and Fifth yanks me back up to my feet. His colleague shoves him gruffly aside as she clicks a restraint around one of my wrists, attaching the other loop to Mandy before we are both tugged back toward the dark opening in the ship's wall, stumbling to keep up with the long strides of the Nahx.

When we get inside the ship, the first thing I notice is how empty it is. When I was here before, there were crowds of dazed humans lined up or being moved from place to place, Nahx soldiers nudging them along with rifles in their backs. But now the large cargo bay is empty but for a few Nahx sentries standing stiffly near entrances and exits to dim corridors, weapons at the ready, as though expecting some kind of mutiny.

A long time ago, when I first realized that the Nahx must have their own thoughts, it undid me. I still can't help but wonder what they are thinking when I see them. Are they as scared as I am? As resigned to their fate? Which of these grim sentinels would be likely to discard their weapons and orders and head west, up into the mountains to join the Rogues? Sky told me she could tell high ranks from low ranks by their posture, but if such distinctions exist, they are too subtle for even my finely tuned mind to detect.

The sneering Fifth shoves me as we reach the inner exit of the hangar and I go sliding knees first into the snow, pulling Mandy down with me. As we clamber upright, the higher-ranked female berates Fifth with sharp signs.

Mud head. Touch them again and I'll crush your neck.

I have to try so hard not to laugh, my eyes water, and despite my efforts the female Nahx is not impressed with me. She grabs me by the arm, shaking me, signing with one hand.

We know what you did.

The blush of shame that crawls over my skin is like something from another life, and I'm suddenly that scared human girl in the park again, a huge police officer crushing my arm with his fingers as he drags me into a police car. I can even smell the smoke of the bandstand burning and hear Tucker's protests as they drag him off in the other direction.

"She started it! It was her idea!"

I didn't properly hear those words at the time. I was gasping for breath, heart pounding, blood rushing, ears ringing. But my mind captured it anyway and slotted it away. And now that I'm a computer, there it is, as clear as a recording. I can even tell it was Tucker, not Topher, who tried to sell me out. Topher never said a word—not in his own defense, and not in my defense.

How this moment fits into my vast database of memories is telling. It's prominent, almost like a flag on the collection of thoughts relating to Tucker. That night in the park in Calgary, the fire he set, and the trouble we all got into because of it—that's not only his defining feature, but the inciting incident in the timeline that led me here, to my being conscripted into this battle, to Topher being emotionally destroyed. And to Tucker being dead. He started it all with his impulsive folly.

He didn't do it to impress me, as Topher once suggested. I know this now. He did it because he was an incorrigible ass.

I might never understand why we two sensible, intelligent people both let Tucker treat us like that, and what it was that finally caused him to make such a devastatingly unselfish choice for once in his life. My brain will be able to solve many things, I anticipate, but never that.

As though inspired by his memory, I open my mouth.

"It was all my idea," I say. "Mandy had nothing to do with it."

"Rave . . ." Mandy starts to protest, but the female Nahx just sighs, as though selflessness bores her.

Take that one back to the sand, she signs. The sneering Nahx unshackles us and drags Mandy off without another word.

"I'll find you!" I shout after her, though logically, I know that's unlikely. I'm only happy because if she's going back to the dunes, she's not in line for the punishment they have in mind for me, and also that the sneering Nahx won't be involved in whatever that is. He's obviously not a fan.

The female Nahx releases my arm and I tug it away.

Follow, she signs with a growl.

We head out into the vast empty stadium that makes up the hole in this doughnut-shaped ship. The snow around us is stamped flat by thousands upon thousands of footprints, each one like a signature of someone who can no longer remember their own name. Items have been discarded among the footprints, hats, mittens, even coats. Most affecting are the eyeglasses, tossed away, broken, trod into the snow. Whatever they did to us, apparently it corrected vision problems.

Halfway to the center of the arena, the female Nahx leaves me with a curt sign.

Keep going. She turns and marches back the way we came as I continue toward the center, aiming for the glowing globe.

I hardly need to hurry. The emptiness of the previously crowded field seems to press down on me. All those bodies have been reassigned to their "fissures," to take positions as the "sentinels" that we are. Very few of them will have an opinion on that either way. As someone whose opinions were so frequently at odds with the world, I'm slightly envious that my conversion wasn't so all-erasing. Then again, if I had lost all my thoughts, would I have remembered to look for August and revive him? He's safe in the mountains for now. Xander and Topher are on their way to the coast at last to be with my parents. That makes it worth it.

When I reach the globe, a First is there, standing droop shouldered and silent, staring at nothing. This one is also more humanlike than Nahx, though it's not the boy with the beaten face. I don't like to think what became of him.

This one is slim and sandy haired with a wispy, unshaven face, probably no older than me. He doesn't react as I approach. The wind gusts across the arena, blowing up snow and rustling some discarded clothes. The First's shoulders rise and fall as he breathes.

"Hello," I finally say, feeling a bit foolish. Who greets their executioner politely?

The First doesn't move. I look around, searching the machinery under the glowing globe and the surrounding expanse of white. The walls of the ship are barely visible as gray blurs in the distance. Looking up, I examine the globe again. The lines demarcating Nahx territory don't seem to have changed, even though their "light prison," the drone web we destroyed, is no more. The light marking our location in Northern Saskatchewan is as bright as ever. My improved eyes can't exactly zoom in, but as I relax, the cells of my retina and optical nerve seem to adjust, and the small light becomes more finely focused. I see that it's actually a thin filament, like a lightning bolt hovering just above the surface. A crack in the sky. A *fissure*.

The other fissures glow at the locations I now know the meaning of. Central Russia. The Mohave Desert. Japan, the South Pacific, and so on. If what I've put together is correct, each location is now guarded by an army of sentinels.

Against what, though? That's the last remaining question.

The First sways slightly when I look back, as though the wind in the arena is gently rocking him.

A tiny vibration tickles my skin, and a second later Blue drifts out of my breast pocket. They dash up suddenly, as though looking around, before zooming back to settle on one of my collar points, their light dimming until they are barely visible.

As I turn my eyes back up to the sky, some of the stars shift out of their positions, moving toward each other until they coalesce into a dense cloud of tiny lights. They flow down past the globe and swirl around the head of the First. As some of the lights disappear into his nostrils and ears, even underneath his eyelids, he seems to come to life, blinking, his body shifting almost warily.

After a few moments, while I resist the urge to run and not look back, the First finally turns to me, his awakening face twisting into an exaggerated frown.

"We are disappointed to see you again, *snezjinka*."

"My name is Raven."

First steps toward me, one step. Not menacing, exactly, but as though he's attempting to establish rank. I hold my ground as he speaks. "*Snezjinka* do not need names."

"Why did you do this to us?"

"*Snezjinka* do not need answers."

"I need answers!" I shout it, foolishly, but I keep going. The First is advancing on me now. I step backward to maintain the distance between us. "I need to know what we're fighting before I . . ."

We both stop as the First regards me, his face now twisting theatrically from anger to puzzlement. I guess that's an improvement.

"What difference will that make?" he asks.

"I'm not going to kill any old thing you put in front of me." I figure the longer I babble, the longer I live, so I keep going. "Maybe the other zombies you made will, but ones like me, who can still think, aren't going to do that. How do we know whatever's coming through the rift isn't trying to rescue us?"

"Rescue you?" First says with a little shake of his head. "Rescue you from what?"

"You, of course! Help us take our planet back!"

The lights around his head shift, changing color slightly, and he actually smiles, if you could call it that.

"*Your* planet? What makes you think this isn't *our* planet?"

"Because we . . . were here first." Even as the words come out of my mouth I know that they're wrong. Because a million things suddenly fall into place, things I've noticed about all of this for the past year and half and not processed. The Nahx are copies of *humans*. Their signs are human gestures. The Nahx technology has that weirdly familiar smell, like smoke or charcoal—an *ancient* smell. No one saw their ships approaching earth before the first attacks, not NASA, not the doomed space station. They were just suddenly *here*, as though they materialized out of nowhere. Or sprang out of the ground.

Or rose up from under the ice.

My mouth becomes so dry, I have to pry my lips apart to speak.

"You're not extraterrestrials."

First shakes his head, the cloud of lights swaying back and forth with him.

"No. We are not."

Why, after everything I've seen and done and lived through, am I more scared in this moment than I've ever been? I'm not running or hiding. I don't hear the stomping of Nahx feet gaining on me, nor the whine of their rifles. No one is dead in front of me, turning gray, their eyes staring at nothing. But all is lost anyway.

We are never getting our planet back.

This is not our planet.

The revelation changes everything, providing the answer I've been seeking since this started. Why did the Nahx invade earth? They didn't. I think they might have risen up to protect it.

"You needed an army," I say as my mind reorganizes, churning so quickly, I can practically smell the burning friction of neurons rubbing together. "Because you're so . . . small. You needed us to protect you? But what are we fighting?"

The First's eyebrows creep upward slowly, as though it's an effort, and he tilts his head to the side. Then suddenly the cloud of lights leaves him so quickly that he stumbles forward, falling to his knees. I have to grab his arm to keep him from face-planting in the snow. As the cloud of lights drifts upward, the First slumps, then regains his balance. He slowly turns his face up to me. His expression is blank, but there is something in his eyes, something so subtle that a normal human with a normal brain might not notice. He hasn't been completely pithed by whatever the Fireflies have done to him. There are traces of the human boy still in there.

"I'll help you," I say impulsively. "We can get out of here."

His eyes roll up, drawing mine back to the globe above us. The cloud of Fireflies is swirling around it, gradually focusing their light into a bright ball over the Gulf of Mexico, which shoots out into the open dark before careening back and slamming into the surface, the pinpoints spreading out in imitation of a huge explosion.

I recognize this demonstration. It was the most exciting part of a dinosaur documentary I watched obsessively when I was little. My brain spits up the name easily.

"Chicxulub," I say. The asteroid impact that killed the dinosaurs. I have no idea why I'm seeing it now, though.

As the mock explosion dissipates, the lights arrange themselves into a jagged filament similar to the other ones around the globe, only bigger. A fissure. It glows brightly, seeming for a moment to gape open before slamming shut. A few lights drift up in its wake and spread around the world. They hover there for a moment as I watch, as though giving me time to process what I've just seen.

I step back as they begin to stream into the First's body again, and avert my eyes once more from the ghastly spectacle of him being brought back to life.

"So . . . an asteroid impact," I say as he wakes and turns to me. "It opened a fissure like the ones we're guarding? Like a wormhole or something? To another world?"

"Correct."

"And something came through it?"

"*We* came through it."

I'm trying to put it together in my head, but it still doesn't make sense. If they came through a fissure caused by the asteroid impact sixty-five million years ago, that certainly means they were here before humans were. Although we *evolved* here, which might give us an edge, on principle, as the rightful caretakers of this planet. But I'm beginning to realize that whole issue might be moot.

"And our nuclear bombs opened other fissures? So more of you can come through?"

"There are no more of us."

"What are you worried about, then? What's coming through the fissures?"

The First stops, gazing at me and swaying as the wind buffets us, lifting the snow up and filling the air with white haze. The cloud of lights around his head seems to pulse.

"We don't know," he says. "The world we left was . . . seething and . . . dark. Those are not quite the right words. There are no words."

But he doesn't need to explain. I've seen what he's talking about in my visions.

Firsts don't show much emotion, at least not in the same way that we do. The color of the cloud of lights changes, but more than that, the body it is operating reacts, his haunted eyes glaring at me, almost as though the ruined human boy left inside understands what we're talking about, or can *see* it somehow. Maybe the cloud mind and the human mind are merged or connected. I don't like to think about it, because I'm worried I might get used to the idea.

One thing is clear, though—both the cloud of lights and the human boy are terrified. I can see it. I can feel it. My heightened senses record everything, and though I'm still figuring out what they mean, my own instincts are familiar enough with the information. I smell their fear. I sense the vibrations coming from the cloud but also coming from the ship, from the lake.

And from the sky. "You want us to fight whatever it is?"

The First nods, watching me with watery silver eyes.

"We meant for the creatures you call the Nahx to fight. But they came out so . . . flawed. We had to start again."

"So you made us? *Snezjinka?* It means Snowflake, right? In what language?"

My cells shimmer, and suddenly the answer comes to me via memories of subtitled news interviews, martial arts demo videos, a couple of scenes from 1980s action movies. It's as though my skin or my muscles recorded it, this other language that should be only vaguely familiar. I can speak it.

"*Russkiy. Ya prav?*" I say. "Russian?"

The First smiles. But all that does is unsettle me further.

"Why Russian? Is that where you did this?" Before he can answer, that comes to me too, as other facts and images slot into place. There are twelve copies of each Nahx, and several million Nahx in their army. So they needed humans to start with—to slice up and copy. And where better to find a million humans that might not be missed? In the years we humans were building up our nuclear arsenals?

"*Glavnoye upravleniye lagerey,*" I say, though I don't even know how I know this. Some random, weed-fueled, middle-of-the-night Wikipedia binge, no doubt, now permanently etched, catalogued, and stored along with everything else. "Gulags." Remote Soviet Russian prison camps. It's deeply disconcerting to think that the boy August was copied from was once in a prison camp. I wonder if he remembers any of that. I sure hope not.

Somehow this last piece of the puzzle is more horrific than every other piece put together. I could keep asking questions or I could make a run for it. I know I would never make it out of the ship, but there is some satisfaction in the idea of dying in motion at least. Not just on my feet but running and cursing and pulling shit over.

But I'm not going to run. I'm going to fight. Because if

whatever is coming through the rift scares the creatures who created the Nahx and destroyed my world with barely an ounce of remorse, then whatever is coming is really, really *bad*.

And there's nowhere left to run now.

The lights flare again, this time with a yellow tinge.

"This one should be discarded," First says. "Her intelligence will distract her. She is incompletely processed."

These creatures have said this to me before, and that time I was ready to defend myself, but now I wonder if there is any point. I might feel superhuman, but these things? They *made* me. They made the Nahx. What do you call a species that makes superhumans? Gods?

Blue, who has been motionless on my collar this whole time, suddenly flares brightly and floats up in front of my face.

"What is this?" First says. I can see he is taken aback from the struggle he seems to be having settling his face into a suitable expression.

"This is Blue," I say. "I kind of accidentally kidnapped them, but now we're friends."

The First's cloud of light veers forward and seems to examine Blue as they float there.

"This is one of our children." The First reaches for Blue, but they retreat back to me and seem to cower under my collar.

First steps back, looking perturbed. I have no desire to

harbor a juvenile delinquent, but I'm also reluctant to hand Blue over, since they seem so unwilling.

"I don't think they want to join your groupthink," I say. After all the time we've spent together I'm protective of Blue, and I don't trust this First and their cloud of lights, which is fair, because they did just threaten to kill me.

First steps forward again, making me edge back.

"You do not understand how our species works. This juvenile must—"

Blue suddenly zips up and charges toward the First, making him stumble backward. They twinkle there, vibrating until a low whining buzz begins to resonate around us. First steps back again as the buzzing gets louder.

"You do not . . . you are too . . . undeveloped to . . ."

A loud popping noise makes me jump, and a bright flash blinds me for an instant. When I blink my vision back, Blue is gone, and in their place is a second cloud of lights, shimmering and pulsing in vibrant shades of turquoise and indigo. As I watch in horror, this new cloud charges the First, enveloping them, merging with the First's cloud and causing the human body to twitch and flail and fall to his knees. Finally the merged cloud fragments, with chunks of it breaking off and swirling away until only single lights escape, floating up into the sky and disappearing.

The First shakes himself and slowly climbs to his feet,

turning back to me as the new shimmering azure cloud settles around his head.

"Blue?"

"It is difficult for our kind to manage disagreements," they say, waving vaguely in the direction of the retreating lights. "They gave up."

He, they, because I think I'm speaking to Blue now, almost look proud. They lift their fingers up and feel the smile on their face.

"What were you disagreeing about?"

"Discarding you," they say, a bit casually for my tastes. "We have been around you and your friends for so long, Raven. *We* know how to manage disagreements."

Blue's cloud shifts as they watch me laugh. They even attempt to laugh themselves, but that only makes them cough. For a second it's as though Blue releases the boy and his eyes flick up to me, pleading, terrified. I reach for his hand just as Blue's cloud seems to wrest back control.

"This body is close to death," they say. "We hoped the Snowflakes might tolerate it for longer, but they wear out, like the others."

"Is there nothing you can do?"

A few seconds go past as Blue moves the boy's hand in mine, as though they are feeling the shape of my fingers, the texture of my skin. I squeeze back.

"I admire your compassion, Raven," they say. "Humans have a lot of compassion under all the . . . other things."

"Yeah. That's kind of our brand."

The boy's body convulses again, bending and coughing blood onto the snow. Blue's cloud contracts around him as though trying to give him strength, but he slumps down, and I barely stop him from pitching forward before helping him settle into a sitting position. Kneeling, I wipe the gray blood from his mouth with a corner of the green dress. I don't know this boy. I don't even know if there's enough of him left in there to be aware that I'm here with him. But no one should be alone when they die.

His eyes unfocus, rolling past me and then back to fix me in an exhausted glare. I can see what a struggle Blue is having speaking through the boy.

"We don't . . . have much time," they say. The boy's voice is barely louder than a whisper. "One of the Nahx will take you back to the dunes. There's a transport waiting."

"Okay." I've made my decision. If I'm honest, I was always going to fight, though I feel stronger knowing what I'm fighting for, and why. "Can I ask you one more question?"

They nod the boy's head. His nose is running with metallic blood now.

"How long do the Nahx live?"

"A long time, like you. If they stay at the high elevations.

And avoid grievous injury." The boy's face brightens for a moment, and he almost manages a smile. "You love that broken one, August, don't you?"

I'm not sure I can blush anymore, but I feel my face heat up.

"Love was something we did not anticipate. Most of the other animals on this planet aren't . . . controlled by it. At least not in the same way. It's . . ."

"Annoying?"

The boy smiles, but his body spasms and he spits up silver blood.

"Blue . . ." I start, because I have a million more questions. But the boy exhales roughly, his mouth bubbling with blood, and then he slides to the side, falling with a soft hiss into the snow. Blue's cloud releases him, drifting up as though watching, settling there above us, bathing the boy's body in gentle light. I watch him for a while, and, seeing he's not breathing, reach forward to close his eyes.

"I'm ready to go now." I'm not sure who I'm saying it to. Blue? Or this unknown dead boy who gave his body and life for a fight he never understood?

"You won't do this anymore, right?" I say, turning my eyes up to the cloud of lights. "Occupy human bodies like this? If it destroys them?"

Blue's cloud bobs back and forth, holding position for a few seconds as though watching me. Then they just drift off, expanding to a less dense cloud, their light dimming as they disappear into the open sky above.

As though some signal has been sent, a small transport rumbles behind me, rising out of the distant hangar and, seconds later, setting down nearby. The sneering Nahx appears on the ramp.

"You again," I say.

Mud brain, he replies as I board, before returning to the cockpit. He leaves the hatch open when we take off, and I watch the dead boy's body get smaller and smaller as we fly away.

The dunes are silent but for the breathing of the million Snowflake sentinels scattered across the white rolling hills like the petals and leaves of some postapocalyptic tree. Metallic. Not cold, exactly, but impenetrable and hard. Or, at least, we will see how hard.

Many of them, I now realize, have been partially or almost fully fitted with armor very similar to the Nahx armor. This was never offered to me. Fifth shoved me unceremoniously out of the transport two days and nights ago. He had the courtesy this time to hover only about twenty feet above the ground as he did it. I landed easily, turning to return his sneer with a human sign he should probably learn—my middle finger.

He gave me a surprisingly kind benediction, as far as high-ranked Nahx go.

Die without pain, he said.

I was too shocked to think of any clever retort, so I just raised my other middle finger. Two days and nights I've been trying to think of a better comeback, but all I can think is that I hope his Offside recovered.

We have weapons. Fifth gave me a very powerful rifle,

two Nahx knives, and a dozen of their grenades. The other Snowflakes are similarly armed, wondering what we should be aiming at. I pass time by trudging over the dunes, looking for Mandy or anyone else I recognize, but so far I haven't found anyone. Mostly the other Snowflakes ignore me, though some seem mildly interested.

"When will it happen?" one of them says to me on the second day.

"I don't know." I trudge on. I don't like to speak to them; their empty expressions remind me too much of Tucker and how easily he sacrificed his life for us all. Maybe that's what these Snowflakes are destined for too.

The sky rumbles, though there is no cloud. The noise jangles my blood, as if making it bubble under my skin. Those who aren't already staring at the sky turn their faces upward to the vast, cloudless blue dome. As I stare at it, something happens to my vision, as though the blood vessels of my eyeballs are shifting slightly, like a prism turning to more properly focus the light. When the change settles, the sky has taken a new shape—no longer a dome but a funnel, the center of it sinking back into a denser, distant core.

"What *is* that?" someone says nearby.

Some, who are closer to the funnel, begin to run, discarding their weapons and leaping down the rolling dunes. The shimmer of energy rushes into my throat, of all places, and fills my lungs.

"STOP!" My voice roars so loud, even I'm surprised. The running Snowflakes skid to a halt, turning back to me, as my voice resonates over the rolling sand and snow.

"We're here to fight," I snarl through clenched teeth. "And there is nowhere to run. Stand your ground."

"What . . . what is that? What are we fighting?" one of them, an older man, says. He's very slight, almost emaciated, and looks like he's never been in a fight in his life. None of these people have had any training. How do the Fireflies expect us to win this battle for them? I look down at my weapons, at my silvery hands, then up at the sinking sky and try not to give in to the despair that lurks in the recesses of my soul.

Time has run out. The sky's rumbling intensifies, the pitch rising until it's like the screech of some gigantic infernal bird. Several Snowflakes put their hands over their ears, staring at the sky with horror. After a few seconds the screeching stops.

I can feel the heaviness of the tunneling sky, the pressure of whatever is behind it breaking through the last barriers, and I know I have seconds, minutes at most. I'm only one person in this million, and I'm furious that those who created us didn't think to do something about our fear. I'm terrified. Along with every other living soul on the dunes, I'm shaking, dry-mouthed, burning-eye terrified. All I have to believe in is myself.

"Look! Listen!" I shout to those within earshot, my voice still preternaturally loud. "Listen to me! Whatever comes through may not be stronger than us, or prepared for us. That's our one shot. Understand?"

They turn and look at one another, but apart from that no one moves.

"You might not have noticed this because I know you haven't been thinking, or you've forgotten how to think, but they did something to our brains. You need to watch and observe—"

The sky shrieks again, and several of the Snowflakes near me close their eyes, cowering.

"No!" I shout. "Open your eyes! Keep your goddamn eyes open! Understand?"

A dark figure leaps over the top of a dune, landing above me, and I lock eyes with Mandy at last.

"Thank God," she says, sliding down the sand. "I thought they'd killed you."

We don't even take the time to embrace, instead grasping arms as I spit out my last hope for life on earth.

"If we can figure whatever it is out before they figure us out, we can defeat it."

Mandy nods. "These zombies probably don't even know what their brains can do."

"Blood," I say. "It's not just our brains. It's everything. Bones, muscles—everything can change as fast as our brains can process the need to. But we have to be hyperalert and trust it. Let it happen."

Mandy's eyes widen. "You're right! My God, that's exactly it. That's the weird feeling. Like when I need to see something?"

"Yes. Your optical cells change themselves. They can *think*." Now my cells are pulsing, as though having figured out this process they can finally kick into top gear. I look down at my hands and make them crackle with electricity, just because I can.

Glancing up at the sky, I see that the funnel shape has changed. It's now spreading out, fracturing like a crack. This is the fissure. Now we really do have seconds.

"Tell them," I say. "Tell as many as you can."

Mandy squeezes my shoulder grimly before turning and running back the way she came.

I gulp for air, feeling the coldness awaken my insides. My vision is shimmering now, and each beat of my heart is like a camera shutter clicking, recording everything I see, smell, hear, and taste. Dropping to one knee, I take a handful of snow and watch as it melts, boils, and then sizzles in my hand. I have turned my skin burning hot with nothing more than a thought. I turn to the Snowflakes around me.

"Observe, calculate, react," I say. "Let your minds relax. Your instinct will tell you what to do and adjust your body as needed, but you need to observe. Keep your eyes open. Understand?"

A few of them nod. The rest just stare, but I think I've gotten my point across.

"If you think of some defense that might work, your body can make it. You need to let it happen. Tell as many people as you can. Hurry!"

They scatter, shouting incoherently. Hopefully the message will get across somehow. I run in the other direction, doing my best to spread the only advice I have, the only thing I can think of that gives us any kind of chance.

"Keep your eyes open. Watch. Analyze. React. Use whatever weapons you have. Let your bodies adapt. Understand? Tell everyone!"

As I run, and as the instructions spread, a feeling of . . . not quite calm, but resolve settles over me. The answer is crystal clear now, like a jewel I could just reach out and hold.

"Eyes open. Analyze and react. You can do it. Lead with your brain. Think."

This. This is why they needed us, not robots, not massive machines, not simple weapons. You can only plan a defense against something if you know what it is. Blue's people don't know what is coming. What they needed was a weapon that could learn and adapt its defensive strategy instantaneously. What better weapon than the most adaptable creature on earth? Us. Humans. They tried to copy us with the Nahx, but it wasn't quite right. But we are their weapons, perfected.

The *snezjinka*.

"Don't overthink it. Go with your first instinct. Observe. React."

Load us up with weapons, make us practically immortal, rid our minds of the usual garbage that makes us inefficient, speed up our processing time. Make us superhuman supercomputers and let us come up with a plan. It's brilliant, really. I'd be impressed if I wasn't so pissed off and almost sure I'm going to die in the process of saving the world.

Most of us are going to die. That's pretty clear. But there's a small chance we can stop whatever this is. I focus on that, focus on Xander and Topher and Mom and Jack and my little stepcousins and anyone else who survived the first attacks and the Nahx darts, on every human life we might be able to save. And this beautiful planet.

And August. Oh God, I almost laugh with joy at the knowledge that he's not here. Then my eyes fill with tears because I'll probably never see him again.

There's a terrible earsplitting noise, like nothing I've ever heard in my life, like nothing natural, like something from another world. My body shimmers, filling with electricity and fire and acid and any other weapon my cells can conjure.

I raise my rifle, moving to stand back-to-back with a few other *snezjinka*, all of us gasping, turning our eyes upward so we can face death unflinching, like the soldiers none of us chose to be.

The sky opens.

And the real war begins.

Acknowledgments

Every book I write I spend 50 percent of the time thinking "This is the hardest book I've ever written" and the other 50 percent of the time thinking "This would kill me if it weren't for all these people supporting me."

Given the above, it's probably not surprising that the first person I want to thank is my therapist. But right after that is my agent, Barbara Poelle, and everyone at the Irene Goodman Literary Agency, for taking all my calls, listening to my paranoia, fixing looming disasters, and just generally being reassuring.

Next is of course Zareen Jaffrey, my editor, and everyone else at Simon & Schuster USA—Lauren, Alexa, Justin, Lisa, Dainese, Michelle, Amy, Bridget, André, cover designer Lizzy Bromley, illustrator Larry Rostant, and interior designer Hilary Zarycky. Of course everyone at Simon & Schuster Canada deserves thanks too: Sarah St Pierre, Rita Silva, Jacquelynne Lennard, Mackenzie Croft, Felicia Quon. I'm sure I'm forgetting someone, so if that's you, just send me a ranty e-mail and I'll send you some stickers or something! Of course everyone at Simon & Schuster UK deserve thanks, as do Brilliance Audio for taking care of the audiobooks and Oceano for the Spanish edition, Intrinseca Brazil for the Portuguese, and Dogan Egmont for the Turkish! And thanks of course to Heather Baror-Shapiro for arranging all these foreign language editions. My first non-English books ever!

Thank you to the experts who helped me get cultural, scientific, and geographical stuff right—Lily, Alice, Natalia, and Calais, and Kiran and Margie at the Bennett Dam Visitor Center. And my engineer husband, Len, an expert in what he calls "plausible sounding bullsh*t."

A bunch of people helped me get the word out for this series, including Storygram Tours, Rockstar Book Tours, and countless bloggers and reviewers. Thanks to the *Writer's Digest* Novel Writing Conference, Anderson's Young Adult Literature Conference, the BC Book Prizes, TD Canadian Children's Book Week, the American Library Association (and of course ALL librarians!), and the Creative Ink Festival. Big thanks to everyone on my street team, the Rogues, and especially Nikki and Kelly at the Inside Story for a review video that saved me in my darkest hour. I love you guys!

Thanks to my bookish colleagues with whom I regularly rant and complain and scheme about this crazy industry—you know who you are.

My sisters, Monica, Kathy, and Tess; my mother, Audrey; my husband, Len; and my daughter, Lucy, are my biggest cheerleaders and constant inspiration. Thank you all.